The
Heart
of
Everything

Henrietta McKervey

HACHETTE
BOOKS
IRELAND

First published in 2016 by Hachette Books Ireland

A CIP catalogue record for this title is available from the British Library

ISBN 978 1 44479 416 8

Typeset in Cambria by redrattledesign.com
Printed and bound by Clays Ltd, St Ives plc

Hachette Books Ireland policy is to use papers that are natural, renewable and
recyclable products and made from wood grown in sustainable forests. The logging
and manufacturing processes are expected to conform to the environmental
regulations of the country of origin.

Hachette Books Ireland
8 Castlecourt Centre
Castleknock
Dublin 15, Ireland

A division of Hachette UK Ltd.
Carmelite House
50 Victoria Embankment
London EC47 0DZ

www.hachette.ie

For Cal and Rosa

MONDAY, 7 APRIL 2014

She was doing lists way before Mr Whatshisname ever told her to. The cheek of him, speaking to her like she was an eejit. And him no older than her own son, Raymond. He had the brains to be a consultant too, if he had wanted to. Well, a GP. Maybe. Or a dentist. Raymond was sure to have got the points for dentistry if he'd only bothered himself with his Leaving Cert. For the life of her, Mags will never understand why her son – a boy with brains to burn, as every single one of his teachers had told her at one time or another – was content to waste his life. Working in a library, of all things! Cork, of all places! He had barely put his eyes to a book as a child. And before the library, what about those years he'd wasted on that television soap? To be fair, he *had* earned good money from the acting. For the first few years anyway. At least he'd never been in one of those awful medical dramas, where every time a new character appears you wonder is something terrible about to happen, and the wards are full of people flouncing through doors, tugging their drips behind them.

Mags frowns, rooting around in her bag for today's list. She doesn't like to dwell too long on Raymond.

If a list doesn't seem long enough she'll often include a couple of extra little errands, or maybe write something down that she secretly doesn't intend to do, so that she'll have the next day's list already under way. Her notebook has a picture of a baby panda slap-bang in the centre of each page, and the best lists are the ones that obscure his fat little tummy, stretching down as far as his furry toes. Rebecca dates the pages for her, weeks into the future at a time. She's a lovely granddaughter, Rebecca. Such a kind girl. Thoughtful. Anita was the same at her age, though the kindness in her has dissipated, watered down like cheap milk. Anita is a good daughter to Mags, it's true, but since Jack... Something about her doesn't ring true any more. Mags feels as though Anita is self-consciously assisting her, that helping her with anything, from a lift to the shops to buying something on the computer (the day Tesco delivered twenty kilos of red onions and ten jars of pickles, Mags decided shopping on the internet wasn't for her, after all), is a task to be borne stoically; another testament to life's mean trials.

When the girls were young she bought them comics every week: *Mandy* for Anita and – no matter that she was ten years younger and couldn't read yet – *Twinkle* for Elin. The back covers always had illustrations of women and a selection of clothes, dotted lines printed around the lot. (*'Remember, readers! Ask Mum before using scissors!'*) The same Germolene-pink bodies and plain white underwear each week, but different outfits and hairstyles. Paper shoes and handbags too, but they were fiddly and would rip; they had Elin in tears within minutes. These days, Anita reminds Mags of those flimsy paper dolls, what with the lovely rig-outs and the jewellery and always being so immaculately turned out, even though she's got a bit of weight on her, despite forever talking about being on the SimpleSlim. But behind them is only an outline of a woman, her expression frozen, standing alone in her underwear. Poor Anita.

There's the page! Wasn't it sitting waiting for her on the table all this time. An otherwise-blank *Monday, 7 April* sheet awaits her command.

Small milk, she writes.

Paper.

That's two things. But she gets them pretty much every day, so they're no more interesting than the thin lines of the page. She forgot them towards the end of last week, though, or must have, because when she went to the fridge on Saturday what was left of the milk was gone off and there was no spare.

Dog food. She gets a tin once or twice a week so that she'll have something for next-door's terrier when he comes calling. Poor little scrap is left to fend for himself all day long. She gets bread every other day, and yesterday was Sunday so today is a bread day. She'd never buy bread on a Sunday as it would be Saturday's loaf.

Bread.

Rebecca had given her a fancy notebook called *Shopping in a New York Minute* for Christmas. It had all the lists you could ever want already printed out! You just had to tick next to the thing and tear off the page and pop it in your purse. She'd enjoyed being the person who might require such exotic shopping: chilli beef, zucchini, lemon thyme. She'd imagined herself – young and busy, casually beautiful and decidedly taller, with a pot-luck chilli the envy of her friends

– living in an apartment overlooking Central Park. She wasn't exactly too sure what Central Park would look like from that apartment, but it was sure to be a vast space in a huggle of high buildings. A place where slices of watermelon-green grass flickered through trees thick with orange and red leaves. Her living room would fill to bursting with the smells of candles and happiness, and from her window – no, better than that, her balcony! – the treetops would glow like sugar on fire in the autumn sun.

She'd ticked a few things in Rebecca's notebook just for the hell of it – *water chestnuts, radicchio, molasses* – but she'd never have bought them. That would have been taking the thing too far. One morning she'd asked the greengrocer for lemon thyme. He sucked his teeth, shook his head. When he repeated it back to her, it became *lemontime.* Ah, sure wasn't that a boom-time herb, he told her. No call for it any more. Pity. She liked the ginny, cocktail sound of lemontime.

She'd kept *Shopping in a New York Minute* in her bag for a while, but it just wasn't the same as her little recycled-paper notebooks with the chubby panda cub. She likes the date written in by hand and the wire across the top to tuck her pen into and her own writing that she can cross off when it's done. Ticks are fiddly little things anyway. Mags Jensen likes nothing more than a good fat biro line put through it when a job is done.

Done and dusted.

'Keep a record of your daily activities,' was what that consultant told her, not interested that she's always lived life to her lists. 'So you can refer back.' Refer back to *what* exactly? she'd wondered silently. Back to myself?

Yet she has more lists these days. Has had them for a while.

Secret ones – not even Rebecca knows about them. (And the doctor certainly doesn't.) She writes a new list in bed at night in a notebook that she keeps tucked away at the back of the locker under a box of tissues because Anita's not above a quick gander around upstairs, she's sure of it. She writes the day and date at the top of the page and on this list she writes everything that troubled her during the day: the things she forgot and how she was reminded of them, or what happened by her not remembering. She tries to think of her pen as a fishing rod and the notebook her net, but some days it's no good: she still can't reel the thoughts in. These lists – her roll of shame – frighten her some days. They make her feel that there's a black hole in her life somewhere and she's going to fall down it one day, completely without warning. And what's worse is that she doesn't know if it's in the past or the future.

Last night's roll of shame reads: *Sunday, 6 April. Toast in toaster at lunchtime. Earrings in cutlery drawer. J card. Raymond?* Mags had reread this list again first thing this morning. What about Raymond? What was it she hadn't remembered to remember? Don't focus on one thing too hard: isn't that what she was told? Stop worrying and let it come back by itself. The doctor had been right about that much: trying to get the thought back when she's in this mood is no better than tugging at a stuck lid. Even if she were eventually to pull it open, the box would be completely empty, with not even a crumb or a wrapper inside and no clue as to what was ever kept in it.

She pops her notebook into her bag: milk, paper, bread, dog food, post office. She has a charity letter to post: she'll need a stamp for it as well as one for the card. It annoys her the way charities do that, and she dislikes herself for feeling irritated by it. No matter how big a cheque she's put in the envelope, or what she may be denying herself so that she can help out someone else, when she licks the envelope shut, there it is on the front next to a photo of a little boy, all ribs and huge brown eyes: *No stamp necessary but using one will save us money.* And then all the good she might have felt about herself, all the connectedness to the flesh and blood of strangers and their lives, their homes and hopes, drains away if she doesn't go and buy a stamp to stick on the wretched thing. She gets loads of these charity letters, she doesn't know why. Tortured young men, abandoned animals, children dying for want of a cup of clean water, entire villages gone blind . . . A new appeal arrives on her doormat ('Cap in hand,' Anita calls it) pretty much every week. Mags reads every one, though she's sure she never filled out any form asking for them all to write to her.

'You're on a list,' Raymond told her, when she asked him had he any idea of the cost to train a guide dog. Charities buy lists of people who are known to donate. He had sighed down the phone from Cork. 'Your data, Mags. You're being bought and sold.' His words had a you-should-know-better-at-your-age tone to them, but then his accent always sounded more Cork on the phone than in person. She wants to reply to all the letters, to send everyone something, but how can she? It feels like a tide coming in the front door. Waves of sadness and misery – those starved orphans trapped under a burning sun sure to die without her to save them! – rising higher and higher in her front room until all the pain in the world will be caught there, pushing her tight, trapping her against her own ceiling.

'Oh, get a grip, woman.' She puts the envelope in her bag, ashamed that she ever begrudged the little lad his stamp.

And, anyway, seeing as how she has to go to the post office, she might as well get the new TV licence while she's at it, no matter that it's a week early.

Good, all done. Her pen speared a great catch this morning. Mags realises she's hungry. She mustn't have had her breakfast, after all. She switches on the kettle and turns up the radio again. She always has the radio on if she's in the kitchen or pottering around the house, and it's been sputtering away quietly in the background since she put it on to catch the morning news. The headlines had see-sawed same as always, one person shouting *bad* to another's *good*. There was a report about a minister who hid in St Patrick's Cathedral in order to dodge a group of pensioners protesting at the withdrawal of their medical cards. Mags felt embarrassed for him. The fool. After that there had been a piece about three army men caught joking on tape about molesting two colleagues and how they'd get away with it too, because the women would know better than to make a complaint. The officers are innocent of any crime, it's been decided. She wondered were those women in their homes, listening to the same news bulletin as herself. She'd imagined them gripping the edges of their kitchen tables and breathing hard to steady themselves while this further undeserved humiliation was told to people quietly chewing their cornflakes. She'd thought of the women – she hadn't caught their names – and remembered how she had once gripped this same table but in a different kitchen. That memory was clear as day, she could smell as well as see it: burned toast and the teapot stewing on the Aga. That awful White Musk perfume Anita wore night and day. The earthy stench from the mud on Raymond's rugby boots, dumped just inside the back door as usual. That long-ago morning she had clasped the wooden table so hard she'd thought her fingers would snap. She'd had no choice. It had been either that or lift every single piece of crockery off the table, pull Elin's cereal bowl out of her little hands, everything, and hurl them at the shut window, screaming the entire while.

There are situations in life when sanity can be a choice, she has always believed that. She had tried to explain it to Anita once, during that awful time after Jack died and Anita was falling apart, barely eating. But Anita looked at her like she was stupid – worse, as though she was a stupid, interfering stranger – and walked out of the room. Pain is the devil's own liar and you have to fight back, was all she had been trying to explain to her daughter. Pain tries to trick you, to make you believe that it has taken up residence in you for ever. That it will own you. And look at the way Anita is now, with little Cuan. So uptight about his well-being that she can barely enjoy his company. When he's not in the room she's always asking where he is, or discussing his health or whatever, as though the *fact* of his existence is the important thing, not the living, breathing, flesh-and-bone messy parcel of him.

Do people still keep tiers of wedding cake for the first child's baptism, she wonders. She had kept an entire layer of her own – they'd had it at Anita's christening. How long would she have hung on to it if she'd had no children? When do you give up and throw it out, mouldy and sunken? Cuan is being minded like he was a precious layer of cake. Being saved for the future, no matter what that is doing to the present. Poor lamb.

Mags had turned the volume down midway during the break in the news when one of those 'Save time when you book online' ads came on. They're all the same, she thinks, those websites with names that are meant to sound all friendly, so you'll forget it's computers you're dealing with rather than real people. The nation's obsession with saving time drives her mad. She'd like to squander it. Wash herself in it. It's all she has some days: time.

Her favourite talk show is about to start, so it's safe to turn the radio back up again: '. . . and with Easter nearly upon us,' Pat Kenny is saying, 'for parents all round the country the Communion season must be well under way. And I'm sure we all thought the excesses of the Celtic Tiger were firmly behind us by now, but . . .' He pauses here, like a horse before a fence. It irritates her when presenters do this. It's your show, she thinks. Don't be waiting for me to finish making your point just so's you can steam in and prove me wrong. As if he's read her thought, Pat canters to the end of his sentence: '. . . it looks like there's some spending we're not prepared to let go.' There are no communicants in the family this year, thankfully. Anita's twins, Rebecca and Ailish, are well past all that – they'll be doing the Leaving Cert next year – and at six Cuan is too young still.

A minute later there's a woman on the phone-in. 'Over a hundred just for the dress,' she complains, 'and that's before the veil or anything. And the tears when I said no to a bouncy castle!'

'Have we learned nothing from ourselves?' Pat asks.

'Not around here they've not.' She sounds unsurprised, a woman comfortable inhabiting the failures of others.

Mags sits at the table and finishes her toast and tea. Pat and his callers aside, her kitchen is quiet. She has the curtains pulled as far back as they can go and the room is bright. Peaceful. The fabric has a pattern of wine bottles, fruit, and long, sandy-coloured French loaves. Anita claims her mother must be the last woman in Ireland with curtains on her kitchen window. But so what if they're twenty years old? When did it become mandatory to change your kitchen curtains every five minutes? They do as good a job here as they did in the old house in Shankill. So what if the painted bunches of grapes are too big and the *vin du table* bottles are faded the colour of old radishes? Raymond, too, had been in the room the day Anita told her she should change them, and he'd looked up, smirked – unusual for him to pick up on anything his big sister said, he normally didn't bother – and added, 'Those French sticks are well stale,' which had made them all laugh.

A starling dab-dabs the crumbs Mags left out on the windowsill, the iridescent flare of his feathers flickering in the light. She looks past the bird to the long, narrow garden and its high, elephant-grey stone walls. At the bottom of the garden is the vast oak Cuan loves to climb when his mother isn't looking. Mags's back garden can be so silent sometimes it's hard to believe that, only a hundred yards away, at the bottom of Booterstown Avenue, there are four lanes of traffic. During rush hour beleaguered cars hurtle down the avenue eager to get to the Rock Road at the bottom, and to work; eight, nine hours later they reappear, just as keen to do the whole thing in reverse.

On the far side of the Rock Road there is a salt marsh nature reserve. Just beyond it lies the thin line of the DART track; and beyond that again, the curling, sealy-blue waves of Dublin Bay. It has always seemed peculiar to her that a nature reserve can be boundaried by a dual carriageway on one side and a train line on the other. Not very natural, is it? During winter she has spotted geese come all the way from Canada, teal from Russia, and those lovely redshanks, stopping by on their journey from Iceland to Africa. She's stood near the entrance to the DART station and watched them until her hands were gone numb inside her gloves. What amazing creatures! Free in the air but controlled by a destiny outside themselves, an instinct that propels them across frozen continents to this small, grubby stretch beside a busy road in a busy city. She'll have a good look today, she decides. See if she can't spot a few new ones.

There's a muddily sort of walk, part proper path, part coastline, that goes two miles from the nature reserve and into Blackrock village, then past the ruins of the old swimming pool – a disgrace, the council letting all the old baths go to rack and ruin like that – and a few miles further, as far as Dún Laoghaire. These are places she knows well from a life spent in Shankill, five miles further again on the far side of Dún Laoghaire. It must be twenty years since she's done that walk. There was a time when they'd tramp this full stretch of coast in summer, the kids playing in rock pools along the edges of the sea, stopping for picnics whenever they fancied, and everyone with pinked-up shoulders by the end of the day, all crinkly and overheated and panting for an ice-cream cornet in Teddy's on the way home.

At night there is still just enough life slipping up and down the avenue to make her feel connected to the world. She listens to it when she can't sleep, when she's staring into the dark wondering is she alive at all. Wondering which night will she close her eyes never to open them again. There was a prayer they were all taught as children: *Now I lay me down to sleep, I pray the Lord my soul to keep. If I should die before I wake, I pray to God my soul to take.* The 'if I should die' part had terrified her six-year-old self, her hands clasped piously together as she knelt on the scuffed, oxtail-brown boards of her bedroom floor, her dolly jammed under her arm. Until she'd heard that prayer it had never occurred to her there was the slightest chance she might die in her sleep. The faith she once had is long since spilled, her God kneaded into nothing by the hands of those meant to be doing his work, yet she recalls that prayer often. When she finds herself thinking of the words 'if I should die', she pauses. It's the *when* of death, not *if*, she thinks. Understanding that, being content with that: that is the impossible trick. We all become fallen soldiers one day. Her lists do the job of religion for her now. Faith, delivered by repetition.

At night she lies there and listens to the sounds of the avenue outside, hoping to hear happy voices from people walking down from Hennessys pub, or the crunch of shoes heading up from The Magpie at the bottom. She concentrates so hard that she can hear past the tipsy messing. Past the chatter and down the road and across the dual carriageway until, through the salty air, she hears the faint, rolling whispers of the sea calling to her, telling her it's time to go home. She lies quietly in her half of her half-empty bed and listens.

Listens hard, and tries to remember.

She is in the hall now and stops by the phone table. What did she come out here for again? 'Oh, hurry up, Mags,' she chides herself. 'Stop your foostering around.' She has a lovely bag she uses for shopping, black leather with a coloured tapestry panel on the front, only she can't put her hand to it now. Never mind. The one Raymond sent her last birthday is hanging up on the peg by the door; it'll do. It has long handles and the words *I'm a canvas bag* in big letters down the front. The height of nonsense, she'd thought. Of course it's a canvas bag. She'd imagined for a moment if everyone had to declare themselves so clearly, to have a slogan of themselves on display. She'd have *'I'm 69, not invisible'* embroidered all down the back of her coat. What slogans would her children have? The daughters who no longer speak to each other, her son who doesn't seem that bothered with any of them. Little Elin, the child she rarely sees and doesn't hear from as much as she'd like, and her only over in Scotland. On the odd times Elin phones she ends her calls with 'I'm always thinking of you, Mum,' so maybe that should be her slogan. When Raymond calls it's usually a couple of minutes before *Coronation Street* starts. Does he think she's so dumb she doesn't know what he's up to? Putting her on a leash like that. She always answers the phone, though. How could she not, and him her own son? There's never much sense to be got out of Raymond about his life, and Jean, and his job in the library, so maybe his slogan should be *I'm not an open book*.

'Well done, Mags,' she says out loud. 'That's a good one.' And Anita? Who's to know what slogan Anita would have? She's not even sure Anita would know herself. There's a phrase seems to be everywhere these days: Keep Calm and . . . Oh, something or other, she can't think of it. Anita said, *Keep calm*, to her over and over when they were in the consultant's office that time, when Mags had got a bit upset and distracted and forgotten herself. Right out of the blue when they had been talking about nothing more than the trouble Anita had finding a parking space near the clinic, the consultant said, 'And tell me, what age are you, Margaret?' and she had no idea, just none. She didn't even understand what he meant by it, what sort of information he was trying to get out of her. For a minute – no, less, only a few seconds! – he might as well have been speaking another language, one in which she had no translation for the word *age.* She pictured her brain as one of those old grey filing cabinets, and her as the secretary she once was standing in front of it. She could hear the clunking sounds it made as she yanked the drawers out in turn, desperately trying to find the right piece of paper in time to answer the man's question, but it wasn't there.

For all her GP had said about it being a good idea to 'have a chat' with a neurologist, Mags had gone into Mr Cooney's office assuming the problem was her thyroid. It had played up a few times as she'd got older, and she'd get all out of kilter, over-tired and a bit bothered and fuzzy, until her medication was adjusted. But that didn't seem to be the issue this time, because then he was saying, 'We'll monitor it for now and schedule a few more tests,' but she had got upset and that had made it harder to follow what he was talking about. Doctors do that, they confuse people. Ask anyone.

'Keep calm and breathe, Mum,' Anita kept saying.

Keep calm and breathe. That must be it. Maybe Anita had seen it on an inhaler.

Back in the kitchen the teapot's in its proper place and the taste in her mouth tells her she's had her morning tea but she puts a fingertip to the ceramic spout just in case. It's barely warm. That's grand. She's had her tea for sure, so she'll have a coffee later on. She has Anita's old coffee machine – Derek got Anita the newer model for Christmas. Mags has taken to leaving the machine with a fresh pellet ready inside. Sometimes it's happened that even before she's put the milk on the ring to heat she's forgotten if there's a pellet inside or not, and has to check. She must be wasting loads that way. *Enough*, she chides herself. Let that be a problem for later. Something to look forward to, she thinks drily.

There's the post! She loves the slither of a letter dropping onto the hall floor. It's an invite to a wedding – how nice. Her friend Maeve's only granddaughter, Eleanor Reynolds-Hayman, is engaged to a chap called Thomas Murray-O'Donnell. She turns the pearly white card over in her hands. It's packed full of surnames. Don't they realise how silly it seems? Words like ivy, to choke them at the altar. *Mrs Margaret Mary Veronica Bernadette Burns Jensen will be so kind as to accept your so-kind invitation.* Mags imagines the children this couple will have. Babies with all four surnames bolted onto them for life, pulled down by the rusty anchors of their parents', and grandparents' affectations. And then what happens if they marry someone whose parents were as daft? On and on it would go, spun out of all control. She's glad Anita hadn't gone in for such nonsense. She pops the card into her bag. Mags loves a wedding.

Shopping bag, handbag, coat, scarf. It's mild, a lovely bright morning, but she slips her umbrella in too, because the one thing you can tell about Irish weather is that you never can tell. Mags enjoys the routine of her stroll down Booterstown Avenue and on to Blackrock, though she always gets the bus back because of the shopping. The name 'Booterstown' comes from 'town of the road' in Irish, which is a silly something-and-nothing sort of a name, really. One of those letting-on ones. There's nothing towny about the avenue – it's only the two long strings of houses, the church, two pubs and a struggling clutch of shops that seem to be forever changing hands and rarely make it past a year. Best Buds is her favourite of the current crop. Liz, the owner, is lovely. Chatty, but not in a did-you-see-*EastEnders* way. She asks proper questions, offers opinions. She pauses before she answers, her head tilted to one side. Her big brown eyes remind Mags of a poster Anita used to have tacked to her wall as a teenager: a puppy, all huge eyes and fur the colour of Cadbury's Buttons. Not that she'd ever tell Liz that, of course. Liz slips in a few extra stems whenever Mags buys flowers. She drops bunches up the odd time too, old ones that are on the turn or whatever. Just last Friday she appeared at the door, her hands full of daffodils. She said they'd not last the weekend and Mags would be doing her a favour to take them. They're still blooming away happily, though, and Mags wonders did Liz make a mistake but doesn't want to ask her in case she sounds rude, telling Liz how to run her business. She hopes Best Buds survives. It's a pity the country can't grow more shopkeepers like Liz.

Blackrock is different. It's a big, overgrown village so people know each other in that towny way. Conversations are rehearsed exchanges, a push-and-pull answer and reply system. People don't like it if you respond to 'How are you?' with anything other than 'Grand, thanks, and you?'

'I'm rubbish, to be honest,' she said one day to the butcher in the Frascati Centre as an experiment, and added, 'I'm particularly out of sorts today,' and the man went as red as the lamb chop in his hand before shaking his head and spluttering something that might have been 'oh dear' or maybe 'old dear'. She wasn't sure and suddenly didn't have the courage to query. The chemist generated better results, but he wanted a list of symptoms and before she knew it she had wasted nearly twenty euro on a packet of senna tablets and a box of fancy-looking sachets of powdered fibre. She doubted she'd ever need them, but her purse was certainly lighter for the experience. Experiment concluded, she decided.

There's a note in Anita's neat script pinned to the mirror in the hall: *Will collect u at 2 p.m. Monday – dentist.*

She had forgotten, it's true. Mags opens up her little notebook and writes *Anita dentist 2*. She'd better leave the table set for her lunch in that case, to save time when she gets back. As she passes the open door to the sitting room, Liz's daffodils bob their heads in greeting from the mantelpiece. They are in the Belleek vase that was a wedding gift to her own parents and hasn't a single chip or crack in it seventy-five years later. She never tires of that vase. She's been tracing its intricate patterns all her life. She smiles back at the pert yellow heads, bobbing like meerkats above the buttercream porcelain. Lilies trapped in porcelain, for ever open, their stigmas and stamens exposed. Alive and dead, all at once. She can see the same vase full of roses instead of daffodils on the mantelpiece in the good sitting room of the house in Shankill. Her mother had a great way with roses; she could make flowers bloom in a desert, Dad used to say. During the day the scent was delicate, exotic. In the evening, the smell disappeared as the room filled with the sulphurous crackles of the coal fire.

Laying the table doesn't take long: plate, cutlery, butter dish but not the tub of spread, cup in the saucer and what else? She looks around. Where's that . . . thingy? She has no idea what she's looking for but can't give up on herself. She has a hand raised to the press over the table so she must have been after something. She takes a two-finger KitKat from the shelf and puts it next to the saucer. She knows it's not really what she was looking for, but this way she's remembered something so, by her accounting system, it can be considered almost a finished job. A half-remember. A thin line through the list.

She stands in front of the hall mirror. The eyes that look back are pale and tired, threaded through with red. They are no longer the blue of a summer's day but more its thin reflection, captured in a tired sea. She puts on her beret and adds a spray of cologne to her wrists and neck. A few weeks before she had caught Anita's reflection in the mirror as she did this. A curious look had crossed Anita's face, as though she couldn't understand why her mother was bothering to make herself smell nice, there was no need for it. That's Anita to a T right there, Mags thinks: a woman who wears perfume only for others.

A million years before, when Mags and Per were first courting and wouldn't be able to see each other much during the week, he would telephone her at home every evening from his digs. For ages, she would never answer it herself, just to keep him waiting, even though she always knew it would be him.

'You're looking lovely today,' he would say, when she came to the phone, and then something like, 'That colour, it suits you,' or 'Is that cardigan new?' and it always made her laugh, every time. She smiles now, thinking of it. For a long time she couldn't think of anything about their life together without that awful white-hot anger seizing the memory, mauling it. But not any more. She has no fury left for a dead man. He made his mistakes. They both did. If only Anita could lose her anger. It's as if she has taken her rage about Jack's death so far within herself that it can't find a way out: she has consumed it more than been consumed *by* it.

'Are you ready at last?' she mutters to herself, as she takes out her lipstick. 'I am indeed,' she answers, and carefully paints her mouth, blots, then does it again. 'You're looking lovely today,' she says, suddenly needing to hear the words aloud again, threadbare echoes from almost fifty years before.

The old woman in the mirror stares back, doesn't reply.

The front door squeaks, a thin sound that she pictures as a mouse pushing a chair. Anita's always at her to oil it, but she never does. The squeak, the *thunk* of the door's wooden lip lifting up from the step, the satisfying thud when she pulls it to behind her: these are the sounds that introduce her to the street and the world beyond. They are the soft tap-tap on the shoulder that shakes her gently awake from the solitary Rip Van Winkle life of home.

And with this thought in her head, Margaret Jensen locks her front door behind her and takes herself away.

Cross, cranky, snappy, snarky: call it what you will, it's what she was. Anita was to think back often on that day, and every time she did she would hate herself for how cross she had been. Cross that her mother had gone out without letting her know what her plans were for the morning, cross that she was late coming back. Cross at the nerve of her, wasting Anita's time like that. Anita had sat at home in the lounge (Derek always referred to it as the 'back room', which sounded just terrible to Anita, and though she gave out about it, it never stopped him) and looked out at her long, neat garden and tapped her feet. Honestly, Mum really would get your goat. She had dialled her mother's number. She was to collect her for the dentist at two and wanted to remind her to be ready on time because the rest of Anita's carefully scheduled afternoon would fall apart if they ran late. No answer. Mobile the same, though she hardly ever answered it, so nothing new there. Hadn't she left Anita sitting waiting for hours just a few weeks before, when Anita had come to collect her for a day trip into town? She'd forgotten and headed in on the bus herself, was all she'd had to say, which wasn't much of an apology in Anita's world.

Anita sat and, at first, fumed. Mum is never on time; she is one of those people. Dad used to hate the way he'd be kept waiting for her. *That woman would be late for her own funeral,* he'd mutter. In his Norwegian accent the words had sounded so gloomy. It was true, though: she's the type who'd keep you hanging around waiting, then make a big entrance in a scatter of scarves and umbrellas, armed with some story about a bus taking a wrong turn, or getting delayed by a tourist who was lost and needed directions, and sure isn't it as easy to just *bring* them to wherever as direct them? ('It's always you they stop and ask,' Anita said once, her patience at an end. 'Always you, no matter what country you're in. Funny, that.')

But Mum was becoming more than *one of those people* now; she knew that. The consultant had told them so. Mr Cooney had turned his iPhone over and over in his hand the entire time they'd been in his office, and was talking into it before they were out of his door. Barely bothering to lift his eyes from his notes, he had spoken about symptoms of cognitive impairment this, and the complexity of memory-related conditions that, and the need for early-dementia-monitoring the other. And, of course, that – my God, that word! That horrible word! – was a shocking thing to hear, and her mother had been upset and Anita had been upset, but the reality of the situation (a favourite expression of Derek's) was that Mum hadn't seemed any different from usual since. Anita had begun to wonder if the whole episode wasn't just a blip, and the GP had overreacted. She's had some funny turns in the past with her thyroid, after all. It had come as a surprise to Anita that the GP even suggested they see the consultant in the first place. A surprise to Mum too; Anita was sure of it. It can be a slow process, he'd told them. Complex. For some. We'll monitor the situation, of course, he'd said. We'll speak again soon, he'd said, and told them his secretary would be in touch about the additional tests he wanted to run. He wouldn't prescribe any medication just yet, he'd told them, when Anita asked why he wasn't giving them a script. 'Diagnoses are a complex business,' he said, looking down at the dark screen in his hand.

She'd left the consultant's office in silence. Mum had said very little on the drive home, just sat there with her handbag clutched tight as an injured pet on her lap. Was it possible the doctor had been right? Maybe her mother was more out of it than she had thought; maybe she couldn't take it all in. They were nearly back at Booterstown when Mum said, her voice almost a whisper, 'But isn't everything in the world *memory-related*? Isn't memory another word for life?'

And in the long days and weeks and months that on that day were yet to come, Anita was to look back at the morning she sat in her lounge and wonder why she wasn't immediately worried, didn't get panicked. Why she hadn't immediately searched for clues that could have been hidden in her mother's behaviour, ready to be picked out like Hansel and Gretel's trail of breadcrumbs through the forest in Cuan's book of fairy tales. And she would always wonder did that say more about her, Anita, than about her mother? Could that be possible? Because for years Anita had believed that she was the only one who cared. Raymond couldn't give a fiddler's, and as for Elin . . . Well, Anita tries never to think about Elin. No, it's always been Anita. *She* was the one who was nearby, who wanted the best, tried to mind their mother and help her with everything.

But in those long days and weeks and months that were to follow, she would have time to wonder if that really was the case. Up until now she had told herself that the reason she didn't notice any significant difference in her mother was because there was no difference to spot. How can you ignore nothing? But could it be true – as Raymond was yet to accuse her, but he would, he would – that what she was doing was trying to deny Mags the right to grow old? Refusing her *the messy humanity of ageing*, is how he will phrase it, though neither of them knows it yet. Anita was like a child, he would hiss at her, a child with her hands clamped over her eyes, cawing, *You can't see me*. During the horrible week that on this afternoon hadn't even begun, Raymond was to shout that she was trying to capture their mother.

To trap her: a butterfly fixed with a pin.

But for now, on this Monday lunchtime, all Anita can do is to redial. No answer. Mum's pulled too hard at the hoover cable and unplugged the phone by accident. God knows that's happened before. Anita drums her fingers against her mug. She's enough to do already without this. She has to pick up the twins after school and bring them into Leeson Street for their grinds – English and maths for Rebecca, and Irish for the pair of them, not that it'll do them any good afterwards, terrible waste of money – and Cuan will have to be collected from his playdate before five, and then she'll have to turn around and head back into town with him to collect the twins for half past.

At two on the dot Anita lets herself in. Jesus, the noise of that door! She'll have to find the oil and do it herself – it's not like somebody else has any intention of getting around to it. Her own neat note is pinned to the mirror. She shouts up the stairs even though the stillness of the hall tells her there's no one home. Dust motes float in a stream of sun through the fanlight and distractedly she watches them flutter and twirl, tiny warm flakes fading before they hit the floor.

'*Muuum?*'

Anita walks down the passage to the kitchen. The table is shipshape and set for one. There's even a fun-size KitKat patiently waiting next to the empty teacup. Didn't know she liked them, Anita thinks. The sugar bowl is missing from its place next to the empty milk jug on the table so she fetches it down from the press.

Mags buys boxes of sugar sachets now rather than a big bag, and the thin paper packets with SUGAR written across one side remind Anita of the time she was in hospital with her blood pressure when she was pregnant with the twins. The private rooms were all full – a disgrace, considering the cost of their health plan – and she'd been unceremoniously plonked in the middle of an overheated public ward.

'Public is right.' Derek tugged at the curtains around the bed, but they had no more stretch in them than a J-Cloth. The ward was full to bursting, as were its occupants. Ten women in the beds, twelve babies in the women. Anita, exhausted and hormonal, had cried at this: her life sounded like the start of a bad riddle. The girl in the bed next to her was five months pregnant and anaemic. She looked no more than sixteen and didn't get a single visitor the three days they were side by side in the ward. The girl lay on the covers, her curtains open, and stared at the TV that hung from the ceiling in the middle of the room. When the TV was off, she drew in a colouring book. Every meal arrived on a tray. The first time the trays arrived the girl had held up two sachets and asked Anita which was *sugar* and which was *salt*. At first Anita thought it was a joke, a wind-up, and pointed at the packet of sugar. The third time it happened she said, 'S-U-G-A-R: the one with more letters is *sugar.*' Immediately she began to fret that she had sounded sarcastic or just *mean* in the indefinable way that having knowledge can confer, so she smiled and added brightly, 'Though nothing could make this food taste better!' The girl, lipsticked with grease from the dinnertime fry already half gulped down, had looked puzzled. Anita blushed. More proof, if she really needed it, that she was a terrible teacher.

The sachet has ripped from her fiddling. Her old Nespresso machine has a capsule ready to go so she makes herself a coffee, sits down at the table and stares out at the garden. She's hardly ever here alone. The clock in the hall ticks neatly, and beyond it she hears the faint rumble of buses from the Rock Road. The house is tired-looking, bits of paint peeling here and there on the woodwork. Those silly curtains and the furniture brought from the house in Shankill, which

Anita always thought was a mistake. It's all too big for this small place, too old-fashioned and heavy. Anita's offered to help her change it, to freshen the place up and give it some *personality*, as the interiors magazines say, but 'It's grand as it is for me. I like my bits and bobs,' is all the response she ever gets for her trouble.

The old house is in a terrible state – she took a detour past the place only a few months before. When they had owned Eastcliff House (she used to love saying the name as a child, delighted that where she lived was a cut above any of her friends' homes, which began with a number), it was set apart from everything around it, like a storybook castle hidden behind an ivy-covered wall, but now it is exposed and raw and sad. The council had bought almost the entire back garden under compulsory purchase to widen a road, and the little that was left made the house look unbalanced, in shock. The place had never really recovered. Then a developer had bought it and what was left of the garden from Mags with the intention of converting it to apartments, only to scuttle off to New York not long afterwards, declaring himself bankrupt. The house was left to rot, tied up in legal knots and unwanted by anyone. For a while Anita would occasionally make a detour past when she was on her way to the mobile home at Brittas but she doesn't any more. It looked tattier each time, more and more faded. The council put a wooden hoarding around it a while back so, some day, it will just be gone, she thinks, disappeared behind the plywood curtain, a misty morning dissolving the bricks like an acid bath.

The vast oak in Mags's back garden is in leaf, soft green nubs beginning to cover the rough brown. Anita doesn't like bare branches, those dark exposed skeletons. Cuan thinks the tree is the best adventure and his grandmother encourages him to climb it, which Anita hates. Jack used to love that tree too. He'd be up and into the branches, like a monkey, and he never got stuck, never once. She tries to remember Jack scrambling up the trunk: now, out there, as if he was in the garden. As if he was living, breathing, panting. Grabbing onto the rough bark, the handholds just out of reach but grabbing, grabbing until he got what he wanted. Some days she frets that it is becoming harder to picture him. Her memories are taking on the over-coloured quality of an old movie, which is ridiculous because it's only been seven years, four months and twenty-seven days. He'd be thirteen now, in his first year of secondary school. There are solitary moments when his face is as clear to her as if he had just that second left the room and rushed out into the garden with his football. Other times she struggles to picture him and can single out only isolated features: the big new teeth in his gappy mouth that made the remaining baby teeth look soft and small as pearls; his freckles; those dark, watchful eyes. Often she imagines him and realises she is picturing a photograph or video still of him – a capturing of him that is both him and not him all at once.

In these moments it amazes her that she ever lets Cuan and the girls out of her sight for a heartbeat, even to go to school.

Jack Jennings was a good name, she thinks. Solid. Honest but friendly with it. When she was pregnant with the twins she did wonder if they shouldn't give the children both surnames, but Derek thought *Jensen Jennings* sounded ridiculous, more like a firm of ambulance-chasing solicitors than a family. Mags had agreed with him. Anita wasn't that bothered; she'd been glad to drop her own Jensen when she got married, fed up of all that *No, no, not Johnson: J-E-N-S-E-N . . . No, Norwegian.*

The hall clock hitting the quarter past jolts her back. She didn't even notice she'd done it, but the little KitKat is gone. Christ, not again. She'll not make her target this week either, which will be three weeks in a row.

Anita redials Mags's mobile only to hear it ringing upstairs this time. She finds it in the pocket of her mother's dressing gown, bundled up with some old tissues and a half-packet of Polos. She checks her watch again. Twenty past two. She'd better call the dentist first, she supposes, sighing at the prospect of an earful from his snooty receptionist.

4.40 p.m. His mobile is switched off so she Googles the library number. You'd think they'd have proper hold music on the library phone system, or even an audio book, but there's nothing, just a crack as the phone is thumped down on the desk. She can hear Raymond's voice muffled in the background and tries to picture what his library looks like, but can't. All she can summon up is her own branch in Blackrock, with a surprised-looking Raymond beamed down behind the issues desk.

Out of nowhere Anita has a memory – clear, sharp as glass – of being twelve and hearing their phone. It used to make a tiny sound before the first ring, a wheezy inhalation she was always tuned in for. She remembers running downstairs. The phone books, her mother's flip-top address book and a notepad for messages all lived on a spindly table near the front door. The idea of a phone being anywhere other than the ankle-nipping cold of the hall was impossibly exotic, like something out of *Charlie's Angels*.

Elin appeared, toddling at such speed down the hall that Anita had to push her out of the way in case she'd reach up and grab the phone first. She recited the number, proud of her phone manners. 'May I help you?' It was her father, calling from her grandparents' house in Oslo. She held the phone to her chest and shouted, '*Muuum*,' up the stairs, and when she put the handset back to her ear her father had said, his voice clear and deep and warm over the long-distance hum and static, 'I could hear your heart beat.'

Another harsh crackle, then a familiar voice: 'Raymond Jensen.'

'Raymond? It's me. Anita?'

'Oh, hi . . . Hang on a second,' he replies. 'Murder?' he says and it takes Anita a second to realise he's speaking to someone else. 'You want Crime, General.' He sounds bored.

'Bloody crime.' His voice is clearer, he must be talking to her again. 'Crime and fantasy, that's all anyone wants. It's been a while Anita, how's things?'

Jesus, is Raymond's first reaction. She said her own name like it was a question. Does she think me that bad that I wouldn't recognise my own sister?

'Have you spoken to Mum today?' she says. 'We arranged I'd bring her to the dentist, but she wasn't here when I called for her and she hasn't come back yet. I waited as long as I could, then had to go and collect the twins for their grinds.

Has she phoned you?'

'No, I've not spoken to her yet this week.' It's not untrue, he thinks. He hasn't. But he mightn't have spoken to her last week either. Raymond loves his mother, he would say so without hesitation if asked, but over the years that love has become an abstract, calcified into an uneasy-but-dedicated admiration. It lies somewhere above his respect for indie music, below his love for Guinness and Krzysztof Kieślowski films. Yet as a child he had adored his mother. With a fierce, possessive passion, he'd believed the two of them to be inseparable; that he was as vital an appendage to her as her own leg or arm. (He has often wondered since why she encouraged him in such fervour. Or, at the very least, not *discouraged* it.)

Raymond believes that the bond between them began to short-circuit when his schoolwork started falling off. His mother believes that he lost interest in anything academic when he started acting, but in truth he had long since stopped caring by then. He'd got the role in *Baysiders*, and instead of being excited, proud, thrilled – *any*-bloody-thing, in fact – she was . . . *nothing*.

'So,' she'd said, her voice careful, 'does that mean medicine is out of the question? You'd make a lovely GP.'

'Mum, I'm never going to do medicine, no matter what,' he'd replied. 'You know that, I've told you before.'

'Dentistry, then?'

He'd stopped calling her *Mummy* years before, but it was then that *Mum* had begun to shrink. The letters became harder to form in his mouth, turned awkward, slippery and dangerous as marbles. It was *Ma* next, and then one day *Ma* came out as *Mags*. And that was it. Severed. She was no longer Raymond's ally, his protector, his limb. She was Mags.

'So you *haven't* spoken to her?' Anita is saying. 'Well?'

'Huh? No, sorry. She probably just got chatting to the neighbours or something. You know what she's like.'

'I've tried them, the few who are home during the day anyway. Nobody's seen her.'

'Have you tried her mobile?'

'For heaven's sake, Raymond, I'm not stupid, you know. Of course I have. She left it here.'

'Okay, okay. Look, Anita, you're worrying about nothing. It's only, what, a quarter to five?' He glances at his watch. Nice one, he thinks, only fifteen more minutes to go. A dull hum in the background tells him that the shutters are already coming down on the building. Despite what he (mostly) privately thinks about his managers in the South Mall Municipal Library, he values their ability to have the library closed on the dot of five, a practice that is achieved by beginning the close-up at half four. Earlier, if it's quiet. He sees the Guinness waiting for him, its soft, creamy head waiting to kiss his lips. *The day is over*, that touch whispers to him. *You're safe now, you're free. I'm here. I've been waiting for you, faithfully, just as I promised I would.* There's a magic to the first pint of the day that is never captured by any of those that follow it, no matter how hard he tries. God loves a trier, isn't that what Mags says? He'll just have the one tonight, though: he's been promising himself he'd knuckle down to the screenplay.

'But, Raymond . . .' she is saying, and trails off when he tunes back in. He was sure she was about to say more, to berate him, but, unusually for her, she doesn't. Anita is a relentless quizmaster: when she wants to know something she goes on and on until she gets the answer she's looking for. And all the better if it is the exact response she predicted it would be, because then she's proved right on two counts.

'What can I say? Who wouldn't want to skip out on the dentist? She's probably just gallivanted off into town for the afternoon. Didn't this happen a while back? Mags told me how pissed off you were that she went shopping without you.'

'That was different.'

'In what way?' How typical of Anita. Of course it wasn't different. Anita is taking it personally as she always does everything. 'Look, Anita, I'm a hundred and fifty miles away, and I'm at work, so I really have to go now. What do you want me to do? If she calls me, I'll tell her to phone you or I'll text you myself. How about that?'

Bzzz. Jensen, University of Life: *No points.* Anita's silence informs him that he gave the incorrect answer. He hangs up, thinking, *Typical.* That's just typical of Anita. When he phoned her just before Christmas to ask what should he buy Mags, Anita moaned about how busy she was, and how much work it all was, and had ended the call with 'Thank God, this time next week it'll all be over.'

'Bloody hell.' He turns to Pauline. She is stamping out three large-print Jo Nesbø books. She leans hard on the date stamp and doesn't look up. He likes the rhythm of it, the dull *duh-DUH*. 'Jesus! She can really push my buttons.'

'Who can?'

'Anita.'

Pauline closes the final cover, hands the books up over the counter ('There you go, Mrs Butler. Two weeks of mayhem there. Enjoy yourself') and turns to him. 'Of course she can, Raymond.' She smiles. 'She's your big sister. She installed your buttons.'

Flannerys is five minutes' walk from the library, which

is about right, Raymond thinks. Just enough to get a breath of air after the dust and smell of grubby plastic covers and overheated pensioners, but not too far that he'd be tired and ratty when he arrived. He switches on his phone. Nothing. Jean must be working late again.

'Evening,' says the barman.

'Precisely,' he replies.

And that is all it takes for Mick to reach down under the bar for a clean pint glass. This code is a source of pride to Raymond. It's belonging, it's kinship. A perfect pint is more than just a drink – that's what the ads don't get right, he thinks. All that focus on the pour, the head, the natty-looking bar staff, the gang of lads around you all drinking the same thing . . . That's not what the perfect pint is to him. It's more than the wait between the first pour and the finish. It's his favourite stool at the bar, no one on either side but a few other faces for a bit of chat if he feels like it. It's the conker-brown sheen of the countertop. The melted-cheese smell from the toasted sandwich maker out the back. Even the occasional fart of bleach when the door to the Ladies is opened. Flannerys looks like it hasn't changed in decades. Mick has told him that during the boom they'd taken to putting crisps and nuts out on the tables every evening: 'But all you'd hear would be the giving out: *Doesn't everyone know stuff left out in bowls is always covered in piss, blah-blah.* Sure you'd be driven demented.' Mick had added, 'Not like the bowls weren't always empty by the end of the night, mind you.' They stopped bothering with the free snacks when the recession hit.

Mick places the pint on the bar and they silently admire it. Raymond bends his head and takes a long sip, the bitter black under the white head reaching his lips like communion. It had taken him a while and many false starts to find Flannerys when he moved to Cork, and now he can't imagine his day without it. Just the one this evening, though. He's got work to do at home. That screenplay won't write itself.

'How're all the big thinkers in the library today?'

'Grand, Mick, they're grand.'

Few of the library *customers*, as they're now meant to call them ('What's wrong with *users*?' Pauline had grumbled), look like big thinkers. There are days when Raymond's not even sure how many of them are readers.

'The wife gave me a thriller, Tom Clancy or one of them lads. I must show it to you, I've it out the back in my jacket to read on my break.'

This is one of the – admittedly few – occupational hazards of his job: everyone he meets assumes he wants to hear what they're reading. People produce books and hold them up to him as though they are cats dragging half-dead bounty across the kitchen floor. E-readers now, too, which he dislikes even more, because he's expected to admire the device as much as the content. When he'd moaned about this to Pauline, she laughed and said, 'When my auntie heard my brother got a place at art college, she phoned to ask him what colour she should paint her bathroom.'

He puts his glass down. It's a good third empty already. The day must have taken its toll – he's thirstier than he realised.

'Two lads in last night,' Mick says, continuing a conversation Raymond didn't know he was having. 'And they were on their mobiles as good as the entire time. Your Facebooks and your Twitters and what-have-you. I goes to one of them when the other was in the jacks, *Would you not just have a chat with each other?* and he looked at me like I was mental. *We are,* he goes to me and shows me his phone, and there's the other lad – the one in the jacks – and his Facebook page and hasn't your man put a picture of his pint on it and the first lad only gone and liked it?' With a sigh that is world-weary and bemused all at once, Mick moves down the bar to a new customer.

Another regular. Raymond nods over a greeting. 'All right?' the man says.

'All right?' Raymond answers. But is he? He doesn't know. There is a little voice in him that the first pint no longer shouts down. It's more than just the blank screen containing his unwritten screenplay at home, it's more than the confusion that thinking about Jean brings on, it's more the fissures of irritation Anita's call gave him. The little voice is that of fear. Fear that he's in the wrong life and there's nothing he can do about it because thinking of how to escape the maze is so exhausting, so entirely consuming and stifling, that he loses the heart even to try. Some days he feels so completely left behind by his life. It is the difference between being in print and online, he reckons. His life is a story lived as a piece of string, a traditional narrative with a beginning, middle and end. Everyone else around him – Jean, mainly, but even Pauline, in her own way – seems to be living a life full of hyperlinks: exciting alternatives and new tangents just waiting to be clicked and chased down. He plods along, and even when he does begin a new chapter, the content will essentially always be the same. His dust jacket gets dustier.

He scans the bar taps that mount the counter and mentally rearranges them. Another occupational hazard. *Beamish, Carlsberg, Guinness, Guinness, Heineken, Heineken, Murphy's, Murphy's, Smithwick's.* He sighs. Look at you, Raymond Jensen, he thinks. Reduced to alphabetising beer taps. And you a star, once. Okay, he gives a mental shrug, not a huge one; not a mobbed-in-the-street movie star, but a perfectly respectable hey-aren't-you-that-guy-off-the-telly? sort of star. *Celebrity*, he corrects himself. Just after finishing his Leaving Cert Raymond had gone for an open audition and ended up in RTÉ's most popular home-grown TV soap. He'd never acted before and only went along because he was bored and the lads had him convinced there'd be all manner of actresses strolling around RTÉ, if not exactly in the nip, then not far off.

The audition was in two sections. First, he had to read a scene with an older man, supposedly his dad, in which the dad tells him he's moving away to London because, unemployed and fifty, he's on the scrapheap as far as Ireland is concerned. The second scene was a solo one, in which he was upset because his girlfriend had gone off with his best mate.

He aced it. This was life: he hadn't even needed to act. Raymond Jensen became Tommy Maloney in *Baysiders*. He got an agent, who found him a few TV and radio ads too. He and Tommy had years – great years! – together. And then. Then it happened. The day every long-running soap actor secretly dreads: the storyline in which he was killed was handed to him, his death neatly typed and photocopied and stapled. Tommy was to be shot by a drug dealer called Steve 'Masher' Maher, a man who'd only been in the show for a month. Masher had gun-for-hire written all over him: he wore a suit and smoked with his hand cupped over the cigarette as though permanently trapped in a high wind.

Afterwards Raymond could see that he was the only one not to notice the spectre of death moving ever closer until it hovered behind Tommy's head, as discreet as a bad guy in an episode of *Scooby Doo*. Certainly his co-stars didn't seem surprised. Over the previous year Tommy Maloney had been slowly going to the bad. A scrape with the local gardaí, then another. A bad crowd was written in, and suddenly Tommy ('And him still in the Scouts when he moved to Bayside!' Mags commented, displaying what was for her an unusual level of interest) was in the thick of it. Drugs, petty theft, muggings. Raymond was disappointed by Tommy. After so many years together he felt that Tommy was letting himself – both of them! – down. And Tommy had started with great ambitions. The only one of the Maloneys to want to go to university, he had taken a part-time job in the corner shop to help pay for it, only he'd let his books burn to ashes around his feet. Raymond had come secretly to despise Tommy's sense of entitlement, his greedy, knee-jerk life, but no way, *no way*, would he have killed him off like that.

'I'll commit suicide sooner than be shot by that fool,' Raymond had said to the senior producer.

'Do you mean Tommy would or you would?' Malcolm answered, alarmed.

'Tommy would. Will.'

'Raymond,' Malcolm sounded impatient yet spoke slowly, as if talking to the hard of thinking, 'for the last time, *you* have no say in what Tommy does.'

The prop gun is fired. Tommy falls to the ground gasping and calling for his long-lost dad. And: cut. Thanks, Raymond, it's been great. The episode breaks all previous ratings.

His pint is down to its last thin inch of black. It's years since Tommy exited *Baysiders* in a hearse, but Steve Maher lives there still. He got off the murder charge on a technicality and bought the local pub. Raymond looked for acting work for two years afterwards but couldn't get anything worth having. And then one day he suddenly understood why: he wasn't really an actor. Tommy was a one-off, just another version of himself. Raymond hadn't created him: he'd just let a different bit of himself out for air during working hours.

It's a good while now since anyone has asked Raymond wasn't-he-that-guy-from-*Baysiders*-who-got-murdered?

Tommy wasn't the only one who never made it to college. After a couple of years on the dole a friend's mother found Raymond a part-time shelf-stacker job in the public library in Dún Laoghaire. And that, he thinks, was the start of a glittering career in the public sector. Mags was so disappointed when he got the full-time job in Cork. He was surprised by how much. It was a job, wasn't it? She certainly hadn't liked it when he was living on the scratch. It must have punctured her last hope that he might yet go to university.

'You'd be a mature student, so you don't have to sit the Leaving Cert again,' she kept saying. 'Even with results as desperate as yours, you'd get in. The rules are different – I've checked.'

His mother feels let down by him, he knows. She never says it, there's just a general shrug of disappointment around her when he tells her anything. He's applied for promotion to cover the assistant librarian's maternity leave. Both Jean and Pauline reckon he's got a good shot at it but he hasn't told Mags yet. No point. He'll tell her if he gets it. Because if he doesn't get the job, she won't see it as an attempt, she'll see it as another failure. He thought she'd be okay about his working in a library. After all, what's not to like about a warm room full of books? Mags herself used to bring them to the mobile library every Tuesday when they were kids, forever banging on about how libraries were proof of a civilised society and a perfect example of free education and free thinking. He sips again, remembering the rickety steps up to the stuffy mobile library, the often-sparse shelves, the fibrous texture of the tickets. He'd never understood what she meant back then.

On his first day in Cork, Pauline was assigned to show him the ropes. Her whistle-stop tour ended at the issues desk. 'Dedication or medication, that's all you need to work here, Raymond.' She grabbed a box of inter-library loans and walked away. 'Either way, you'll be grand,' she called back over her shoulder.

He puts his glass down and checks his watch. Five forty. Mags must be well home by now. He supposes he should text Anita later to check what time she arrived back; he'll stay in the bad books otherwise. Anita is such a fretter, always creating these dramas, manufacturing scenes that have herself at the middle of them, controlling them. That's what comes of not being busy enough. Anita has nothing but her kids and her pain and that bore of a husband. Poor old Mags, he thinks, rambling back home after a jaunt into town only to find Anita waiting inside the front door, fizzing with irritation. Who wouldn't want to turn tail and head straight out again?

Raymond puts his drink back on the counter. A creamy slug trail runs down the inside of the empty glass. Best to make a move. He clenches his buttocks, testing his body's enthusiasm for moving off the padded stool, for leaving the soft, conker-warmth of the bar counter. Mick catches his eye and smiles, raises an eyebrow. Monday's not a good night to begin writing – he's sure he saw that somewhere in *Now Write That Screenplay!*. It's not something to plan: you need to nearly sneak up on yourself, find yourself sitting at the computer with the internet off and a fresh idea ready to spill out. Tuesday is probably a better day for it. Raymond relaxes his buttocks back down onto the stool, enjoys the comfortable squish-squash of the *faux*-leather under him. He raises his empty glass a few inches from the bar, inclines it towards Mick and nods.

That's one thing decided at least.

Elin puts her pants back on to walk into the bathroom. She's no idea why – it's not like Marty hasn't seen it all before, hasn't just rolled off her and is now leaning over the bed and fumbling for his cigarettes on the floor.

'Want one?' he says, clicking the lighter.

'I'm giving up, remember?'

'I thought you were having the odd one. Special occasions and all that.'

'You're very sure of yourself, aren't you?'

'Will we go a takeaway tonight?' he says. 'I've a gob on me for a Chinese.'

'Sure,' she calls through from the tiny bathroom. Sitting on the toilet, her knees touch the sink. 'Can you order it? I left my mobile in the studio again.' She can see part of her head in the mirror above the basin. Her cheeks are flushed, her hair is fuzzy and ragged, pulled half out of its ponytail. She scrapes it back. When she stands up to wipe herself, a headless torso appears in the mirror. A slim torso, but without any discernible waist. When Elin was a teenager, Anita used to call her the human ironing board. Has she put on weight? The shoulders in the mirror shrug. There's a slight roundness, a spread, to her hips that's new. Her nipples are large pink eyes staring back, her belly button a mouth in her soft stomach. 'You look,' Elin whispers, 'like an old owl.' She touches her stomach and her hand briefly covers the owl's mouth.

She flushes the loo and runs into the room again. Her flat is freezing. Marty thought she was mad to rent this place – three tall, narrow and chilled rooms over a Turkish grocer's in Leith – when she could have got a tiny-but-newish apartment for nearly the same money.

'Just think,' he had said. 'Warm air. Hot water on tap, so to speak. Broadband.'

Elin had smiled. 'Just think,' she'd replied. 'Stacked into tiny cages with dozens of other little hens.' As she often does when she's trying to figure something out, she had done a little drawing of it. A little egg box with her possessions neatly divided between the six chambers.

She hops back under the duvet. An old-fashioned alarm clock tick-tocks next to the bed. There is a heavy *thwock* as it clicks to eight o'clock. The hands always seem to stick on the top of the hour as though they believe their work to be done, only to find themselves shoved forward again, propelled by something other than time. She rests her head on Marty's chest. Small streams of sweat are trapped between rolls of skin on his stomach. She runs her fingers through them.

'My mother would say you've a grand bit of flesh on you there.'

'For someone you don't talk about much,' he says, 'this seems like an odd time to bring her up.'

He's right, on both counts. But, then, her choice of flat aside, Marty usually is. It's one of the things Elin thinks is so great about him. He's right about stuff. She can ask him things – capitals of countries, the best place for a coffee in the Old Town, what the codes on her tax return mean – and he'll know. He is immune to doubt, is Marty. She knows, too, that this should make him an insufferable pain in the arse, but it doesn't. He wears it lightly. To him, it's all just *stuff*.

'I finished the first draft today,' she says.

'All of it or just the text?'

'The lot.' Elin has written and illustrated three children's books about an enterprising tufted puffin called Neep and his friend Nucho, a flamboyant fish dressed in a luxurious brown fur coat. Her publisher is Peakes, a small Scottish press. She got chatting to Randall Peake in Marty's bookie's one rainy lunchtime. She has friends who attribute their successes solely to their own talents, but Elin suspects chance has more to do with it than most people will admit.

Her usual method is to write the story first, then illustrate it when she's roughly happy with how it flows, but this time she has found herself working through both at once. Certain words have compelled her to a picture – a line, a shade, a thought desperate to build itself a home on the page – even though she was halfway through the storyboard before she saw what she was doing. It felt strange, as though her right and left hands were working simultaneously, yet insisting on hiding their work from each other. She reminded herself of the ad she loved as a child in which a harassed housewife, besieged at her kitchen sink by yet more dirty dishes, is rescued by the assistance of a third, disembodied hand. Was the ad for gloves? She couldn't remember. Washing-up liquid? Maybe a new and improved brand of housewife. Bet Marty will know, she had thought, as she laid out the last finished spread to dry.

She leans over and takes a drag of his cigarette. 'I'm not sure about this one. I think it's too abstracted, even for kids,' she says. Elin believes in being completely honest with children, in starting from the premise that they understand the fundamental lack of meaning of the world in a very basic, obvious way, one that is not predicated by cause and effect. Children are born with a black and white understanding of sadness and happiness, of good and bad. It is growing up that teaches them shades of grey, indecision and hesitation and confusion. Maturity fosters the urge to please, an ability to nod and smile through the misunderstood, half-baked whims of others.

'You always say that.' Marty smiles. 'You weren't sure about the last one either. For weeks after you finished it you were still saying maybe it wasn't right.' It's not diffidence that makes her hesitant. He's told her that often enough. And it's not lack of conviction about her own talent either: she has that, no matter how little she might articulate it. She's just not a very sure sort of person in lots of ways. *Hithery*, is how Marty describes her. As though she doesn't quite believe the ground is firm. He once told her she behaves as though there is shifting sand hidden below the surface, no matter where she puts her feet.

In this new book, the moon is sick and tired of playing second fiddle to the sun. The moon has had enough of tiny stars and their inane, twinkling chatter. She waited long enough for humans to land – and the first chap who did vowed to return, but never stopped by again – and she has had enough. Enough of being nothing more than the tired, age-spotted mirror the sun uses to reflect its light. The moon has been chasing the sun for so long, desperate to make friends, but the sun never stops. The sun, the moon decides one day, is nothing but a big, gassy snob. Neep wakes one morning and sees the sun desperately trying to rise but the moon is zipping around the sky, blocking his path. Neep leans out of his bedroom window and calls up, asking her to go home because he wants to go out and play with Nucho, but he's not allowed outside until after sunrise. With a tilt and a flounce, the moon refuses. Point blank. No way. Not for all the cheese in the world.

'So what happens?' Marty blows smoke upwards towards the spidery, cracked lines of the broken ceiling rose.

'Neep and Nucho pack a picnic and travel up to meet the moon. When they discover the moon is lonely rather than bad-tempered, they set off again, this time to visit the sun and explain. He has got rather self-centred, the sun, what with all those ancient gods named after him, and leaves and flowers staring at him all day, not to mention the fact that the earth depends on him for survival. He has come to believe his own hype. But he's a kindly enough fellow underneath all the heat, and agrees that he will meet regularly with the moon from now on.' She takes another drag from Marty's cigarette. 'It ends with Neep and Nucho watching the first eclipse.'

Marty laughs, which is reassuring, yet the story is worrying her. Is it about trying to change what you don't understand? About turning the murky, grown-up greys of the world back into white and black – which was her intention – or has it somehow become a cotton-wool tale of compromise, of giving in to the will of others? She's afraid that some darkness has leaked out from herself into Neep and onto the page, and no amount of smiling, cuddling mummy puffins and fantastical fish sashaying around in fur coats can mop it up.

As a child in bed after lights-out Elin would read under her duvet for what felt like hours and hours, until she was hot and lightheaded from the lack of fresh air. Her torch beam was a searchlight on the pages, a pointer to other lives, which seemed so much more real than her own. That she desperately preferred to her own, although she was never sure exactly why. When she first found herself drawing Neep and Nucho during that winter in Tobermory, forced to it by the lack of a life as well as the lack of money, she had been sure that her creation would be nothing more than an anagram of all the books she had once loved. She was convinced that, without ever intending to, she would pluck a plumage from here, thieve a scarf and mittens from there, steal a glint for an eye from who the hell knew where. But she hadn't. Doesn't. Her books are purely herself.

She had met Marty in Tobermory. She'd spent eight months there, cold and lonely and troubled. He had appeared out of the mist, a stag on his brother's stag weekend. It was March, and the sky was still so dark and thick that every night was like being sealed in a bell jar and dropped into the ocean, fathom-deep and alone. Unlike some of the bars and hotels on the island, the owners of MacLarens, Jimmy, a sour, red-faced alcoholic and his sour, pale-faced wife, Maire, stayed open all winter. They never did the business in the summer that the seasonal pubs did, which was a source of great irritation to Maire particularly. It made her resent the locals who drank there in the winter because she knew they'd defect as soon as they could. It made her resent the tourists who drank there in the summer because they'd not be back come winter. Maire's irritation flowed freely over the bar in MacLarens. To Elin it was the magic porridge pot of the fairy tale. Bitter ire spilled over the counter, puddled around their feet until it piled up so high that Maire and her family were trapped inside, drowning in it. *Stop, little porridge pot, stop.*

In the summer the pubs and guesthouses and hotels peeked above ground, like snowdrops, and showed MacLarens for the grim winter weed it was. It was the only place hiring when Elin had appeared on the island, that cold November day, with no plans and no prospects. She'd chosen Tobermory because when she arrived in Scotland she had exactly enough money for the fare. It felt like Fate. And on that day, she'd had nothing else but Fate to lean on.

'You're *what*?' she'd said, as she leaned across the bar with Marty's tray of whiskies. 'That's thirty-six pounds, please. You're on a stag weekend? In Tobermory in this weather?'

'Shite, isn't it?' he said, and laughed. 'The best man has quite the sense of irony.'

'Is that what you'd call it?'

'No, that's what he calls it. I call it shite, but . . .' he shrugged and nodded towards the eight lads at the table playing cards while they tipped pints and chasers down their throats '. . . they're enjoying themselves right enough.' And whenever she looked over at their table, from then on he was looking over at her, smiling, pushing hair the colour of a sweetmeal biscuit back from his eyes. Two hours later it was his round again and his cheeks were pink and shiny from drink and the fire. 'Would you like to go out with me?'

'Thanks, but I'm working.'

'No, no, not now, next week.'

'Aren't you all leaving on Sunday?'

'I'll come back next weekend. Take you out somewhere.'

'Somewhere on Tobermory?'

'Sure.' He grinned. 'Here.' He pointed to the pub's mean little fireplace with its bare few logs spitting and throwing sparks onto the tattered sofa by the hearth. 'I'll take you for a drink here next weekend.'

'Not here,' she says. 'Christ, anywhere but here,' and she'd smiled at how daft, how keen and determined he seemed, his red cheeks shining above a scrappy beard, the biscuity hair flopping around because he kept pushing it back. It was a line, course it was. And a dumb one at that. Did he think she'd put out in advance, as though they were discussing some sort of hire-purchase agreement? Spread her legs as a deposit on a date? There was no way on God's earth, she thought, that he had any intention of coming back.

He came back.

Elin pulls the duvet up under her chin. 'That radiator can't be working properly. It's freezing in here.'

'You've to bleed them,' he says. 'Don't make that face, it's only water. I'll show you. I've got a thing for it at home somewhere.'

'The . . . bleeder?'

'Exactly. Now, if you want to warm up, Jensen,' he stubs his cigarette out, takes her hands and moves them further down under the duvet, 'I've just the thing for you right here.'

It's nearly nine when Raymond gets home. The apartment is quiet. Was Jean to be out tonight? He can't remember and she hasn't texted. Her work spills into the evenings regularly and they seem to communicate mostly by text or Post-it during the week, so he's not sure. People always seem surprised when Raymond tells them about Jean. When she is within earshot he refers to her as his *partner*. He'd prefer to say *girlfriend*, though Jean reckons it sounds tacky, what with him being forty and her thirty-five. But Raymond likes the sound of the word *girlfriend*. It sounds young, eagerly happy. Giddy, almost. *Partner* sounds like they're stuck with each other, trapped in a gone-rotten business arrangement that no longer suits either of them. 'Ladyfriend?' he had suggested once, but she snorted and walked out of the room.

Raymond had met Jean Jordan during his first week in Cork. He'd gone for a drink after work with his new colleagues and Jean happened to be standing next to him at the bar, trapped by Pauline's brother in a stilted conversation. It was one of those horrible superpubs, he remembers; he'd never gone back. Everything enormous, especially the prices. Scaled up, a temple to booze. She had glanced up at him, crossed her eyes and smiled, her head to one side. 'I thought you were Pauline's boyfriend,' she told him later that night, when they were both pissed. 'And I was like, wow, she's done alright for herself.'

It had been his idea to get a place together. He'd first suggested it when they'd only known each other six months. It took ages to get her to agree. He had found her reluctance exciting: it brought an added chase to her, an elusiveness he enjoyed simply because he had never encountered it in previous relationships. There have been times since that he wonders whether his eagerness to wake up next to her every day was born out of a desperate need to be near her all the time, or because the relentless best-foot-forward business of dating was too exhausting. He wonders, too, whether her initial reluctance to wake up next to him every day was her spinning out the pursuit for her own enjoyment, or because she wasn't sure about him, yet gave in simply because her life was so busy and it made everything easier.

'Found her filed under *J*, did you?' Anita's husband Derek joked, the first time Raymond brought Jean to Dublin for the weekend. 'On the shelf, was she?' Jean had smiled politely by way of reply, which had made Raymond stupidly happy that he alone understood her expression for what it was: the response of someone who is squirrelling away the absurdity for later, savouring it for when they were alone. When Derek went to open the wine Jean had brought ('Sancerre? Lovely choice. Hang on to this one, Ray, eh?'), Raymond turned to her and, mastering his impulse to say something mean about Derek's perfectly pressed raspberry Chinos, instead whispered, 'Well, wasn't I right? Doesn't he put the *offensive* into *charm offensive*?'

'He's fine. Be kind.' Her whisper was so delicate and warm against his ear it gave him an erection.

Raymond and Jean have an apartment – he has learned not to call it a flat – on Mardyke Walk, near the university, where she works as the director of Business-Academic Liaison Services. When they first met she, too, had laughed at the unfortunate acronym, but now whenever he makes a joke about her job being *a load of*, she frowns and says she doesn't understand why he's putting her down. But how can he be putting *her* down by slagging off her job? He can't figure out why she sees it that way. He couldn't care less what anyone might say about the library. He likes the library and, anyway, he's not going to take anyone else's opinion personally.

Jean is petite and pretty, with short blonde hair and greenish eyes. She wears rectangular-framed Prada glasses that cost a fortune and make her eyes look bigger, if slightly prim (Raymond knows better than to tell her this). She wears black trousers almost always, has a whole row of them in her wardrobe. Unlike all the other short women he's ever known – and most definitely unlike his elder sister – Jean never wears heels. Always slim-cut black trousers, fitted tops and narrow, flat shoes. A ballerina on a day off. She always wears the same shade of red lipstick. He likes that about her, her faithfulness to one colour. When the lipstick is empty she goes out and buys a replacement, never being swayed by the vagaries of fashion. He went to get her one as part of her Christmas present one year, only to discover at the make-up counter that the name of the brand wasn't enough. Who'd have known there were so many variations on red? He couldn't tell the difference between most of them. Tired of dithering in the overheated shop with the assistant pointing out one after another, as though he was incapable of reading the labels himself, he had chosen Restless Heart. The expression on Jean's face when she opened her present told him he had got it wrong. When he's not with her – that is, most of the time – he has a court artist's impression of her in his mind, all glasses and ruby lips. A clumsy sketch that isn't her at all.

Raymond thinks he would like a baby. Jean would not. When they first met neither of them was that bothered about having children, although those early conversations left him with the distinct impression that she just wasn't bothered at that time, and it was something that would, some day, find its rightful place in her life. But in the couple of years since, she has become gradually less and less interested while it seems as though his own procreative dial has tick-tocked all the way around to *really bothered* without his noticing it was happening. It makes no sense because, despite wanting a child, Raymond can't really imagine being someone's father. The idea strikes him as preposterous, as alien as if he had been scouted as a professional footballer or – and this is even more preposterous because he can't understand the game, despite living so close to the college ground – for the cricket team. And yet, he reasons with himself, there's plenty worse than him become fathers. His own, for one. And that's a start in itself, isn't it? Knowing what *not* to do?

Never during pint one, but usually during pint two, Raymond wonders whether Jean is planning to leave him. He works it through as the level sinks in his glass. First: she's very ambitious at work; he's not. Second: she's earning good money; he's stuck on the same public sector pittance. And finally: her life is getting bigger; he often wonders is his own shrinking. Why should she stay? By the end of pint two he will be sure that she wants to move out (or more likely, wants him to), yet so trapped in that surety that he can't bring himself to do anything about it. On pint three he'll reason, *No, hang on*: why would she? Okay, so he doesn't get the same level of attention as he once did, but he's still a good-looking guy – he can tell from the reactions he gets over the counter in the library and when they are out at night. They have a nice flat – sorry, apartment – and an easy life together, for one. He knows that she knows he won't be pushy about having a child; they both understand he's too lazy for that. Plus, she likes being the one in charge: he's not sure how happy she'd be with the male equivalent of herself. And not forgetting Dermot! The most serious weapon at Raymond's disposal. No one is quite sure why, but Jean's father has been mad about Raymond since the first day he met him. ('Maybe he's a fan of the soaps,' Mags suggested.) Dermot doesn't give Jean's two sisters' husbands the time of day and is only marginally friendlier to his daughter-in-law. Because Jean and her three equally successful siblings are terrifyingly competitive with each other, Raymond worries that Dermot may become the only card he will have left to play.

And that's pint three finished.

Drinking is like digging. Every mouthful of Guinness takes him deeper down to where the truth is. He pictures himself as a character in *The Great Escape*, scrabbling at the soil under the prisoners' hut, desperate to get under the surface, to run away from himself.

By pint four his mind will have moved on. When he's having his few pints, Raymond's brain is a show-jumping arena. Around and around he goes, completing the circuit each time while accruing faults here and there until it's time to trot back to the loose box. It is a slightly different performance each time but the end result is always the same.

Tired now, Raymond wanders into the kitchen to make a ham sandwich. A snack, a look at the sports news online, a cup of tea and an early night, he decides. That way he'll be fresh for tomorrow, so that he can get stuck into writing the minute he gets home. His *Ideas Notebook* shouts at him from the desk drawer. He flicks through it. Some good stuff there. He flicks again. More pages than he remembered are blank. Not to worry, he'll have a good read through it tomorrow as part of the warm-up routine *Now Write That Screenplay!* recommends. He catches sight of himself in the little mirror Jean keeps on the table for when she does her make-up in the mornings. His face is getting fleshier, jowlier. He sucks his cheeks in. That's more like it. If only he could keep it like that. He has his mother's pale blue eyes. 'Striking' was the word *TV Soap!* magazine often used: *Tommy Maloney's striking good looks gain him another conquest this week.* Are they the eyes of a younger man? On him do they look tired, permanently hungover and slightly seedy?

He fishes around the bottom of his bag for his phone. It's stuck in a folded copy of the previous Friday's *Irish Times*. Shit. Four missed calls.

'Sorry, were you trying to get me?'

Anita is shrill. 'Jesus, where have you been? She's not back.'

'Mags?'

'Who the hell else?'

'All right, calm down. Has anyone seen her?'

'No, and I've been back around all the neighbours and the local shops. Look at the time! I don't like to think of her out after dark by herself.'

'She's not a child, Anita. She's perfectly safe outside in the dark by herself.' *Shit*, he thinks. *Raymond, you thoughtless arsehole.* Quickly, he adds, 'Did you call her friends?'

'The few I have numbers for, yes. No one I spoke to heard from her today.'

'She's out, that's all. Theatre or cinema or something. You're working yourself up over nothing.' As always, his habitual reaction is to say anything that will placate his sister enough to get her off the phone. 'She'll get a taxi if she's going to be out late.'

He can hear Anita bristling. 'And what if she's had an accident?'

'Anita, it's hard I know, but . . . Look, I'm sure it's nothing like that.'

'You've to be gone for twenty-four hours before you can be reported missing to the guards.' Even by her always-on-high-alert standards she sounds upset.

'The *guards*? Fuck's sake, Anita. You don't go to the guards because your mother has gone out for the evening. They'd laugh you out of the place. Where are you now?' He wouldn't put it past her to be phoning from outside a garda station. How like Anita to add two-plus-two and get 999.

'In Booterstown. Derek's at home with the kids – it's lucky he wasn't working late. She must be gone since sometime this morning. That could be twelve hours!'

While she is speaking Raymond has walked to the sitting-room window. His gaze follows the soft, eggy glow of streetlights marching up the road to town. In the other direction lies the dense blackness of the cricket ground, the cherry trees at the entrance invisible now, their tiny buds swallowed by the dark. A woman's shadow spills into a pool of streetlight, then is gone. She is walking swiftly, handbag lodged tight in her armpit. It's gloomy, that path between the apartments and the cricket ground. He's always telling Jean to be careful coming home late at night.

Anita is still talking. She and Mags speak on the phone pretty much every day, she's telling him, so when Mags *does* have any big plans, Anita is always sure to have heard about them, usually more than once. Yes, fair enough, of course she doesn't know minute by minute – *the blow-by-blow*, she calls it – of every single day, but if Mags was going away *overnight*? On a day when they already had an arrangement?

Could this be what is really bothering his sister? Her problem isn't that Mags hasn't got back home yet, but that Anita wasn't in on her plans?

'I hear you, I do, but I don't think you've anything to worry about,' he says again.

Anita just can't help herself – and who can blame her, really, what with Jack and everything – but, Jesus, her always-on-red-alert state can be really hard to deal with.

The window is cold to touch and he can smell his own pub breath, stale and ferrous. So he closes the curtains and turns away, to face his quiet Jeanless flat.

TUESDAY, 8 APRIL 2014

The slightest noise, and Anita is on the move. She notices the sharp, lonely click of her heels along the black-and-white-tiled hall every time. A creak from the gate, the bang of a car door . . . anything, everything, and she rushes to the front window. The net curtain is creased from her incessant shoving. *You're not as laundered as you ought to be*, she thinks, sniffing the dust stirred up from within its folds. Unlike the curtains, the glass is perfectly clean. The smudge of her breath appears and disappears on the glass, puffing back to her in a thin mist.

There's a man on the pavement on the far side of the road. She hasn't seen him before, or the woman moving several slow and steady steps behind him. His red hair is faded with age to a sort of strawberry roan, the colour that never really goes grey. She watches his mouth move, and a second later the woman's mouth moves too, and Anita realises they are together. What can they be talking about, she wonders, that it doesn't matter that they aren't next to each other?

She recognises several neighbours, each one beginning their ordinary, same-as-yesterday day. Teenagers bent low under their rucksacks trek to the school halfway up the avenue, the girls' voices loud and shrill as they repeat each other's words backwards and forwards, telling each other what they have just said. They are covered with make-up, their lipstick matched to the same shade as the trowelled-on foundation. They are identical: mouthless and silenced. Pasty chain-store mannequins come to life. Rebecca and Ailish would be slathered just as bad, if they had their way. Commuters swim downstream to the bus stop and the DART and their desks and their computers and their . . . what? Water-coolers? Anita has never worked in an office. Apart from dropping by Derek's the odd time, and visiting the school secretary or doctor – and they don't really count – she's not been in that many offices, not properly, not for years.

The house directly across the road is painted a lurid purple. A sculptor lives there; she did the place up herself the previous summer. Anita remembers her up that ladder in her filthy overalls ten hours a day every day for a fortnight. The interiors magazine that featured it heralded the design as a triumph of Andalucian influence, and Mags says it's great; claims that she loves it. But, honestly, it's horrible, a Ribena-ish lump of a thing, with a streaky green panelled door, as though a pre-schooler had crayoned it. Mags had frowned and told Anita she was talking a load of nonsense. Getting out of bed and looking across at Daphne's place is gorgeous; like beginning every day with a cocktail, she claimed.

Tuesday is recycling day and Anita must have watched every single neighbour put out their wheelie bins. For something to do, she dragged out Mags's too, though it's barely a quarter full. Does her mother not recycle? Anita spots potato peelings curled on top of the old newspapers. A few used teabags. They're not meant to go into the recycling, everyone knows that. Sod it, she thinks, it's not my problem, and she dumps it on the kerb anyway. Five minutes later, she's back outside wearing her mother's Marigolds, her head and shoulders bent low into the murky green plastic.

Not paying enough attention to small things is what causes the boulders to roll in your direction. This single belief is the closest Anita has ever come to having a personal philosophy, and it has been hard won. It took her a long time not so much to *believe* it as to absorb it. The obstacles thrown at her by God (or whoever or whatever, she's not sure, and sometimes frets about that too; about being unsure even though she insists the twins and Cuan go to Mass and she wouldn't hear of them going anywhere other than Catholic schools), these are outside her domain. Not paying attention to the small things is what brings about bad luck, bad times. The black cat unacknowledged, the kindly shop assistant unthanked, the good fortune selfishly whispered too soon . . . these everyday jinxes can be avoided. There are days when Anita feels as though her life is lived with a piano over her head, suspended by a single thread. And in such a situation, why wave scissors around?

Anita could no more have left her mother's bin like that than she could have ignored her son's tears.

One of their books growing up was a collection of Norwegian fairy tales. Anita never cared for it much, she was an Enid Blyton girl herself. Dad produced it after a trip home to Oslo. His favourite book as a child, he'd told them, as he lifted it from the suitcase. His pyjamas were wrapped around it and it was odd watching him unfurl one deflated paisley leg at a time. The cover was the colour of a muddy lake. For his entire childhood, he told them solemnly, it was the best book he'd read. She couldn't see why. The stories all had silly titles, and every tale was so straightforward, every creature either so-very-good or so-very-bad that, even as a child, she'd understood she was meant to be taking some other message out of them, that there was some crafty *adulty* lesson disguised among these animals and their stupid carry-on, though she could never figure out exactly what it was. There wasn't an *in the beginning* or *happy ever after* in sight.

'You're so literal,' Raymond had remarked, when she took him to task over some nonsense comment he'd made at Mum's birthday tea the year before. 'For God's sake, Anita,' he snapped, 'it's like you're hearing everything in translation.'

Anita had gone home the previous evening for a while, to check everything was okay. She'd looked over the twins' homework, perfunctorily done as usual despite the grinds, but she'd not had the time to argue them into redoing it. The girls made such heavy work of their English essays on *Circle of Friends*. But it's a lovely story: how hard could it be to write an essay on which of the characters you would choose to be? Anita remembered being fifteen and struggling with *Silas Marner* and that other one . . . *Vanity Fair*, was it? *Barchester Towers*, maybe. Books that were taught in such a way as to have all the pleasure of reading drained out of them, where every chapter felt like a new door closing quietly in your face. But *Circle of Friends*? When Anita was at school she and her friends swapped Maeve Binchy books under their desks when the teacher was having a fag break.

'How long's yours?' Rebecca said, tugging at the corner of her sister's copybook.

'Four pages.' Ailish – always the slightly harder worker of the two, to be fair to her – pulled the page back.

'You witch!' Rebecca shrieked. 'I've only two and a half!'

'No way,' Ailish said. 'Is that all?'

'Fact,' Rebecca said, sounding proud of the ineptitude that was bound to bankrupt them. 'Literally.'

Anita had got Cuan ready for bed and made the lunchboxes for the morning. She'd rung Mags a few more times but there wasn't any answer so she got ready to return to Booterstown to wait. Cuan had been upset, scrambling up on her lap, tethering her to the chair. He didn't like her to leave him while he was going to sleep. Ever since he was born, Anita's habit has been to hold his hand and sing or tell him stories until he nods off. It can take ages, sometimes nearly an hour, but Anita loves holding her little boy's hand in her own, tracing tiny circles in his palm with her finger, casting spells of love and safety and warmth over him. He lies there, his eyes drooping but not closed, and sometimes she will run her fingers over his forehead, down the slope of his nose and off the end like a ski run. And though his eyelids might briefly protest, they always give themselves over to her gentle swoop. She alone is the owner, the protector, of his sleep. And what is that, if not love? Cuan is her harbour; she keeps him safe and he her.

Derek finds the whole business exasperating. Cuan should be going to bed by himself, he says. She's babying him. Mammy's boy-ing, he calls it sometimes.

'Mothering,' she had snapped back once, only she was sure he'd replied, 'Smothering, more like,' under his breath.

'What did you say?' she replied, thinking of the moment

when Cuan has given himself over to sleep and she tweaks his duvet straight and rises to leave and his hands faintly bat her away in a weak wave.

'Nothing,' Derek muttered, from the depths of the sofa in the family room. He had flicked the news on, and shouted, 'Becca?' in the general direction of the kitchen. 'Bec? Any chance of a cup of tea?' He twirled the remote in his hand. Derek loves the remote control. Anita wonders does he sometimes wish he could point it at her and click her out of sight. Or, at the very least, mute her.

She lifts her head out of the recycling bin. She wraps the peelings and tea bags in an old newspaper before interring them in their proper grave in the kitchen.

Raymond is on his way to Dublin. He said there was no point facing into rush hour; he would get in the car at ten. Though why he couldn't have got up when she phoned him at eight and avoided rush hour that way – or caught the train – she has no idea. To keep busy while she's waiting, she has another hunt for Mags's address book, finally locating it in a press in the kitchen. Some sort of burglar-proofing strategy, no doubt, as Mum always kept important numbers, like bank account details, written inside the back cover. Mum has had the same address book for years, yet its contents make meagre enough reading. Some entries have a line drawn through the address and a new one – or more than one – written in the margin. She recognises the name of one of Mum's old friends. 'Osborne House, Bray Ave, Sandycove', underneath 'Maria Keady', was crossed out, and so was '4 Seabay Apartments, Grove St, Dún Laoghaire' beside it. Scribbled in the margin was 'Avonmore Nursing Home, Pembroke L., Glenageary'. From avenue to street to lane: life's tracks narrow to a point.

Some entries have a line drawn through the name. Her mother's relationships are crumbling at the edges, a cliff under attack from the sea.

Phone! She fumbles it out of her pocket, cursing the shake in her hands. *Finally*, she thinks, and for a split second she permits herself to be angry at her mother's careless selfishness. She hadn't even realised *how* angry until it comes over her, now that the worry is over, that she is about to talk to her.

'Mum?' she says. *'Mum?'*

And then, 'Oh. No, nothing yet,' only it comes out more of a whisper. She hears the siren of an ambulance on the Rock Road, and then its own plaintive echo, a wounded cry, comes over the phone as well. Liz must be calling from the shop. 'I will, Liz, yes. Thank you, you're very good.'

She puts the phone back into her pocket but doesn't let it go. It's warm in her hand. Her reaction when it wasn't her mother at the other end tells her what she hasn't admitted so far: she's more than merely annoyed now, she's frightened. Mum isn't just late getting home; she's not gone away and not bothered to tell her; she's not delayed somewhere. She has been gone all night. Gone and not told anyone. Surely that means something is wrong. Desperately, horribly wrong. That is how the world works, Anita knows it.

But until Raymond arrives, and the twenty-four hours before they can go to the guards have passed, she doesn't know what she is meant to do. So she treads the path between the kitchen and the window. What else can she do while she's waiting? She had walked up and down the street the evening before, then drove into Blackrock and stopped by Mags's favourite café, a cutesy enough little place on the main street, all Cath Kidston oilcloths and bloated raspberry scones that must be, what, four, maybe five SimpleSlim points each?

'Haven't scones gotten desperate big?' Mags asked her once. 'What's that about, do you think? Why scones? None of the other pastries have changed. I've been checking.' Anita didn't remember what her reply was, but suspected it was of the *oh-what-are-you-like* variety. The café had masses of books piled up any old way on shelves next to the tables, with *Please read, please enjoy, please return!* handwritten on thumbtacked cards. She reread the notice a few times over, but couldn't decide whether the owner's intention was for the books to return, or the customers.

'I was meant to meet my mother,' she'd explained to a hollow-cheeked blonde waitress and flicked through the photos on her phone for a picture to show her. She hadn't known she wouldn't tell the truth until she heard herself lie: 'Only I can't remember was I to meet her here or in the supermarket, and she's no mobile on her. This is her, on the left. Has she been in here today?'

'Oh, I know who you are talking of,' the girl – Eastern European, they usually are – replied. She had braces strung across her top teeth. The clear sort that are meant to be discreet but aren't really. 'That lady comes in for a cappuccino and a pastry, two, maybe one times a week. But only in the mornings, never late like this. And not today at all, sorry.' She'd reached her hands above her ears and smoothed her hair back into a knot. Her white blouse was stained dark in the armpits and a smell of heated milk hung around her. 'We always like to see her,' the girl said, after Anita had thanked her and turned to leave. 'She's friendly.'

And so Anita stands alone at her mother's front window with the strangest sensation that she needs to count every breath she's taking. To listen as hard as she can to the resolute tick of the clock in the hallway. To stare at every dust mote that floats above her until they all settle somewhere out of sight. To study the spidery cracks in the ceiling. To hold it all inside her because everything is about to change and she is going to need the strength formed in the distraction that watching the strangers going up and down the avenue outside can give her.

Then Raymond is at the gate. Anita hadn't noticed his car pull up, and she immediately feels guilty, as though she's been wasting time, hanging around doing nothing.

'So, what's up?' He knows he's spoken too quickly, she's barely got the door open, so he adds, 'Hello, Anita,' and bends over to give her an awkward sort of hug.

'Nothing. Liz from Best Buds—'

'Best *what*?'

'The flower shop? Near the corner? She saw her yesterday morning, waiting at the pedestrian lights on the Rock Road. She thought maybe Mum was heading for the DART station, but that's it.'

'Was she by herself?'

'Yes.'

Just inside the door, Raymond drops his bag as Anita says, 'Give me that,' and reaches forward to grab it from him. How like her, is his automatic reaction, to act like this is her house. That's what twenty-odd years of Derek will do for you, he thinks. Derek is a man who treats everywhere as though it's his own, or as good as. They stand there for a moment, the bag on the floor between them. Anita turns away first. 'Come on through,' she says, then goes down the hallway and into the kitchen.

Anita had rung him first thing to say Mags wasn't back yet. She demanded he come up to Dublin straight away. 'Will I get you a ticket for the next train?' she asked. 'I can do that now and email it.'

'No, no, it's fine,' he had replied, groggy with sleep yet quick to buck under her attempts to control his movements, as though he wasn't even capable of arranging a simple journey. Not that he needed to go anywhere, he was sure of it. When he had told Jean the night before she had immediately twigged what was going on: Mags had taken a notion to visit Elin in Edinburgh but – completely understandably, to his way of seeing it – thought it better just to head off and do it, rather than tell Anita in advance and have to put up with the pursed lips, the unspoken accusations, the *buthowcouldyous* that she must know would be her daughter's parting gift. He couldn't believe he hadn't thought of it himself. He'd texted Elin but she hadn't replied. Nothing new there. He had been hoping that if Mags hadn't reappeared by the morning Anita would have reached the same conclusion herself, but it didn't seem as though she had.

He pictured the scene now: Mags returning a day or two later, caught rotten, that nice *I'm a canvas bag* carrier he'd given her crammed with shortbread, having to explain her actions to her elder daughter. It's a shame she forgot about the dentist appointment, because she'd most likely have got away with it too, if she'd just said she was going to visit a friend down the country or something. Anita's the type from whom it's better to ask for forgiveness than permission. Raymond's worked on that basis since they were kids.

'Look, Anita,' he'd said, keeping his voice low so as not to disturb Jean. 'She's probably gone away to visit someone. It's the most likely explanation . . .' he really hoped he wouldn't have to say their sister's name '. . . and, um, forgotten to tell you. People head off all the time and come back in a day or two. It's odd, yeah, but I don't think we've anything to worry about, I really don't.'

'Her suitcase is here.'

'People buy new suitcases, Anita. Just because you didn't know about it doesn't mean it didn't happen.'

Jean was awake, and looking at him curiously. Had he sounded harsh? 'I didn't mean that the way it came out. I'm still half asleep.'

'Raymond?' Anita's voice was hard, bitter. 'I found her passport in a drawer.'

He'd sat up in bed. So Anita had read his mind, even if she wouldn't come straight out and say so.

Now, stiff-legged from the three-hour drive, he finds himself obediently following his sister down the hallway. 'Okay, so tell me again, who have you checked with already?'

'Here, I wrote it down, look.' She shows him a notebook. The secretary sort, with a spiral top – Mags always keeps one on the phone table in the front hall, has done for as long as he can remember. His mother's handwriting has a spidery, unfamiliar look to it. It's become the writing of an old person. He looks at his sister's list: neighbours, the local shops, the two pubs, a few of Mags's friends, her cousin in Dundalk. St Vincent's Hospital.

'We should go to the guards now.'

'Jesus, Anita, are you sure? I think you're making way too much of this. Let's just phone around everyone again. That woman from the flower shop—'

'Liz.'

'Yeah, whatever. She saw her when? In the morning? Right, let's—'

'No, Raymond, you're not listening to me, this is different. The doctor . . .' Anita stops.

'What doctor?'

'Consultant, actually. Has Mum spoken to you about him?'

'What consultant?' He knows he sounds tetchy but honestly, Anita, he thinks, it's not as though he's querying the doctor's qualifications. Typical of her, to start something then back away. To leave it hanging there, like a fart in a lift. 'Anita? What consultant? I don't know anything about this.'

'Nothing. It's just her recall has been . . . off,' she says, and looks oddly pleased with her description, as though *off* is fine, because it's merely the flip side of *on*.

'Her *recall*?' He feels exhausted suddenly. This is what being trapped in a student play must be like. 'Her recall is off?' he parrots. 'That's a diagnosis, is it? Or does she have a switch we knew nothing about?'

'If you're going to be like that!' Anita snaps.

'Sorry, sorry.' He raises his hands, takes a step back.

'If she didn't want to tell you, then it wasn't my place to. She made me promise not to tell anyone about it yet!' Anita is bristling, ever-righteous. 'Anyway, last night on the phone you kept fobbing me off with all your she'll-be-at-the-theatre talk. She saw a consultant three weeks ago. She's been having trouble with her re-' she hesitates. 'Her memory, though you'd

66

not know it. Well . . .' she almost shrugs '. . . not really, not most of the time. Haven't you noticed anything?'

'What did he say?'

'She's maybe . . .' she swallows '. . . she's possibly in the early stages of dementia.'

'*Dementia?*' His voice goes up a notch. 'She's got *Alzheimer's*?' He can't believe it. It's not true. It's a mistake. Mags is easily distracted, absent-minded sometimes, but who isn't? That's all.

'There's other types too,' Anita is saying. 'It's complex, that's what the consultant said. She's to have more tests to be sure exactly what's going on. It can take months to reach a complete diagnosis.' She picks up her handbag. 'It's twenty-four hours now,' she says. 'The guards will know what to do.'

While Anita calls a friend to make arrangements for Cuan, Raymond goes upstairs to the toilet. He stops on the landing, in front of a long, narrow window inset high into an alcove. On either side of the alcove, built into the very walls of the house, are two wide cupboards. The auctioneer who sold Mags the house said de Valera had hidden out in one of them – she wasn't sure which exactly, but it was probably the one on the right, because it was the nicer of the two, in her opinion – for a few days in 1923 during the Free State round-ups. A likely story, Raymond thought; a pleasing yarn spun by an opportunist estate agent, and as transparent as the smell of fresh-baked bread and coffee that Mags had said permeated the house the first time she'd viewed it. Yet she'd been delighted with the notion. That's what had sold the place to her, she'd said. And whenever she wanted something out of one of those cupboards, she'd say, 'Go get the folder of phone bills, and ask Dev does he need a cup of tea while you're at it,' or 'Will you fetch down that box of books for the charity shop, please, love? Dev had better not have been sitting on it after the dent he put in the last one,' or whatever. Dev took on the flavour of a resident guest, pliable and peaceable as a poor relation.

He wipes his damp hands on the back of his trouser legs and tries to remember when he was last in this house. He hasn't been to Dublin to visit his mother for three months. No, four; he remembers the dutiful visit at New Year, and this is now April. *Early* April, he reminds himself. So three months, really. He can hardly recall that visit. He tries to remember what they spoke about the last time he phoned. Did she sound different? Forgetful? He wasn't aware of anything. And if he wasn't aware of it, how can there be something wrong? It can't be possible to conceal the loss of your own self. It's not the same as pretending an awful pain in your chest is a spot of indigestion and you'd best lay off the beer and spicy foods for a few days. He pictures old people – proper old, not his-mother old. Women in faded flower-print bed jackets in care homes, their faces blank as babies'. Strangers, even to themselves, lost for ever in Ga-ga Land. Mags doesn't fit in the scene.

Dementia?

Bollocks.

And bigger bollocks: why hadn't anyone told *him*?

'You know what, Anita?' He's halfway down the stairs and sees her waiting by the front door, coat on and handbag over her shoulder. 'Okay, so you're telling me that she might have a problem with her memory, though I've not noticed anything and I'm not at all happy that this is the first I've heard of it.' She is about to interrupt so he keeps going: 'And, yes, she's not here and didn't tell you where she was going . . . but there is no *actual* link between them. None. Whatever connection you've made is one you've imagined.'

Anita is capable of drawing a line between any two things and coming up with disaster. He can't blame her for that, but he doesn't have to let himself get dragged into it. No way. She says nothing and walks outside, ahead of him. She pulls at a tissue in her hands and tiny white shreds flutter to the path at his feet.

Garda Ivan Petkova doesn't look much older than the twins, and Anita has a sudden image of Rebecca and Ailish trussed up in garda uniforms, drafted into the force for a fortnight on a transition-year project. He is short and stocky. His thin blond hair is cropped and sticks straight up, like a baby chick's. There is a smear of shaving foam on his right ear. Anita sees Raymond spot it too. She'd never let Derek out of the house like that – does the man not have a mirror? When he excuses himself to fetch the station book, Anita whispers, 'Should we ask to speak to someone else, do you think?'

'That's racist, Anita,' he smirks.

'That's not what I meant! I meant a . . .' she falters '. . . a—'

'A grown-up?'

Anita feels herself flush as Garda Petkova reappears and wonders if they could have been overheard.

'Sorry for wasting your time. I mean, you know, it's probably nothing,' Raymond begins. Anita wants to give him a dig in the arm for his patronising don't-mind-my-stupid-sister tone. She would have done it, too, when they were kids.

'You're not. If you were concerned enough to come here, then we'll discuss it,' the garda replies. 'Do you have a recent photograph?'

'No.' Raymond sounds surprised to have been asked at all.

How like him, just to reply without checking with her. Of course she has a photograph! She opens her handbag. 'It's all I could find in a hurry.' She can hear the apologetic tone in her voice. 'It's from last Christmas. I don't have any more recent ones.'

Mum is sitting to Derek's right at the table and the twins, with Cuan between them, are sitting across from her. They are wearing party hats and Cuan is waving a ripped cracker in his hand. A plum pudding in a halo of flames waits on the table beside Derek, the blue flickering a beard in front of his face.

'This will be fine for now.' Garda Petkova puts the photograph on the desk beside him. He takes out a ledger and a sheet of questions. It's left up to Anita to answer them, of course, just as she knew it would be. Raymond is useless as ever. The public office of the station is cold: she can feel a draught from the door nipping around her ankles. It's an ugly room, peppered with formal-sounding signs about passport applications and driving licences. Scraps of old sticky tape hang from the walls. Some posters ask what you've seen, others tell you what to watch out for. It makes her nervous, to be in a garda station. It makes her feel guilty. They must design these rooms for that purpose, she thinks. She sees Raymond sneaking glances at the photo of their mother, over and over. Upside-down Mags is smiling, untroubled, her paper crown low over the forehead that takes the place of where her chin should be. Upside-down Cuan is grinning at his grandmother rather than the camera, his mother.

They are standing at the public desk, talking through an open hatch. It's not quite big enough for both their heads to peer through at once, so she's doing the talking. Raymond sticks his head in and out from the side when he wants to add something, which isn't often. It's like he's under the control of an incompetent puppeteer.

The other hatches facing onto the long counter are shut, and while she explains about Mags and going to collect her for the dentist the day before, she becomes aware of a straggling queue building alongside them. A spotty teenager, mobile clamped to her ear, fans herself with an application for an Age Card. She's standing too close to them and Anita's brain quickly conducts an automatic algorithm and comes up with *Age Card + teenagers = drunk twins*.

'I know!' The girl's voice is shrill. 'I mean, lols? Like, I know!'

A woman with a tattoo on her neck is complaining that they'll never get the bloody baby's passport done on time now. Why could he not have got the bloody thing sorted when he said he would? She pushes a buggy back and forward aggressively, and with each shove a small, grizzling face appears briefly by Anita's knee, only to jerk back again in a horizontal bungee. 'Go way,' the man with her hisses. 'Go way and shite with your carry-on.'

'Next question.' Garda Petkova scowls at the baby. 'Have you details of any known medical condition, physical or mental disability?'

'Well,' Anita begins, 'she takes medication called Eltroxin for an underactive thyroid. I get the prescriptions filled for her sometimes.'

'Anything else?'

'Well . . .' Anita says again.

The passportless baby lets rip a loud cry and its parents unite in anger as they look down and yell, 'Shut UP,' at the buggy.

She has to raise her voice to be heard over the lot of them. 'Her memory.' It comes out too loud, a shout. Garda Petkova looks up and frowns. The girl on the mobile, the man, the woman, they all stop. Their stares burn hot on the back of her head. Only the baby ignores her and continues to squeal.

He puts down his pen. 'Wait here, please,' he says, and walks away, through a door Anita hadn't even noticed was there.

Sergeant Call-me-Rena Corish's handshake isn't a shake at all, more of a politician's thorough clamp-and-release. Anita's hand disappears entirely inside the woman's paw. Anita doesn't know what to say and so, 'Right so, then,' the sergeant continues. She gestures to them to sit down and sips from a mug she's had clutched in her other hand since she walked into the room. Rusty tea stains streak down the mug's side, bisecting the words *I've Tried the Tri-Athlone*, whatever it might be. The interview room is dull and grey, two stacking chairs on either side of a grubby, scratched table. Sergeant Corish sits across from them. She is a tall woman, not far off Raymond's height, and broad with it. She takes up more space than the seat provides and seems to spill over it and under the table. Her nails are cut low and – surprisingly, because it doesn't fit with the rest of her – painted a thin opalescent pink, a colour Anita hasn't seen in years. She didn't know you could still buy it.

Sergeant Corish puts down the mug and takes off her glasses almost as a single movement. Tea slops over the side and puddles on the table, but if she sees it, she doesn't care.

'To explain: the term *missing person* is used by us to apply to anyone whose whereabouts are unknown and the circumstances of the disappearance presents a risk of harm either to themselves or any other person. But, most importantly, what I need you to understand is that going missing is not a crime,' she says, looking straight at Anita. She feels herself blush guiltily again. This woman's not going to do her for wasting police time, is she? Derek will have something to say if she so much as tries! Sergeant Corish continues, 'And you may not have known this, but every year thousands of people are reported missing in Ireland. Last year it was the best part of eight thousand. Almost nine thousand the year before.'

Anita feels she ought to protest at this. As if she cared about anyone else. It's just the one she's here to talk about.

'Now, I'm not saying any of this to belittle your concerns,' Sergeant Corish continues, as though she knew what Anita wanted to say, 'and, yes, that's approximately twenty people reported missing every day. But the vast, the *vast*,' she says again, as though a single vast couldn't possibly do justice to the scale she has in mind, 'majority turn up safe and well within a couple of days. And why am I telling you this?' Anita has time to wonder are they meant to answer before Sergeant Corish adds, 'Because if they didn't, you know what? You'd hear about them. From last year's cases, there are only a dozen outstanding missing persons. The word *missing* is a very emotional one, Mrs Jennings, and our advice would be not to focus on it.'

Easy for her to say, sitting there swigging tea like she's nothing better to do.

'What we find,' she continues, 'is that in some cases the person may be escaping from real or perceived conflict – within the family, say – or they may be victims of foul play, though from the information you gave my colleague Garda Petkova, I think that's highly unlikely to be the case here. And,' her voice softens, 'there are also instances of people feeling that they need to assert their independence or to take some time out for themselves. This may be hard for you both to believe, but there are people who simply forget to make contact. These are all much more common reasons than you might suppose, because these are the ones that the media don't pick up on and that don't make the news. In such situations we usually begin with what we call a *watching brief*, where we monitor the situation until we have reason to believe the information has changed in such a way as to move it off this grid. Okay?' They nod. 'So, Mrs Jennings, do you have any reason to believe your mother could be in any of the categories I've outlined?'

'No.' Anita's hands twist in her lap.

'Is it possible that she might have made a new . . . friend, maybe?' Sergeant Corish leans heavily on the word, weighing it down.

'Who?' Anita asks. 'What do you mean?'

'A new relationship, possibly? One you don't know about.'

'Of course not!' The very idea.

'Why not? It could happen.' Raymond speaks for the first time since entering the interview room.

What is *up* with him? 'I'd have known if she had. No, this isn't like her at all, Sergeant Corish,' Anita interrupts, her voice flat (she can't bring herself to call a garda *Rena*).

'Em, Anita? What about a few months ago when she was to go shopping with you and went off into town by herself for the day? You weren't calling her "missing" then.'

'But now . . .' Anita hesitates '. . . there's the recall issue.'

'Yes,' Sergeant Corish says quickly, eyebrows raised and head tilted to one side. 'Yes, tell me some more about that.'

'She's been having some problems with her memory recently. We thought it was her thyroid at first, because when it's out of kilter she often feels a bit fuzzy for a week or two. Her GP referred her to a consultant a few weeks ago and he thought, said, I mean, that, well, she was in the early stages of dementia, though nothing is confirmed yet and she hasn't seemed particularly . . . ' The words Anita might use without thinking about someone else's parent – *doddery, batty, not-herself* – don't apply now that it's her own mother. But she's not sure what to say instead. She knows the sergeant is waiting for her to finish, but she can't. Her thumb bumps into something hard on the underside of the table. It breaks off and falls onto her lap. A scored, greyish lump of old chewing gum.

'There is a separate protocol in situations where the person has any form of dementia,' Sergeant Corish says. 'But this sounds slightly different, as there isn't a formal diagnosis in place.'

'Does that mean you're not going to look for her?' Raymond says.

'You have to!' Anita butts in. 'It's over twenty-four hours now!'

'It doesn't mean any such thing.' Sergeant Corish gives him a curious look. 'And by the way, Mrs Jennings, there is no need to wait twenty-four hours to report a missing person. That's a common misconception.' Anita flushes. More ammunition for Raymond against her.

'But first,' the sergeant continues, 'we have to find out if she is, in fact, *missing*.' She holds one finger in the air as she speaks, presumably to remind them of her earlier warning about the M-word. A stale whiff of cigarettes floats across the table. 'It's possible that she's staying with a friend or has gone on holidays or . . . well, there are lots of scenarios relating to family circumstances or unplanned trips away or new situations, as I explained earlier.'

Anita frowns, sure that Raymond is silently *told-you-so-ing*. 'I can't think of who else to try,' she says. 'It doesn't make sense anyway, that she wouldn't have mentioned it. And I called St Vincent's too, in case, you know, of an accident.'

'Have you contacted any other hospitals?'

Anita shakes her head. 'Only Vincent's. It didn't occur to me to try any others. I assumed she'd be nearby.'

'Not always,' the sergeant says. 'Just last week in this station there was a situation where a young local man was knocked down by a car in Howth and was unconscious. His phone smashed, he'd no ID on him, and his parents assumed he was out in UCD as usual, so they didn't phone hospitals on the northside when they starting looking for him. He'd been in hospital for twenty-four hours when they found where he was.'

Of course! How stupid of her not to have thought of that. It's almost a relief. But then she pictures Mags in a hospital on the other side of the city, a tube in her mouth, her identification gone, waiting for her daughter to come and claim her. Christ, what if she was mugged in town? Knocked unconscious and her bag stolen. Alone and confused, pushed down some filthy laneway. Sergeant Corish takes out the station book and looks over the answers they gave to her colleague. She reads quietly to herself, as if they aren't even in the room, touching her mug gently against her teeth over and over. Anita mentally runs through what she has just told them, prodding the statistics, desperately wanting these new assertions to be strong enough to take Anita's weight, to keep her upright. Everything that has been said pretty much boils down to: *don't worry*. Anita pushes against this thought. It creaks, sways. It is nothing more than the soft green bones of a child. Sergeant Corish must know this.

'Did you give Garda Petkova your mother's mobile number?' Sergeant Corish asks, without raising her eyes. 'We can ping – track – it to establish where it might have been used.'

'She left it behind in the house,' Anita replies.

'Have you checked whether her bank accounts have been accessed?'

'Isn't that something the guards do?' Raymond asks.

'If we have to, but there is a legal sequence we have to follow that can take time. It's probably quicker for you to check yourselves.'

There is another silence, then Anita adds, 'Sergeant Corish? What happened to him?'

'Who?'

'The guy, the one in Howth.'

'He's going to be fine, Mrs Jennings. That's my point. At this stage, in this situation, we would be very confident of a positive outcome. Very confident indeed, and I would ask you both to take note of the statistics I quoted and remember that.' She looks up. 'Okay? Right so. This is what is going to happen next.'

Naked walls painted an unconvincing grey gloss, metal table, stacking chairs. The sergeant's pumping handshake that went on so long Raymond felt as though she wasn't so much shaking his hand as holding it. And then she had just sat there in front of them, slowly reading everything the child-garda had so laboriously written down in his hard-backed ledger. Not a sign of a computer anywhere. It was disappointingly commonplace, in fact, rendered completely familiar from years of TV dramas and his own supposed drug-fuelled wrangles years before in the plasterboard garda station on *Baysiders*. The interview room might as well have been a set, and a cheap one at that, he decided. Raymond had trained himself always to have one eye out for details he'd need for the screenplay. It made him feel good, the awareness that he was observing things. The anticipation of the quiet happiness that letting this inner world out would bring him. He was a camera, cool and impartial, his brain reconfiguring the meaningless upside-down images of life into art. It was a sort of pre-writing, necessary and important. The fact that his packets of A4 continued to remain unsullied was almost irrelevant. Life translated was what was important, and it was stacking up on the inside, waiting for him to unlock the door and channel the ideas that would flow.

Apart from that glance she'd given him when he'd asked about searching (the last thing he needs is *another* woman looking crooked at him), Sergeant Corish had been very straightforward. Even her fag-stained, air-quoting fingers and that triathlon mug – no way was that her own – were oddly reassuring. Anita seemed to believe her way more than she had believed Raymond, even though the sergeant had told her pretty much the same thing: yes, lots of people disappear, take time out, whatever phrase you want to put on it, but nearly all of them reappear within days. (Anita's face when Corish suggested Mags might have got herself a man!) People make the decision to go, people return. Sergeant Corish had told them so, loud and clear. Raymond had decided not to mention Elin because then the sergeant would have been sure to say, *Who's that?* and the whole awful history would be started up again, whirling around them. What difference would it make anyway? he'd reassured himself. Without a passport or any other photo ID, Mags hasn't gone to Edinburgh. Some sort of accident is a possibility for sure, horrible an idea as it is. Raymond is kicking himself that he hadn't thought to phone around all the other hospitals earlier, before going to the garda station. That's the next thing to do. It made so much sense that he'd wanted to elbow Anita in the ribs when Sergeant Corish said it. Mystery solved. The momentary relief had nearly made him lightheaded, the same foolish upswing that sees the entire country, tipsy and giddy and shivering, drinking their pints outside on the first fine evening of spring.

The beat when Sergeant Corish *tap-tapped* her mug against her teeth had put Raymond in mind of the issues desk at work. Pauline has a particularly rhythmic way of stamping out books. If only he *was* in the library – a first for him, to wish that – instead of here, now, in Anita's car on the Rock Road, waiting for the lights to change so they can turn right onto Booterstown Avenue. He's tempted to tell Anita that he'll jump out now. A quick pint in The Magpie may help him think. He flicks the electronic control of the window, moving the glass up and down a few inches at a time. Outside in the nature reserve birds hunting for food drop into the long green grass, their descents as smooth as tiny, doomed planes.

Click click. Click click.

'For heaven's sake,' Anita snaps. 'Will you give over?'

Raymond sighs. Everyone is a recalcitrant child to his sister. Uncontrolled, a gun that fires blanks. But he drops his hand to his lap all the same. To be fair to Anita, she had known the answers to all the questions. Raymond himself wouldn't have made it past the first round of Garda Petkova's 'Know Thy Mother' quiz. Raymond silently runs through a few of the questions again. He remembers when he last saw his mother, and the call log on his mobile had revealed when he'd last spoken to her: those he could have answered easily. But that's not what he's searching his memory for. No. He's trying to spot exactly where on the checklist it was that he'd slipped: where it was that he'd slid from information to speculation, and then down into the darkness, into ignorance.

Raymond is trying to pinpoint exactly when it was he – and only he – lost his mother.

Name, address and telephone number of person reporting and relationship to the missing person. An easy one for starters, Raymond thinks. Thanks, Guard. Anita Jennings, 33 The Pines, Carysfort Grange Road,

Blackrock, Co. Dublin (081) 2009004, daughter; and Raymond Jensen, Apartment 6, 7 Mardyke Mews, Cork, (081) 2356911, son.

Name and age of missing person. Again, no problem. He'd aced it. Margaret Jensen, sixty-nine. She'll be seventy on 10 August, added Anita. Typical one-upmanship.

Details of any vehicle or other transport used. Raymond was first to the buzzer again. Bzzz. None, Guard, none! When she moved to Booterstown she got rid of the car. She doesn't even have a current driving licence any more. Seven years ago, that was; she had been living in Shankill her whole life before that, Anita broke in over him. But she could have got a taxi, couldn't she? Anita had added. Or a lift. Or a bus or a DART or . . .? Yes, yes, Raymond replied, aware of how harsh he sounded. We get it. Tears glistened in his sister's eyes. Sorry, he whispered. They were sitting side by side and he reached out to give her shoulder a squeeze, only Anita suddenly bent over to fumble in her bag for a fresh tissue. I've got the measure of you, he read in the young guard's eyes, as Raymond's hand wrapped around the back of his sister's neck instead.

Details of social networking sites, chatrooms or blogs, e.g. Facebook, Myspace, Kidzworld. They had both stared, wordlessly. No, I suppose not. Garda Petkova had shrugged.

Assessment of the person reporting. Garda Petkova flushed as soon as he'd spoken. Sorry, he said, glancing at Raymond. That's one for me, I think, for later.

Description of person. Raymond had gestured to his own shoulder to illustrate that Mags is so-so in height. Grey hair. What else would he have said? Blue eyes. About normal size and shape for a woman her age? He corrected the thought: about average size. Friendly. Curious about people. Healthy? Yes. Or, at least, he had thought so. But honestly, how bad could her memory be, if she hadn't even been prescribed anything? Hadn't even been diagnosed, for God's sake! Would he describe her as a happy woman? he'd asked himself. Yes. Would he describe her as disappointed in him, her only son? Definitely.

Anita gave Margaret's height as five foot four, which made her smaller than he had thought. Weight about nine stone, maybe less. She had lost a few pounds recently. Slim build, anyway. Hair worn in a high bun. Almost entirely grey around her face but dark at the back, under the coil of the bun. Pale skin. Lovely skin.

Raymond recalled Anita as a permanently flushed and freckled teenager who had always envied their mother's colouring. No matter how much of that green Corrective Crème muck she slathered on, she had never achieved Mags's even, pink-tinged complexion.

Poor old Anita, Raymond thought. How is she to describe Margaret, as both the guards referred to her? Margaret is an abandoned widow of one. Margaret is a mother of three. Margaret is a grandmother of four, one of whom is dead. She is all Anita and Raymond have left of their own childhood. She is the keeper of the family's memories.

Then the lights turn green and The Magpie slips silently past.

He should have got out.

Click click. Click click.

Jesus, what is he like, flicking the switch again, after she'd told him not to? 'Raymond, Jesus! Will you please cut that out?'

'What?'

'That!' Anita flaps her hand, irritated. 'Give over the messing. You'll break the mechanism.' She pulls up outside Mum's. She's sure he's still annoyed with her for not telling him about the doctor before today. She'd been about to last night on the phone, but had stopped herself. She had pictured the words – *memory loss* – being beamed up into the air, bouncing from tower to tower across the land until they dropped down to Cork and his ear. *No, no*, was what she had thought. Not now. But no way is he going to make her feel guilty for not running to him with what Mum had made very clear was her own private business. He is annoyed with her for not telling, and Mum will be annoyed with her that she *has* told. Typical, Anita thought. Damned, no matter what she does.

'Whatever you might think, Raymond, I don't believe you when you say you're not worried.' She pulls the handbrake up, hard. 'And do you know why? Because you're here.'

Neither of them moves for a moment. They stare straight ahead at the car parked in front. At the street where their mother isn't, but should be. At everything, at nothing.

'You know what we have to do?' Raymond speaks without looking at her. She has her hand on the clasp of her seatbelt but suddenly doesn't have the energy to push it. She can tell that he's been building up to this. Well, let him. Let him struggle to say something: she's not going to meet him halfway, that's for sure. Let it be difficult for him. It is for her, every single bloody day of her life.

'I can think of a hundred things.' She hears the chilly tone in her voice and is glad of it, of its surety. She takes out her mobile to call Derek even as she's pulling the fob from the ignition. *We generally find, and the Missing In Ireland Support Service would concur, that it's best to keep yourselves calm during this time and take it step by step.* Wasn't that what the sergeant had said to them just before they left the station? Well, that's what she's going to do. She knows Raymond is waiting for her to take the lead. Fine. She is. 'You heard what the guards said,' she continues, ignoring his discomfort. 'We've to call the hospitals, all her friends, check with her bank. All that.' She is all business. There is work to be done, control to be pulled from chaos. Catastrophe must be contained, must be ordered. The spent parachute folded and returned to its backpack.

'No,' Raymond replies. 'You know what I mean.'

And suddenly she is a cartoon character hurtling over a giant crevasse in a rock, her little legs whirring and flailing as she hovers over the edge for one, two, five seconds. She's waiting for this to happen, and yet it still comes as a shock to hear him say, admittedly gently enough for him, the name.

'No, Anita. First off,' he says, 'we have to talk to Elin.'

And Anita is nothing more than a blur of black lines and

rotating arms, toppling and turning, whizzing to the bottom of the canyon.

That whooshing sound! And again, only closer that time. He didn't have to open his eyes to know it had landed on top of the wardrobe and its long arms, thin as branches but strong as tree trunks, were scrabbling above his head, desperate to grab him. To shove him under the batwing of its black cloak and disappear.

Raymond and Anita weren't allowed out of bed after eight, but a vampire on his wardrobe had to count as an emergency, even for Dad. The lights upstairs weren't kept on at night because the house *gobbled electricity*, Dad said. His first plan was to sneak out and wake Anita, but her room was at the opposite side of the house from his. He'd have to survive the landing that led to the top of the stairs and then another corridor to her room. She'd probably tell him to get lost anyway.

Instead he crept down the pitch-black stairs, the chattering of his teeth keeping him company. Anita told him she'd once seen the creature that gobbled their electricity, a huge warty thing, crunching light bulbs between its fangs and spitting splinters in all directions. Dad knew how scared Raymond was of the dark that took over the world at night. (It was to be many years before Raymond twigged that switching off the landing lights was his father's way of keeping his children tucked up in their beds.)

Raymond would have loved to live on an estate, like the ones most of the boys in his class came from. Everything neat. The houses all warm and bright, each with another house joined to it, like a best friend. Windows that closed tight as lunchboxes, and cupboards that joined up with the ceiling. Raymond hated his house, a big grey stone building, with trees all around it and a garden the size of a field on three sides. Anita thought the house was cool: her friends envied her, saying it was like living in a castle. He hated the windows that always let in cold air whether they were open or not, and the cracked glasshouses that rattled like marbles when it was windy. Their house was at the far end of Kilmarth Road, which was nothing more than a lane. Every garden had a thick border of trees. A few yards from the gate at the top of their driveway Kilmarth Road ended abruptly in a stile. To the left, thirty steep steps led down to a beach. Over the stile there was a large park, with a path that meandered alongside the coast for a bit, then turned back towards Shankill village. He didn't like having the sea so near: the beach was stony, and the water full of seaweed and jellyfish. Poo as well, Anita used to tell him, and dare him to walk into the water with his eyes shut.

By the bottom step he could hear their voices coming from the back of the house. Mum was in the dining room. A wind was getting up in the garden, tugging at the glass. He navigated rug by rug on tiptoe down the hall. The dining-room door was half open, but something about the voices inside made him pause, his hand already flat against the wood. He put one eye to the door jamb. The thin slit framed his parents as though they were on a tiny stage. Dad was smoking by the window while Mum sat at the table, her dinner pushed away from her. Raymond could see the mound of beef stew – Dad's favourite – on her plate. Raymond had been in the kitchen with her when she made it but no way would he taste it. Bulges of marrowbones bobbed up out of the broth, bodies thrown overboard. He had sat at the table and played chess by himself while she chopped and fried and stirred. She hardly said a word the entire time. Maybe, Raymond thought, she didn't like stew either.

Mum was apologising for something.

It's bad timing, she was saying. *I'm sorry.* She had a good dress on and was wearing make-up. When had she put it on? She definitely hadn't looked like that when she'd tucked him in at bedtime. Her hair was free of its usual hairband and hung loose below her shoulders. Her hands rested on the table, in the place where her plate should have been. Did Mum carry on like this all the time after he went to bed? Her hair brushed flat and long and shining like a conker and the dining table set for good, like it was Christmas Day? He always had assumed her day ended at eight, same as his. And yet there she was, looking different. Acting different. Carrying on without him. It didn't make sense. If he could sniff her, he'd be able to make sure. He'd be able to smell her perfume and cigarettes, and under them, her real self – the thick, meaty cooking smell of the stew.

A small black plastic bull dangled from a ribbon tied around the neck of the wine bottle. In the kitchen earlier Anita had claimed this *Torres!* as her own, even though she had lots of them, way more than Raymond. She always grabbed stuff like that, and Dad let her. Every time.

Dad continued to smoke and look out into the dark garden. Mum sipped her drink without taking her eyes from the man in the window. Then she looked down at the table and her hair fell into curtains at the sides of her face. She must have lost her band somewhere. *I know how much it matters*, she said. *I won't forget.*

Could Dad tell he was hiding behind the door, afraid of the dark and desperate to slip into the tight wrap of his mother's arms? Cigarette smoke puffed into the room, and Raymond turned and went back upstairs, quiet as he could. Back to the terror waiting on top of his wardrobe.

The sun through the net curtains is heavy on his eyelids, not so much a colour as a yellowish haze, the dense, exhausting weight of hot, summer sand. He opens his eyes, and the long-gone ghost of his father turns an imaginary corner, disappears down the rabbit hole. Raymond blinks. He remembers that night clearly: he'd had a fear-of-vampires thing for ages around that time. It didn't fade until after Elin was born and Anita swore the noise of her screeching kept all the monsters away. (But just to be on the safe side, for his eighth birthday he had asked for a built-in wardrobe.)

It is two hours since they left the garda station. He knows he should be outside now. Asking, looking, phoning. Doing something, doing anything. But he isn't. He's standing at his mother's window, the net curtain a ticklish filling in a sandwich of forehead and glass. The dusty nylon holds a faint whiff of the scent Mags has been wearing for as long as he can remember, though he's no idea what it's called. He twitches his nose at something else: Anita's perfume. Her face, too, must have been pressed to this window recently. His heart unexpectedly aches for his sister. He can hear the mountainous climb of her voice from Mags's kitchen, though he can't make out exactly what she is saying. It rises then falls, interlaced with thick moments of silence when she reaches the brow of each hill. Lulls, carved out by his sister trying not to cry. He should go to her. Only he can't move.

No one has seen or spoken to Mags for thirty hours.

This is where they are.

Mags is missing.

Despite everything Sergeant Corish said, and everything he himself has said over and over again in the last two hours to reassure Anita, he can't stop the word *missing* running through his head over and over, in a panicked ticker-tape parade. He is trapped behind the glass, looking out at a street that has changed completely in two hours without changing at all. The sky and the ground are the same ones the sun rose on, but everything between them, uniting them, has been tilted on its axis.

Anita called all the hospitals. Nothing.

'Circle the wagons,' Anita told him Derek had said. What a very Dereky thing to say, Raymond had thought. But Raymond should be circling a wagon, he knows it. More than one. Yet, right now, all he can do is press his head against the rough crosshatch of the net curtain. There's a tatty navy tartan travel rug on the back of Mags's sofa and he wants to climb under it and hide. He pictures Jean's gaze, eyebrows shooting up over the top of her glasses. *Hide and seek is for children*, she would be sure to comment. *When adults do it, it's just hide.* Jean would know what to do. He's called her four times in the last two hours only to get her voicemail each time. She's not called him back, and he hasn't left a message. Why should he? A non-message is a message in itself, isn't it? A summons, a plea for help, a cry that is both loud and unspoken. This is what couples are meant to do, isn't it? To communicate in code. Doesn't she just *know* he needs her?

If only he could be in Flannerys and that today was yesterday. No, more than that: he wishes that today was last week. Last year. And he could forget all of this because it hadn't happened yet. Nor would it because he'd stop it coming to pass somehow. He'd reach into the future and derail this day. He'd . . . He isn't aware that his eyes have closed again until the window vibrates under a hefty *rap-rap*. He jumps and stumbles backwards, and whacks the back of his knees against a little table. A wordsearch book – *Bumper Issue! Puzzle Mania!* – and a TV guide slip to the floor. A biro rolls out from between two pages of the book and trundles out of sight under the sofa.

'You're Raymond.' The woman from the window is at the front door and has shaken his hand before he's even realised he offered it. 'I'm Liz Buckley. I have the flower shop down the road. Any word from Mags yet?'

He shakes his head. It's odd to hear his mother's name fall so familiarly from the mouth of yet another stranger. Unlike Sergeant Corish's deep-dug pronunciation *Maaargrit*, Liz's voice is soft and low, her *Mags* a breathy sliver of a word.

'Shit,' Liz says, and he nods.

Get a grip, Raymond, he thinks. Do more than mime your answers. 'Yes,' he says, and in the long pause they both understand that that single word was the best he could do.

Liz leans forward and puts her hands on his arms, just above his wrists. Raymond finds himself being turned around and led back towards the sitting room. 'Staring out the window won't find her,' she says, and he wants to bristle but he can't because it's true. He can hear the trace of a smile in her voice as she points over his eyebrows and adds, 'You've the print of the net curtain on your forehead.'

Anita, still on her phone, appears briefly in the hallway, and Raymond watches the quick flash of unspoken exchange between her and Liz: a shrug and shake that said *hello* and *no* and *can I help* and *yes, you can* all at once.

'Your colleague went through that with me already, yes.' He hears his sister's irritated tone as her voice recedes once more. 'And, as I explained to her twice already, I'm not trying to check how much money my mother has. I don't want to *access* her account. I need to find out whether she's used it this week or not.'

He is led to the sofa, pliant as a shy child. 'Close your eyes for a minute and breathe slowly,' Liz tells him. Her voice is a metronome clicking in harmony with the old grandfather clock by the front door. 'In and out, take your time,' she says. His first thought is of the stupid trust exercises the *Baysiders'* directors insisted the actors do before filming a difficult scene. He recalls the time he had been blindfolded and then led, his feet jutting stiffly in front of him, as if he were a toy, by Masher Maher around the RTÉ car park. All he had needed, was his bitter thought at the time, was to be wearing a high-vis 'guide dog in training' jacket. An hour later the cameras had rolled and Maher shot him in a single take.

'I've come to help,' Liz says, replying to a question he would never have asked.

Help, he thinks. And whether it is because of the word, or the thought, or just the kindly voice of Liz, sitting next to him with her hands loose in her lap, right now, and for the first time in a very long time, Raymond wants to cry.

Best Buds, Liz decides, will be a better location from which to coordinate a search. 'You don't want to use the house,' she said, and before Raymond could ask why not, Anita had appeared, her phone call finished, and agreed.

'It's not a good idea. For security. Anyway, I don't think your mum will want to hear you'd had strangers trooping in and out of her home,' Liz adds, nodding. 'She's too private a person for that.' *Is she?* Raymond has never thought of Mags as private. (Or public, or otherwise.)

'Can I have a recent photo?' Liz asks. 'Then I can do a poster for us to hand out. I've a printer in the shop.'

A *what*? He wants to shout at her to stop, to leave them alone. His mother's disappearance is becoming hyper-real. He desperately wants to slow it all down, as though the activity is creating her absence rather than responding to it. First he had to watch it get written down by Sergeant Corish, and now a *poster*? All this officialdom is making it worse. Of course she is no more missing than she was an hour before, yet somehow she is. She has become that thing he's seen on the news: A Missing Person. Only this morning she was nothing more than his mother, off on a jaunt in Edinburgh or wherever. But now the scene has changed. Her character has been rewritten by Anita, by the guards. She is an old lady. She is nowhere to be found. She is missing.

She is going to be a poster.

Anita doesn't have the picture taken at Christmas: she left it behind at the station. 'Raymond,' she tells him, 'go back and collect it.'

'No, no, it doesn't matter,' Liz replies. Are they talking to him or about him? He pictures the thin gold paper crown Mags had on in the photograph. Was she having a nice time when it was taken? He hopes she was happy with her grandchildren in her fragile, Christmas kingdom.

Liz goes over to the mantelpiece where a couple of framed photos prop up flimsier bits and pieces, cards and letters. Anita takes up a reminder from the dentist and sets it down again. They choose a photo of Mags dressed for a winter day, her beret at an angle and covering her bun, a bright pink scarf wound around her neck. She has a fleshy double chin he's never noticed before. Is there something not quite right to her eyes? Is he imagining it or is there a slight disconnection? A blurriness? Her smile is the same, though, the wide beam that lit up his childhood. It looks as though she was trying to make the photographer laugh. She must have liked whoever it was.

While Liz and Anita discuss the wording for the poster, Raymond puzzles at the photograph. Mags is at a slightly odd angle. The camera was pointing up, which is why her chin looks soft and doughy. It must have been taken by someone much shorter than her.

Liz is at the door, ready to go. 'Talk to you later, Anita,' she says, 'I'll keep in touch.' And with that, she is gone. She didn't say goodbye or look at him. They must both think him a useless lump, he decides, one that is better ignored than involved.

'Raymond?' She's back. Or, rather, her head is, poking around the door. 'Why don't you come with me?'

They haven't got three houses away before Anita is shouting at them from the gate. 'Liz?' She mimes a rectangle in the air. 'Have you the photo?'

Liz breaks her stride for a second and turns around, holding it aloft between forefinger and thumb. Mags sways to and fro in the slight breeze.

'Right,' Anita shouts, and is gone.

'I was driving from here to Blackrock one day,' he can hear himself babbling, as he follows Liz down Booterstown Avenue. 'Last year sometime. And there was a trail of clothes scattered ahead of me, in the middle of the road.' He has no idea why he's telling her this. 'I saw a T-shirt first, then jeans, shorts, and a beach towel with tyre tracks running over it.' There had been boxers too, several pairs of rain-soaked boxers, but he doesn't mention them, only he's not sure why – Liz doesn't seem as though she'd be the prudish type.

She looks at him curiously. 'Do you reckon they fell out of someone's car? Maybe a caravan on its way to Dún Laoghaire for the ferry?'

He shrugs. A badly packed life, unravelled in a stranger's boot. A grubby, sodden striptease, exposed to everyone and no one caring a bit. He looks down at Liz's hand. Mags stares out at him, the pink scarf a gash around her neck. From across the Rock Road he can hear the thundery crack of a DART approaching.

Of course! It was Cuan who took the photograph.

Thank God. He's gone at last. Loping down the street behind her, like a cross child in a supermarket. The relief when Liz offered to take Raymond to Best Buds! Though what good he'll be is anyone's guess. What is he like? When you might actually, for once, need him to *do* something.

'Liz?' The door is squeaking louder each time, she's sure of it. They're a few houses down already so she raises her voice. 'Liz! Have you the photo?' Liz waves it above her head and gives a thumbs-up. Mags is a blur, a flash of pink and white.

Anita returns inside, muttering, 'It's not a flag, you know.' Liz is being very kind to help out, and Anita's grateful, of course. Still, though, there's no need for her to come in and act like she owns the place, all *Mags-wouldn't-like-this* and *Mags-wouldn't-want-that.* Giving Raymond the eye, as women always did. And that denim skirt! Bare knees are for the under-sevens.

Anita heads back to the kitchen, and her phone, and her lists.

She has been working her way through Mags's address book since she found it, making a note of everyone she speaks to and when. She can't seem to get it right. When she's too casual – *Just wondering if you've heard from Mum this week or know what her plans are?* – it comes across as though she doesn't care, that she's ringing up to enquire after a lost umbrella. But when she sounds worried – *Mum has been missing since yesterday morning!* – it panics people. She threw a second cousin she hadn't seen since her own wedding into such a complete tizz that Denise was all for jumping into her car and heading for Dublin.

She reaches the end of the address book quicker than she thought she would. She only got to speak to seven more people, five of whom are now praying for them. There were three wrong numbers. Two names turned out to be patients in nursing homes and either couldn't or wouldn't come to the phone. Three didn't reply (who doesn't have an answering machine or mobile these days?) and two were dead. She reaches for her pen and puts a line through their names.

She rereads the information Sergeant Corish gave her, even though she practically knows it off by heart already. She's been on to the Missing In Ireland Support Service too. Garda Petkova is contacting the DART stations and Dublin Bus. Liz said she would organise people to go looking (Anita is convinced Liz had pulled herself back from the word 'searching') in the area. Anita decided the best thing she herself could do was to stay at the house and wait. After all, Mags could be on her way home, and if Anita's not there, how will she know what's been going on? The upset that's been caused? Derek is coming over, and Cuan is at his friend's again this afternoon: she's checked that Rob's mum collected him from school and that they are back in Rob's house. The twins can manage at home by themselves, though she knows full well that without her there to tear them away from Facebook and Snapchat there won't be a scrap of homework done.

She is a child on a high swing, kicking between anguish and hope. 'It will be fine,' she says aloud, to the kitchen. She can hear the lack of conviction in her voice. She says it again, more confident this time, quicker, her tone the one she uses to reassure Cuan when he falls and gets a scrape. Her words sound odd in the empty room. There is silence, apart from the birds on the feeder outside the back door. Their bodies have the gone-off, greenish colour of fish scales and she wonders what breed they are.

Liz had been so convincing on the phone earlier: yes, of course the best thing was to get out there and look for her, but it was bound to be a misunderstanding, and Mags would be back, right as rain, wondering what all the fuss was about. Anita had listened and nodded and added this to Sergeant Corish's 'positive outcome', and even Raymond's earlier assurances before he'd gone all quiet and stupid, and they all equalled: *yes*. A calmness had settled over her, tucked in around her, like a cot sheet. Yes, everything was going to be all right.

But now Liz has gone and, with only the birds and the sound of her own voice to break the silence, Anita can feel her conviction slipping away. She might as well have two hands behind her back, and when she taps one she gets 'good' and the other 'bad', with no predicting which will be which. And, sure enough, it's the bad hand's turn now, so *It will be fine* dissipates, replaced by a grim certainty. How the hell can Liz be so sure? She's no clue what's going on either. Almost nine thousand people in a year! That's one person every hour. And so what if the majority of missing people return quickly? What does Sergeant Corish know, *really* know, anyway? Because someone – no, many, many *someones* have to be the ones who don't come home, the ones who make the statistics what they are. The ones whose mothers, fathers, daughters and sons wait in vain. Anita knows this: she watches the news. She's seen the photographs of the women who set off early to work and never return, the young men who don't make it home from a night out, the sleep-heavy children stolen from their tiny beds. She's watched their families, punch-drunk and crying on the televised appeals, then the reminder at one year on, the dull-eyed teddy bear, the memorial tree planted to mark a decade, the age-progressed images. And she'd be looking at the news and thinking, How shocking, there hadn't ever been a trace of that little girl in all these years or whatever, before flicking over to another channel. The photos grow more poignant, more fragile, every year. All these people, lost to their own families, lost to themselves. Trapped while the spinning world relentlessly pushes the rest of us into the future.

'Don't go there, Anita,' Derek had warned her, when she'd said as much to him on the phone. 'Don't, now. Remember what you were like when you were expecting Cuan? You got yourself all worked up, obsessing over the foetal abnormality statistics, asking for all sorts of unnecessary tests, and you'd not been given any reason for concern. None at all.'

She never was able to make her husband understand that someone has to be the one.

That someone is *always* the one.

The noise of the bin lorry coming down the street makes her jump. Its dinosaur roar echoes louder here than it does in her own cul-de-sac and she recalls an item in the news a week earlier, about a man who was deaf from birth. He'd had cochlear implants and now he could hear for the first time. It showed his transition from *deaf* to *not-deaf*; the moment in which his life changed for ever, a switch to his world flipping from *off* to *on*. His hands had shot up to cover his ears, as if the sensation alone, the expectation of what was to follow, was too much. After a while, he decided that some voices and noises sounded exactly as he'd thought they would, but others? Anita remembered his wide, surprised look when he said that other sounds were completely different, the concept of volume, the lights and shades within sounds so at odds with what he'd always imagined. She wonders did the man in truth prefer his own silent versions, would he inevitably end up feeling uncomfortable in a world that was no longer what he had always believed it to be.

A bag of fun-size KitKats lies empty on the table. She has no memory of consuming them, of steadily working her way through the bag. Yet her mouth is sweet and sticky, and she has that jittery, full-of-sugar feeling. The evidence lies before her, flattened out, tidy as fresh-made beds. She doesn't remember doing that either. She picks up the wrappers one by one – there are six, she counts, despising herself more with each number – and shapes them into a little nest.

On the windowsill over the sink is a large radio, kitchen-stained and streaked with grease. Mum's had it for ever; even when Anita got her a new one she didn't use it, making up some rubbish about the display being too small to read. It's the same radio they were listening to that day the man phoned about the competition. She must have been, what, just sixteen? She was home sick from school so it was just her and Mum in the house that morning. He was from a local radio station she'd never heard of, told them that their number had been picked at random from the phone book to enter a competition. Lucky them! She'd never listened to a local channel, but no way was she going to admit it, in case he wouldn't let her enter after all.

She stood in the hall in her nightie and slippers, with Mum sitting on the bottom step of the stairs smiling and giving the thumbs-up when Anita put her hand over the mouthpiece to quickly relay the list of prizes. He was polite, a bit posh. He sounded handsome, was what she thought at the time; an older, handsome adult. A Magnum PI-type. He wanted to know her name and age, and what school she went to. She was thrilled. Wait till tomorrow, she crowed to herself. The girls will be mad jealous when they hear about this! Just another minute, then he'd be putting her live on the air for the competition! *Would you like that*, he asked, speaking more quickly, *I'll have you, Anita, I'll have you live on the air!*

And then he said, his voice getting faster all the while, breathier, *just another minute Anita, and tell me, have you a boyfriend, Anita?* She had a moment of panic, aware both of her mother now standing next to her (they never, ever, spoke about boys) and the odd way he kept repeating her name. But she was desperate to appear grown-up, the equal of this handsome man who was going to put her on the radio. *A boyfriend? I do, yes*, she admitted, not looking at her mother. *I knew you would, Anita!* He said. *And what do you do to him, Anita, what do you do to him? Do you do this? Do you? Anita?*

There was a loud, strangled cry and the line went dead. Her hand shook. She felt awful, pushed through a door into a foreign room she'd never want to go into. The way he kept saying her name, like she was a dirty word!

Mum grabbed the receiver out of her hand and slammed it back down. 'You have a *boyfriend*?' She sounded furious. Anita turned away in tears, hot and shamed and betrayed.

She stands up, walks over to the window and picks the grubby radio up by crooking two fingers around the handle. Mum just doesn't notice these things. She puts it into a cupboard, right to the back, then sits down again, in front of the empty KitKat wrappers. She takes her phone out again, switches it off and puts it carefully down. The blank screen is a waiting baby, staring up at her from a silver manger. She lowers her head and the sweet, melted-chocolate smell rises from the foil and greets her with a sickly kiss.

When they got back from the station, Raymond had spoken to Elin. Anita didn't ask him to repeat their conversation. Elin hadn't been in touch with Mags for over a week was all he said, and then he'd paused for a minute before adding, 'If there's no news in the next few hours, she's going to come over tonight or in the morning. Depends on when she can get a flight.'

Anita hasn't spoken to Elin since Jack's funeral. Before the tears there is a familiar pain. It begins both inside and behind her head all at once. A thousand darts pierce the skin around her eyes and forehead. Her scalp hurts with the effort of pushing against this weight. Her throat constricts, as though unseen hands are wrapped around her neck.

To forgive and forget is the most ridiculous expression. How can she forgive if forgiveness is the very thing that will allow – more than that, will embrace – forgetting? To forget would deny him his life and she won't allow that. The very thought of it frightens her.

Her face slumps into the sweet wrappers and she cries. Everything is about to end and everything is about to start and she doesn't know which scares her more.

Buckets of flowers and potted plants crowd the walls of the shop, with an empty space about the size of a lift in the middle of the room. A thick smell hangs over everything. He sniffs again. Lilies. Through an open sliding door behind the untidy counter there is a little room that looks like an office, storeroom and kitchen all in one.

'You'd best wait out front for now, while I get sorted,' Liz says. 'It's a bit of a squeeze back there.' He glimpses a cardboard box tottering on top of the microwave that in turn rests on top of a tiny fridge. Stick a single bed in there and hey presto! His first flat, recreated Francis Bacon-studio style, right down to the chaos and the crumbs.

'I hope you didn't miss out on any customers while you were closed.'

'None, probably, more's the pity. Tuesday isn't peak time in the floristry business. Anyway, I wasn't gone long. Catch!' She throws him a damp cloth. 'Those plants by the door get dusty from the traffic.'

On his first day in his first-ever library job he'd been told to go and clean the plastic covers in the large-print section. He'd worked his way down the stacks nearest the issues desk, giving spine after spine a desultory wipe, before hovering in a quiet corner and flicking through the books instead. It wasn't that long after *Baysiders* – couple of years, tops – and he hadn't fully adjusted to acting not being his life, to his not being the shifting person that was half Raymond and half someone else.

'People look at the spine, but they touch the front and back,' the assistant librarian snapped, when Raymond reappeared, his eyes smarting from two hours spent reading sixteen-point type, his mind dulled by cream-tea crimes in dappled, green-leaf villages. 'If you have to be lazy about it, then be lazy the smart way: ignore the spines, if you must, but clean the bloody covers.'

What passes for his career in the library has been based on this single conversation. Now, he always does what is asked of him, but with no thought other than what has been specifically requested. This lesson in easy acquiescence taught him that life in the library moved in an opposite way to *Baysiders*. On television all that had mattered *was* the spine, the side on display. When he was acting, life was a cover jacket with no book inside.

Liz is in the storeroom with her back to him. He can overhear her on the phone, asking people if they will volunteer, an irony he notices but doesn't comment on. He cleans leaf by leaf, gently dusting the underside as well as the top of each.

'Mags,' she's saying. 'No, with the bun . . . Yes, that's her . . . No, not since yesterday morning.' He imagines the response at the other end, from *Who?* to *Oh, no,* to *What did the guards say?* Her ponytail is straggling, and she twists the loose hair around her finger and pulls it straight, high above her head. The skin of her neck stretches with it, her hairline pulled taut and fine. Under the bright light of her tiny storeroom, the curls have the sharp, reddish sheen of a copper beech.

'Yes, I'm sure it will be,' she replies. 'This is, you know, just in case—' She glances up and spots him staring. She turns away again and the rest of her words are lost.

The smells of ink and warm paper mingle with the flowers as her printer churns out copies of the poster. By five o'clock her volunteers are assembled and waiting for their instructions. Her tiny shop is packed with bodies: the assistant manager of the local Centra shop on his tea break ('It'll be grand. Bound to be'); a smiling, off-duty barman from Hennessys and his teenage son; Daphne from number twenty-four and her partner Susan, a slim blonde whose face is so covered with dark freckles that she looks oddly pixelated.

Liz introduces him, but once he's thanked them all for their help and their time, he can't think what else to say. They all look at him curiously. Amateur actors watching him deliver his lines, following the movement of his lips while they wait, nervously hoping they remember their cues. How well could these strangers really know his mother? he wonders, then thinks: *But they're here, aren't they?*

'No problem, glad to help out, like,' Killian from Centra mutters, and takes a drag on his e-cigarette. Raymond can't get used to seeing people with these, and that the pull isn't followed by an exhalation of proper smoke always looks wrong to him. Unfinished. He's glad he gave up smoking when the ban came in. He'd hate to be sucking one of these stupid things, an adult perpetually tugging at a small, silent tin whistle. 'Your mother was in with me on Saturday, getting a card,' Killian adds. Jerome from Hennessys, bearded and beer-bellied, bobs his head and smiles. He has a small patch of pure white next to his mouth. A smear of toothpaste stuck to his beard? Raymond looks again and sees it's a tiny island of perfectly white hair. Jerome's son looks up from his iPhone to check that no one is waiting for a response from him. It is the quickest of glances, the disinterested, efficient flick of windscreen wipers.

'We're mad about your mother,' Daphne says, looking at him. 'Mags is . . . she's so, I dunno, *herself*, wouldn't you say, Sue?' Susan's reply is a loose-limbed movement, a shrug, smile, nod in one.

Liz gives the volunteers their instructions and they depart in a fuzz of conversation, each with a sheaf of posters and a roll of sticky tape. Her allocation of the routes was methodical; a world divvied up, its territories redrawn, with Booterstown Avenue the epicentre. From behind the counter he watches her waving goodbye on the pavement outside. She is a zephyr, her goodwill blowing these kind strangers gently along their paths.

Raymond's phone rings. *Finally.*

'Is everything okay, love? I saw your missed calls.'

So, you decided to bother, he wants to retort. *You found time to phone back.* He's annoyed with Jean for taking so long to call, but annoyed, too, at how relieved he is now that she has called. *Mags is missing and the guards fear the worst*, he wants to say. *And I needed you, but you weren't there.* He has power over her in this moment: the power to panic and to punish her. *And I needed you, but you wouldn't answer your phone.* He pulls himself back from this brink just in time. Hang on a minute. If he lets rip at her, all sarcastic and angry, he will lose her undiluted sympathy, and that's not what he wants either. His brain has automatically clicked through all these permutations of response in a half-second and is still debating his next move when she continues, 'Because I had that all-day thing in the new medical-instruments lab. I told you about it earlier? Mobiles aren't allowed, and I knew you'd have remembered that, so when I saw the missed calls I got a fright.'

Bam! And she's got him. Again.

'Is it Mags?' Jean continues, worried. 'Is she ill?'

It is some consolation that she sounds upset, though he hates himself for feeling gratified by it. He had completely forgotten what she was doing today. It was her most important BALS meeting yet, a project she's been trying to bring in for well over a year that could make a lot of money for the college.

As usual, he's in the right and he's in the wrong. His customary response to finding himself in this situation is an irritation, an itch he has to rehouse elsewhere in their relationship if he's not to scratch himself raw. But today he doesn't have the energy or the will to pack his reaction up and move it around. He tells her what's happened, as plainly as he can.

'The *guards*? Oh, Christ, Raymond, that's terrible! What do you want me to do? I can get in the car now, and be there by, I don't know, half eight? Nine at the latest.'

He can still see Liz through the glass panels of the door, waving Jerome and his texting son along their way. A breeze pulls at her hair and plasters loose strands to her mouth. What is she saying? he wonders, watching her lips move as she scoops the hairs back with one finger. 'There's no need to come up tonight Jean, honestly.'

What a shit he is even to consider being angry with her. None of this is her fault. No, no, he reassures her. Mags hasn't come back yet, but the guards are confident that everything is just fine, and Jean's had such a long day at work already . . . It would be too late. *Tomorrow*, he tells her. Tomorrow, maybe, though Mags will most likely be back by then and there'll be no need, he's sure of it. He hangs up, promising to call her again later or as soon as they have news, feeling relieved and hating himself.

There hadn't been much for him to do while he waited in Best Buds. He had dusted the plants, sold a pot of hyacinths and an Easter Bunny arrangement. He'd moved things around in the front window to hide the gap when the Easter Bunny hopped away. Smells aside, it wasn't that different from being in the library. After a while he'd even been able to ignore the lilies. For Liz's sake, he hopes this has been an unusually quiet afternoon: he can't see how she makes a profit otherwise.

Liz empties the till and goes into the back room to bag Raymond's few takings. A dark-skinned teenager clatters into the shop, all arms and legs. He is tall but hunched, a child still unused to finding himself in a young man's gangling body.

He looks surprised to see Raymond standing behind the till holding a *Missing: Have You Seen Margaret Jensen?* poster.

'Danny!' Liz's head appears around the sliding door.

'Mum.'

Mum? Raymond looks from one to the other. The boy's black hair is cropped close to his head. Stripes of acne run across his forehead and down the sides of his face, around the lines of his jawbone. It reminds Raymond of the protective headgear he had to wear for rugby.

'How was school?'

'All right.'

'And CoderDojo?'

'All right.'

'I need you to mind the shop until closing, okay, love?'

'All right.'

'And you're not to shut early, do you hear me? That bouquet by the door is to be picked up just before six. It's already paid for.' Liz throws him a bunch of keys.

Danny nods towards Raymond's hand. 'Isn't that the old lady from up the road?'

'Danny!' Liz sounds horrified. 'Her name is Mags and this is her son. I'm sorry, Raymond.' Liz rolls her eyes, her face contorted into a loving what-am-I-to-do-with-you grimace.

'It's all right,' he says, and immediately wonders will Danny think he was mocking him. He holds the poster up so Danny can read it. 'She's gone missing.'

'Shit.'

'Yes,' Raymond says. 'You've hit the nail on the head there, Danny.' He nods. 'It's completely and absolutely shit.'

'Usual drill with the alarm, right?' Liz turns back to Danny. 'And double-check it this time. Straight home after, there's a pizza in the fridge. If I'm not going to get back by eight I'll call you.' This must be a routine they have, a private two-hander refined over the years.

'All right.'

When he smiles Raymond can see his mother in him after all.

Elin's hard plastic seat is at the gable end in a conjoined row of five. A toddler two seats down is kicking the underside of her own chair so hard Elin feels the vibrations in her thighs. The little girl is wearing a faded pink cotton jacket in a design of tiny purple and white daises, with matching plimsolls. There's something familiar to the pattern. Elin stares at it, willing her memory to fall open at the right page. And, sure enough, her flower blanket, her favourite comforter as a child, floats hazily into view.

A Christmas present from Grandma Sigrid in Oslo, Elin had never seen anything so delicate, so pretty before. Sprigs of tiny lavender daisies embroidered on one side and an intricate trellis of climbing purple flowers on the other. She preferred the daisy side, but wasn't sure which was the right way around. Should the best side be the one that touched her – imagine sleeping under a bed of daisies! – or the side that faced into the room? If she had to sleep under the flower trellises, she was afraid it would remind her of the glasshouses in the garden, and their cold, crunchy glass panes.

'There's no right way to it,' Dad had said, pulling Elin onto his lap and wrapping the blanket around the two of them.

'And do you know what that means?' He held her closer. 'It means there's no wrong way to it either.'

The seat between her and the child is empty. She wishes that Marty was travelling with her, that she was in the airport because they were going on holidays. That he was at a window nearby, staring at the planes rising one after the other, flying into the inky night like the Children of Lir; or knocking about the shops; or popped across the lounge to the loo. And any minute now he'd reappear, the *Racing Post* and a smoky single malt from Duty Free under his arm, and he'd take her hand and off they'd go, up, up and away.

He'd tried to insist that he go with her, of course he had, but she'd refused. And now that she's waiting for the flight to be called, sitting near a mess of people behaving as though they're trying to flee the *Titanic* rather than board a plane that they all know has enough seats for everyone, she really wishes she had been able to have him with her. It would be no bother, he'd told her. The bookie's would run itself without him. Sure what was the point of being the boss if he couldn't pull a sickie for a day or two when he needed it? When *she* needed it, he had said, and put his arm around her. No, no, she had protested. Really. But thanks. It was bound to be a misunderstanding; Ray was overreacting. Marty has only met her brother the once, so he is not to know how unlikely it is that Ray would overreact to anything. Ray – who used to call her Spuddy when she was little because when she was born he decided she looked like a Mr Potato Head, and was such fun that she spent entire afternoons padding around the house after him in her Minnie Mouse slippers, desperate to join in with whatever he was doing, and he never told her to go away, never ever, not once – wasn't really one for *reacting* any more, let alone overreacting. Elin should probably come back home, was what Ray had told her. It sounded strange, to hear him say 'home' like that. Even to him, she suspects. Home isn't Dublin any more. Sometimes she wonders if it ever was. Elin has a new shape for home now: it's a chipped and flaking flat the size of a Tupperware box; it's Leith; it's Marty.

But Marty's not here. He's not not-sitting in the plastic seat stuck to her own. Because how could he go to Dublin with her? It isn't possible. Because he'd meet Anita. He'd meet Derek. And more than that, far, far worse than that: he'd find out about Jack. And then he'd know the truth about Elin. He'd leave her, if he knew about Jack. He might love her still, but he would have to leave her. For who could not?

She would leave herself if she could.

It's so hard to believe that, only a few hours earlier, everything was different. Everyone was where they were meant to be; life was perfectly ordinary. Her plan for today had been no more than a continuation of the day before: the illustration of Neep and his friends watching the eclipse wasn't right yet. Wonder was missing from it: a sense of a limitless horizon spinning on a sixpence that she'd not managed to capture. She wasn't meant to be at the airport late in the evening, watching strangers, wondering if she was the only one at the gate who had woken up with no idea that this was how her day would end.

As strange days always do, it had started ordinarily enough: she'd had a meeting with Randall first thing in the morning, so it was after lunch when she'd got to the studio. She'd barely had her key in the door of the studio when she'd heard her phone ring: the Jackson Five, 'I Want You Back'. She was right: she had left her phone charging on the workbench again. (A few months earlier Marty had sneaked her phone out of her bag when she was in the shower and set that song as her ringtone. She hadn't even got to the end of his street when he had phoned her. It had been one of those mornings where the porridge-coloured clouds that were winter's roof over the city had lifted for a few hours, and the sky glowed blue and white and gold. She had stopped on his street and laughed, her face warmed by an unexpected January sun. She had laughed, and turned around, and gone back to his flat.) The memory had made her grin as she'd kicked the studio door shut behind her.

'Ray? What a surprise!'

'Have you heard from Mags?' How odd he'd sounded. Buffeted, as though he was phoning from the bottom of the sea. And not even a *hello*. Something about his tone untethered something deep within her. His voice registered in her head and her heart and her bowels and her hands. The takeout cup she was holding in her right hand shook violently and coffee splattered onto the open pad on her drawing table. 'Ray? What's going on? It's not Cuan, is it? Has something happened to him? To Anita?'

'I've been trying to get hold of you.'

'Sorry. I didn't have my phone since yesterday afternoon. What's wrong, Ray?'

'It's Mags.'

'What about her? Is she—' Elin began to cry. She couldn't say *dead*. She knew her throat would close sooner than let the word out. 'Ray, is Mum sick?' The pause before he replied lasted for a hundred years. Wars were won and lost, cities sacked and remade in that single second.

'We don't know where she is.'

Elin couldn't take it in, not at first. She made him repeat himself, more than once. No one had seen or heard from Mags since the previous morning. Elin glanced at her wristwatch but her brain had run away screaming and she couldn't force any sense out of the numbers. No hospital had any record of admitting her, they had phoned them all; she hadn't shown up in any garda station. Her friends hadn't heard from her. They had no evidence that anyone had been in the house with her or that anything bad had happened. Their mother had disappeared into thin air.

Ray reeled off some statistics about people going missing and reappearing. He kept repeating the words *positive outcome*, which sounded like such an un-Rayish phrase. Elin listened in tears. Some of it she recognised as her mother, yet some she didn't. He thought she should come over, if not that night then on Wednesday morning.

At some stage she had picked up a pen to write down what he was saying but, from habit, her hand had automatically scribbled a rough version of Neep's home beside the spilled coffee. Ice blocks arranged in a rough hemisphere, with a tall chimney right in the middle. Two blocks removed for windows. But these windows were smaller than usual, mean and pinched. Her hand had cross-hatched lines, darkened up the panes. A house cut off from outside, trapped beside a dark brown moat. Immune to the power of sunlight.

'Ray?' She took a deep breath. 'Does Anita know you're phoning me?'

'Yes.'

'What did she say?' Elin looked back at her notebook. A large, dense circle was scribbled in the sky, right above the chimney and wider than the ice-house. A ball, falling from the heavens, hurtling towards Neep's roof. Dark and angry-looking, a black ink-dot trail flaming behind it.

So, for all Raymond's *positive outcomes*, all his *I'm-sure-it-will-be-fine-but-just-in-case*, whatever was going on had to be serious.

Because Anita has agreed Elin should come back.

'I was only nineteen having him,' Liz says. They are sitting at the bar in The Magpie ('You look shattered. Come on, a ten-minute pit stop won't hurt'). It's only twenty-four hours since he'd walked into Flannerys but it feels like a week, a year, since he's had a pint. She's right, he is shattered, though he's only just noticed it.

'I thought my life would be ruined but it wasn't. That's just the way it goes, I guess.' She smiles. 'Danny's great, I've been very lucky. It took me a while to accept it, was all. And some people were a pain in the arse at first.' She sips her orange juice. 'You know, about his being mixed race. Though you can be sure that wasn't the term used, if you get my drift.'

'Where is his father from?' What he really wants to know is whether or not she and his father are together – he reckons not – but can't think of a way to make that question come out right. What he does instead, he realises, as soon as the words leave his mouth, is to sound racist. You eejit, Raymond, he silently chides himself: why not go the whole hog and start banging on about *them*? Them coming over here, taking our jobs and our houses and our dole.

'Manchester,' she says, and a tiny burp escapes with the *s*.

'Scuse me. They see each other a few times a year. Maurice has got other kids – littler ones – but he was never good at regular contact, even before they came along.' She shrugs. 'It's tricky, being Danny's mother and father. But when I can't figure out how to be his dad, I settle for being his friend, and that gets us by. Most of the time, anyway.'

Lucky Danny. Raymond stares into his glass. A creamy pond, pockmarked with tiny, gassy craters.

'Your mum talks about you at that age, you know.' This surprises him. 'Like if I was telling her something about how Danny is getting on in school, she says, *Oh, my Raymond was good at science too*, or whatever.'

'Let me guess: I could have been a dentist?'

She laughs. 'Now I've met you, I can't see it myself, but yes.' She shoves her sleeve back from her wrist. 'Go on.' She sighs. 'Don't hold back.'

'What?'

She holds up her hand as if showing him a watch. On her wrist are two black stars, their inked edges blurry. It seems pretty restrained to him, considering some of the full-sleeve tattoos he's spotted recently. 'One for me, one for Danny,' she says, and pushes her sleeve down. 'But thanks for not saying it.'

'What?' he repeats, clueless.

'That I'll only last three weeks in the freezer.' She puts her unfinished drink on the table. 'Right, will we make a move?'

The route Liz allocated them is a path that follows the line of the DART into Blackrock and beyond, as far as the stop at Seapoint. On the way, she talks about Mags, about how she regularly pops into Best Buds on her way to Blackrock in the mornings, about their chats. Liz encourages her to call by. *When I see your face at the window I know it's time for a break*, I said to her last week. *You're like my Teasmade.* She talks about Mags with ease and affection, and now that he thinks back over phone calls with his mother, she has often mentioned Liz, but because he didn't know her, he never paid that much attention. She was just another walk-on part in Mags's cast of characters, a bit player in a production he would never see.

At a corner about fifty yards past the entrance to the DART station a white bicycle is chained to a clearway sign. Plastic flowers are neatly laced through the spokes. Raymond has read about these memorials to dead cyclists, yet this is the first he's seen. It is entirely white, even the saddle, which makes the heavy frame strangely ethereal, as though his hand could pass straight through the metal. 'They're weirdly beautiful, aren't they?' Liz says. 'The ghost bikes.'

From a distance, they must look like a strangely robotic pair as they walk on. Their heads flick from side to side constantly, unnaturally, with abrupt stops every few yards to Sellotape posters to lampposts and bus stops. Liz ambushes everyone who passes by and insists that they give the poster their attention. 'Just in case,' she says, over and over. 'You can't be sure if you don't take a look.' Rush-hour traffic crawls by on their right. Packed DARTs trundle past on their left, each train leaning slightly towards the sea as it traces the line of Dublin Bay. Hundreds of lives he will never interact with, hurtling past. And whether they are bigger, smaller, sadder, happier than his own, who's to know? It is a world packed with strangers. In the last twenty-four hours even people he knows are being presented as strangers to him.

What Anita had said about Mags and her memory is

troubling him more and more. Sure she can be forgetful, getting names wrong or mixing up dates or whatever. But who doesn't do that sometimes? During their visit after Christmas, Mags had told Jean the same story twice in one afternoon. Was that a sign he should have picked up on, instead of teasing his mother about it to cover his embarrassment?

'We all have our senior moments.' Jean had laughed it off when Mags apologised. 'What harm, Mags?' she'd said. 'Sure doesn't your son do the same thing himself all the time?' Raymond had laughed, noting privately how kind, how *even*, Jean always was with his family. But it's easier to be kind when you don't really care, isn't it? He dismisses the thought instantly, hating himself for his meanness.

Even if there does turn out to be nothing to it, he wishes he'd known about the doctor. How very Anita-ish, to withhold information, then be sniffy with him for not knowing it, to cast *him* as the callous, careless one.

'Liz, has my mother said anything to you about seeing a doctor recently? A neurologist,' he adds, because who knows? Mags might have seen other doctors for other ailments that no one has bothered to tell him about either.

'Yes.' Her reply is immediate, and he's not sure whether it's the ease of the *yes* that annoys him or that it's not the *no* he wanted. He squeezes the roll of posters in his left hand. This is all wrong. It's half past six. It's a Tuesday. The shutters should be down, locked. He should be in Flannerys; the world should be turning towards the easy, unplanned expanse of evening. But it's not. It's not day, it's not night. The shutters are stuck, neither up nor down, and here he is, accosting people on the Rock Road, asking them have they seen his mother, this woman who is beginning to feel as much of a stranger to him as she is to the passers-by. He squeezes the roll tighter in his hand, creasing her face.

'Right, yes. Of course. Of course she did.' That's just bloody great. Everyone must know. Everyone except him. 'And let me guess, she had a chat about it with whatshisname over the cooked meats in Centra? And Daphne? Probably shouted it across the road to her.'

'Not that I know of.' She frowns but her tone doesn't change. She doesn't break her stride.

'Really? Because you all seem to know a hell of a lot more about my mother than I do.'

'Nobody's told you, you mean?'

'Yes!' Thank you! Finally, someone's looking at it from his perspective.

Liz stops at a lamppost. She wraps a poster carefully around it, then leans against it while she tears a strip of Sellotape with her teeth. His black and white mother peers out at him from under Liz's forearm, her grainy face curved around the metal post.

'Raymond, you are in a very difficult situation, and I can imagine how stressed you must be feeling, but can I say one thing? And I mean this with all respect: don't be an arsehole.'

She walks on.

What the hell does that mean? What the fuck is her problem? He is fired up, righteous and sure-footed in his anger. So what if Liz has nothing better to do than hang around her stupid, empty shop, having cups of tea with his mother? That doesn't give her the right to talk to him like that.

'Mags knows that my father had mixed dementia. He died two years ago,' Liz says, without looking back at him. 'I assume that's why she decided to tell me, because she knew that at the very least I'd understand.'

So what? He chats to old biddies in the library week in week out, and he's never once assumed he knows them better than their own children do. He tests his annoyance, needing it to be solid, to arm him with the right retort and bounce him right back. He needs more from it: for it to transform into a rage that will rear up and carry him, roaring, far higher than this.

He prods his anger, but it's too late. He can feel it deflate, a spent whoopee cushion. 'Oh,' he says. 'Sorry.'

'About my dad?'

'For being an arsehole,' he replies, by her side again, and then, 'And, yes, I mean, no, for your dad too.'

'It's often much easier for people to talk to a stranger than someone in their family.'

Kind of her to let him off the hook. But it doesn't make him feel any better. If anything, it makes him feel much worse. Under normal circumstances, he would have parked this conversation long before now. It has already strayed much further into someone else's life – their real life, not their favourite-films-did-you-see-the-match life – than he normally wants to travel. But what's normal about any of this?

'Liz, do you think her going missing has something to do with her seeing the doctor?'

'She might want some time to think it all through by herself, you mean? Yeah, that did occur to me.'

'Even though she's not been diagnosed, not properly?'

'Do you always need someone else to tell you what you already know? Your mum is frightened, I think. Who wouldn't be? It's a terrifying prospect, especially in the early stages, when you know yourself that something's not quite right, and even though you feel fine, you're constantly policing your every move, watching in case you betray yourself.'

'Is that what happened with your dad? Mixed-up dementia, was that what you called it?'

'Mixed. It's common enough for people to have a mix of two different types of dementia. As if one wasn't cruel enough. Dad had a combination of Alzheimer's and vascular dementia.' She glances at him, then adds, 'It means the blood supply to the brain is damaged. My dad had been having silent strokes for years before he was diagnosed, and we'd no idea. We weren't looking, that was the problem. All we could see was the version of him we were used to. Oh, shit.' She's dropped her roll of Sellotape and it takes off, wobbling towards the gutter. It reminds him of *The Runaway Pancake* in the children's library, with its conga line of man-to-mouse, each character with its arms wrapped around a smaller one. He grabs the tape before it reaches the drain. 'What happened then to make you realise?'

'There wasn't a single, defining incident, if that's what you mean. It would have been so much easier if there was, and we could have said, aha, okay, so this is where we are now, we've gone to some weird new place. No, it was nothing like that. It was like watching him leave himself bit by bit over seven years, until an outline of him was all that was left. But the worst of it was knowing that it felt like that for him, too. Right up till almost the end he'd have moments when he was completely clear and knew exactly what was happening inside, and it terrified him. You know *The Wizard of Oz*? Imagine being on the Yellow Brick Road, and from far away, across all those unnatural bumps and twists, someone you love is watching you. They can see you, and you wave and wave until your arm aches, but they keep getting smaller and smaller until they're only a dot on the path. It's not only about memory. His behaviour changed, the way he would communicate with us. Everything.

'He used occasionally get the notion that he wanted to go home. *Home-home*, he would say, and we would keep on repeating, *But you are home, Daddy*, until eventually we figured out he wanted to go to the farm in Leitrim where he grew up.'

'And did that help?'

'It wasn't there to go to – my uncle sold it off twenty years ago. It's a golf course now. Dad wouldn't have recognised a blade of grass in the place. So when he'd start going on about it, and get agitated and want to leave the house, we'd distract him. We had this old coal scuttle and I filled it with Styrofoam peanuts and put things in it he'd have been familiar with as a child. Sunlight soap powder, and his penknife with the blades taken out, and some old copybooks Mam found in the attic. That sort of thing. And he'd get as far as the front door and stop by the bucket and start to fooster about, delighted with whatever he'd discover. And then he'd forget about going home.'

'A treasure chest.'

She smiles. 'The books call it a Rummage Bin, but you're right. Treasure is closer to it. For months after he died those Styrofoam peanuts would turn up in the oddest places.'

'I ran away from home once, when I was sixteen.' He's not thought of this in years. 'I was annoyed. I'd had a fight with Dad so I legged it to my mate's for the day. When I went back late that night Mags was furious. I'd never seen anything like it. She was so angry she could hardly get the words out at first, which isn't her style at all, as I guess you know. *Honestly*,

Ma, I kept telling her, *I was fine*, and then she began to shout at me from across the kitchen: *I wasn't to know that, you stupid child.* She was white with anger, roaring at me: *That's the point. In my head, you were dead.'*

It's impossible to imagine his own mother, the woman who'd screamed at him for his carelessness, for the casual ease with which he had disregarded her love for him, fading away until she is no more than a shell. Is he going to have to stand by and watch helplessly as her constancy, her very Mags-ness, dissipates? What was it that Daphne said earlier? *She's so herself.* Is this to be part of his future too? Watching a light bulb with a dodgy circuit fizzing endlessly until everything goes dark in a final, jaded *pop*?

'All he wanted in the end was for us to be there with him. *Once I've my little buddies beside me*, he used say to me and my sister, *I'll be grand.* Even on the days when he didn't know who we were, or the days when he got very angry – and there were plenty of them – he always trusted us.'

Raymond takes an imaginary leap forward into such a future. Mags, confused and angry and afraid, her mind a jam-jar with a broken lid that won't budge no matter how hard she twists. There could be years of this ahead, of his mother needing him, Elin, Anita and God knows who else by her side just to function.

'And were you with him every day?'

'Pretty much, yes. Mam, my sister Aileen and I had a rota. We got a few carer hours from the HSE, but not nearly enough. Mam expected it from us girls, that we'd be there with her, to mind him at home. She would never have asked my brother to go part-time in his job so that he could help out every day too.'

She doesn't like that she's bitter about that aspect of it, she tells him, but she can't help it. Why should love be a level playing field while care isn't? And it is a completely separate thing from her feelings for her dad, but it annoyed her that only women are supposed to be tirelessly, endlessly flexible. Willing – and, worse, *able* – to pop in and out of the working world as their lives outside work need them to. By the time he died she'd had to pare back her hours in the Botanic Gardens – she had trained as a horticulturalist – to such an extent that she'd no real job left to go back to.

'And you didn't get any other help?'

'Charities and support groups, if that's what you mean? Mam was keen on meeting people in the same boat as us so I took her to a few meetings. I couldn't be doing with them for myself. Half the people in the room have a better situation than yours so you don't want to hear about them. The other half are worse off so you can't bear to hear about them. Who are you left with? No one. Yourself.'

No one. Yourself, he thinks. That's life right there.

Neither of them speaks for a while. The traffic is dying down, rush hour ending for another day. The cars that pass now are fewer but travelling faster. The silences between trains have lengthened. Raymond knows he is putting one foot in front of the other, looking around, sticking posters to lampposts, but even as he is doing so, he can tell he will have no recollection of it later. All he can think about is this – his? – grim future, which is also Liz's recent past. How could it work? It's not like he could come up from Cork every day. And would Jean give up her job to move to Dublin, too? Hardly. Dermot would be more likely to want to go with him than his daughter would. *No, no.* He pulls himself back from worrying about Jean's response: that's too much, too far ahead. That's the small print, even now. Nothing has been diagnosed, he reminds himself again. Nothing is certain. All this worry is probably completely unnecessary. It has to be. Because the idea of him and his sisters coming together, forming a magic ring around their mother's old age, is unimaginable. How could his sisters come together to protect a life when death has already split them apart?

Liz described her father's illness as his leaving himself behind. And gradual as that departure may be, doesn't it imply there is a tipping point? A day when so many connections have withered that his mother could be alive but no longer herself? He pictures the last chapter of a book, sentence after sentence, page by page, disappearing until there is nothing left but pure white sheets in a cover. This thought frightens him, but the next scares him more: what happens if he *already* no longer knows her well enough to recognise when that will be?

'What could be left,' he wonders aloud, 'if everything that makes a person themselves has gone, even though they're still living and breathing?'

'Ah, you can't start talking souls,' Liz replies, her tone suddenly quite different, tired. He shouldn't have asked such a personal question: she clearly wants to change the subject. 'Don't you know, Raymond, us Irish aren't allowed talk honestly about souls until we've had at least four pints?'

It's nine o'clock before he gets back to Booterstown Avenue. His fingertips are cold and smooth from the touch of so many lampposts and his teeth rough from the Sellotape. Rain spatters down through the dark. His shoulders ache and he's lightheaded from tiredness and, suddenly, hunger.

'You'd better have kept some pizza for me,' Liz had said on the phone to Danny, and though Raymond couldn't overhear her son's answer, it must have been more than a monotone *all right*, judging from her laugh.

Beep beep. A text from Elin. Wednesday morning's flights were full, so she got a seat on the last one today. She hopes to make it to the house by midnight.

Anita is at the window and gesticulates wildly as soon as she sees him at the gate. She was just about to phone him, she cries, excited, the front door open wide. She has news. Sergeant Corish just called.

'Just this minute,' she says. 'She's just gone off the phone this minute.' She's talking in staccato sentences, starting and stopping in mid-breath.

'The man working in the ticket office at Shankill DART station saw her yesterday. They had a chat, his wife has the same beret. He was off today, which is why the guards didn't hear about it sooner, but didn't he drop by the station earlier because his wife's chiropodist is near there and—' She flaps her hands around, a conductor who has lost control.

'Where?' Raymond butts in, sharply. *'Shankill?'*

'Yes. Odd, isn't it? She never said a thing to me about going to Shankill – she's not been there for, I don't know, months at least. What must have happened is that Mum completely forgot about the dentist and arranged to meet someone out there – she still knows loads of people, I'm sure, though she hardly ever mentions the place . . . I can't think who she might be visiting that I don't know . . . Oh, maybe they've just moved there! That would make sense, wouldn't it? She might have been going to see their new house or whatever and it got late and she decided to stay over, though why she couldn't have called me I don't know.'

'Good news, eh, Ray?' Derek appears from upstairs.

'I was so worried that she was in hospital somewhere.'

'But you phoned them all,' Derek says. 'You knew she wasn't in hospital, Anita.'

'Like whoever would be on the reception desk would know everything! There are people lying on trolleys in hospitals for days at a time. Oh, the relief! *A confirmed sighting*, Sergeant Corish said.' She leans heavily on each word, repeating them. She even sounds like Corish.

Derek puts his arm around her. 'Come on, let's get you home.' The twins have been babysitting Cuan all evening, though Derek suspects it's more likely to have ended up the other way round.

'I told the sergeant she's to phone me first, but call me if you hear anything, won't you?' Anita smiles when she says goodnight, for the first time since Raymond arrived that morning.

He shuts the front door behind them, switches off the lights and stands in the hallway. After hours of walking alongside busy roads in the cold, he is glad of the quiet and the familiar gloom. Mags was at Shankill DART station, a place he hasn't been for the best part of a decade.

'Eastcliff House, Kilmarth Road, Shankill, telephone 886283,' he says it aloud but what he hears is his own voice aged four, a childish sing-song. Mags insisted on them learning their address and phone number off by heart as soon as they could. She used to test them on it. In case they ever got lost, she claimed, and it was years before he thought twice about this. What did it say about her parenting that children too young to be going to school might be wandering around lost and reciting their address to strangers? Was it a realistic understanding of her own potential carelessness? Surely not. A prudent safeguard, then? He never did decide whether it was a sensible just-in-case defence, or quite the opposite: a pessimistic fear of a world full of risk?

Confirmed sighting. Great news. Of course it is. But where is she now, right now? Because who knows what happens out there in the dark when the laws of daylight have sluiced away? When the old, the young, the weak, the vulnerable are abandoned, left to defend themselves?

He feels on the edge of empty and *confirmed sighting* isn't scaring away the fears about his mother's future that are newly lodged in his guts. What Liz had said about her father wanting to go back to his boyhood farm in Leitrim has lodged in his head. Isn't it just possible that his mother, in her fear or worry – or whatever, he thinks, but doesn't linger over the many paths *whatever* could drag him down – decided that she wanted to visit their old house? Isn't it possible she was going home?

Home-home.

WEDNESDAY, 9 APRIL 2014

The twins are sixteen, so why does she have to treat them like toddlers? Anita has been having pointless one-sided conversations with her children for a thousand years about *finishing*. Bowls of mashed banana, their business on the potty, jigsaws, games, their chores and now, relentlessly, homework. When will the need for this constant admonishment and encouragement end? She used to be the source of everything, but now they see her as little more than a taxi fitted with an ATM and GPS set to the Abercrombie shop in Dundrum.

'Why didn't you get your Irish done?' The see-saw had flipped, and instead of the twins constantly asking her questions all day long, she has become their interrogator. She doesn't know when it came about, that reversal, but she knows it is here to stay. She dreads it happening with Cuan. 'Well? Why?' Anita is aware of the sharp *snap-snap* in her voice. She decides to leave the steel trap there, and if Rebecca gets snared, then so be it. Anita isn't a woman, she is a threat who cooks and cleans and drives. She is half a carrot, half a stick. And, right now, she's no interest in being either.

'I forgot.' Rebecca piles Special K into a bowl and sloshes milk onto it. At least she always has a decent-sized breakfast, certainly by comparison with Ailish's reluctant, doll-sized portion.

'You forgot.' Neither question nor statement, it is a dangerous hybrid of both. A storm warning, broadcast in two words.

'Yes.' White drops splash onto Anita's new linen tablecloth. Milk blurs the baby's-breath pattern. 'Pretty much.'

Anita leans over Rebecca to dab at the cloth. She never sits to have breakfast with the children, preferring to busy herself with the school lunches instead. Her habit is to eat something later on after she's dropped them to school and there is no one to watch her. No one to give her a look when she goes for an extra slice of buttered toast, or to sneer, 'You're not at that again, are you?' when she has only half a grapefruit and a pot of black tea. She reminds herself of the landlady in a B&B she and Derek stayed in once. The woman reluctantly offered hospitality – own-brand cereal in boxes the size of packing crates and flaccid sausages glittering with grease, a stink of cigarettes hanging over the lot – while all the time clearly wishing they would just pay up and get lost.

Rebecca glances across the table at her sister. She is gearing up for what they all know comes next: the telling-off, the argument, then, finally, when they are bloodied by battle, the resolution. Rebecca and Ailish know the steps of this dance perfectly and move within it with the practised rhythm of jaded ballerinas. They know how to fold their swan wings in beautiful, perfect death on stage, then immediately the curtain falls, yawn and stretch and suggest, maybe, just for a change, how about a burger for supper?

But Anita says nothing. She doesn't take the invisible hand willing to whirl her away. Instead, she shrugs and walks to the island unit in the middle of the large, glass-walled kitchen. The room is long and wide. The kitchen takes up two sides, with the rest of the space given over to the dining area. The wall behind her long oak table is papered, an expensive embossed turquoise and silver print of leafless branches that Derek said reminded him of that hotel he'd stayed in when he was in London on business. She had been quite pleased with that – what's not to like about a smart hotel? – until ages later she'd overheard Raymond remark to Jean that boutique hotels were *up themselves*. 'Over-priced restaurants with bedrooms attached,' was what he'd said, and Jean had laughed even as she chided him for being such an inverted snob.

This is the right layout, according to the design magazines, but she wishes her sink overlooked the garden, the way Mags's does. Anita's sink is landlocked in the island unit, the taps facing away from the garden and towards the wall oven. Forward and back, oven to drainer, her kitchen is a series of blocks in differing temperatures: hot, cold, frozen. Even with the cleaner coming in once a week, her life mirrors itself: one task forever watching the next. Anita has old friends from college who work full time and employ other women to run their houses and their children, yet when she complains about the thankless drudgery of housework they wince in sympathetic recognition, which she finds difficult to understand.

She continues to squeeze the cloth under the tap, though the water has long rinsed clear. The silence from the table tells her that her decision to sit this one out has bewildered the twins. Good, she thinks. Let them figure out what to do next for once. Why should it always be her who knows what to do? This is what we do to our parents. We dip into them as though they are a box containing all the answers we need, yet insist on shutting the lid down tight to deny those we don't want to hear. Did she do this when she was a teenager? Treat her mother as though she was both problem and solution all wrapped up together? And, with the water running cold over her fingers, she finds herself thinking about a morning many years before. A chilly, shivery morning. Before Cuan, but in this case also before Jack. *Before Jack, after Jack,* this is how she has learned to categorise time. His existence – no, not that: his lack of existence – is the pendulum around which all other time swings. Each hour, each day, each week were written large in grief and rage for such a long time on her private calendar. It is not as bad, not these days. His death does not completely empty and consume her all at once, as it used to. These days she turns each new morning over to uncover a dull, hungry sadness. It has become somewhat stable, a constant for which she supposes she should be stupidly thankful. There are rushes of pain still that catch her unawares and make her lose her balance, as if she's standing on the edge of a cliff, but it is not every moment of every day as it once was.

Jack was born in October 2000, so it was the first spring of the new millennium (though who gave that a thought? The whole Y2K thing had been a damp squib all round. Just another Happy New Year, and not The End). It must have been March, April maybe . . . yet it doesn't feel like spring. Maybe it does to everyone else but so what? To Anita, it is the dead heart of winter. She shivers despite her dressing gown, despite the central heating. She has a hunger like that of a shaky, trembling hangover, yet every attempt to eat makes her nauseous. The twins are being difficult. She wants to say *bad*, the twins are being *bad*, but her *Double the Love: Parenting Twins* book tut-tuts at this. *Challenging. Exploring boundaries.* The book sighs and gives its perfectly manicured pages a haughty flick. Or, if she really insists on being so terrible, so frighteningly un-maternal, then maybe *boldly behaved*. But whatever it is, the twins are it. They are masters of chaos and completely irrational, both of them. Wild animals, chasing their prey until it collapses, exhausted, abandoned to its fate. With their toddler telepathy they just know when she is too flattened by tiredness to manage them properly and then *Aha! Got her!* zaps between them and they go in for the kill.

Mags is in Anita's kitchen making a pot of tea. Mags loves her tea stewed dark as mahogany but never has the patience to wait. *The bag-strangler*, Raymond used to call her. Derek has already left for work. He goes early, whether he needs to or not. She is so tired this week that Mags offered to come and spend the morning helping with the twins after she'd dropped Elin to her bus.

'That sister of yours is very cranky these mornings,' she remarks. Why is Elin *your sister* when you're annoyed with her, and *my daughter* when you're not? Anita silently wonders. 'Too many late nights with her new crowd, I think,' Mags adds, impatiently opening the teapot and crashing her spoon about inside.

'Careful, Mum, you'll crack it!' Anita is desiccated with tiredness. The sound of the spoon clanking around the inside of the pot rings loud as a church bell. 'That teapot cost a fortune.'

None of Anita's school friends had gone to art college and she reckons Elin's set are a scrubby-looking bunch, determined to be alternative for alternative's sake. Stoned and over-confident and lazy.

'What? Nonsense,' Mags replies. 'Crosspatch she may be, but she hasn't missed a day, and from what she says about her pals they're the same.'

Anita wonders is this a dig at her, at the degree and then the H. Dip. she worked so hard for, only to abandon it after two years' teaching at that secondary school in Bray. She's never been able to explain to her mother how much she hated teaching business studies. Everything sifted from high, falling as either a pro or a con. Life as a scales tipping back and forth. Good, bad. Profit, loss. And those hands waving up at her! Pick me, pick me. *Muinteoir, Muinteoir.* Drowning arms, desperately wanting her to drag them out, only she didn't know how. The teachers all had to wear black gowns with wide, draped sleeves, and she was forever catching hers on the door handles. She'd be crossing the threshold of her classroom and *boing*! She'd find herself tugged back into the corridor to a chorus of loud sniggers. Most days she wanted to chuck the gown out the window and run away, never to return. Getting married and pregnant had saved her from that life. Derek had saved her.

'Elin said to tell you she'll come straight over after college. About five, she thought.'

'Will she stay for the girls' bedtime?'

'She's free all evening is what she said.'

Elin plays silly games with the twins, ones that have no rules other than chasing and catching and chasing again.

Games that end with them all lying on the carpet, the twins panting and sweating they're giggling so hard (the sort of games that Anita never has time for, and isn't very good at). Elin makes up stories and acts them out, giving the characters their own voices, their own shapes. She is so animated, so completely engaged when she talks to her nieces that when she turns her attention back to the grown-ups Anita can see her struggle to refocus. A shadow will pass her face, a shift from one version of herself to another. Anita is more familiar with the child version. A decade older, she can't get used to Elin being an adult, and alongside her. She wonders does Elin now see herself and Anita as grown women. As equals or as big-sister-little-sister?

Anita was a toddler when Raymond was born; she couldn't remember before-Raymond. But Elin? That was different. Anita was ten. Old enough to be content with the status quo: to love the two-parents-two-children symmetry of life. There was always enough of everybody to go around. And then Elin appeared. Blonde and pretty; her colouring Dad's and her smile Mum's. Anita and her friends' big thing at the time was making perfume. They'd spend ages picking flowers, then squash the petals in water with drops of food colouring. But it never worked. That feeling she got when she went to inhale her creation and it smelt only of the plastic of the bottle! The sudden certainty she had somehow made a complete mess of it. That was how she felt about her baby sister. Anita must have done wrong, failed her parents somehow, and that was why they needed another daughter.

'Ellie?' Ailish claps her hands and looks around as though Elin is stashed behind Mags's back, like a packet of sweets, a treat hidden for later.

'She's not here.' Anita waves them away. *Double the Love* taps her firmly on the shoulder. *Ahem?* it says. *Firm yet clear, and always positive. Remember?* 'Ellie later on,' she adds, 'at dinnertime.'

Elin wears thin nylon slip dresses and thick boots and has black sloughs of eyeliner, but the roughness of her style can't hide her Nordic prettiness, her sweet grin and wide cheekbones. Raymond and Anita are dark-haired, unmistakably their Irish mother, whereas Elin is blonde and blue-eyed, her naturally sallow skin – on holidays Elin tanned while Anita went from white to pink to burned in a day – made pale by foundation. Easy for Elin to look good, Anita thinks. She's not covered with food and God-knows-what and bent double from running around after toddlers all day. Her sister is a shimmering ghost, smelling of Rothmans and shod to climb a mountain.

'I don't own the look, Anita! There's nothing stopping you dressing this way, if you want,' Elin had said on a recent visit, her black-rimmed eyes wide, when Anita commented on her clothes.

'*Anita?* Grunge?' Derek choked on his beer he laughed so much and Anita had to slap him on the back, hard. She is twenty-eight and wonders what age bracket her husband has redeployed her to. It doesn't take a generation to have a gap: a decade seems to be enough. Only last week she had said something about travelling and he had laughed and said, 'Anita, people like us don't *travel*, we go on holidays.'

'Raymond called in yesterday, Mum,' Anita says. 'On his way to some audition or other.' This is how they talk about Raymond's occupation – well, it's hardly a career, is it, his acting? His *or other*, his *whatever*. Rebecca pops out from behind Mags's chair and wiggles her hands. She has a dog made out of felt on one index finger, a cat on the other. 'He brought those animal finger puppets for the girls. He thought they might like to put on a little show.'

'Woof-woof,' Rebecca says, and her left hand jumps on her right, 'Woof-woof, Catty!' She runs off, miaowing fiercely, one hand chasing the other around her back. Anita always puts small triangular dribble-scarves around their necks. Her daughters are tiny slack-mouthed outlaws.

'That was kind of him.'

'They were so screechy he didn't stay long.'

You get the children you deserve, Raymond had called over his shoulder to her as he was leaving. She had laughed. Not because it was funny, but because she needed to be sure that he was making a stupid joke, and laughing seemed the only way to confirm his intention. But he had waved and said nothing further, just kept going down the driveway, and only when he was out of sight did she admit crossly to herself that she had no idea whether he'd been joking or not.

'I always thought you get the children you need,' Mags says. She believes that in a family the children's lives are a big broth, different shapes and textures all mixed up together. Sometimes one ingredient grows stronger than another and temporarily determines the flavour of the dish, but it shifts and changes as you stir. Anita, her arms full of the washing she forgot to take out of the machine the day before and which now will have to be done again because it'll have gotten smelly and there's no space for it on the airer, and there's already a load in the dryer, thinks this is more of her mother's fanciful nonsense.

Mags is thrilled that Anita is pregnant again. 'When you were born, Anita, I couldn't wait to have another. I used to wish *you*'d been a twin, sometimes, even though I had work enough with the nappies and the bottles for one.' It was the shape of it all felt wrong to her, she explained. It wasn't a family shape, it was a pyramid. Parents downstairs in the evenings and just that tiny person upstairs, alone and fragile in a cot in the middle of the large, high-ceilinged bedroom. The three of them a crystal triangle pointing into the night. It was different when Raymond was born, she'd decided. The robustness, the square solidity of her little boy made her think quite differently about it. 'Perhaps,' she wonders, 'the trick of it is to have your second child first.'

'But I've already had my second,' Anita wails. 'You've got it all wrong, Mum. I'm *already* outnumbered.'

When Anita was first pregnant with the twins she'd been shocked by other women's description of their unborn babies as parasites. Those off-hand, pop-it-out women she'd get chatting to at the obstetrician's. Women on their third or even fourth, who treated the waiting room as a café, a place to rest and gossip and catch up on the magazines. They were another species by comparison with her, nervous and overdressed, waiting on the edge of her chair for her name to be called, as though it was a job interview she'd somehow forgotten to prepare for. She'd been so nervous at the first scan that when the midwife said, 'I can hear two heartbeats,' she had started up from the bed and cried out, 'My baby has *two hearts*?' Derek had told Raymond, who teased her about it for weeks. But even when the realisation sank in that she had two babies living inside her and feeding from her body, the word *parasite* struck her as cruel and unnecessary.

But now this new, mistaken pregnancy, this it's-too-soon, why-me one, has thrown her into a panic. She understands *parasite* now. Not only that but she uses it. A lot. And worse: the children she already has are vampires. Nocturnal, destructive, desperate to drain the life force from her even as they burrow into her shoulder, sweet mouths against her cheek, fumbling arms determined to fold themselves tight around her neck. Clutching her harder, tighter, the more she tries to escape.

'You need to rest.' Mags lifts the damp, trembling pile from Anita's arms and dumps it on the kitchen table. 'Now, right now. Go back to bed.'

Anita doesn't even have the energy to protest – this is her house, her sticky, jammy-handed mess to sort – yet she ignores the cold and baleful eye of *Double the Love* and lets herself be led upstairs, like the child she still is. The bliss of feeling the duvet tucked around her leaden body! Of resting her back against the mattress, of watching through already drooping eyes while Mags draws the curtains against the morning. The joy of the door closing on downstairs, cutting her off from the girls, their cartoon blaring from the sitting room and the voices from the radio in the kitchen. Sealing her, alone. She lets her eyes close. No, not alone, she thinks and wriggles her hand between two buttons of her pyjama top. She rests her palm on the hillock of her stomach. There is only one baby in there, thank God. And even though that is one more than she had wanted, she finds herself feeling sorry for this baby and its solitary life. The twins will always be whole and a half all at once, yet this little thing bumps around inside her womb alone. She pictures two little beds inside her, one mournfully empty. It is a boy, she is suddenly sure of it, though she doesn't know why. She is his shell, lined with the silvery slug trails of stretch marks. She is hard-ridged and solid, a ribbed cage around the softness within. He isn't a parasite: he is a pearl, being formed in the layers of her own grit.

'Your sisters have each other,' she whispers to him. 'But you'll have me, so you won't ever need to feel alone. We'll always be together.' He is saltwater, taking from her even while he is giving to her. He is her, she is him. She is wondering what name she'll give him as she nods off. Something strong, she decides. Something strong and big and brave and able to take on a world in which he, too, is already outnumbered.

'Jack,' Anita whispers, but only she and the dripping tap and him, the never-never-child forever alive inside her alone, can hear.

The third step of the stairs lets out its distinctive creak. Derek. She refills the kettle and switches it on. She hears him cross the hallway to the den and the mumble of his voice asking Cuan something. Searching for his iPad most likely, which you can be sure Ailish has stashed in her room. Getting the twins an iPad to share was such a mistake. They're forever fighting over it and the one who loses helps herself to Derek's, which only winds him up. She knows she'll end up giving in and getting a second for them sooner or later.

She inhales loudly. She's tired, more so than usual. Cuan was up twice in the night for the toilet and, because he doesn't like being alone at night, she always goes with him. She is so used to waking at his touch on her shoulder that sometimes she wonders if she sleeps at all, or merely lies there in suspended animation waiting for him to appear. A human snooze button. Derek used to turn on his side and grumble, *Cuan is old enough to go by himself, the landing light is on, blah-blah*, but she ignored him. Cuan has learned to tap her to life without speaking and now Derek sleeps through. Why shouldn't she go with him? What's wrong with a little boy being nervous of the night? She is a marker on his map, a beacon. Every journey he makes is made via her. She remembers sitting up at night in bed feeding him when he was a baby. That quiet communion in the dark, just her and him. Her arms and shoulders and nose cold. Derek snoring and Cuan snuffling and sucking. She was the only soundless one of the three as her body went to work, even though her mind was barely awake. Sometimes the sleep-deprived dark confused her. She would look at the tiny mouth as it opened for her, wide and obedient as a bird, and, for a moment, would be sure the baby at her breast was Jack. She hadn't fed the twins herself; the first time she'd tried was with Jack. And just for a second a miraculous joy would charge through her entire exhausted body. And then she'd wake up fully and remember it was Cuan, and hate herself for the bewildering confusion of this baby not being *that* baby.

'Are you okay, Mum?' Rebecca asks suddenly, and the unusual sight of a frown on her daughter's forehead makes Anita feel terrible. Rebecca is easier-going than her sister, harder to upset. They are light and shade. All Anita's children love their granny, but Rebecca is closest to her – she has been for years. For the last year Anita has allowed her to get the bus to Booterstown by herself on weekend mornings to 'hang out', as Rebecca refers to it. Anita, who can't imagine her own mother 'hanging out', often wonders what on earth they could be up to. The two of them pottering about with whatever daft project they have on the go.

'Any news?' Derek is hovering in the doorway, the iPad in his hand. Why doesn't he just come in or go away? Hanging around near her, like she's an animal that might go for him, drives her spare.

'I'd have told you if there was.'

'Do you want to get off? I can hold the fort here before school.'

She shakes her head. *Hold the fort.* How like him to refer to looking after his own family that way. Something that needed only brief, showy flares of his protection until she returns to take *the fort* back into her own hands. For years, he used to describe staying home while she went out as babysitting until she shouted at him one day to stop: how could it be babysitting when the children are your own?

The previous evening Derek was all for sitting the three kids down and explaining that Granny had gone away somewhere and, because they didn't know where, they were worried. But Anita couldn't do it, no way. The genie would be well and truly out of the bottle then and she'd never be able to stuff it back in. And when they got news of Mum being seen she had persuaded him to hold off. Her job is to protect her children, so why expose them to something when she herself doesn't even know what it is? Children are like dogs, she thinks. They can smell your fear. Awake at six, she made the mistake of looking up the missing.ie website. Again. Name after name, plea after plea for help, for information. An air of bafflement hangs over the entire thing because every disappearance has a different cause and not one of them makes any sense. And behind each photograph is a family cracked open, exposed and bleeding.

Her phone rings, and even though it's been either next to her on the countertop or in her hand since she woke up, the noise makes her start. Her fingers are damp and she fumbles to pick it up, cursing under her breath. She has been awake for hours already, but only now is the day beginning. She takes a deep breath and gestures at the twins to keep the noise down as she hurries out of the room.

Wednesday, eight a.m. He sits on the spare bed, staring down at the blue pile of his mother's dressing gown. The top-to-bottom zipper turns the fabric into a long, bumpy path. Aside from being short, it fits him fine. Well, fine-ish. So on his mother it must be vast; the wide-sleeved cloak and train of a picture-book witch. The stare Elin gave him last night suggested she thought he was weird to have put it on, but it's not like he's going to walk around in his underpants in front of her, is it? Had Anita been there she would most likely have scolded him for not packing 'properly'. Doubtless she has a sartorial strategy for dealing with missing mothers. He allows himself to visualise Anita in full combat gear, her make-up a careful series of battle marks, a designer flak jacket protecting her from the fallout. A crisis wardrobe.

He lets himself fall back onto the bed again. If only he could take off the dressing gown and go home. But he can't. Christ, he thinks, where *is* she? Who is she staying with? That bloke at the DART station aside, no one has spotted or spoken to her in nearly two days. She didn't have a suitcase or even a big bag with her when she walked down Booterstown Avenue on Monday morning. Liz had told them so. ('Just the usual handbag,' Liz said. Raymond didn't reply, so after a pause, Liz had described it.) Mags's bank had finally offered up the information that seventy euro withdrawn eight days ago was her last ATM transaction. She'd used her debit card in the Centra at the corner on Saturday. DART station aside, it's as though she's disappeared into thin air. This makes no sense. This is what happens in the first act of a thriller; it's not how life plays out. Life is bloody, pointless and messy and – births and deaths the obvious exceptions – refuses to conform to any pattern.

A distinctive scent, newly liberated by his own body heat, rises from the dressing gown. It's not perfumy, it's not even particularly fresh, but it's incredibly familiar. It's Mags. Undeniably her. If he'd been asked before today he would have said there was no such Eau de Margaret, or not one he was aware of anyway. Yet when he holds the sleeve to his nose, she could be in the room with him. She is part-tea, part-soap, part-rasher. He puts the sleeve to his cheek. The touch of the fleece is a caress. He sniffs it again. Maybe that's all any of us is, he thinks, an ever-shifting collection of smells. What would his own be? Two parts Guinness to one part Hugo Boss? A distillation of old paperbacks sweating in plastic covers? The top note a flourish of pure, concentrated desperation.

He closes his eyes. Breathes in and out, inhaling his mother, imagining that she is there with him, but moved out of sight. The child in him stamps a foot. She *is* there, she has to be. Messing about with Dev in the cupboard outside his bedroom door, or standing in front of the window on the landing, quietly watching the shimmering greens coming to life on the tree out the back.

Feeling foolish, he creeps out onto the landing and puts his ear to the cupboard door. A scratchy sound makes him jump. A dead president, a live mouse, something rebelling against his mother's unwieldy and erratic storage systems, who knows? And as he so often does when he feels wrong-footed, he finds himself automatically categorising this moment, putting a genre on it, filing it so it can be understood. If this were a thriller, he decides, it would be a historical one, and he'd open the cupboard into 1923 to find de Valera himself in there: all six-foot-whatever of him hunched up, bent at the waist, as though he were on a hinge, with one large, authoritative foot tap-tapping against the door. Fantasy, and it would be an armour-plated mouse, swollen with testosterone and ready for battle. Crime, and it would be an unknown body.

But of course it is none of these. It is life: immune to classification until much later, after the emotion has dried like ink on the pages.

'Mags?' It is so faint as to be not much more than a single breath. 'Are you there?'

He jumps at the sudden noise and, blinking and disoriented, he fumbles his phone up to his ear. His 'Hello,' comes out a croak.

'Morning, it's Liz. Sorry, I know it's early but . . .'

The spell is broken, the witch and her magic cloak zapped back onto the shelf. He is a middle-aged man in his mother's dressing gown. Categorisation returns. *Stack, stack, stack.*

'Hi, no, yeah.' He clears his throat and returns to the bedroom. 'Sorry, yeah,' he says again.

'Raymond? You okay?'

His stomach gives a lurch when she says his name, as though he has just remembered something so significant that it should never have been forgotten. He'd had the same sensation the week before, when he spotted a friend of Pauline's on the street near the library. Nice bloke. Tom? Tommy, possibly. And as he watched him cross the road fifty yards ahead of him, Raymond had been completely shamed by a memory of having a long, life-affirming, life-changing drunken exchange with him at Pauline's husband's fortieth a few weeks before – the sort of intense, boozy discussion Jean describes as 'wronging rights' – but until that moment on the street, he hadn't remembered the conversation at all. Not a word. Worse than that, the man hadn't even featured in his mental rewind-and-replay of the party the next day. Seeing Tom/Tommy had made him feel sweaty and panicked, fearful as to what he might have said. As though he had pushed open a door to a toilet only to find himself walking onto a stage, the curtain back and the audience sitting there, expectant. When Tom/Tommy had turned out of sight onto Patrick Street, Raymond had gone back to work, unsure whether he was concerned about what he might have revealed about himself while drunk, or what he might have concealed.

Raymond? You okay? stirs up this exact feeling again. The sweaty, panicked fear of someone who knows they have done something wrong but isn't really sure what, and knows that their definition doesn't matter anyway, for who is ever truly allowed to be their own judge? He'd overstepped the mark in asking Liz so much about her dad – oh, Christ, and worse, about her *son's* dad – he's sure of it. He knew he shouldn't have asked her all those questions, shouldn't have allowed the weirdness of the circumstances to make him so needy and garrulous. He should apologise, he knows it, should say,

Listen, Liz, thanks again for all your help yesterday but we can manage it ourselves from here on, and I'm sorry for asking you such personal questions – that was rude.

'She went to Shankill. She was at the DART station on Monday morning,' is what he says.

'I know. Anita texted me last night.'

Ah, yes, of course she did. Anita must think he can't manage the simplest thing.

'So I was wondering how you want to manage everything today. I'll organise whatever you need from the shop, no problem. I came in early to do up some more posters. Anita wants to go around Shankill village and check out the estates nearest the DART station.'

'Yes, I know.' Why does every woman he knows insist on keeping ahead of him all the time? His phone beeps discreetly in his ear. Another call. He ignores it.

'I can close up the shop for the morning, and go out there too,' she says. 'If you'd prefer?'

    – Phoned but it went to voicemail. What's happening? Am worried. J xx

    – Sorry was on a call. Nothing new since last night so going 2 Shankill shortly x

    – Elin ok? Is Anita there too?

    – yes & no

    – U ok?

    – Yes pls don't worry

    – I'm going to leave now, will be in Dub b4 lunch.

    – What about work?

    – All sorted. See you later. x

Beep beep. It's Anita this time.

    – Sgt C will b @ Mum's 9.30 to discuss plan for today. See you then.

    – ok he texts back.

He sits on the bed, turning the phone over and over in his hand. He needs to call Pauline, but it's a bit early yet. He phoned in sick yesterday. After breakfast he'll give her a bell and explain what's going on. He reads Jean's texts again. A few minutes pass before he replies to her last one.

    – Pls bring me some clean clothes?

And a minute later.

    – Thanks. x

He slips the phone into the pocket of the dressing gown. Anita will be arriving in an hour so it's time to wake Elin. At nine thirty, and for the first time in over seven years, he is going to be in a room with both his older and younger sisters.

    Jesus, what a prospect.

Elin wakes up in a single bed shoved against one wall. She had to move boxes of Christmas decorations in order to get into it the night before. This room is more of an oversized cupboard than a bedroom, crammed full of stuff from the old house in Shankill. The clutter comes from growing up in a big house, Mags claimed. She never had any need to edit her possessions, because there was room for everything. Moving to this house was meant to be a downsize, but judging by the hoards piled against the walls, Mum hasn't changed much.

When Elin pushed the boxes to one side the night before, she'd spotted a sheet of cardboard sticking out of a plastic container marked 'fairy lights'. It was the calendar she'd made the first year that Dad was away. She used the corner of the bedsheet to wipe layers of dust from an exposed corner. She remembered the afternoon she'd spent painting the backing sheet red, then cutting out fourteen doors, one for each day until he got back. (She must have been, what, eight? Raymond had promised to help, only when she went looking for him to get the scissors down from the press for her, he wasn't in his room doing his homework and his coat was gone from the stand by the front door.)

Elin had tugged the little doors open to see the pictures she'd cut from magazines and glued in or drawn onto the card behind. Two doors were missing. A faded robin with a green bow drawn around his neck filled 17 December, and slivers of silver foil peeled from the exposed rectangle beside him. What was the eighteenth meant to be? A star, maybe? She couldn't remember.

She had looked at every picture but one the night before and now she leans out of bed and picks the calendar up from the floor. Elin edges this last door open with her thumbnail: 23 December. A photo of a man outside a house, Elin had cut most of the picture away to make it small enough to fit. Anita had lost it with her when she saw it, she remembered. But it had been the only photo she could find that would fit such a small space. Anita wouldn't listen when she tried to explain. She had shouted at her to stop always taking her stuff, that it was her photo of Dad and Elin had no bloody right to look through her things. Raymond walked into the kitchen as Anita was yelling that Elin was barred from her bedroom.

'Grow up, Anita,' he said. 'You're ten years older than her. Don't be so mean.'

'Yeah, well, you're barred too,' Anita snapped at him. She leaned over the kitchen table and began to scoop up jagged pieces of photograph into her hand. A trellis here, the bonnet of a car there, two disembodied legs in suit trousers. 'Don't think I don't know you sneak in and steal my magazines. From now on, both of you leave my stuff alone!' She stormed out of the room with one hand cupped over the other, as though the thin slivers that were all that was left of the photograph could escape from between her palms.

Elin flicks the cardboard door open and shut between her fingers. Dad's face reappears and disappears, over and over. 1990 was to be the only year she made a calendar. In December 1991 they had all gone to Oslo for Christmas, and by the time December 1992 came around . . . There was no Christmas that year, not really. He was gone from them by then, gone with a recently-divorced woman from Stavanger he had gone to college with. Elin leans out of bed and tosses *Dadvent 1990* on top of the box of fairy lights. As she lies back against the pillows, 23 December springs open one last time.

She hasn't slept in this room before and now that she looks around properly, she can see it is a weird distillation of their old house, with anomalous representatives from various rooms unceremoniously shoved together, like ingredients in a spell. The wardrobe facing her from the far wall was Ray's once, judging from the faint outlines of the Panini stickers that hopscotch down the veneer. And though the headboard seems to have disappeared (weird, who'd want just a headboard?), the familiar lumps under her spine tell her she is lying in the very bed that was bought for her when she outgrew her cot. She slept in it until she was twenty-two and moved out of home to another life, to a series of beds in rented flats, their stained mattresses turning her into a fussy princess, layering sheet after sheet, yet never able to forget the blotchy and suspicious shadows underneath the white. The curtains were from her parents' room in the old house; Mags had had them cut down to fit in here. Elin wonders where the rest of the seventies Victoriana has gone: the matching pillowcases, bedspread, dressing-table frill and cushions. When Elin was little she used to see the red, white and orange pattern as a series of frogs jumping up the walls and over the bed. Their bedroom had been so completely, relentlessly, coordinated that when her parents were both in it they looked disproportionate and out of place. Some patterns aren't made to be broken.

It's nine months since Elin was in this house. For the last few years, visits have coincided with Anita's summer holidays in Portugal. Mags would happen to mention, casually, diplomatically, that Anita was going away; Elin would happen to mention, casually, coincidentally, that she was thinking, maybe, how nice a few days in Dublin with her mother would be, and so, with careful non-timing, it would be done. Anita's absence always hung heavily over them. It was an echo, the way a door slammed in temper is, even when the argument is long over.

'It's cowardly of me to visit only when she's away,' Elin once said to Ray on the phone. 'But what else can I do?'

'Nothing, I suppose. Apart from hoping you don't bump into her in the airport.' He didn't sound that interested, and had gone on to talk about other things: the film he'd just seen, the long hours Jean was putting in at her job. Anything, Elin suspected, rather than talk about his sisters. Or should that be to his sisters?

Without lifting her head from the pillow Elin stretches her hand down the duvet cover until she touches the book. She had fallen asleep reading it, just as she often did as a child. *The Pantheon of Norwegian Folktales*, its title debossed in gold type on Prussian blue card, lies splayed open at what had been Dad's favourite story, 'Ape Likes Her Own Children Best'. This book had helped him learn English when he was a child, he said. Neither Ray nor Anita was ever interested in folktales, so even before she could read properly, Elin had been determined to love Dad's stories. She liked that they were different to fairy tales; that they lacked weeping princesses, desperate for happy-ever-afters. She never told him that Ray and Anita used say, *You're not reading that silly thing again are you?* (Ray); and *Stories without people are dumb* (Anita).

As a child she had preferred the titles to the tales. In just a few words, the heart of each story was laid out. She loved illustrations for the same reason: their ability to explain everything all at once even as the details sent her imagination racing in a hundred new directions. Each story title was illustrated by a single black and white woodcut. An animal, its body wrapped around the words and forming a letter, sometimes two. She would have liked lots more illustrations, ones that made the story feel bigger, that became its arms and legs. Pictures that breathed life into the words. That kissed them and set them free to jump and hop, skitter and scatter across the pages.

As soon as she'd spotted it on the shelf the night before, Elin remembered a summer spent lying under her blanket, its daisies shining like tiny purple stars over her head, reading that book over and over after lights-out. She remembers the year well because it had been one long, loud conversation after another between her parents. ('Argument, you mean,' Ray, a narky, angular teenager with his hands jammed in his pockets, had said. *It takes one to know one*, Elin had thought, worried into disloyalty. Ray's voice had broken, only Elin wasn't used to it yet, and often thought he was cross with her when he wasn't.)

The same thing, over and over. Leaving and staying; coming and going. It was all they seemed to discuss. *I put it off once before*, she overheard Dad say. Then: *the summer,* and *options*. And again and again, *opportunities for the future*. He sucked the words smooth as butterscotch. The way he said them you'd think their family had never come across an *option* or an *opportunity* before. Yet everything referred to another time: next summer or the one after, to some vague, unspecified 'future' or to something gone awry in the past. There was no *today,* no *now* in any of it, which confused the eight-year-old Elin, for whom the past, present and future weren't the distinct entities they were to become with adulthood, experience slowly sealing individual parts of a jigsaw together, bending the edges of the pieces to make them fit. Rather, time was roughly blended, a series of likes and dislikes that floated alongside her, that swirled around her head like ribbons. Her past existed only as yesterday's version of the present: 'I love painting the best'; 'Why won't they let me cycle to school?'; 'My brother says I can live with him for ever.' Elin never did understand why her family could rage at each other over and over, repeating themselves endlessly, only for their words to stay as words, never to take shape in actions. A book of stories without any drawings.

When her parents' conversations stopped she'd thought everyone had forgotten about it, but she was wrong. It was quite the opposite. They had gone quiet because it *was* happening, not because it wasn't. Dad was going to AHO, the Oslo School of Architecture and Design where he had done his degree twenty-five years before, on a research contract in September.

'It's very exciting.' Mum's lipstick was patchy, dried threads of dark pink. 'A great opportunity.'

Elin had stared at the creased pink bow kissed onto the white teacup.

'If it's so exciting, then why aren't we all going?'

'Because, Raymond, we decided it was best not to disrupt you children, as you well know.' Mum was snappy. 'Your schoolwork needs all the help it can get. You've no hope of getting a good Leaving Cert if you don't get your act together. Starting now.'

'I'm not a child.' Anita didn't look up from painting her nails.

'You know what I mean,' Mags replied. Anita shrugged. Even Elin, for whom teenagerhood was an achingly distant and unattainable goal, could interpret Anita's shoulders: *I don't care what you mean.*

Elin flicks through Dad's book and remembers how she'd lie in bed that autumn wishing Ray would come upstairs and sneak into her room after lights out and read aloud to her, the two of them snuggled up under the daisies. But he wasn't home. He and Mum argued. Lots. Shouts that would get louder, then: slam, silence and he'd be gone, off to rugby training or a friend's for the evening. Places that were outside the life he lived with her, his little sister. It worried her that Ray might leave too and forget to – or, worse, not want to – take her with him. That Ray might find *opportunities, options*. A new future, one in which there wasn't space for her in summer – or any other season, for that matter.

It wasn't easy, being the youngest. It felt like her siblings and parents were somehow in on everything before she was; that being the most junior member of the family was an internship. There were rules, codes, but because the others already knew them, it never occurred to anyone that she didn't: that she might need a map to navigate the stormy waters of her family.

She hadn't bothered to close the curtains the night before and the room is dull, the morning outside still shapeless and grey. Elin holds the book close and flicks through the pages until she finds the fox. Half-open buttony black eyes stare out at her. He has a pointy nose and his tongue sticks out, thick and heavy. As a child, the way his tongue draped over his little teeth and lolled damply towards the ground made her feel uncomfortable. His brush was long and curled right around the words, tiny inked lines of the woodcut wrapped tight as ivy about the final letters of the title. She holds the page up close to her face and looks him in the eye. The lines are thick and badly etched, the fox beady and out of proportion, his tongue the same length as his paw. Faint rubbed-out pencil lines have left tiny indentations on many of the pages, thin grey marks. It's not a particularly good illustration, she can appreciate that now. The fox wasn't scary, he was just badly drawn.

And such were the ooh-aah glories of summer 1990, she thinks. And when Dad's contract went into its second year, Mum said they couldn't go because Ray was sitting the Leaving Cert. And then Dad met Her, and he was never coming home.

He'd had a heart attack and died there, fourteen years ago. By the time that happened she had got used to telling people her dad had 'gone away', and almost without thinking, she began to say 'gone' instead.

It's eight o'clock and she's been awake for well over an hour. The snoring from across the landing had stopped a while ago: Ray must be awake now too. He'd looked so tired the night before. Poor Ray. She pictures him lying there, physically nearer to her than he has been in years, yet she can't bring herself to get up and knock on his door. He and Mum were really close up until the time Dad went away. It was as though their family was modelled on an inefficient public service, and through a quirk of the system Ray, by virtue of being male and there, found himself promoted to chief executive officer. But he hadn't applied for the job of man of the house, or wanted to fill the vacancy created by their father's departure. Mum had made it all seem so reasonable: the time would pass quickly, she'd said. And he'd be home during the holidays. That it was more important to focus on their education became the party line. Education mattered a lot to Mags. Elin has often wondered since does her mother think what a waste this was: Anita has done nothing with her qualifications, Ray doesn't have any, and Elin makes children's books for a (just about) living. With hindsight, it seems such a strange thing to do, to choose to fracture a family, even if they really did believe it would only be for a year or two.

An Irish divorce? the neighbours had whispered at first (and were to be proved right in time).

She wishes they were more like Marty's family. Marty and his three raucous, beery brothers play everything out in the open and at speed. It is a sport. They agree, they disagree, they slag each other off, and then it's done. They argue, yet they always manage to be on the same side.

'Don't make my lot out to be something we're not.' Marty laughed, when she envied the easy way his family are around each other. 'When we were little lads and Ma would stop us hitting each other, we'd punch each other's teddies instead.' Yet it seems clear who they are to each other: the straight man, the funny man, the fool, the smart guy. They each know who to be. He'd looked at her strangely when she'd said this. 'And which one do you think I am?'

Marty has phoned several times since she left Edinburgh but she hasn't picked up. She's texted instead, but can't bring herself to speak to him. If they can just catch up with Mags today, Elin reckons, she can be back home again tomorrow. Tonight even! She will call him then. Friday at the latest. Edinburgh is her suit of armour and as soon as she lands she will climb back into it and be protected again.

It had been after one a.m. when she arrived in Booterstown Avenue, her plane delayed by a series of ten-minute hold-ups that sounded like nothing when announced individually over the Tannoy, yet slowly added up. Her ugly relief that meeting her sister was to be postponed until the morning was followed immediately by the deeper, more ingrained dread that a fear postponed brings. That powerless, panicked waiting room feeling, when the patient ahead of you at the dentist is taking too long. But she had arrived to good news: someone had spoken to Mags on Monday, and in Shankill too, a place Mags knows well, where she must still have lots of friends.

But then . . . there had been more, which Ray hadn't told her on the phone. About a consultant. *A neurologist*, he had corrected himself, before Elin had had time to ask. Mum had been getting a bit confused and forgetful, according to Anita, though he'd no experience of it himself. ('No real experience,' he said, and it was only afterwards she realised that she didn't understand – was there *unreal* experience?) There wasn't a diagnosis so they shouldn't distract themselves. Shouldn't 'worry unnecessarily', he'd said, as though that was a reasonable request in the circumstances.

Though he'd sounded upbeat enough, his face was flat-looking. Tiredness had turned his eyes from their lowland-lake blue to the grey of old bath water.

'I mean, you know, we should be confident,' he said again, 'of a positive outcome.' Ray has long eyelashes. A girl's eyelashes, the pretty, curling sort that people say are wasted on a man. He blinked slowly as he spoke, and she noticed the thin spider-leg lines drooping to his skin each time. Had Mags already told Elin about seeing the doctor? he'd wanted to know. She shook her head, bewildered. She knew nothing: the youngest once more, her child's tiny voice unheard, her opinions unsought.

She lies there, stuck to the bed, running this conversation around in her head again and again. She wants to get up, to leave this cold room. She wants to begin this day and, by doing so, get it over with. And yet she doesn't want to, for exactly the same reason. She knows she should be up, doing, doing, doing, but the very thought of it terrifies her and makes her want to dive under the bedclothes and hide. A constant *beep beep* of texts echoes from Ray's room.

It's strange, but last night Ray had seemed oddly relieved that Elin knew nothing about *the doctor thing*, as she thinks of it. She feels the need to smother *doctor* in another word, as though she could diminish it, rub out its edges.

'Are you sure,' he had repeated, 'that she never said anything to you?'

'No, Ray. Like I said, this is the first I've heard.'

And he had nodded, almost pleased-looking. It made no sense. She must have misunderstood him somehow. She pushes the book away and turns on her side, her face close to the wall. The wallpaper is the William Morris pattern *Acanthus*. Narrow leaves pressed together, all dark greys and soupy Victorian browns. In first year they had an old fart of a lecturer who regularly quoted Morris's belief that decoration is futile unless it reminds you of something beyond itself. How odd a concept that seemed. Doesn't every decoration, every drawing, every design, do that anyway, for good or bad? There is a tiny rip in the join between two strips of paper, just big enough for her to edge her fingernail under the paper. She pushes and it buckles away from the wall. A loose isthmus of wallpaper swings out, the tear much bigger than she had intended. She presses it flat against the wall, pushing the torn strips back together. There is a pause of a few seconds before the paper flops out again, a bird's wing unfolding. She puts her hand out to flatten it to the wall again but instead finds herself grabbing the edge. She pulls, hard. Gunmetal leaves rip away, torn up like weeds.

'Knock-knock.'

Quickly she pulls her hand away and wriggles to one side so she is half sitting against the wall. Ray appears slowly around the door. His eyes are a match for the baby blue dressing gown but he looks ridiculous. He has it zipped up to his chin but it is far too tight, and falls to just below his knees.

'You're awake,' he says, and then, with a snort, 'Christ, Elin! You've not changed much.'

She follows his eye to where ripped leaves droop away from the wall beside her and the exposed lining paper is the colour of communion wafers.

She pushes the paper back and wriggles against it. 'Ray, do you remember this?' She holds up the book. 'You used to read to me from it.'

He yawns. 'Nah, I don't think so. Listen, I've been thinking about today—'

'Are you sure?' How can he not recognise that distinctive dark blue cover with gold lettering? 'But we used to read it together. Lots.' That book connected her and him: it was the string that pulled two tin cans together, creating the sound that travelled between them. Elin's memories of her childhood are so tied up with her brother that it's hard to imagine his aren't the match for them. Of course they weren't always together, far from it. But Ray has a starring role in pretty much all of the memories she dusts down, and cares for, and keeps faith with. She no longer has an adult life in common with her brother, no day-to-day currency to squander or save. But surely their past is lodged in a joint account. It has to be, doesn't it? Because if it's not, then it's spent for ever, slipped like water through her careless fingers.

She lies down and silent tears run down her temples and are lost in her hair. He takes a step forward, lifts the book from her bed and quickly flicks through a few pages.

'Oh, yeah, I know it now.' His laugh is a short bark of a thing, all sound and no emotion. 'I remember you added your own drawings, and Dad was pissed off. He said you'd ruined his book.'

Elin has lost the bony, fragile quality she used to have, is her first thought. And then: how beautiful her sister is still; the only one of the three who took after Dad. A third thought rears up. A rabid dog, it grabs her *beautiful* and tears it to bloody shreds.

Anita was standing in the doorway tugging her key out of the lock when Elin appeared, startled by the noise of the front door. It is the mildest morning they've had for ages, though heavy rain is forecast for later in the week. The contrast between the sun on her back and the cold hallway makes Anita shiver. Mum's ill-judged sense of economy means she refuses to switch on the radiator in either the hallway or the landing. 'If I don't sit in it, I'm not going to warm it up,' is her refrain whenever Anita gives out to her for letting parts of the house get so chilly. Yet she doesn't seem to think twice about leaving the immersion heater on while she's out. Even Rebecca's had a word with her about her carbon footprint, for all the difference it made.

'Anita.'

The nervous squeak in her sister's voice reminds Anita of the door. She drops the key into her bag, aware of a familiar, dull ache in her fingers. Once again she had slept with her hands clenched tight as a boxer's, curled up and ready to strike. 'Where's Raymond?'

'He's – he's in the shower.'

Something about her sister's voice is different too. Deeper, maybe. Must be still smoking. Anita checks her watch. Exactly twenty-nine minutes past. Bet Raymond has done this deliberately, she thinks. He's hiding out in the bathroom. For all his sneering about Sergeant Corish, it seems that Raymond is the one who needs garda reinforcements.

'Anita, I . . .' Elin's mouth trembles and the thick shape of a lump moves in her throat as she swallows. Anita shakes her head, dismissing her sister's right to tears. She's seen enough of them. Anita wonders is she the only one who cries any more. She will not look at her sister when she speaks to her. It's been seven years, four months and twenty-nine days. She's counting, even if nobody else is.

She walks past Elin and down the hallway to the kitchen. Sergeant Corish is due any minute and it's not like anybody else will have thought to put the kettle on so they can offer her a cup of tea.

'Morning.' Raymond's head appears around the door a few minutes later. His hair is damp. She shoves the packet of chocolate digestives back into the cupboard, only to be instantly annoyed with herself for acting guilty. She didn't have breakfast, and it's only a biscuit. Two. There is a pause before the rest of Raymond's body joins his head. His left arm is the last part of him to appear, the hand conspicuously clutching his coat and bag. *He's leaving!* She is suddenly panicked at the thought of Raymond abandoning her to deal with everything. With Elin! No! He can't. She can't be in the same room as Elin, she just can't, because that will— She can barely breathe at the thought of what that might mean. Useless Raymond may be, but he's better than nothing. Is it her? He has a shrugging passivity that makes her want to force action on him, but has she pushed him too far? She's been cranky with him, she knows it, but it's a terrible situation, and he didn't believe her at first. She has had to be firm to make him understand. She is furious. He can't dump everything on his older sister because he doesn't want to deal with it; can't just up and go because it suits him. Not this time. She won't let him!

'You're going to Cork, aren't you?'

He looks surprised, then irritated. *'What?* Why would I do that? I've just called my boss and explained what's happening. I'm going to Shankill now. Phone me after you talk to Sergeant Corish. There's no point in both of us being stuck here all morning.' As he turns to go he says, 'Oh, and I'm taking Elin with me.'

It's like she doesn't know him at all any more.

She is the second Mrs de Winter – an ageing child-bride wandering through a dream, a world in which Manderley has been abandoned to weeds and brine, its glories forgotten. A jewel, dropped by a careless hand into long grass.

On this side of the plywood wall only the roof is visible. Some tiles swing loose, others are missing altogether. Ray pushes the panels of the hoarding nailed to the garden fence until one gives against his hand. He disappears behind it, leaving her standing alone on the scrubby edge of Kilmarth Road. There are no pavements at this, the very end of the road, where it meets the coast. Back in the village, as they waited to cross through the oncoming traffic and onto Kilmarth Road, she had noticed a pair of trainers dangling by their laces from a cable overhead. She's seen this before, in Leith; Marty told her it's an international code for *dealers operating here.* Do different types of trainers mean different types of drugs? she'd wondered, and squinted to look up, one hand shielding them from the glare of the sun. Filthy old Nikes, strung up, hanging heavy as the dead. *Just do it.*

At the village end, Kilmarth Road is a series of predominantly semi-detached houses in a jangle of styles and sizes, a many-faced, multi-sided suburbia. Some are unchanged since they were built, aside from the addition of an aluminium porch here, a garage conversion there. Others look as though they have been dropped in from another city, with vast, sharp-angled extensions and natty cobble-lock drives. About a mile along, the road turns an unexpectedly sharp right and heads off under an old railway bridge. There, the suburbs fall away abruptly and the trees begin. The houses on this part of Kilmarth Road are more sporadic, every one different and set back in its own grounds, sprouted at random, wherever the brick seeds fell. There are no footpaths, just muddy ditches running alongside a pitted road that goes from one nowhere to another. It eventually gives up almost entirely, petering out at a steep flight of stone steps that lead to the rocky beach below to one side and a stile leading to a large park on the other. She peers up a driveway at a house she remembers as the Reynoldses' only to jump back in fright. A large dark owl is suspended, heavy and sacrificial, from a wire stretching over the path to the house. 'Ray, look!'

'I think people hang them to stop birds shitting on their cars.' He glances at her face. 'You didn't think it was *real*, did you?'

The new R something-or-other, built to link the motorway to the coast, runs through the far end of what used to be her back garden. She can hear a faint tidal hum of cars, the symphony that plays the same in every city. She imagines the traffic smashing through their greenhouses, bumping in and out of the scummy green pond her father hated because it attracted flies to the vegetable patch. Ray's car is the only one parked on the road. Somewhere nearby a dog barks, low and constant.

Trees and bushes grow rough and unchecked around the hoardings and cluster overhead, obscuring the sky. The light reflected on the branches is a curious reddish colour. Unnatural, a colour from a dream. Half a red apple, perfectly cut, its creamy flesh just beginning to yellow at the core, is speared on a low twig. Tacked to the hoardings that have replaced the fence are: a laminated planning notice seeking permission for ten one- and two-bedroomed apartments; an estate agent's board – *Deposits taken now!* – offering a unique once-in-a-lifetime opportunity to buy stunning sea-view apartments 'fresh off the plans'; and a council 'Keep Out – Site Unsafe' order. Desire, greed, damnation: eight years, in miniature. Scrawls of graffiti run up and down the chipboard panels: *Veronica sucks cock. Nailor was here. Happy dickmas.* A large dark brown water stain runs nearly the full height of one of the panels and someone has drawn on ears and paws, a rough yet perfectly executed snout. It has become a huge brown bear, the word *Hug?* hanging bereft in a graffiti speech bubble over his head. A small piece of paper sticks to her left shoe. It's white, clean-looking; she can make out the outline of a little panda cub on the whiskery page. She plucks it from her heel and throws it away.

'Ray?' then louder, *'Ray!* We're not allowed in there! Look at the sign.'

'Sign my arse,' invisible Ray replies. 'I'd say half Shankill is on the lash in here at night. Fuck!'

'What?'

'Broken glass. Here.' He flips the loose board out and up so she can climb through. 'Come on, I know what I'm doing.'

The fence behind is rotted and broken. Ray's right, there must be kids in here all the time. She bumps against the fence and scratches her hand. 'Ouch!' She licks drops of blood from her wrist.

The house is Georgian, built for a farmer. A bucolic squire with money to spend and rowdy children to house and teach to become just like himself. Elin always loved how simple-looking the building was. A big panelled front door with paned windows on either side; three windows above and a high roof sitting like a lid over the lot. Two attic windows jutted out of the roof, tall and narrow, perky as a dog's ears. The paintwork of the window frames is chipped; what was once a rich brown has gone the colour of winter puddles. The front door is lost under thick layers of paint and dirt. The clean, sharp lines of the panels are rough contours. It is a blurred shape, the door to a dream.

Elin dutifully follows her big brother. She hasn't been in Shankill since before Mags sold up. The front garden is so overgrown that it's hard to see the edges of the path leading up to the front door, and the crunch of broken glass is sharp as snow under their feet. There are no bird sounds, only faceless rustlings from the dense, overgrown hedges. It's turned into a warm morning, yet she shivers because it's weirdly colder here than it was just feet away on the other side of the hoardings. She stands in front of the house and stares up at it. The downstairs windows have been boarded up, while upstairs are merely empty black rectangles. The attic panes are either broken or cracked. She wants to cry. Her house has been stoned, blinded. Worse: her house is dead. She pushes open the letterbox and peers in, smelling shit and cider in the damp air. She hopes her mother hasn't been here since the day she turned the key in the lock and gave it to the auctioneer. She can't bear the idea of Mags knowing that the house that had been in her family for the best part of a century was so broken. That it had been abandoned to its pain.

'I'm so sorry,' she whispers, through the front door. She hears the slamming shut of the letterbox as the house refusing to accept her apology. *Fuck you*, it says. *Everything I did for you, for every one of you, and for what? What did you do to protect me?*

Ray is all for trying to break in.

'There's no point, Ray. Even if Mum did come out here on Monday she'd never have climbed through the hoarding the way we did. Please, let's just go.'

As Ray drops the panel closed behind them she glances back. Sunlight glints on shards of glass in the attic window frames and flashes like code. *Help me. Save me.*

Elin wipes her hands on her jeans. 'Do you think she knows this is here?' she says, nodding towards the rough two-foot-high letters next to his head.

'Who?'

'Veronica, whoever she is.'

He snorts. 'She probably wrote it.'

Elin looks down at the scratch on her hand, a thin track running around the curve of her wrist. Tiny scored lines, like tailor's marks, a cheap cartoon Frankenstein. She is bits and pieces of a real person, put together any old way. She glances into her side mirror as they drive off. The big water stain on the hoarding is just visible. *Hug?* she thinks. But the bear puts his snout in the air and turns away.

Driving along the coast road, Elin says, 'If Dad hadn't gone away . . . do you think he'd have met someone else anyway?'

'What?' He has been staring out his window at the sea but he turns and looks at her. 'Why do you ask that?'

'I felt bad about it for years, that it was my fault he left, that he met her . . . everything.'

'What do you mean?'

'Mum told me once that he'd been offered a similar job eight years before and he'd turned it down because she was pregnant with me and she didn't want to have her baby in a country she didn't know, where she didn't speak the language or have any friends. They had a deal, she said, that if it came up again he could take it, if he still wanted to, no matter what.'

'I never knew that.'

'I didn't know it myself until after Dad died. She said it out of the blue, I'm not sure why, but it made me feel really guilty because he'd never have met Nina if he'd stayed here, with us.'

'Children look at their parents through the wrong end of the telescope, I reckon,' Ray says slowly. 'We see them all out of perspective. How can we ever know whether he hooked up with Nina because he didn't love Mags any more or whether it was meeting Nina made him fall out of love with her?'

Ray has always suspected Mags thought their father had an itch to be back in his birthplace, and once he'd scratched it he'd remember why he'd left Norway in the first place. He'd return to Ireland and it would be truly *home* to him; he'd finally feel about it the way she did. Ray is sure Mags was really taken aback when he told her at the end of the first year he was staying for a second, but how could she admit it? His contract was for up to two years. How could she have owned up to her assumption that he wouldn't or couldn't want to see it through? She would have had to admit a fundamental lack of faith in her husband. In his ability to understand his own motivations.

'Maybe she was right, though.' He shrugs. 'As it turned out. That's what I think anyway.'

Elin tries on his theory for size. She and Marty both get what they want all the time simply because they're happy together. It's all tied up, an investment made by both of them in both of them. Has she been wrong to believe this? Living in a silly bubble, and assuming that life could go on this way for ever. Why should she be any different from any other couple who rewrite their contract to accommodate something other than love? It's possible that what she believes is the heart of her relationship isn't a heart at all because it hasn't been tested. It's red and the right shape and beats, but that's it.

Had anyone asked her before now, she would have sworn that she would follow Marty to the ends of the earth and be grateful for the chance to do so. So why does she suddenly remember a day the previous year when he'd casually mentioned an area manager's job he'd heard might be coming up soon?

'*Leeds?*' she had scoffed, 'Christ, who'd leave this gorgeous place to go live in Leeds?' Without missing a beat he had moved on to chatting about something else. Until this minute she hadn't understood that he had been gently, carefully, asking her a question. She had chosen to believe his comment was an affirmation of his being happy with his status as *Manager, Edinburgh*. As *Lover, Elin*. He'd not mentioned the job again. He'd dropped the thought of it, for her, and she hadn't even understood that she'd asked him to. Elin puts her hands to her face.

Beep beep. Ray checks his phone. 'We'd better get back to the DART station now. I told Liz we'd be there at half eleven.'

'Okay,' she says, staring out her own window, away from the sea. Marty deserves so much better than her. Who needs an empty liar?

'It's weird to see the house in bits like that,' Ray says. 'The hoardings around it reminded me of a set, the front designed and painted into whatever it needs to be, but behind, it's all just sheets and sheets of plywood and everything's the same. Both sides are an illusion.'

'What do you mean?'

'Back there in the garden was like being lost behind the scenes, only the set was the wrong way round.'

'And?' Her voice is flat.

'Nothing. It doesn't matter.'

She looks out the opposite window. White horses prance their circus act in the distance. Blue diamonds twinkle on the surface of the water. A shadowy moon hovers, reminding her of Neep and Nucho. Of her lovely studio, her crappy flat. Of Marty and Edinburgh. Of home. She leans forward and looks past Ray and out his window. The curve of the bay is beautiful, sandy arms stretching out yet failing to wrap themselves around the icy water. And invisibly, far away on the far side, Marty is sitting in his windowless office at the bookie's, his chipped *Heart of Midlothian Scottish Cup Winners 1998* mug next to him and the day's racing papers strewn over his keyboard. She pictures him as clearly as if his desk had dropped down on the road outside her window: slurping tea, shirt sleeves rolled up to his elbows and the gold strap of the watch she gave him gleaming through a thicket of arm hair.

Her heart is aching. The memory of Anita's face in the hallway earlier is trapped right at the front of her head: she can't dislodge it. The iceberg fury of her stare. Her only words those thrown over her shoulder as she strode past her: *As soon as Mum comes back, you leave.*

But where is Mum now, right now? Where is she to come back from?

Twenty retweets in the first ten minutes! Liz's text says. Mags wouldn't even know what putting the poster on Twitter means, Raymond thinks. Though, to be fair, there were plenty at work wouldn't know either. He and Elin are waiting for Liz in the car park at Shankill DART station. *It's gone pay & display*, her text had warned him. Is there any eventuality she doesn't prepare for? She and her volunteers have been out here for a good hour already. They've done some house-to-house, and Liz said she had someone at the DART station as well as outside the Supervalu in the village. Was it the guy from Centra, Raymond wonders – he's forgotten his name – and, if so, would he have to take off his Centra-branded fleece? Anita texted too: Sergeant Corish wants to meet them at Shankill garda station at three thirty for what her message called *a status update*, and that a guard from the local station is reviewing CCTV footage in Shankill village.

A woman wearing an inky-blue robe and black hijab is waiting by the entrance to the station. He watches her, vast and solid, talking animatedly on her mobile. A gust of wind tugs the material up and around her, submerging her face in a dark sea and briefly exposing bright red trainers. On the wall behind her is a large and colourful mosaic, *A Whale of a Journey*. The whale's tiled body is a sanctuary, giving up the shapes of other, smaller, creatures sheltering inside it.

'*Missing Person Margaret "Mags" Jensen: please RT and contact local garda station with any information in Shankill area*,' he reads the tweet aloud, squinting at the screen. 'That doesn't make sense. Are people meant to contact their local garda station or the Shankill one?'

'Don't know.' Elin shrugs, her door open before he has the key out of the ignition, as though she can't get away from him quick enough.

'Will I ask her to change it? Or would that be weird?' He pictures the expression on Liz's face if he were to start fussing about the wording – that *don't be an arsehole* look she had given him the evening before.

'Don't know.'

It's like talking to a child. She got very quiet on the drive back from Kilmarth Road. But he'd thought she was doing okay at the house. She was upset by how rank the place was, yes, but who wouldn't be? As they'd left, he was sure he'd heard her mutter, *Doesn't anybody care?* to herself. Has something happened? he wonders, then corrects himself. Has something *else* happened?

Raymond's car is old and stuffy and his back is sticking to the cheap donkey hide of the seat. The sun is high and strong, an unexpected hit of heat that in April never lasts longer than an afternoon and invariably ends in rainy tears. He's sweating after clambering around back there – Liz will be sure to notice it. He debates whether he should ask Elin if there's a wallop off him. When she was little he would have waved his arms around to waft the smell onto her and she'd have giggled, rolled her eyes in disgust and pretended to gag while grinning at him all the time, delighted with the skit.

In Best Buds the day before he had spotted two buckets

of old flowers in the corner of Liz's little office. All different types jammed together, with no care given to colour or arrangement or scent. Bouquets for losers. 'Not fresh enough to sell, not dead enough to dump,' was Liz's comment, when she saw him looking. He had bent down and sniffed them, all fleshy and damp. Sure enough, when he got close he could smell it: decay, claiming its birthright.

Liz tweets a follow-up, and he reads this aloud too.

'"We are concerned for her welfare,"' Elin repeats, each word an ill-tuned note flatly pounded out.

'And? What's wrong with that?' he asks, though in truth he, too, is disconcerted by Liz's *we*. It feels a bit pushy. Accusatory, even: a finger pointing at him, the son who continues to fail his mother at every turn, even on social media.

'Because "we" aren't concerned, are we?' Her voice is getting higher. 'At least, "we" haven't been until yesterday. I don't know about you, Ray, but I barely give her life a thought. I love her – I think she's good and kind-hearted and everything the world brings us up to believe mothers ought to be, but I don't *consider* her. I don't sit at home and wonder what she's doing with her days. Her *welfare*? For fuck's sake, Ray, I hadn't even noticed there was anything the matter.' Her voice cracks on the last word.

She's right, of course. He has no meaningful idea of how their mother spends her time. He knows she loves Dickens and enjoys a good crime novel ('as long as there's not too much blood squirting around'). She has a soft spot for Gay Byrne and never misses *The Archers*. She never bothered with *Baysiders* much, but she enjoys *Coronation Street*. He knows this because when he phones her, he often times his call for a few minutes before *Corrie* is due to start. He blushes, ashamed of his meanness, the casual cruelty with which he has measured out his attention. But the last film she saw in the cinema? No clue. The last CD she bought? Ditto. And this is only the meaningless stuff, the ephemera that he knows in his heart doesn't matter. The stuffing in the cushions we pad our lives with. Just as he had in the garda station the previous day, he wonders where was it on the path of his life that he lost his mother. But it's more than that, now. Now he also wants to know *why*.

We are concerned for her welfare. We are, he thinks. Christ. But not just now, for today. What about next week and next year? He's not going to be able to give up his job and mind her when she needs constant care. He wants to, of course he does. But, despite his earlier promises to himself, how feasible is it really? It's just not a realistic option.

'No, me neither,' he replies quietly and shifts about to unstick himself from the seat. He's tired and thirsty. This is all too much. He's been thinking hard over the last two days, desperately trying to come up with some nugget that would prove he had been paying attention. A confused phone call; an unwitting repetition; an angry, resentful forgetfulness. *Try and recall any detail*, Corish had said, *no matter how inconsequential it may seem.* But how can he? He can't define *inconsequential* because he has no idea what it means in relation to his mother's existence. So here he is, he thinks. Drowning in the consequences of *inconsequential*.

'Ray, what are we going to do about this . . . dementia thing?'

She says it as though it's a woman's name. The evil nemesis of a pulpy, sci-fi thriller. *Strangled by Time!* starring Dementia Thing.

'I don't know.'

'It's not like I'll be able to come back.'

Woooah there! Why the hell not? He has a panicky flash-forward five, ten, fifteen years. Sees himself trapped and living alone with a mother who has become lost to herself and the world alike. Frail and speechless and slowly dying, every new day a vicious indignity. Quiche in a blender for her and sneaky, guilty half-hour runs to The Magpie for him, his hands doughy and shaking. Anita, her kids grown up, buzzing in and out as self-crowned matron of this solitary hospital. Existence, not life, for him and Mags both. And the additional pain that would come with the knowledge that he would be one of thousands of people living that life all around the country, every single one of them hauling themselves out of bed every morning to face another day of the living dead. Alone in a solitary, relentless world, forever out of step with everyone else.

It's not just up to me, he wants to shout, immediately hearing the silent echoes of Anita's anger. He wants to inflict on Elin the shame and guilt Anita offloaded on him. Family dominoes. One push and *click-click-click* the whole lot comes down, the tiles landing in a curling helix.

'*What?* Why? Why can't you come back?'

'Anita,' she says quietly, and drops her head into her hands.

'Now hang on . . .' he begins, but stops. Liz is walking into the car park, the guy from Centra by her side. She spots the car and waves at Raymond to come over. He raises a hand and gestures back, nodding. Elin is crying muffled, snotty, messy tears beside him, her feet on the ground outside. It will have to wait, he decides. Anyway, what argument could he and Elin really have about their mother's future? With barely a solid fact between them to fight over, they would be no more than mangy dogs scrapping over a shadow.

Doesn't anybody care?

'Ray?'

'What?'

'Do you think, I mean, is there any chance that Mum might have . . . might be . . .' She trails off.

'Dead?'

She nods.

'No! No, I don't!' What Liz said about Mags needing time to think, that made a lot of sense to him. Who doesn't need time out? She's a grown woman, who – this thought makes him sweat – owes her children nothing. Maybe she was teaching them all a lesson, a desperate attempt to force them back together. Perhaps Mags saw what Elin clearly doesn't – that they can't all abdicate their responsibility to the family indefinitely.

He leans over and awkwardly puts his arm around her shoulders. The gear stick jams into his thigh. 'Time to go,' he says, as softly as he can. She mutters a reply through her fingers. He knows he has nothing to smile about, but when he catches his own reflection in the rear-view mirror, he sees that he's grinning.

'You stink,' she says.

The first pint didn't even touch the sides. The second more so. By the third he could feel himself calming down. His angry gulping gave way to the slower, easier sipping of a nearly sated baby on a bottle. He looks around Nolans. The pub was shadowy dark when he first walked in, and the shift from the glare outside into its gloomy, cigarette-butt-strewn lobby made him dizzy. A soundless wall-mounted TV is tuned to Eurosport, to the International Giant Competition 2014. Men with shaved heads that sit ridiculously small on their mountainous bodies are hauling tyres around a field somewhere in the arse-end of Poland. At this end of the bar he has only a discarded *Racing Post* and the fatty-meat smell coming from the carvery for company. Through an open door to a kitchen he can hear a man's voice whining on a radio phone-in, though his words are muffled by the music coming from a speaker over the bar. He remembers this place as The Hole in the Wall, a dingy local, whose undiscerning owner sold the village teenagers pissy pints of Fürstenberg and Foster's until they vomited them back up into his grubby toilets. He looks around, trying to remember the room as it once was. Lager never did suit him, and what was once the men's, where so many of his nights in the Hole regularly came to a sorry, heaving end, is now an unroofed smoking area.

Anita and Elin will have come to blows by now, he thinks. Just as well they were already at a garda station. Sergeant Corish will have drafted in the army peacekeepers. He imagines her tucking Elin under her long arm and spiriting her out of the room. Easy done, she's so slight. Anita would need a bit more heft.

Raymond straightens the beer mat and puts his glass back down. He had been trying his best, he really had. He had stayed calm. But they'd forced him away, sure as if they'd booted him out the door. Tugging at him like he was the last fucking Christmas cracker in the box!

He sinks a good third of the pint. Nolans isn't so bad, now

he's had a proper chance to look around. Standard-issue suburban boozer. It's a decent pint of Guinness, though; he has to give them that. Just the right temperature. Whoever Nolan is, he keeps his lines clean. Anyway, right now if it was a choice between drinking in a toilet or being with his sisters, he'd take his chances in the jacks. He runs the scene in the garda station over in his mind and confirms with himself that, yes, he's in the clear. He was doing what he could so that his sisters didn't have to speak directly to each other but that just wasn't enough. No. They had left him no choice. He should have known better.

It was just after three when he and Elin finished two hours of house-to-house in the estates nearest the DART station. His feet were killing him, and he wished he'd thought to ask Jean to pack his trainers. Liz had done up a list of locations for him and Elin before nipping back to the shop for a few hours. She'd be back later in the afternoon, she'd said.

Half the houses were empty. By the end of the first street they'd learned to look through the letterbox for signs of life before ringing the bell and hanging around to see if anyone was home. In Halldean Drive, Raymond's heart sank when his old history and Irish teacher opened the door, recognised their surname and kept them jawing for fifteen minutes. An easily inflamed nationalist, 'Rashers' Ford was renowned for doling out extra Irish grammar to anyone caught talking in class.

'He said he loved Irish but he used it to punish you?' Elin remarked, when they'd escaped Rashers' clutches. 'That's weird.'

'S'pose. Everyone in the class hated Irish by the time he was finished with us. Even the few who once liked it.'

'Did he seem lonely to you? He kept asking us to go in.'

Raymond shrugged. 'Fuck him.'

Most people had had their dismissal all teed up before he and Elin had even had a chance to speak. What quirk of human nature compels us to open our doors but doesn't want to give the stranger on the doorstep a hearing? Elin had got an immediate *no* and two *not todays*, and he'd been the recipient of an energetic *fuck off*, all in the first twenty minutes. They soon learned that it helped when Elin stood in front of him and held up the poster. Once people gave them a chance to explain, the stony *What is it now?* expressions usually softened in concern.

An elderly lady with the makings of a decent moustache and a sun-faded picture of Padre Pio pinned inside the glass of her front door let Elin use her toilet. Elin had to edge sideways up and down the stairs as most of the space was given over to a clunky stair lift. As they left her house, Elin thanked her again and said, 'But, you know, you really shouldn't let people in your house like this. I could be anyone.'

'We all could, my dear,' said the woman, Padre Pio's face looming over her shoulder, one hand lifted as though he was waiting to haul her back indoors. 'Isn't that the point?'

An exhausted-looking young man, with what appeared to be a half-dozen small children milling around behind him, was very sympathetic. He hadn't seen Mags, he said, but then he'd not been out of the house for about a hundred years because two of the kids had chickenpox and a third looked like he'd be down with it by the end of the day. He was waiting for his own mother to come and take over only she'd been delayed at work. When they turned back down his driveway a flushed toddler in a Thomas the Tank Engine sleepsuit zipped past them. Raymond grabbed his arm and returned him to the doorstep.

The man hooshed the boy inside. 'It's like herding poxy cats.'

They could hear him calling at the kids to get out from under his feet as they walked away. 'I wonder do the people on this estate know each other?' Elin said. 'I bet those kids would love a go on that stair lift. Isn't it weird, Ray?' she continued, as they crossed the road to call at the odd numbers. 'By rights we should never in our lives have met any of these people, or heard of them, or seen them, but we have. And they'll all tell someone about us calling to their door today, and then that person will mention it to someone else, and it will ripple out, like a pebble in a pond.'

But ripples fade into nothing, he thought: the power is all in the centre, where the stone lands.

They drew a blank at every house. No one knew Mags, no one remembered seeing her, no one had been at the DART station the previous day. The only person who had even heard her name before was Rashers and, as he put it himself, he'd not seen *hide nor hair of her* since a particularly frank exchange of views at a parent–teacher evening in 1990.

They trudged into the garda station, worried and thirsty and fretful. Anita was already there. 'About time, Raymond. I've been waiting for ten minutes.'

'Half three, you said. We're not late,' he answered, hearing his *we're* loud and wondering did it sound as heavy in the air as it was in his head. He tried not to see her ignoring Elin, and tried not to see Elin not knowing what to do about it. Before Anita had a chance to get any narkier, Sergeant Corish arrived and ushered them into a room with three chairs in front of a desk and one behind it. Anita took the left, Elin the right, leaving Raymond no choice but to sit in the middle. He could barely breathe.

Sergeant Corish pushed a large map across the desk. Raymond could feel Anita bristling next to him.

The DART employee was definite it was Mags he spoke to, Sergeant Corish began. 'We're checking all available CCTV footage in Shankill village to establish her route from the DART station. As I believe you have, we've called out to her former house in Kilmarth Road and there is no evidence that anyone has been there.'

'Hardly,' Raymond said. He hadn't realised he was annoyed about the vandalised state of their old home until he heard the sarcasm in his voice.

'So we have two areas of focus. The first is local, in the Shankill area. Between your volunteers and ourselves our intention is to get as far as Ballybrack on one side and the golf club out on the Bray Road on the other today.' Her hand on the map obscured Shanganagh Park and part of the coastline.

'It sounds to me like you're not really looking anywhere else,' Anita interjected. 'Fine, so she was seen at the DART station, but how do we know she didn't get a DART away from here again?'

'A perfectly reasonable question, Mrs Jennings. Because she has a free travel pass, we cannot ascertain her plans by checking tickets. However, the DART employee who spoke to her was on duty from eleven in the morning until the ticket office closed that evening, and your mother didn't return in that time. In addition, we have reviewed the CCTV footage taken at the DART station and we are confident that she did not return there that day.' She spoke with a rehearsed *Crimewatch* ponderousness, but no one else seemed to notice.

'But that just means she wasn't getting the DART,' Anita persisted. 'She might have been planning to get a bus. Or a taxi.'

'Which is why the local gardaí here in Shankill are contacting other transport operators in the area. I said we have two areas of focus. The second is maintaining the general search, other family members, perhaps some friend she mightn't have mentioned to you.' She folded up the map. 'But now I'd like to hear more about your mother's state of mind in the recent past. No diagnosis has been made in relation to the problems you told me she had been experiencing with her memory, is that correct?'

'I told you about this yesterday,' Anita said.

'Would you tell me again?'

There was a pause. Raymond glanced at Anita, as the owner of the information, to answer. Elin looked down at her lap and said nothing.

'She'd been getting mixed up. Not vague exactly, because she can be a vague sort of person anyway, you know, about times and things like that . . . but confused,' Anita said reluctantly, adding, 'Sometimes.'

'I have made contact with Doctor Molloy, your mother's GP. She told me that she had discussed this with her on a number of occasions in the last few months, hence the neurologist referral. Did you know about that?'

Anita blushed. 'No. The first I heard was when Mum told me she had an appointment with Mr Cooney. I've never been to the GP with her, she never asked me to. I wasn't to tell anyone until the doctor finished the tests,' Anita added, looking at Sergeant Corish. 'I couldn't go against her wishes, could I?'

Raymond recognised his sister's defensive tone, her customary fall-back position since childhood. *Didn't want to*, he thought.

'Excuse me?' Anita turned to him. 'What the hell do you mean by that?'

Shit. *Think bubble, speech bubble*, Raymond. Yet rather than grab the words back out of the air, swallow them with his pride, he heard himself continue, 'Admit it, Anita, you know you should have told me, regardless of what she said.' Information is his sister's currency. The panicky, futile power of knowing something – having something – that no one else does affirms her view of herself.

'Like you'd have done anything if I had!'

'Of course I would!' He bristled at the accusation.

Anita leaned across the table closer to Sergeant Corish. 'I had to offer to pay his train fare to get him up here at all.'

'That's bollocks! I can pay my own way, as you well know.'

On his other side he sensed Elin edge into the back of her chair as if she could push herself through it and, like Alice in Wonderland, disappear down a rabbit hole into a world where none of this was happening. Oh, for God's sake, he thought. Here we go again. How bloody typical. One furious, one chewing the furniture. But having gone this far he might as well keep going.

'Anita, the reason you kept quiet is because you can't accept there might ever be something wrong with her. You never want anything to change – you didn't even want her to move house!'

'That's not true!'

'Yeah? If it was up to you, she'd be stuck in that huge place all by herself with a motorway going through her back garden and kids taking pot shots at the windows.'

'Really, Raymond?' Her tone slows. It is the solid gathering of ammunition. 'Really? You're saying this' – her gesture takes in the shoebox interview room, Shankill, Dublin, their entire stupid fucking lives – 'is all my fault?'

'No, you're not listening! It's not anyone's *fault*. What I'm saying is, if you'd told me what was going on I'd have been able to help. *She* wouldn't be missing and we wouldn't be sitting here.'

'You wouldn't, that's for sure. Everything is always left to me.'

'*I* would, if you'd only let me!' Elin. Her voice trembled. Raymond had a sudden memory of her, barely taller than their dining table, begging to be allowed to play Monopoly with him and Anita. He always had fun with Elin goofing around next to him, a tiny adoring audience of one, and anyway, who cared if the board got messed up? It was only a game (and he was losing), but Anita had refused: *It's not a game for kids*, she'd said, and shooed Elin away.

'Someone tell her to shut up.' Anita's voice was too loud in the small room. 'She's no business here.'

'Mrs Jennings, please!' Sergeant Corish raised her hands.

Yeah, Raymond thought. Do yourself a favour, Guard, and surrender now, while you can. It'll save you the grief in the long run.

'*Well?* Raymond?'

'Mrs Jennings!' Sergeant Corish was louder as she glared at Anita. 'This is a very upsetting time for you, but please take my word for it when I say that arguing among yourselves will not help.'

Anita ignored her. 'You have no right to accuse anyone of neglect.' She turned back to Raymond. 'I can see what's going on here: you've all decided it's my fault, even though *I*'m the only one who pays Mum any attention at all. You blame *me*.'

'Fuck this,' Raymond replied. There could only be one destination for this train and no way was he going to be hanging around the station when it crashed. In a single swift movement his chair juddered back and he was standing at the door. Just before it slammed behind him he shouted back, 'Yeah, Anita, do you know what? I do.'

What little had been in Elin's stomach is gone, spewed down the wheel arch and tyre. She bends low between two parked cars in the forecourt of the garda station. It was as far as she'd got before she began to throw up. The bonnet under her left hand is hot and gritty. She is all tears and vomit and snot, her body made only of liquids, all of which are desperate to leave her and deposit themselves on the car and the tarmac. She has done this once before. A night she can barely bring herself to think about, even though she's sure she thinks about it all the time. It is constantly playing in her mind somewhere, a radio tuned to a channel that can never be changed, playing loudly in a locked room. Propaganda, blasted out to a field of silent workers who can do nothing but toil and listen. Since Jack's death – she has to force on herself this neutral description; it has been hard-won – she has come to believe that *Try not to think about it; It won't help; Don't dwell on it* is social code.

What is meant is: *Please, don't talk about it; Don't open your Pandora's box of sadness into our lives.*

A tissue appears in front of her face. 'There you go, now,' says a voice. 'I'd say you'd be glad of a drink of water too.' Elin takes the plastic cup and doesn't look up. She wipes and gulps all at once, swilling the water around her mouth to get rid of the taste of her own bile.

'I'm sorry about the car.' Her throat is sandpaper.

'I'll tell one of the lads to run a hose over her.' A hand takes her arm and straightens her up. 'Come on, Elin,' Sergeant Corish says. 'I think it's probably time you and me had a chat.'

He orders another pint. Three down, who knows how many to go? The way he feels now, he could drink the bar dry and then some. He is hollowed-out and waiting to be filled, weighed by alcohol. He has calmed down at least: the second pint took care of that. Decompressed. His anger is gone, replaced – maybe displaced – by an eager thirst. His phone is in front of him, beeping continuously. Jean's on her way, stuck in traffic. He'd forgotten to tell her he was in Shankill, not Booterstown, so she'd gone there first. Liz had phoned from the shop just as he was finishing pint one – he could hear Danny in the background. Both Elin and Anita have called several times but he hasn't answered. Let them find another wishbone to crack in two.

This place isn't a patch on Flannerys. Who is sitting on his usual stool now? He should ask Pauline to go and buy his seat a drink. Give it a little pat and tell it not to worry, he'll be home soon. She'd probably do it too – she's goofy like that.

She'd text him a photo of the glass and stool together, with a sad face drawn on the head of the pint.

There are two men sitting near each other at the bar counter. He doesn't realise they know each other until one returns from the toilet and the other nods and says, 'You're still happy with the power washer?'

'I am,' his friend replies. 'I am.'

He's noticed this before. He does this too. You'll be sitting at the bar next to someone, chatting away, and they get up to go and smoke or piss or whatever. And when they return you don't greet them. Instead there is silence until one of you just says the next thing, like a programme starting again after the ad break. Women do the opposite, he's noticed. Jean would come back from the loo, having noticed something or someone on the way, or clocked how busy the place has become, or tell him something she'd remembered while washing her hands. Everything would be woven and continuous, not this fractured, clunky interaction.

He doesn't want to be at a bar counter that isn't Flannerys, so he moves to a table towards the end of the room, as far away as possible from the two men. He's not used to drinking before early evening, and the bright afternoon outside is a disorienting reminder that everything is wrong, that this is no carefree, careless *ah-sure-why-not* holiday session.

'So there you are!' A curly-haired blur drops down next to him.

'How did you know I was here?' He looks past Liz, towards the door, suddenly fearful and hating himself for it. 'Anita's not with you, is she?'

'First, because you texted me a while ago. Don't you remember? And second, no, she's not.'

He offers her his packet of peanuts, but when she goes to shake some out, it's empty. Didn't he just buy them?

'What's happened?' she asks, licking her finger and running it around the inside of the pack to catch the last grains of salt. 'I spoke to Anita and she sounded very . . .' she pauses '. . . um, very . . .'

'Angry? Mental? Vicious?' he asks, thinking, Oh, well done, you, alphabetising adjectives.

'*Worked up*, I was going to say,' she replies.

He laughs as though she hasn't spoken. 'Angry, mental, vicious . . . Sounds like a shit death-metal band, doesn't it?'

'What?'

'Nothing,' he says. 'Drink, Liz?'

'Sure,' she replies easily. 'Unless you've already had enough.'

'I'm just getting going.'

He squeaks his bum along the padded seat to escape the booth. The table must have shifted: he's hemmed in like a toddler in a high chair. He bangs his knees when he stands up.

'You okay?' She half rises too. 'Will I go up instead?'

He waves her back down and strides off stiffly. He's fine. Fractured both kneecaps, most likely, but he's fine.

The barman takes his order with a silent nod. Raymond looks at his reflection in the mirror behind the optics. Mirror-Raymond is framed by bottles, vodkas to one side, gins to the other. He stares at himself and sees, not quite a stranger, but a collection of features that he neither understands nor likes. He looks into his eyes and his mother's look back. He blinks, she blinks.

His mouth tastes sour and metallic, and the peanuts have made him thirsty. He runs his tongue around his teeth. *Keep it together*, he warns himself.

'Ma.' The figure in the mirror whispers a word from another time, another life. *Ma. Where are you, Ma?*

'I just remembered something Mags said to me last week.' Liz is laughing as he puts the drinks down. 'We'd been talking about my dad's early symptoms and I said something about him not being able to do many things at once, that he was best with short, defined sequences. So, no difference there, really, I told her, because he'd always been as bad at multi-tasking as most blokes. And she said: *So a woman with dementia is a man?*'

And then it's another pint later and Liz is sitting close to him, telling him not to worry, that it will all be okay, that it's a terribly emotional time but she's sure it will all work out. She's so understanding, Liz. He wonders does she know it? Maybe he should tell her. He will. Good idea. He will tell her. Of course, why wouldn't he? And he's just starting to, or maybe he'd just finished telling her, he's already not sure which, and then just as she's saying, 'Raymond, that sounds like a five-pint decision,' the door at the far end of the room bursts open.

'Fuck,' he says, aware that some tiny part of his addled brain is filing away *five-pint decision* to come back to later. Anita is framed in the doorway, her face in shadow, light spilling from either side. He hears a twanging Western soundtrack in his head, a mournful *waaah-waah-waah*. Girls in ruffled skirts should be a-shrieking and a-diving for cover, grown men spitting and reaching for guns.

Anita seems to split in two – Christ, is he seeing double? He's not that drunk, is he? No, hang on. It's a second person, someone right behind his sister. Someone much smaller. Blonde. Jean!

The two women stop, pause, spot him and hurry over. Anita wins the race.

'I knew you'd be in a pub,' she says, before she's even reached the table.

'Don't start, Anita,' he begins, grasping for the row earlier, desperate to anchor himself to it. If it's all to kick off again then, fair enough, he's game. More than game. It's gone a bit fuzzy, but he'll give it as good a go as he gets . . . If only he could remember what happened properly, before she sticks him with one of her vicious *your exact words were* daggers.

'No, no, what I mean is, I've been looking for you,' and only now does he notice that she's smiling, laughing even. They both are. 'We've found her! Raymond, we've found Mum!'

THURSDAY, 16 NOVEMBER 2006

Is it wrong to have a favourite? To prefer one child to another? To two others? So much else in life is meant to be pick and choose, isn't it? Select and click and pay and wrap and done. Better than, lesser than. But when it comes to *people*, we're just meant to wrap a one-size-fits-all blanket around the entire family. Divide our hearts into equal cavities, and slip effigies inside each one, like those creepy shrines you come across down the country, tucked high up to the side of the road and invariably well tended, though you'd never see a person near them. It doesn't make sense. How can it? Why should we be obliged to love everyone equally when they're so different? Bloodlines can be thin, trickling mountain streams or vast, hard-working estuaries. The water flowing into the two might spring from a single source, but they're not the same. No way. Not at all.

Favourite. That's the real F-word. Other mothers had favourites, she was sure of it. She knew what that panicked, greedy love looked like. She could occasionally catch a guilty glimpse of it in a friend's face, fearful and defensive. She was tuned into a certain tone of voice used when speaking to one child rather than another. It was to be found in an expectation of irritation rather than the anticipation of pleasure. Yes, they all had favourites. Her mother did (Raymond). Her father did (Elin). There was no hereditary privilege operating in the Jensen household. No primogeniture of love handed down that she, Anita, was taught to adhere to and live by.

Only eight but going on teenagers to hear them carry on, the twins didn't look particularly alike, they didn't act particularly alike but they were undeniably a unit. They shared a room, friends, clothes. Homework too, Anita was sure of it, though they always denied it. Except on the occasional days when they'd had a falling out, they looked to each other first before they ever asked her about anything. And even when they *were* arguing, they rarely brought their complaints about each other to her. Their common code was deeper than life as they lived it on any single day. But Jack! Her baby in six-year-old's clothes. Her little man! He might be in the middle of watching a DVD in the playroom but he would hear her in the kitchen, or maybe she would call him to her for a minute, and he would appear for a quick cuddle, then take himself off again.

He was her favourite. She was his. And it didn't mean she didn't love her girls. God forbid, of course she loved them! She would have been horrified had anyone suggested otherwise. But it wasn't the same. The shard of love that lonely single-baby Jack had planted in her body six years before had gone deeper. Every mother was the same, in their heart of hearts. It was just that most of them would sooner die than admit it.

'No, no, don't come near me. I'm smothering.' Anita opened the front door further and coughed. 'Did you get the bus or the DART?' Elin heard the heavy cold, thick and cracking, in her sister's voice. Anita turned back down the hall, not waiting for an answer. 'Come in a sec till I find the car keys. Thanks for collecting him for me.'

'It's okay.' Elin shook her umbrella out and winced as drops splattered the runner on the floor. Elin has no idea why her sister chose a cream rug for her hall – she was forever complaining about how it showed the dirt – but Anita had walked away so she reckoned she'd got away with it. Just in case, she opened the front door a crack and slipped her umbrella out onto the step. 'My shift doesn't start till seven, so once I leave here around six I'll be fine. Plenty of time.'

'I can't face going out again, especially not to a kids' party. The way Ben's mother stared at me earlier you'd think I had the plague!' Anita coughed again and put a palm to her forehead. 'There's no way I'll make it to the girls' school concert this evening either. Mum said she'd go instead with Derek, did she tell you? Raymond's dropping her over. She must have bribed him. They're going to look in here first. At the rate I'm going I won't have the dinner made by then – I'm sure that's what he's hoping for.'

'No idea. Does Jack know I'm collecting him?'

'No. But it won't be a problem, he'll be thrilled to see you. He's mad about you. Here, don't forget this.' Anita handed her sister a parcel.

He's mad about you. Yet it hadn't sounded like a compliment, not really. There was, always, a sharpness to Anita. She had put on a few pounds over the last few years, and though it suited her, made her look softer, filled out her otherwise pinched-looking face, on the inside she seemed to be getting thinner. How was it Mum had described her recently? That she was edgy? Or was it *all edges*? Elin can't remember. She shivered as she fumbled with Anita's car fob in the driveway. She had only been in the house for a minute yet she'd had to take her coat off. The place was always roasting. *Jesus, Anita, we're not hothousing tomatoes*, she'd heard Derek say more than once.

It was one of those purely wintry afternoons when, even though there were decorations up everywhere and the shops were stuffed full of silver and red and white and fuck knows Cantuccio's was already heaving with early Christmas bookings (her calves gave a tired, Pavlovian twitch at the thought of the sweaty, remorseless evening shift that lay ahead of her tonight and it was only Thursday: she was on the rota till Sunday), the dense grey cold made Christmas Day feel further than five weeks away. Most of the neighbours in Anita's fancy-pants estate (Ray used to make Elin laugh by imitating Anita's voice and going, *It's a development, not an estate, you oaf*) have put as much effort and money into decorating their gardens as they have the houses. Elin wondered did they have a residents' meeting to discuss the parameters of Christmas or was it through some sort of middle-class osmosis that they all knew the sort of decorations to buy? Strings of delicate white and silver lights curled like candy cane around trees and looped over hedges – each one, she noticed, carefully adhering to its own territory, even if it meant a line like a score mark running along the top of a shared hedge. Season of goodwill it might have been, but

Christmas was not a time for the disrespecting of expensive land boundaries in Anita's *development*. Elin had said as much to Ray on the phone and he'd laughed and replied, 'Sure why should they pay to decorate next-door's hedge? The price of those houses, every leaf cost a hundred euro.'

Where Elin lived in Dún Laoghaire there were no such considerations to be made. For the previous fortnight her bedroom window had looked out on a six-foot-tall Santa scaling the house behind. One plastic hand was pinned to a peeling window ledge on the first floor and the other hauled a vast sack, its shape picked out in fluorescent tubing. It was hard to know if he was arriving or leaving: he had the look of a man who could have been taking as easily as giving. The lights in his beard had short-circuited on the second day. She always slept with her bedroom curtains open, and for the previous few weeks had lain in bed at night and watched a pale reflection on the ceiling as his chin flickered on and off.

It wasn't that far to Jack's friend's house but because it was so wet Anita had asked her to drive. 'No point him getting a dose too,' she had told her on the phone. 'Anyway, I forgot to bring the present when I dropped him off, so when you come here for the car you can collect it and save me a job tomorrow.'

Elin threw the box across to the passenger seat. The wrapping paper was expensive, a fashionable reprint of some retro comic, all space-race and boys in short trousers. The printing was slightly off-register and blurred lines of colour ran to the edges and thickened the lettering. *I've got you now!* she read, in a speech bubble, and then, *This is the end for you, Villain!* Classic Anita, to sign you up for one task only to have another lurking underneath it. *Oh, don't be so mean,* Elin thought, recalling the ball of tissues in her sister's hand

and her rheumy, pinked-up eyes. As she reversed down the driveway she noticed a forlorn wave from the front window.

Rain was pelting down, heavier than before. Her coat got soaked through just running up the driveway to Jack's friend's house. (Better it than her stupid uniform, though. A black skirt and red blouse with black buttons and a vast crimson pussy bow at the neck, Elin hated being seen in it outside work. Raymond had laughed his head off the first time he saw it and called her *Killer Clown*.) Despite being the only child left at the party by the time she eventually found the right house, Jack had made a fuss about having to leave and she'd been left standing outside the front door in the rain while a knackered-looking au pair chased him up and down the stairs. He could be hard enough work at the best of times – Elin has overheard Mum describe him as 'maybe a bit over-indulged', only for Ray to retort, 'Spoilt rotten, you mean' – and the party had him wound up like a spring. She got him into the car, only then she'd forgotten to give Ben the present so she had to go back, and when she got back to the car again Jack began to cry because he'd forgotten his party bag so she had to trot up to the door again.

'Again?' the au pair said, opening the door to Elin for the third time. 'What you want now?' She must have thought Elin was hired help too. Some people found it easier to be rude to their own: waitressing had taught her that. There is little solidarity to be found in the minimum wage.

On the drive home Jack fired a stream of questions at her. She hadn't driven Anita's car in the dark before and was so preoccupied with getting the wipers back onto the right setting that she could barely keep up with the questions and demands being shouted at her from the back.

'*Well?* How much?'

'Sorry, Jack. What was that?'

'My tooth!'

She glanced in the rear-view mirror and noticed the new dark gap in his mouth.

'Rebecca said I'd only get ten cents for this one. She's a big fat liar. Mummy said the tooth fairy would give me five euro.'

'*Five?* Isn't that a lot? I must be very out of the tooth loop, if you know what I mean.'

His car seat was fixed behind the passenger seat. He had a balloon on a long string and was pushing it forwards and diagonally through the gap in the front so that it rubbed against her hair. 'Willn't you, Auntie Elin?' he was saying now. She hadn't been listening properly: she'd missed something else. 'Well? Willn't you?'

'Sorry, Jack, what? Oh, bollocks!' she cried, as all the car windows zipped open simultaneously. 'How did I do that?' Rain sprayed onto their faces.

'You said bollocks!' He was gleeful. 'You said bol-locks!' Chanted it. 'Mum is going to be really mad at you when I tell her!'

'Don't tell her, then.' She wiped her sleeve against her cheek. *You little shit*, she added, under her breath, and immediately felt guilty for it. He was full of sugar and overexcited, that was all. 'What was it you were asking me, Jack?' she said, when she got the windows closed again. Maybe if she kept him talking he'd forget the bollocks thing before they got home.

He had made up a story, he told her, and because she was good at drawing he needed her to help him write it down and do the pictures. 'It's about a penguin.'

'Good choice.' She stared at a red light, willing it to change.

'Penguins have very good adventures.'

'How do you know?'

'Some of my best friends are penguins.'

'Oh, yeah? What are they called?'

'Um . . . ' She was only half listening again. 'Timmy, Tammy and, eh, Tippy.'

'Where do they live?'

'The zoo.' That sweaty rubber smell went up her nose again as his stupid balloon batted against her cheek. 'Jack! Stop distracting me! For the last time, it's dangerous.'

'Can I meet them?'

'Huh? Who?'

'*Hello?* Timmy, Tammy and Tippy, of course.'

'Yeah, I guess so. Sure.'

'Today?'

'No, no, not today.'

'When?'

'I don't know.' The car was hot and fogged up. She fiddled with the buttons on the dashboard, wondering which of the squiggly lines might symbolise *demister*. Demystify is right, she thought. Might as well have been trying to land a plane for all the sense she could make of the controls of Anita's jeep. What did Anita even need this thing for anyway? The overflow car park at Superquinn was the closest to off-roading it would ever do. 'Oh, there it is.' She pushed a button with the side of her hand.

'Auntie Elin! I said, *when*?'

'What? Oh, right. Saturday? Sunday?'

'Just by ourselves?'

'I guess . . . It'll have to be first thing though. I'm working from lunchtime all weekend.' Plastic nuzzled her ear. 'Jack, for the last time, put that balloon down or I will stick a pin in it. I can't see out the rear-view mirror!' *For the last time.* She sounded like his mother. Anita was capable of issuing feeble *for the last times* indefinitely, her discipline that of Scheherazade. There didn't appear to be any genuine last times in Anita's world, no final sanctions or punishments. It would be good to get to work today, Elin decided. The hardest-to-please, shittiest-tipping, most pissed-up office gang would be easier to deal with than the single tyrant currently harassing her from the back seat.

As she turned left from Carysfort Grange into Anita's cul-de-sac she heard a loud, insistent beeping. A few yards ahead a large van was parked lengthways, partly blocking the road. She braked quickly.

'Oh, piss off,' she muttered, as the driver behind her thumped his horn. *Who're You Going to Call? Drain Busters!* faced her, the words taking up one entire side of the van. Orange lights were a blurry glow in the rain. Like the arc of a lighthouse, the pulsing flash illuminated two men in oil slickers. They were standing over a manhole in the middle of the road, unfurling a hosepipe. She could probably drive around the truck, she reckoned, if she went up onto the footpath on the far side. But it was darker on that side of the street and there was a big hedge running along the edge of the path. Anita would bloody kill her if she got a scratch on the side of her precious car. It just wouldn't be worth the risk. She'd still be hearing about it Christmas twelve months. She pulled up on the footpath by the corner and stuck the hazard lights on.

'Cool,' Jack said. 'Look at that truck.'

'Right, Jack, grab your stuff. We'll have to move quick. It's pelting down. Let's get you into the house, then I can come back for the car in a while, when the truck is gone.'

She opened her door and got out. Shut her door then walked around the front of the car to the passenger side to open his door. But then. Then. Then she wasn't breathing properly because somehow he wasn't in his seat any more. The door behind the driver's seat was open. A car that had been behind them wasn't behind them any more: it was up ahead and she heard a popping noise over the thud and the thud over the beep even though the beep was so loud and then it was stopped and Jack was on the ground and the driver was out and it was wet everywhere and she heard herself scream his name and the men dropped the hose and ran over and and and

and he was on the ground and still and his eyes were open and he was there and he was gone.

He's mad about you.

A roar in her ears. A blood-red alarm rang around her body. She looked down the street to Jack's house, where the trees were covered with tiny white lights. But he was on the ground and she was next to him, shaking him, gently, then not gently, and his eyes were open and he was staring at her but not looking and he was there and he was gone. The driver of the car was running at her, shouting and waving his hands at her that it wasn't his fault, it wasn't his fault, how could it have been? What the fuck was she doing letting him out like that? He reached her and stopped shouting and looked down at the crumpled boy on the ground. 'Is he okay?' he said. He put his hands to his face. 'No,' he said. 'Please no.'

One of the men who had been carrying the hose had his phone out and over the incessant *beep beep* of his van she could hear him asking for an ambulance and the guards. The other guy had dropped the hose too and was suddenly next to her. 'Jesus,' he said. 'Holy Mother of God.' She felt the touch of his hand on her coat as he said, 'You poor love.'

And even as it was all happening around her, and there was shouting and voices and panic, and her head was cold and burning all at once, she could feel her mind scrabbling about, desperate to land on anything that might take her out of this, that might lift her up and put her down somewhere else. Desperately trying to rewind a minute, a day, a lifetime. Her fingers twitched. Wipe away the paint and make the brushstroke again. Control Z. Undo, undo. She saw her own hand reaching out, her own arm moving, as though it belonged to someone else. And for a second her eyes landed on the signage on the side of the drain truck. 'Haven't you ever looked at your own van?' she imagined herself saying, as her brain liberated her for a bare second. She imagined herself reaching up and grabbing his hand. Telling the man whose fat glove squatted on her shoulder like a toad. 'What?' he would say. 'What do you mean?' And she would point to where someone had scribbled out the apostrophe in the first word and he would look over and read it, and he would laugh and she would laugh and it would all be over because it had never happened.

'Christ,' he said, and lifted his hand from her. 'I'm so sorry.' His voice cracked. 'Your little boy.'

Elin rose and looked again down the dark, rain-sodden street at the decorations – cold and tasteful in silver and white – that stared back from Anita's garden. They glowed perfectly, clearly, for a second, the whiteness of the light burning her eyes, then they blurred. She walked past the truck. *Whore You Going To Call? Drain Busters*. She pushed past the car driver, past the other drain man, on the phone still, giving directions to the guards.

There are people who will always claim that they *just knew*. That ring at the door late in the evening; an unexpectedly shrill peal of the phone; the weighty pause before the stranger speaks . . . They *just knew* it was something bad, something that would remake the world. Time for ever after would be re-formed into life before that moment and life after. People who instinctively understood when the path underneath their feet invisibly turned into a one-way, single-track bridge.

Anita wasn't one of those people.

There was a drain-cleaning truck blocking the top of the cul-de-sac, she had just been telling Derek on the phone. He had promised that morning he'd be home in time for the girls' concert, but he always needed reminding. She wanted to give him advance notice that Raymond would be going too. If only Raymond wouldn't treat Derek as though he was mentally defective. There was never any talking to him about it, though: Raymond's response *sure I'm only having a laugh* used to drive her nuts. Such an Irish defence, Anita thought: that not being able to take a joke was a more heinous offence than meanness or bullying. When she was teaching she had watched how some of the children – hardly that, really, she was in her twenties and they were barely ten years younger than her – would tease and mock each other, so horribly cruelly sometimes, and it was all meant to be okay because sure weren't they only messing? Having the craic. She seemed to be the only one who was annoyed by the way Raymond treated Derek. Treated them all, in fact, when it suited him. Mum claimed it was in her imagination, but then she would think that: she never could see anything wrong with Raymond. Derek didn't seem bothered, and the kids thought he was good fun. The twins particularly. 'Once your brother stops drinking my beer and eating my food, that's when I'll know he's got a problem with me, Anita,' Derek said, and told her not to get herself so worked up.

Anita stood at her front window, the curtain pulled back, and looked down the street. Elin should have been back by now. 'You'll be fine, Derek. I'm sure the truck will be gone by the time you get home,' she was saying. 'It's at Tara's, as far as I can see. She's had no luck with her drains since she did the extension.'

'Who?'

'Tara. You know – at number two?'

'Number two?' He laughs. 'Sounds about right for that problem.'

'You're as bad as your daughters.'

She stayed at the window after they said goodbye. Will Elin have remembered to give Ben the present? She wouldn't be surprised if she'd forgotten, left it sitting in the car. That car has been nothing but trouble. Honestly, the nerve of the garage to keep her waiting for a single spare part after all the money they've put their way . . . She did tell Elin about the broken lock, didn't she? Anita puts a cold hand to her hot forehead. She's aching all over. She just wants the day to be done so she can go to bed. Her favourite Christmas song came on the kitchen radio. She had always loved the way it was about the world getting smaller, purer. Shrinking into itself until there was nothing left but home, and the people in it.

'*Home with my lovin' faces,*' she sang along softly, her cold making her voice crack more than usual. She hadn't a note in her head at the best of times, Mum used to tell her. There was something comforting about the truck shielding her from the world beyond. A drawbridge dropped down to protect her from the desperate sleigh-bell hassle of the run-up to Christmas. '*Home from a million places.*' They never got much snow, more's the pity. If she were to be trapped indoors for a day she wouldn't mind it at all, once Jack was there too. And the girls . . . She must have a temperature, to be thinking such nonsense. As she turned to go back to the kitchen she wondered did she hear a bang, maybe a yell? It was hard to tell, so faintly the sound came through the cotton-wool muffle in her head, the faint hum of the engine and the radio. When she glanced out again, nothing had changed. All she could see was the dark shape blocking the light and the fat hose snaking towards poor Tara's bunged-up pipes.

Anita will wonder over the years – the decades, even, that are yet to come on this Thursday afternoon – how many times she is to relive what happened next. What had already happened to her, though she doesn't yet know it. It will be thousands, she is to decide. Hundreds of thousands. For a long time it will be every night in her sleep as well as every hour of every day. *Tragic accident.* She is to hear those words uttered within minutes of it happening. But how could that be possible? Those were words she knew well. Until this moment, they were familiar yet almost meaningless: a phrase made for drowned holidaymakers, cut off by unfamiliar tides; for wandering farm toddlers slipped and fallen into slurry tanks. These words, too, will haunt her in the years to follow. And from this moment, whenever she will hear them spoken, or read them in the paper, she will be forced to square up to them, to shake the familiar, bony hand. From this moment, *tragic accident* is to be as close to her as her own name.

She will hold these words in her mouth in the time to come, when the coroner's verdict is delivered and the man walks free who has at this moment hit her son so that he falls and bangs his head against the kerb in such a way as to kill him instantly; and the sister who has let her son hop, skip and jump to his death also walks away, blameless and sympathised with. Scot-free in Scotland. Everyone, on that day, will be sharing these words. And that sharing won't diminish the words, won't spread the pain around. Instead its very promiscuity will render them crueller, dirtier. Everyone else is free then to drop these words and move on. But not her. She will continue to live narrow days, days in which she is breathing only for others, and never once for herself. This, she will think, on one such morning when a summer sun is blistering down and the twins ask if she will take them to Brittas for a picnic, this is what *life support* means.

She will hold these words in her mouth in ten months' time, when she will force herself to take most of Jack's clothes to a charity shop. Cuan will be with her: safely inside her and asleep; a water baby sucking a barely formed, wrinkled thumb. But this will be 2007 and the charity shop will refuse to take her bags. *It's all donations and no sales*, the elderly man, who volunteers because he wants company that isn't remote-controlled, will tell her. *But you must*, Anita will protest, sweating and teary. *I can't take them home again, I just can't.* And when he shrugs and looks bewildered, she will grab the bags, walk around the corner and leave them in a grey, piss-stained laneway at the back of the shop. And she will get up in the middle of that night and slip out of the house and go back for them, hungry – desperate, even – for another touch of fabric that once housed his skin, but the bags will be gone.

She will hold these words in her mouth in six years' time, when Cuan is in hospital for a hernia operation. She will refuse to leave his side until an irritable anaesthetist finally puts her out of the theatre. A nurse will offer to show her where the café is and, when she won't budge, a vending machine. With a tired sigh, this nurse will finally offer to bring her a cup of tea and a sandwich when Cuan is back in his little bed and still unconscious, but she will refuse with a shake of her head, desperate not to let go of his hand. *The mums always fast too*, the young woman will remark. *Always.*

Night after night during the years – the decades, even, that are yet to come on this Thursday afternoon – she will find herself standing back at the window. Sometimes in this waking dream the phone in her hand will be ringing, but whenever she tries to answer it she will never find the right button. The screen will shift and pulse under her fingertips and the buttons slide around. Her hands will fumble with the phone over and over, even when she is old and her life is misting over within herself, with dream fingers as arthritic and creaking as those that get her through day after exhausting day, even then the ringing will continue, insistent and shrill.

Some calls are never to be answered.

As she dropped the curtain and moved away from the window she noticed someone appear from the shadows behind the van. The figure was moving towards her house. *Elin?* What on earth was she doing? The rain was pelting down, she looked drenched. The car couldn't have broken down – Anita had got it serviced the week before. Derek never had time for that sort of thing. Where was Jack? Jesus, was her sister good for nothing? She could see Elin was shouting, her mouth flapping wide, her arms whirling wide arcs as she ran towards the house, to her sister at the window.

Someone had switched off the engine and the hose that had been lying on the ground twitched convulsively, then began to shrink away, flaccid. Anita could hear sirens getting closer. His face glowed in a pool of streetlight. They are for me, she thought. This is what it feels like when a siren calls your name. A dark smear started at the flat pink line of his mouth and ran up his cheek. Was it blood? She leaned over the small wet face and licked it. Chocolate. As a faint, damp sweetness spread over her tongue a chasm opened inside her, and she knew without looking into it that it would be as deep as the loneliest ocean, as dark and as silent.

Anita lay on the ground, listening to the siren's breath getting closer. The shitty smell of drains and diesel hung around him. Around both of them now. The wet road pressed its cold and gritty self against her scalp. Her hair was soaked immediately. She kept swallowing and her aching throat burned each time. It didn't hurt enough. Rain pelted down, thick drops falling straight into her ear, burrowing into her head. This was impossible. Impossible that he could be lying here on the ground, traces of Ben's party still on his face. Impossible that he wasn't breathing, that his body was robbed of its own air. She put one arm under his neck so they were level, head to head. She was aware of a man bending close as if to talk to her and she stretched her arm back to push him away. She wrapped Jack's closed left hand up in her own so when she straightened her arm his obediently followed, his hand warm and obliging. They might have been dancing. There was a stickiness to the back of his head that was warmer against her fingers than the wet ground. He was holding something in his hand. She gently pulled back his fingers and unwound a slim silver string from where it had caught around his thumb and forefinger. She tugged it, pulling the line in slowly until a limp piece of plastic lifted from the ground and dangled from his hand, hanging in the air over his head.

Front doors began to open. 'Oh, my God!' Tara. Anita knew it without looking up. 'Oh, my God!' And the sound continued to get nearer and nearer, with Tara's prayers audible over the siren. A child screamed and was shushed, told to get back inside and shut the door. *Yes*, Anita thought. *You do that. Shut the door and lock it and never come out again.* She closed her eyes and held him tight. It was impossible. He was at a party: that was all. She had dropped him there earlier, hadn't she? And everything was fine. Hadn't she herself rung the bell? Yes, that was right, she had. She remembered it clearly, how she had winced at the dense fog of noise from the other side of the door, fixed at a particular level that only large groups of small boys can create.

'Be good for Ben's mum, won't you, Jack?' She had looked down at him, about to give him a kiss, and noticed he wasn't carrying the present. 'Oh, Jack, remember how I said you were to bring it yourself this time? No, no, don't worry, it was my fault, I should have reminded you again.' And then this week's au pair had opened the front door and, after a final swift hug of her leg, he had flung his shoes at the girl and shot off inside the house.

Did she kiss him or not before he ran off? Did she? She clutched the wet, sleeping form harder. The zip on his coat pressed sharp into her chest. Good. Let it serrate her, stab her. She put her lips to his forehead, his cheeks, his mouth. She did, she did, of course she had kissed him. Hadn't she?

Anita is also to wonder over the years what she would have done differently if she had known earlier that afternoon that she was saying goodbye to her son for ever. Then, it was nothing. It was just ordinary life. Unremarkable, uninteresting. One of a million things she would do that day. *For the last time, Jack!*

She knows what she would have done differently.

She would have said *goodbye*.

Mags stared at herself in a pocket mirror, tilting her head from side to side, her movements the neat twitches of a budgie in a cage. She hummed and hawed for a minute, then, 'So, what do you think?' she said.

'Nice,' he said, barely glancing. The rain was so bloody heavy, he should have known they'd waste forty minutes in traffic just getting there. What was it with Dublin that at the slightest drop of rain the entire place slowed down? God only knows what would happen if there was snow. The city would stop entirely, an ugly Herculaneum but trapped under ice not ash. It was probably too early to expect dinner, but Anita was sure to have the makings of a decent sandwich at least. She kept a great fridge, did his sister. He had got up late, had breakfast at midday and nothing since.

'*Nice?* Nice is no compliment at all. You might as well say nothing as *nice*.'

'I'm driving, Mags, I can't look properly. It's lovely, how about that?'

'Hmm, that's a bit better, I suppose.'

'Beautiful. Stunning. *Vogue* will be after you, or maybe even the *Senior Times.* You know, for a pin-up. Miss December.'

'*Vogue*? Sure I had them on the phone before I ever left the boutique. "Not again," I told that Anna Wintour. "You can keep your front cover. I can't be doing with all the fuss."' She snapped away her compact brush and mirror set and folded her hands neatly in her lap. 'The girl in the shop said it was lovely on me too.'

'Has Elin been press-ganged into this concert too?'

'Cheeky. No, she's working. She was collecting Jack before her shift, though, so she might still be here now.'

A silent ambulance slipped past them as Raymond made the right turn into Anita's estate. Out of the corner of his eye he spotted Mags making a sign of the cross as she turned her head to watch it disappear, swallowed by the traffic on the main road. He glanced again in the rear-view mirror. Wasn't that Anita's car parked on the corner? Just up ahead, a big van was half up on the pavement, its arse end protruding into the road. Its rear doors gaped open.

'That van looks like it's mooning, look,' he said. It was only when he went to drive around the far side that he noticed the police car parked just beyond it. A guard appeared, one hand raised to stop Raymond driving any further. He pulled in next to the pavement. 'Look, Mags,' he said, still *not* adding together Anita's oddly parked car and the police car, still *not* coming up with trouble. 'Burglary, d'you reckon?'

The guard began to unfurl a long strip of reflective incident tape.

'Shit,' said Raymond. Yet he was still thinking in neutral about what was happening. This wasn't Anita's bit of the road. She was, what, five doors up? It was still someone else's scene, the action relevant only to him because he had an entrance to make at the end of it and was listening out for his cue with only a feigned interest in understanding the lines that went before.

The back passenger door of the police car was open. A second guard was leaning in over the seat. Was he getting sick? Raymond looked again. No, the man was bending over someone sitting in the back seat. Two boot-clad legs stuck out, just visible through the guard's blue ones. A streetlight directly over the car cast the cheap yellow glow of a spot over him. Two long pieces of material fell to the ground on either side of the boots, and in the rain the cheap sheen of the fabric glistened like blood. Elin!

'Fuck, something's happened,' he said. Mags's head was turned over her shoulder back down towards the corner where the ambulance had gone. Elin looked up when she heard him call her name. 'Mum!' she cried out. 'Ray, Mum, I . . . I . . .' She gulped over and over, swallowing and choking on air and tears and snot. The guard next to her did a neat skip to the left as she bent double and got sick onto the ground in front of her. Vomit slicked down her unravelled bow.

'Where is Jack?' It was the first thing Mags said. Christ, Raymond thought, what a thing to say! (He couldn't get this out of his mind when he was eventually home and alone again. Why didn't she ask about Elin? He was to ask Mags about it, ages later, in one of the few stilted, unbearable conversations they would ever have about that afternoon. He would ask her, and she would tell him, *No flash, no siren, Raymond.* She was already sure that there was a dead body in the ambulance.)

'It's okay. We're here.' Mags crouches down next to Elin but looks up at the guard. 'What happened?'

'It would appear that Mrs Jennings's son exited a car on the corner and was knocked down by the car coming directly behind.'

'And he's in the ambulance?'

The guard nodded. 'And you are?'

'Margaret Jensen, Jack's grandmother. This is my son, Raymond.'

'Mrs Jennings has gone in the ambulance,' the guard said.

Raymond and the guard nodded at each other. It's not like this on TV, Raymond thought. With TV you get the bad news straight away. Even too early: the camera tells you with an angle, an expression. Just the fucking actors they use are a tip-off as to what's happening – that randomer you've never seen before who's woken up wheezing and can't find his inhaler? He'll be on a trolley in cold storage before the first ad break. And on the telly there's music as well, a score to tell you how to react, what you should be thinking, and why. Real life is much slower. We're all stupider, rudderless. We're each the main character and the randomer both, which was what made acting real life so very hard. But no one had said the words yet, and until someone said it, there was just a chance that it hadn't happened. Wasn't there? That the script could be edited differently or, even better, rewritten with a different ending.

'Jack, is he . . .' He was about to say the word, opened his mouth to say it, but he couldn't. He felt it as a lump in his throat, a solid piece of gristle that he would never be able to cough back onto the table. He had a vivid memory of getting a phone call years before from a friend to tell him that a mutual friend had hanged himself. 'Something bad,' was all Mark would say at first. And it was only long after Raymond hung up that he realised neither of them had used the word *dead* once. Raymond hadn't seen Mark in years.

Raymond swallowed the word back down inside and grasped for another. Its opposite. 'Is he . . . alive?'

The guard looked at Mags when he answered. 'He was pronounced dead at the scene. I'm very sorry. Now I'm going to have to ask you to move to one side. The forensics are going to need exclusive access to the road for a while.'

Raymond stared at his mother, hunkered on the wet ground. She looked deflated, her new beret wide and flat as a bird table on her head. He waited for her to tell him what next to do, how next to react. He was a child in her presence, then and always. A strange thing happens at such a moment: the valve that will control the grief that is to come flips open. The speed, the duration, the viscosity: all these are created in the alchemy of this second. An unspoken decision is made as to who will take charge, and how. The hysterical panicker, the public stoic, the forever tearless: such people are made at this moment, never to be unmade. Raymond understood that the Jensens, in common with every other supposedly normal family, had an unspoken life behind the scenes, a complex ordering and reordering of relationships and systems, and it was that history that stepped forward in that moment. That other existence elbowed their individual selves aside and said, *Leave this to me. You lot haven't a clue what to do next.*

'The girls.' Mags rose slowly. She pushed past Raymond, down the footpath, and up to Anita's open front door. The hedges twinkled as she walked past, the lights a guilty reminder that Christmas was only weeks away.

Raymond put his arm around Elin. He could feel her teeth chatter as he pulled her against his shoulder. 'Mum?' Elin whispered after her, and then, with a stutter, 'Ray, I'm so sorry.'

'Sssh,' he said. 'Sssh now.' He clutched her tighter, feeling the shiver of her thin shoulders against his arm, knowing that whatever had taken place, Elin believed she had just been found guilty.

The guards took Colm Russell, the driver of the car, to the station. 'It wasn't my fault,' he said, over and over, to the guard gesturing at him to get into the back of the squad car. 'I'm driving thirty years without an accident. He ran straight out in front of me – there was nothing I could do. Nothing! Thirty years driving,' he said again, bewildered and tearful. 'Why did she let him out of the car like that? Why?'

'Let's not get into that now, please, Mr Russell,' Raymond heard the young guard say, as he closed the car door on a final plaintive 'Why?'

'Miss Jensen,' the guard called back to her. 'You're to come to the station too. There's another car on the way here for you.'

'Ray, will you – can you ...' She paused. 'I can't go by—' She stopped. Was she about to get sick again?

'Do you want me to get something for you to wear?' Raymond asked quickly, pointing at the vomit down her shirt. She looked at him blankly, barely blinking. Her long hair was soaked, plastered to her head, her fringe flattened halfway down her eyelids. Black mascara ran in trails down her cheeks. They must have thought the same thing: that he meant *something of Anita's*. He took off his coat and unzipped his hoodie.

'Here,' he said. She continued to stare. She was swaying too, he noticed. And just for a second it occurred to him – was she pissed? Stoned, even? She'd have the odd joint, though he'd never known her to smoke during the day. Clearly there had been some sort of terrible accident, hadn't there? He had been assuming it was that guy's fault and all that *I'm thirty years driving* bollocks was because he knew he was guilty somehow, and what with the rain and everything . . . But? Christ, was it possible that Elin—? Then she blinked and looked at him.

'He got out. I didn't know he could get out of the car by himself and . . .' She gestured to the area near the van roped off behind garda tape. An ordinary bit of street redrawn by death. 'And he's dead.'

'Yes.'

'What has happened.' Her voice was so flat that he was never to know was it a question or a statement. In that second could she see far into the future and know where this afternoon was going to bring them? What it would do to Anita and Elin? There was confusion on her face alongside the shock, a lost expression that he remembered from her childhood. A decade younger than Anita and eight years his junior, Elin was always the little one trying to catch up. *Wait for me!*

'Your shirt's wrecked,' he said. 'Here, put my hoodie on instead.'

She looked like a child in adults' clothes in the back seat of the garda car. The folds of fabric hung like a noose, flapping around her neck. A TV news crew arrived just as Elin was being driven off. She was spared that, he thought. A young woman and an older man got out of the van and began to set up. The man cursed the rain falling on the equipment, and she told him to get the fuck on with it and stop moaning. She held a clipboard over her head instead of an umbrella.

'Get a move on,' she snapped at the cameraman.

'You won't find anyone to talk,' the cameraman replied, surly. 'I told you already, it's too soon. We should come back tomorrow. The gear will get wrecked if we stay out too long.'

'Course I will,' she snapped. 'Devastated local community, lovely child, all that stuff. It's a tragedy – people need to talk when there's a tragedy. I wonder has the local priest arrived yet. He'll do, if there's no one else. Let's give him a shout. Phone Directory Enquiries there, will you? Get his number.'

Raymond watched her size up the few people still hanging around on the fringes. Two men in dirty overalls – guys from the van, he supposed – two neighbours he sort of recognised and a teenager he didn't. One neighbour was bawling, standing behind the police tape like it was some sort of finish line, with her child tight by her side. There was no need for her to be there and definitely no need for the child, who looked terribly upset, to be clutched to her in the rain, like a prop in a mourning scene. He imagined the woman telling her friends about it afterwards, with herself cast centre-stage. One of the van guys was crying too, but softly, entirely to himself. When he lifted his arm up to wipe his eyes with his sleeve his overalls strained tight around his paunch, and greasy stains flickered and glittered in the streetlight overhead. It was the memory of this stranger's quiet tears that made Raymond shed his own, later.

The reporter spotted Raymond and her face brightened. She rushed over, her tight skirt wrapping her legs awkwardly around each other. 'Hey, don't I know you? Cathy Lawlor, NewsZone. You're an actor, aren't you? Didn't you used be Timmy in *Baysiders*?'

'Yes,' Raymond said. 'Tommy.'

'We were on our way to a four-car crash in Sallynoggin when we got the call about this. Seeing as how we were in the area already, we thought, you know . . .' She looked at him again. 'Do you live here? Do you know the family of the boy who died? I really could do with a face-to-camera if you're up for it?'

He turned away, to walk down the wet footpath to Anita's dark door. Mags had closed it behind her. 'No,' he called over his shoulder. 'I don't know them at all.'

By the time Anita and Derek arrived home from the hospital, the twins were asleep. Mags had called the school earlier. Mr Brennan offered to cancel the school concert, Mags told them, 'but I said it was his decision, and he should go ahead if he wanted to. What difference would it make, really?' Anita didn't answer. Derek shrugged.

No one knew where Elin was. Raymond had phoned over and over, but she wasn't picking up. He called the guards but he was told that she had been *released* earlier in the evening. (Was that an ominous word? He tried to recall reports on the news and old *Baysiders* scripts. Did they always use the word *release* irrespective of the context? Victims giving statements didn't get 'released', did they? Did the word somehow signify a crime?) Raymond didn't have contact details for many of her friends, and was reluctant to call the ones he did have numbers for. What was he to say? 'Have you seen my sister? She's missing because . . .' It would be like a dumb multiple-choice personality test in a magazine. There would be no right question, no right answer, only another fucked-up scenario.

'Did the guards call yet?' Anita asked. 'They said in the hospital that the guards have to see us again.'

'Yes, they did,' Mags said. 'They're to come back first thing in the morning and talk to you then. There's nothing to be done tonight, love. You should try and rest, if you can at all. Will I make you both tea? Something to eat?'

Something to eat? Anita thought. She stared at her mother. Why on earth would she want to eat? How could she possibly put anything into her body? She didn't deserve any food. She could smell the hospital on her skin. She hadn't known there was a morgue attached to it, though of course there had to be, didn't there? The woman on the desk had kept forgetting

Anita's name, and referred to her over and over as *Mum* and the word had scratched her raw every time. Anita had watched an official write Jack's details in a ledger. Derek had leaned over the desk and touched the words *Jack Jennings – BID* on the page. 'Brought in dead,' the man said. 'I'm so sorry.'

Just as well the twins were asleep: she didn't think she'd have been able to deal with them both now: the explanations, the tears in stereo. Mum must have gone up and closed the door to Jack's room while they were at the hospital. Anita never shut it, even during the day. The beds were changed every Monday, and this week she had put on his favourite duvet cover. *Triceratops, Apatosaurus, Stegosaurus:* she could hear him listing them from underneath it. He would climb inside the cover and punch his fist against the fabric to make their heads move. There was a tiny rip in the Brontosaurus's neck where the cotton had worn thin from his pulling at it. She took hold of either edge of the tear. The material pulled taut against her. She shoved her knuckle into the gap, breaking the threads apart, splitting them one by one.

She climbed into his bed. Her freezing feet ached and her whole body began to shake, slowly at first then more and more until even her teeth were chattering. She had a fever; the touch of the cotton against her skin hurt. Even her hair ached. She stretched out fully and lay still, the duvet pulled high up over her head. Her feet dangled over the bottom of the bed. She was a body in a conjuror's trick. Sawn in half and the parts mixed up, never to be returned to herself.

Under his pillow there was a small fold of kitchen paper. His tooth. They had put it there together that afternoon. She held the tooth up between her thumb and finger and looked at the bloodied tent pegs of the corners. The worker bee top of it was flattened, with a soft, brown-spotted crater. It was so tiny it was hard to believe it had ever managed to do its job in his mouth. She envied it, that it had been attached to him, that it was truly of his body.

'You were alive in me first,' she said to it. 'I grew you first, before he did.' The tooth inside the baby inside the mother. Without sitting up, she extended her tongue. Could she taste blood? She wasn't sure. There was no weight to the tooth as she swallowed it. She pictured it tumbling deep inside her, pitching down into the dark. A pebble trapped in the grit of her own horrible, hungry, demanding body. A pearl that would never be harvested.

The church was packed, stuffed at the seams with a good fifteen minutes left to go before the funeral began, and a crowd left to hang around outside in the rain. A leaden *plop-plop* on the umbrellas was audible as Raymond and Derek and Derek's two brothers carried the coffin from the hearse up the aisle. Jack's principal and teacher and class were there in waves of blue and grey uniforms in the last few rows by the door. A few of the kids weren't allowed to attend: their parents were afraid it would upset them.

'Fuck them and their upset,' Derek said, and the twins, unused to hearing their father curse, stared at him with round red eyes.

Raymond had been expecting Anita to be hysterical the entire time but she wasn't.

'You can be too tired, even for tears,' Mags whispered, when she spotted him looking at her after they had finally left the coffin alone in the cemetery and were back at Anita's house. Raymond wished someone had thought to get rid of the sodden teddy bears, streaked notes and garage-bought flowers at the kerb by the entrance to the estate. It was horrible, having to pass them every time.

'The teddies are drownded.' A girl from Jack's class began to wail when she saw them. 'Mummy, can't we take the teddies home? They're crying.'

'No! Rosa, Jesus.' Her mother saw Anita was staring at them and winced. 'Sorry,' she said. 'I'm really sorry.'

'She's right,' Mags replied, suddenly at Anita's side. 'Rosa, was it? Right, you help me, love, and we'll get this lot all warm and dry. The rest of you, please go inside. Rosa and I have this under control.'

From the front window Raymond watched them carry armfuls of wet bears up the path by the side of the house that led to the back garden. 'What did you do with them?' he asked Mags later on. 'Rosa lined them up in the utility room to dry. When she left I stuck the lot in a black sack. Give me your car keys and I'll put the bag in your boot when no one's looking.'

'Why?' he asked, confused. 'Why bother to bring them all inside if you were just going to dump them?'

'So who should have done it, do you think? Anita? Derek? And when? In a week, when a dog has been at them and there's glass eyes and stuffing rattling around the road? In a month, when the neighbours have begun to think *litter* but no one will say anything to their faces? I don't like those mawkish memorials. We never used to have them in my day. I blame Princess Diana, all those photographs of the piles of flowers outside the palace. Not that it was her fault, God rest the poor woman. Raymond, none of us will ever need anything to remind us of what's happening. That little Rosa did us a favour.'

Just as the church had been, the house was packed. Raymond stood to one side, near the door to the kitchen. It was so he could help serve drinks and food, he told Derek, but really it was because he wanted to be as alone as he could manage in the crowded room. That and be able to refill his own glass without getting a look from anyone. It was working, because people weren't bothering with him much. His only suit was a bit tight around the waist and he tried to remember when he'd last worn it. There was Trevor's wedding in September, which was what – seven, eight weeks before? And just before that there had been the interview for a library job that wasn't his usual casual shelf-stacker position. He had felt overdressed in the suit that day. He'd passed the interview, they'd told him, so he'd be on the panel for the next jobs that came up. At the interview he said he'd be happy to move anywhere in the country. Delighted at the chance of a change, even. It was a huge lie, of course: he'd no intention of going anywhere other than Dublin. Wicklow, maybe. At a push. But not a country bit of Wicklow, only the bit nearest to Dublin. But why say that at an interview? Better to be offered the job and turn it down after.

Every bereavement has its own pecking order, he thought. Anita and Derek first, obviously. Then the twins. Then Mags, and Derek's parents, Rita and Shay. Jack's godmother Imelda, a woman Raymond didn't really know that well even though she and Anita had been friends for years, seemed high in the rankings too. Funerals and weddings are ramshackle gatherings of people – funerals more so, he thought. He looked around the room. So many of these people would never otherwise meet. And yet something happens collectively, some unspoken calibration. There is a fixing of roles and an expectation of levels of pain. Raymond realised how far down the list he was. Was it to do with the word *mother*? Mother, grandmother, godmother: these were solid roles, linked. Undeniable and conspiratorial. Every other person radiates out from these mother shapes. Elin posed a conundrum: she was the boy's aunt, the previously publicly acknowledged fun, favourite auntie of all three children. And yet she was culpable too. Accident or not, it seemed safe to say that none of it would have been happening had she not been driving, not stopped where she had, known that the child lock was faulty on that side of the car – Anita has sworn blind that she'd told her, *definitely* told her, and Elin is equally sure that she didn't – and Jack could open the back door himself, though he knew he wasn't allowed to.

One can only assume – though Raymond, a man whose fictional shooting he believes to have been the death of him, knows never to assume anything – that had any of these things taken place Raymond would not have been standing by that kitchen door, tugging at the waistband of his suit trousers.

During the service Mags had sat in the front pew with Anita, Derek, the twins and Derek's parents. Raymond was with Elin in the pew behind. He thought Mags looked a bit unbalanced, compared to Derek's parents. He didn't often notice his father's absence any more – he'd been dead six years and living in Norway most of the decade before that so Raymond was well used to his not being around – but he felt the lack of him now.

Elin had bawled throughout the funeral. Derek had glanced back over his shoulder now and again, not unkindly. 'Poor girl,' he whispered at one point to his mother, and Anita leaned over and hissed to him and Rita both, 'What about the poor boy?'

By four o'clock the crowd in the house had thinned out. Most of the neighbours had slipped off, back to their Christmas trees and their warm houses. Jack's school principal had decided that the school wouldn't open on the day of the funeral as a tribute. Anita couldn't bear to look at Jack's friends. She was furious that so many people appeared to think it was okay to have their kids in tow in order to save paying for a babysitter. He had watched her face as she saw people eat, drink, talk. It was as though she couldn't even believe such ordinary things were allowed to happen in this new universe of her own. The plates piled with food made by Rita and Derek's sisters-in-law had disappeared, as had the beer and wine Raymond had picked up the night before. ('Crimbo party, is it?' the young lad in the off-licence had asked. 'Funeral,' Raymond replied, only the guy went so scarlet that Raymond felt terrible and added quickly, 'Nah, only messing. Office do.') Exhausted and bewildered, the twins had gone upstairs together. Raymond heard the noise of the TV in their room when he went up for a piss.

He was at the top of the stairs when he heard Elin's voice, raised and pleading: 'Anita, please, you have to talk to me, please. I can't bear it.'

'*You* can't bear it? Oh, I am sorry.' He recognised that tone:

it was in the same spectrum as the sarcastic and cold edge that had formed a soundtrack to his own teenage years. 'I am sorry that *you* are in pain.'

She looked up and saw him hovering on the landing. Shit, he thought. 'Raymond?' she called up the stairs. 'Elin's sorry. Guess what? She wants to explain it all away, just as she always does. Well, she can't.'

'Anita, please.' He walked slowly down the stairs towards them. The sound of canned laughter from the twins' room followed him. 'Jesus, I know, we all do, how awful this is for you but—'

'You don't know anything about me, Raymond. Now tell her to get out of my house and stay away from me and my family. I mean it.'

In the hallway they each stood to one side of him. Elin put her arms out to Anita, which even Raymond could have told her was a terrible mistake. He glanced at Elin's outstretched hands and shook his head, such a tiny movement that only she could have understood.

Her arms slumped back against her sides. 'You have to listen to me. Ray, help me explain. I've told you, the guards told you, I didn't know. I couldn't have known.'

'You were in charge of him! You! No one else. So, yes, it is your fault.'

'Please, both of you,' he said, swivelling his head from one to the other, desperately wishing for reinforcements. He wanted to shout out, to call for Derek, Mags. The twins. Anyone. *You pathetic shit*, he thought, *a grown man shouting for your mammy at a funeral.*

'So you take her side, do you?' Anita had turned on him. 'Right. I should have known you'd never disagree with Elin, even though your sister killed my son. Which means it was my fault, is that it?'

'No! Jesus, Anita, no!' he said, horrified. 'I'd never say that. No, of course it wasn't your fault.'

'So you blame me?' Elin said. Her shoulders slumped. 'Ray? Do you?'

'No, no,' he said, turning from one to the other. His back was sticky and sweat was pouring from his armpits down his sides. Should he make a run for it? Hide out in the toilet? The TV laughter upstairs got louder suddenly and he glanced up. Rebecca's little face peered around the top of the banisters. She was crying. 'Ellie,' she said, but she spoke so softly that he must have read her lips rather than heard her.

'Ray?' Elin was repeating. 'Do you?'

'I mean, look, it was, I mean, it's the most awful thing.' He glanced up at the landing but Rebecca was gone, so swiftly and silently that he was to wonder later whether she had ever been there at all. 'It was a . . . a tragic accident.'

Anita lunged at him. 'Fuck you,' she screamed into his face. 'You have no fucking idea what you're talking about. Get out of my house! Get out!'

'Anita!' Derek grabbed her arms, pressing them against her sides. As she struggled against him her feet lifted from the floor. 'No, love, no,' he said. 'Come on, now. This way.' Her arms stayed stuck to her sides as he awkwardly pushed past them and half walked, half carried her up the stairs, her steps the jagged movements of a broken toy soldier.

They stood alone in the hall. No one came to check, to see what was happening, though there must have been ears out on stalks in the front room. And was this, too, Raymond wondered, a collective damning of Elin? 'I think I'll go,' he said.

She shook her head. 'It's me has to go, not you.'

And the door was shut behind her. Just like that. His little sister. She was there, then she wasn't. It was dark and wet, too, just as it was when he had watched her get taken away in a police car the week before. He should have gone with her to the station that day. He felt terrible about that. She had looked so scared, so young, in the back of the car. And she must have been in shock. Raymond opened the front door onto the dark November afternoon. Elin was already halfway down the far side of the road. Her coat flared to life under a streetlamp, then disappeared again. The estate itself was so quiet he could hear the soft slick-slick of tyres on Carysfort Grange Road. The world Elin was heading for was one that kept turning. That would never stop, not for anyone.

'They've switched the lights out for the day.'

Raymond hadn't heard Derek come back downstairs. 'What?'

'The neighbours. They've all switched their Christmas lights off. *A gesture,* McDonnell next door called it.'

'Oh, right.' He wasn't sure what Derek was expecting him to say. Surely even Derek wouldn't be impressed – wouldn't care – about something like that. He was a bit of an eejit, for sure, and beyond rugby and wasting money on fancy TVs and gadgets there wasn't much to him, but still.

'How's Anita?'

'I've put her to bed, but whether I can get her to stay there or not, I don't know. I'd like if everyone was gone before she comes down again.'

'Oh, okay.'

'I don't mean you. You and Mags, stay as long as you want.' Derek opened the door to the sitting room. Raymond got a glimpse of his mother standing by the window with a friend. Mags had a hand on Maria's arm. She didn't notice Raymond staring in at her. She looked pale, he thought, her face creased in tears, her lips pursed and narrow. *My mother is old.* 'Tomorrow,' Derek said, over his shoulder, 'they'll switch their lights on again. It'll be business as usual, won't it?'

'Yes.' Normal service resumes. For everyone else.

'I should've told McDonnell, *Go fuck your gesture.*'

Derek shut the sitting-room door behind him. Raymond turned and looked down the street again. Elin was gone. What was he thinking, that he hadn't insisted on going with her? What sort of person would do that?

FRIDAY, 11 APRIL 2014

Raymond and Jean are sitting at Anita's kitchen table. It is nine thirty and Sergeant Corish is briefing them on the plan for the day. *Rena*, he corrects himself. She had introduced herself as Rena when they'd first met on Tuesday but he and Anita had both *Sergeant-Corished* her at first. Had he known then how heartily sick he was going to get of saying it, he would have gone with *Rena* from the outset. He watches Rena's mouth move, saying his mother's name over and over. Mags is being spread so thin, now that she isn't in front of them. And hers such a small name to begin with. What optimism he'd still felt the previous day was gone when he'd woken up, the thread unravelled away to nothing.

'I'm going out now, Mum.' Rebecca – or is it Ailish? – is at the door to the hall. The twins aren't identical yet they are very similar, and what with the dipped-in-gravy make-up and long hair, he doesn't always get it right first off.

'Where?'

'Sophie's. She's not at school either. She's got the orthodontist later.'

'Rebecca?' (He was right, then.) 'Back by lunchtime, okay?' Anita tells the closed door.

The oversized window to his left overlooks the garden, which is low and uptight-looking. Its rows of trimmed bushes and borders remind him of the stacks in the library. The earth is dark and mucky after the rain the day before. A small bird the colour of oxtail soup is tugging at the bed outside the folding glass doors. A grey thread is pulled out of the soil only to disappear again. As he watches, the bird begins a tug-of-war, dipping to and from the ground, fighting the earth for the worm. A meagre sun does its best to beam in, catching the silver on the kitsch tree-branch-pattern wallpaper behind Anita's head. He tunes back in to hear her say, 'But why *pretend* to be our mother?' She's at it again. What is wrong with his sister? 'It doesn't make sense. She didn't even *look* like her. Not really.'

They had been over and over it the day before, yet here she is, literal as always and insisting on arguing every last point. He hears himself snap, 'It's not *Stars In Their Eyes*! I don't know why you're still going on about it.' Anita is sitting with her back to the wall and gleaming twigs rise from behind her hair like antlers. 'For the last time, I don't know why she did it. She's a nut-job who thinks it's funny to pretend to be a missing person.'

'Ray, please!' Jean speaks for the first time since they'd sat down. 'The poor woman clearly has mental health problems.' Anita ignores this, and even though he agrees with Jean's comment, and is glad she said it because he had immediately felt mean for saying *nut-job*, he doesn't have the energy to speak up again. He glances back outside. The worm droops unevenly from the bird's beak.

'Anita?' Jean's voice is softer this time. Jean argues by getting quieter – he knows its velvet-gloved stages well. When she is truly furious, it comes out a bare whisper. 'It was very distressing, we know. Horrible, to get your hopes up like that.'

'I'm upset about all the time it wasted, is all I was trying to say before Raymond jumped down my throat.' Ah, there we go, he thinks. The deflection when she knows she's on a hiding to nothing. Classic sidestep. He looks at Jean to see how she will respond.

'But, Anita,' Jean's voice is unchanged, 'you're going to have to let it go now.'

'Well, the way I see it, Mum's still missing, and no one,' Anita's gaze rests on Rena longest of all, 'is doing a bloody thing to find her.'

'Mrs Jennings.' Rena's pen taps her teacup as she leans forward, as if she is going to make a toast. She is wearing a purple cardigan and cords. She doesn't explain why she isn't in uniform; nor does anyone ask. Her glasses are suspended from a chain around her neck. They swing low, centred over her broad chest in a comical, fake-moustache sort of way. He finds himself picturing two myopic nipples blinking behind the lenses. *Get a grip, Raymond.* 'I appreciate how you must be feeling. It was very unfortunate.' Even Jean's eyes widen at this. Christ, Raymond thinks. *Unfortunate* was putting it mildly, wasn't it? Even for someone whose job it is to keep everyone calm.

'We're doing everything we can to find your mother, as,' she adds quickly (Rena has clearly spent enough time with Anita in the last few days to understand the importance of being quick on the defensive), 'are you all. To review: the CCTV camera trained on the entrance to the village supermarket caught her walking past about ten minutes after she left the DART station. Our review of other CCTV footage in the area has yielded no information in addition to this. The appeal the garda press office ran in the national media yesterday will continue today. My experience of a missing-person situation is that the family really needs to come together,' Rena adds. 'Anita, I know how difficult this is for you.'

Raymond looks at his sister and clenches his buttocks as though he will need the extra spring when he jumps up to leave the room. From across the table Jean catches his eye. With the barest flicker he can tell that she knows what he is thinking. Her eyebrows rise, turning from long hyphens to soft brackets. *Man up*, they tell him.

Rena has picked up her notebook and flicks through it. She is being casually careful, not looking at any of them, when she says, 'But it is important for your family to unite as best you can, irrespective of what has happened in the past and what your relationships with each other and your mother may be.' Then she closes the book and snaps the black elastic around the cover. 'You have a common goal here, and you must make that your priority.'

'I have!' Anita says. 'I'm the only one who has.'

'Oh, come off it!' Raymond protests. 'What do you think the rest of us are doing? We're here, aren't we? And we're trying as hard as you are.' He glances at Jean but she has picked up her coffee mug and is holding it high in her two hands.

'Where were you when she needed a hand with her shopping? Or a lift to the doctor? I never noticed you *trying as hard* then. And you think that's just going to get easier, is it? The woman has dementia, for God's sake.' Her cheeks are flushed. 'You were happy enough to leave everything to me when it suited you, but now it's okay to start telling me what to do?'

He wonders what Rena makes of Anita's incessant harping. Derek takes it – doesn't even seem to notice – but why should *he* have to? Raymond has been putting up with his elder sister his entire life. 'So she's been diagnosed by you now, has she? You wouldn't hear of it the other day. Didn't want to have the word mentioned. Look, Anita, I didn't want to get into all this again but you know what? Since you want to keep pushing it, yes, okay, you should have told me earlier what was going on. No matter what she asked you, it wasn't your choice to withhold it. Did you think that would stop it happening? If you pretended it wasn't?'

'I didn't pretend anything! Mum didn't *want* me to talk about it! It was her business. I've told you that over and over.'

'Yeah, sure. You respect her *business* when it suits you! Jesus, Anita, you're like a child with her hands over her eyes cawing, *you can't see me!*' His voice is louder than he means it to be when he tells her that she wanted to stop her getting old and becoming *a problem*. To deny her the messy humanity of ageing. And worse: that she was trying to capture her: a butterfly fixed with a pin.

'And what about you? You treat her like she's some old dear you barely know but visit out of the goodness of your heart!' Anita turns her head away. 'Anyway, I'm not going to listen to a man who can't even search for his own mother without getting pissed.'

Surprisingly for Anita, this is the first time she has referred to the state he was in on Wednesday evening when, right about the time Liz had arrived in the pub, a woman had wandered into Pearse Street garda station, some fifteen kilometres away from Shankill. She'd seen herself on a poster, she said. Her: Margaret Jensen! Missing! But, look, here she was! She had no bag, no identification, nothing. 'I just want to go home. Is that all right?' she asked the guard on duty. 'I haven't been feeling well. I want to go home. I'm ready now.'

The guard had called Anita and, fools that they were, they had all piled into Anita's car and rushed into the city, tumbling into the station. The woman had stared at them, expressionless. She was a similar build to his mother, her coat the same colour. Her grey hair hung loose and thin around her shoulders. When he closed one eye he could see a resemblance all right, could understand how the guard had believed her, had chosen to interpret her as a dishevelled version of the woman in the photograph. Liz was standing next to him. He was aware that he was swaying, moving slightly closer to her, then tilting back again. Jean slipped between them and grabbed his arm, her fingers curled tight above his elbow. He really needed a piss.

'Who on earth is this?' Anita had asked the guard on duty.

'Are you for me? I'd like to go home now,' the woman said politely, looking from Anita to Jean to Liz. She appeared exhausted, the skin under her eyes swollen and purple-smudged. 'Are you mine?'

The guard wanted them to wait for Sergeant Corish to arrive but Anita refused. Raymond trooped out after her. Liz followed him. Jean followed Liz. They stood in the dark beside Anita's jeep, wondering what to do next. At least, he'd assumed that was what everyone was doing, only Anita had immediately started on about who they should be complaining to. 'Look it up on your phone, will you, Liz?' she said. 'Garda incompetence or whatever. Go on.'

'Go easy, Anita,' Jean told her. 'They only had the woman's word for it. Wasn't identifying her the whole point?'

'When that garda phoned me, he said she was there.'

Raymond stayed silent. Could he slip off for a drink by himself? Would he get away, if not unnoticed exactly, then unshouted at? He knew he was close to the point where it would be too late to start again: his mouth would have gone sour and the faint jingle-jangle of early-evening hangover would have kicked in.

'No, Anita,' Liz broke in. If only he could go for a drink with just Liz! She'd understand – she wouldn't argue or insist on talking the same shit over and over. 'I'm sorry, but that's not quite right.' In the gloom of the car park Liz's curls blended into the dark and he couldn't figure out where she ended and night began. 'They said a woman who told them she was your mother was there. It's not the same, if you think about it.' It was only when he noticed Anita look from each of them in turn that he saw he, Jean and Liz were standing in a row with his sister facing them.

Anita climbed into her car alone. He saw the tears on her cheeks as she drove off. They all did.

'There we are, now,' Raymond said, hearing a Cork accent he didn't know he had. Maybe it had only kicked in when he'd left the place. The city had branded him with invisible ink and Dublin was the heat lamp that made the marks appear. He burped, and the iron tang of Guinness filled his mouth. He took a step back, breaking the line of the firing squad. 'That was a heap of shit, wasn't it?'

Raymond looks at his sister across her kitchen table and remembers her tears. He wonders does Liz's *I'm sorry, but that's not quite right* still rankle. Still, fair play to her for saying it. Someone had to. When he'd first spoken to Anita on Thursday he hadn't referred to her driving off and abandoning them all in town so that they had to get a taxi home – or, in his and Jean's case, all the way back to Shankill first to pick up her car from the pub car park – and she hadn't referred to his being pissed. Fair exchange, he reckoned. She hadn't mentioned Elin either so neither had he. God only knows what's up with Elin anyway. She'd spent most of Thursday out searching by herself or with Liz. When she'd got back to the house in the late afternoon she'd disappeared into her bedroom for ages before telling him that she had broken up with her boyfriend. Raymond had only met Marty the once, but he'd liked him. Straightforward, but craic with it. The serious-messer type.

'What the hell did you do that for?' He'd winced as he said it, realising that he was quoting their father, who had asked him the same question often. To his own surprise, Raymond insisted she tell him what had happened. Was it guilt? Because he'd let her go years before on Anita's doorstep? On that long-ago day he had wished he was the sort of man – the sort of brother – to say, *No. This isn't right, it doesn't have to be this way.* But he wasn't.

Well, he's done what he can today. This time. He hopes it will be enough.

Shit, he's missed something else. He tunes back in to

Anita's kitchen. Again.

'That poor woman won't be charged with anything, will she, Rena?' Jean is asking. No messing about in the *Sergeant Corish* foothills for her.

'Wasting police time or whatever?' Anita snaps.

'No.'

'Well, she should be.' Anita shifts in her seat. 'What did that guard think? All old women look alike, is that it?'

On Thursday it had poured all day, which made the searches even more difficult. Rena had phoned Raymond early on Thursday morning to say that, as a result of what had happened on Wednesday, the guards wanted to run a national appeal. What they had put up on Facebook and Twitter had been a big help, she said, but no substitute for what the television and radio could do.

'In these situations we don't always run an appeal straight away. It can be very upsetting for a family to see their loved one in the media. But ...' She paused, as though reconsidering the implications, the narrow ledge she had pushed him onto with her use of *but*. She continued, '*And* at this point my advice is that running a public appeal would be in the interests of the most positive outcome, so I would like your permission to put that in motion immediately.'

'I'm not sure . . . What happens if we don't want one?' Raymond remembered journalists accosting him when Jack had died. Anita had been so upset to see the accident and inquest reported in the news. Was that why Rena was phoning him instead of her? Probably.

'We have the authority to override a family's wishes if we decide the situation warrants it.'

His throat and his eyes – his whole head, in fact – hurt. He and Jean had given the meagre pickings of Mags's drinks cabinet a go when they'd got back there the night before and now he felt diseased. 'What do you need?'

Four hours later, with Elin and Jean on either side of him, Raymond switched on the TV for the lunchtime news. Mags appeared after a piece about some new economic forecast that claimed the country was on the up again, which seemed unfair somehow. *See, everyone? We're grand, after all. Oh, hang on, except for this lady.*

'Gardaí have issued an appeal for a missing person. Margaret Jensen . . .'

The newsreader had barely begun when Elin started to cry. '. . . was last seen in Shankill village on Monday morning. Her whereabouts since are unaccounted for. Gardaí have asked for the public's assistance in locating her.'

Raymond felt as though he was spying on his mother as he watched her stop to pat a dog tied to a sign by the supermarket entrance. Sergeant Corish had told them about this CCTV footage, but this was the first time he had watched it. His first time to see his mother in four months and all he had was this grainy, jerking image on the news; the same picture everyone else watching had. He imagined people viewing it, hearing about her on the radio and online and thinking, *Uh-oh, poor dear, whatever is up with her?* Whoever his mother had been before this week, her character is rewritten entirely by now: in the eyes of the country she is an old woman, alone and crumbling, scared and lost and lonely. (*Or worse*, is the whisper in his head. *Or worse, much worse.*) Raymond looked at the screen and hated himself.

And then she was gone again, replaced by a report from a film première in London the night before, featuring the latest hot-shot Irish actor. Richard Barter swanked up and down a red carpet, dutifully modest.

'It's far from *Baysiders* you are now, Richie!' the interviewer cooed. Raymond pointed the remote control at Barter's face and fired.

Steady sheets of rain fell from morning until early evening, and by that stage it was getting too dark to do any useful searching outside. The rain had kept the volunteer searchers away too; only five had shown up at Best Buds that morning, though when he was back out that afternoon another four had appeared: four strangers, who had seen the lunchtime news and turned up to see if they could help. Jean was keeping up with Twitter and Facebook; she said there had been a lot more interest since the appeal. Her phone buzzed with offers of help.

But alongside the media attention came the missightings, the misfirings. A boy on a bike reckoned he'd seen her walking three dogs around his estate the day before. She'd been in the first-class carriage of the train to Belfast at the same time as she was down the back of the bus to Galway. A priest said she'd sat in the front row of his Lent Mass that very morning and had taken communion from his own hand. She'd been in Lidl, Spar, Supervalu. The Gresham in Dublin, the Europa in Belfast, The Butler's Arms in Shoreditch. ('A *pub*?' Jean said. 'In the East End? Jesus, that's nuts.') Not to mention the butcher's, the baker's, the candlestick-maker's, thought Raymond, grimly, when they were told of the fifth incorrect sighting.

He hadn't seen Anita at all. She'd told Rebecca, Ailish and Cuan what had happened and they were so upset she had kept them all home from school. She'd had no choice but to tell them, she'd explained to Jean, when it was going to be on the news. Wasn't it better to hear about the situation from their mother than on Facebook, or in school? He and Jean had both phoned Anita several times on Thursday but she was curt (with him) or tearful (with Jean). There was no middle ground. Liz had made sure there was no chance Anita and Elin could bump into each other when they were both out searching. God, that disastrous scene on Wednesday lunchtime with Rena in Shankill! It was no wonder he had needed those pints. It was Jack's funeral all over again: Anita white-hot with fury; Elin cornered, not knowing whether to run away or stay and beg. And them both grabbing at him as though each needed him for their side. He was sure neither did, really. His weight was necessary to bring the see-saw down one way or the other: that was all. Jean has promised to keep them apart again today, but for how long are they meant to be able to do that? It's ridiculous. He's all for letting them get on with it. Slug it out, if that's what they need to do.

('You don't really mean that,' Jean retorted, when he suggested this. 'What you mean is, you want them to leave you out of it.')

He and Jean went to the shopping centres in Blackrock on Thursday evening. 'It's worth a shot,' Jean had said. 'Seeing as how she's here so much, people are sure to recognise her.' He nudged Jean to look at a handwritten sign pinned to a café window: *We will pray for you*. 'Don't knock it till you've tried it.' She shrugged. 'Works for some.' It was late-night opening, and the shops were busy, yet they drew a blank.

Back home, just before midnight, Liz phoned. 'Nothing, sorry, Raymond,' she said. 'It's so wet out there, we hardly even got to talk to anybody. We put leaflets through doors and went table to table in the pubs,' (Christ, he thinks, I should have gone with her), 'but nothing.'

As he said goodbye Jean and Elin were in the sitting room, listening.

'Ray?'

'Yes?' He walked to the doorway but didn't go in.

'We're not going to find her, are we?'

'*No!* Elin, fuck, no. Don't say that. That was just Liz, she—'

'I know who it was. It's four days, Ray. We're not going to find her, are we? She's gone for ever.'

'Don't say that, Elin. She's not. Just bloody don't.'

Jean put her arm around his sister. Their two blonde heads pressed together. 'Sssh, Elin, love.' Jean's voice crooned, a lullaby. 'He's right. Don't say it, don't think it.'

Just thinking about Thursday – only the day before? It feels like a year – exhausts him. Anita has the heating cranked up and the kitchen is stuffy. He goes to take his jumper off. He pauses, arms raised elbows sticking out. The shirt underneath is on its second day: the pits are bound to be a bit ripe by now. He pretends to stretch and lowers his arms again. Jean refills his teacup and pushes it towards him. The table in front of them is covered with maps, scraps of paper, leaflets, posters. Mags's face stares up at them over and over. He finds himself counting the Magses on the table. *She loves me, she loves me not.* He reaches out and gathers the posters into a pile. His hand raised, he stops. He doesn't know what to do next. He's stuck. He can't bring himself to put his mother face down on the table.

'So that's everyone.' Anita is talking again. She stops and frowns at him.

It's as though a huge balloon has been inflated over his head and it's squashing down on him, on his hand. A dark weight forcing him to drop this black and white mother onto the table. But if he does, if he lets go, he's as good as admitting that he's failed her, that she— Jean leans over, prises his fingers open and takes the sheets from his hand. She holds them in her lap, her hands a hug around his mother.

Raymond exhales as Anita continues, 'Every single person in her address book and her phone is accounted for. Even the ones abroad. Every neighbour in every house on the street.'

They have taken the globe of Mags's life and spun it around and around. Her world has shrunk to nothing. Every knowable second of the previous weekend and Monday morning until she flickers into the CCTV footage of the shop in Shankill has been discussed. Every nuance of her behaviour has been discussed, analysed, interpreted as evidence of ill-health, interpreted as evidence of normality. They have gone up, gone down. Spoken to her GP, her consultant. Cried, prayed, entreated, hoped. They have unpicked his mother's life and still not found her hiding within it. (Late on Wednesday night Ray had stuck his head into the cupboard upstairs. 'Dev,' he whispered, 'where is she?')

Rena nods. 'Every avenue has been explored and the public appeal hasn't produced any serious leads as yet. As there is no reliable evidence that your mother left the Shankill area again on Monday, the ground operation there has been stepped up significantly as of this morning.'

Every avenue has been explored. It's a cliché he'd never thought he would have to apply to himself, to his life. Yet here he is, panicked and afraid and sweating. Here he is, in his sister's house, every avenue explored.

Something shifts in the air of the room as the talk turns to *area searches* and *location sweeps*, and how these would be concentrated on a two-mile radius of the DART station. On the Shanganagh Park side, they would cover the area between Kilmarth Road and the coastline. 'To begin with,' Rena adds.

'But we've – well, Raymond, mainly, has been all over Shankill already. And back to their old house and spoken to all the neighbours there. More than once,' Jean says. 'Where else is there to go?'

In the pause that follows, he hears Anita and Jean inhale. From upstairs they can hear Ailish shouting at Cuan to give the iPad back *right this second.*

'A ground search is much more thorough.' Rena measures out each word, giving each an equal weight that may ring an alarm bell over all their heads. 'Our search to date has been to establish sightings. We have primarily been concentrating on areas where there are people: the housing estates, the shops, the transport operators.'

He understands the code: it is time for the earth under their feet to yield its secrets.

'Rena?' Raymond is aware of an unexpected spike of fear, a physical twist in his bowels. 'What sort of . . . outcome are we looking at here?'

'Just tell me!' Anita's voice is so loud and shrill it takes him a second to understand what she's saying. 'She's dead, isn't she? Just fucking well say so! Stop treating us like fucking fools!'

Jean gives a start and the posters slither out of her hands. Raymond pushes back from his seat. Ma is all over the floor! He has to pick her up. She can't be down there like that, puddled around their shoes. He ducks under the table and scrabbles about, sweating and panicked.

Anita points at Rena. 'Just tell me!' And again, louder. 'Tell me!'

He's kneeling now, toddler height to the table, the posters bunched in his hand. Crumpled but safe. He lays them gently on the table and begins to flatten them out, one mother at a time.

The raised voices upstairs, too, have fallen silent. The room is silent. The house, the street, the entirety of Ireland, the world. *Disappeared off the face of the earth* – isn't that the expression? As a child he'd imagined that to mean a globe with a tiny figure the size of a plastic soldier flying out from the side and landing . . . where? He has no idea.

'There is *no* evidence at all to suggest that your mother has come to any harm, Mrs Jennings. Yes, locating her is taking longer than we would like, and I hope I've been very clear with you as to the level of concern my garda colleagues and I have, but as I've said before, we remain hopeful. I'm being honest with you. It's not in anyone's best interests for me to be otherwise.' Rena picks up her notebook and phone.

At least Rena didn't say *positive outcome* again. Anita would probably have gone for her with the bread knife if she had. Anita's face is bright pink. Her eyes are full and her jaw is trembling. Without getting up from his knees, Raymond leans forward and puts his hand over his sister's. Her fingers are hot under his own, and the vast diamond of her engagement ring presses hard against a callous on his palm. When was the last time he touched his sister's hand? He has no idea. His head is so close to her wrist that he can hear the tiny tick-tock of her watch. He looks up. Her eyes begin to flick from side to side, then up and down, quickly, blink-blink. For a brief second he wonders is she about to have some sort of fit, then realises that she is willing – forcing – herself not to cry.

He waits for his sister to tug her hand angrily out from under his own, but she doesn't. She leaves it flat on the table, where his fingers cover it completely.

Tick-tock. Anita's watch reproaches them all. *Tick-tock.* Hurry, hurry, hurry.

What time is it? Nine? No, nearly ten. She was awake and crying most of the night, finally dropping off at five. The silence tells her the house is empty. Did she sleep? She's not sure. She must have but her head has a fogginess she can't shake, the dehydrated blur of a codeine hangover. What day is it? Friday. Yesterday was— Oh, Christ. Yesterday. *Marty!* Her eyes fill. But there is no time to think about that, or about the day before. The days before.

She gets ready quickly, only to find that she's too early. She can't leave the house until ten twenty-nine exactly. She wanders from room to room, haunting the place, too jittery to do anything practical. She picks up her phone and puts it down, over and over and over. The screen stays silent. Angry.

Shit. The doorbell. She doesn't want visitors; she has to leave in five minutes.

A girl is standing on the step, crying. And then Rebecca is wrapped around her, hugging her.

'Auntie Elin.' Rebecca smells of perfume and hair spray and, underneath that, ironing. Elin can feel the line of her shoulder blades under the thick cotton of her hoodie. She runs a hand down the long slope of Rebecca's hair. She was a child the last time Elin saw her, a little girl who loved teddies and wanted roller skates for Christmas. Elin closes her eyes and, for a second, allows herself to pretend that the last seven years have fallen away, that she is at the door of Anita's house, getting a cuddle from her niece, same as always. She opens them again. The child has gone. In her arms is a slim teenager with too much make-up and straightened hair.

'Mum told us about Granny. It – she, like, I mean, she – was on the news.' She wipes her face with her sleeve and smears of foundation and blusher streak across her cheeks.

'I know, love. Don't cry, Becca, it'll all be fine.' You big liar, she thinks. What the hell do you know? 'Does Anita know you're here?'

'Nope. I heard her talking to Dad about you and I guessed you'd be here, so I took a chance and got the bus over. But that's okay?' Her accent turns statements into questions. 'I often come and visit Granny on my own, because Ailish isn't, you know, like, that bothered?'

'It's so lovely to see you again, Rebecca, it really is. But I don't want to upset your mum.'

Rebecca sniffs. 'I don't see how she could, you know, get any worse than she already is?' For a second Elin envies Rebecca's teenage certainty: the ability to see her mother as a lost remnant of an ancient species completely different from her own. To be unable to understand that the sort of grief her mother is experiencing could somehow, some day, be hers too. 'But I wanted to see you. I missed you, Auntie Elin. Ailish, too.'

Rebecca opens her bag and the familiar grins of Neep and Nucho dance into view. She opens the cover of *Neep and the Ice-cream Iceberg*. 'You look just like your picture.'

'So do you. Mum – Granny – sends me photos. Of Ailish and Cuan too.'

'You've never met Cuan.'

'No.'

'I've shown him the books. Granny had them here and she gave them to me. Cuan didn't believe me at first. He thinks if he had an aunt he'd have heard about you before, but ...' She shrugs and trails off, her cheeks flushed.

Elin takes Rebecca's bag and returns the books to it. She doesn't want Neep and Nucho here. This is not their place. They are different. Untainted. She glances at her phone. Ten twenty-seven. 'Rebecca, it's amazing to see you, it really is, and I'm so sorry ... but I'm going out now.'

Rebecca is a crestfallen child. 'Can't I come with you?'

'It's something I have to do by myself. I'm sorry. And if your mum knew you'd been here and talked to me she'd be furious.'

'Yeah, like, I know. But Dad said it was okay. He was fine with it.'

'You have to admit, Anita was right about that much: the let-down was truly horrible,' Jean says, when they are alone again in her car. It's noon. They are all to meet again in Shankill in a few hours, but first he has decided to go back to Booterstown Avenue for Elin. How has it happened that *he*'s the one legging it around? First they're tugging him between them and now he's a ping-pong ball shuttling between his two sisters.

'It was very frightening for Anita, I think,' Jean says, 'having to go to the station to meet that woman. Apart from this being an awful situation, it must bring back such terrible memories for her.'

'Yes, I can see that, but don't see why that woman made it any worse than it already was.'

'I suspect it connected your mother somehow to another person's life, and a tragic one at that. It's like, I don't know . . . it pulled the two things together somehow. *And* Anita's had to tell the girls and Cuan. It's no wonder she's so upset this morning.'

'You might be giving my sister too much credit for empathy.'

Jean shakes her head. 'No. You're not giving her enough.'

They are silent for a moment. Blackrock village slips past them. He recognises the names of shops his mother likes. He feels guilty that he has never been in any of them, goofing around by her side, hunting for bargains.

'I was talking to Liz last night,' Jean says. Uh-oh. Where's this going? 'She told me about her father.'

'Oh, right. Yes. She's talked to me about him too.'

'I know. You and Anita and Elin are going to have to take it seriously, the situation you'll be in when you find Mags.'

'You heard Anita. She won't accept there's anything wrong.'

'No, Raymond.' There's an official note in Jean's voice. She must be a demon at meetings. 'She *does* accept it. What she's telling you is that it's not solely her responsibility.'

'I know that.'

'Liz was very open about how tough it was for her family. It's in the papers every day, stories about Alzheimer's and dementia and the awful battles people have to manage. The new cancer, she called it.'

'I know.' He pictures it as a fog, a deadly gas rolling over the land. Rising higher and higher, swallowing memories, obliterating communities. 'But lots of people are facing this, not just us. Anita acts like she's the only one affected.'

Jean drums her fingers on the steering wheel. 'Everyone is just another funeral you'll have to go to some day, aren't they, Raymond?'

Jesus, where did that come from? He glances across at her but her head is turned towards the side window, checking the turn onto Booterstown Avenue. This is more like the life he recognises. A conversation with Jean in which they both know there is another, silent, discussion going on between them. One in which they are less afraid. Her funeral remark got belched out from that second life. A pop of fire from a quiet volcano.

'I'm going to move back here, and take care of her.' He'll never be sure whether it was a reflex, an attempt to prove her wrong, or a serious decision he has made without knowing it.

'Are you?' Her voice is quiet, neutral. He wonders will these two parallel versions of themselves flip around some day and come face to face with each other for real. Would they recognise each other? Love each other?

'You don't believe me, do you? You don't think I have it in me. I can see it on your face.'

The front door squeaks when she opens it, as does the gate. She waits on the pavement until, at exactly twenty-nine minutes past ten, she walks down the avenue towards the main road. Rebecca is in the distance ahead of her. She watches the girl turn the corner in the direction of the bus stop. At Best Buds Elin pauses again. Ten thirty: the time Mum passed by here on Monday – Liz told her so. There are three buckets of daffodils and two Easter arrangements in the window. The lights are on inside, and she can see Liz behind the counter but she has her back to her. They would have been there that day, too, wouldn't they, these plastic-eyed bunnies, red ribbons like nooses around their necks, and pots planted in their compliant paws? She takes her phone out. *Click click.* But just say they weren't? What are the chances of the exact same bunches of flowers still sitting there four days later? (Unfortunately, very high, as Liz would tell her if she was to put her head around the door and ask.) To be on the safe side, she crosses to the other side of the road and takes a photo of the Best Buds shop front and signage. That won't have changed.

At the Centra on the corner she flicks through the racks of birthday cards. She's looking for one with an illustration, a sprig of flowers probably, and the words *Happy Birthday* swirling around it in gold calligraphy. She knows exactly the sort of thing: she's received it from her often enough herself . . . If she can only find it . . . There it is! That's bound to be the exact one. When another customer distracts the young Chinese woman behind the counter she bends down and takes a photo of the card.

'*Mental?*' The girl frowns.

'You tell me, love. I said: do – you – sell – menthol?' The

man points at the shelves behind the girl's head. He looks around the shop till he catches the eye of another shopper in a conspiratorial *what-the-fuck-can-you-do* glance. 'Men-thol,' he says again. 'The green ones.'

Click. She waits at the pedestrian lights to cross the Rock Road, then heads down the path towards the DART station. *Click*, the car park. *Click*, the ticket machine. Cold and windswept, the station rises like a stage from the marshy field. She crosses to the far platform and stands next to a low wall that looks out over the sea. This nature reserve is *Important for Diversity* claims a poster on the wall. Does that girl in the Centra take the DART? she wonders, imagining her reading the poster every day and thinking that the Irish must care more about diversity in nature than in each other.

There is a ten-minute wait until the next train. The wind is biting. She doesn't deserve any shelter. The tide is so far out she can't make out where it begins, just the silvery blue stretch marks of the horizon. The muddy shore is exposed. A scalp, with tiny white birds scattered over it, like dandruff.

The clack of the DART down the tracks she hears as *Marty Marty Marty*, and she sways on her feet with the tiredness and pain. She chooses her seat carefully: she must get it exactly right. It's important. Definitely the window, she decides. A seat for four. Facing the way the train was going. She chooses a window seat to the left of the middle door. Good. This feels right. The green fabric of the seats shifts under her hand as the train moves to and fro, slipping from suburbia to seaside and back again. *Click.* She takes picture after picture, greedy in her determination to capture as much as her eyes can see and her phone's memory can process. Sloping roofs of tiny railway cottages; blocky, self-important extensions protruding from the back of semi-detached houses, like miniature museums; silverfish flashes of sea appearing and disappearing. Everywhere she gets brief, intimate flashes of other lives: breakfast bowls and teapots abandoned on kitchen tables, lonely swing-sets twisting in the breeze, unmade beds, and apartment blocks where window after window is filled with bulging clothes airers. Patches of graffiti and relentless advertising hoardings insisting she do this, buy that, think about the other. She catches her breath at the unexpected sight of a new playground (Jack!) where a man stands at the bottom of a slide, gloved hands folded patiently behind his back. Cracked oily rainbows lie in the puddles left behind from yesterday's rain.

Everybody around her on the train is normal, ordinary. Are any of them screaming inside, as she is? She wants to stand and shout, a panicked plea for attention, for help. She thinks of the man and his little kids in that housing estate in Shankill. Would he have seen the appeal on the news? Turned to his partner and, excited, said, 'There was people here yesterday, asking about that old lady!' Desperate for a moment to link to the action, before turning away, forgetting about them again.

When her phone rings, she cries as she switches it to *mute*.

At twenty-five past eleven she gets off the train at Shankill. She waits until it has rushed off down the track and out of sight – *click, click* – before she leaves the platform. The ticket office is unoccupied. A handwritten sign, *Back in a mo, use the machine* is taped to the hatch. There is a poster stuck to the side of the hatch. She stands in front of it for several minutes, reading it letter by letter. She reaches out a hand and traces her mother's face with her fingertips. She doesn't take a picture. Two garda cars are parked at the far side. A lone garda is standing by the exit, waiting to accost drivers as they come and go.

Elin stands alone by the side of the ticket office when a familiar figure glides past the exit and slips out of sight, silent as a ghost. There was something about the woman, that slight figure, the beret . . .

Ohmygodohmygod. It's her. It's her. It's over! She can go home. It mightn't be too late . . . Everyone can go home.

Elin is past the ticket office and through the car park in seconds. Tears blur her eyes. 'Mum!' she shouts. 'Mum!' There she is, her head down, leaning into the open boot of a car. Elin rushes over, grabs her. 'Mum!'

'What? Get off me!' the woman shouts. She's young, probably Anita's age. On the front of the beret a skull pattern is picked out in diamanté. Some of the stones are missing. 'Jesus, what's wrong with you?'

'Sorry, sorry.' Elin backs away. 'I thought you were my mother.'

'Do I look like your effing mother?'

Elin turns and goes back in the direction she has come.

When she gets back to Booterstown and the house, Ray will be waiting, angry. He will snap at her that he knows she's upset but, Jesus, she never said she was going out and why wouldn't she answer her phone and, fuck it, does she think they need *another* missing person?

'And anyway, Elin,' Ray will continue, impatient, 'there was no point in retracing her steps, you knew that. It's been done. We don't need to focus on her journey from here. We know she went to Shankill. It's not relevant.'

'It is, Ray,' she will reply, turning her phone over and over in her hand. What a tiny, simple object, yet so stuffed with lives and thoughts and new-minted history. She and Marty are in there together too, safe for ever. She will want to be alone so that she can look at the photographs she has just taken. To flick through them so quickly that she has the power to turn them into animation. Into a life. She framed every shot as perfectly as she could, crouching a few inches lower to get the eye-line right. Seeking out what she was sure her mother would naturally have been drawn to: the colourful, the silly, the perfectly imperfectly human.

'I don't get it.' Ray will lean his head against the wall by the kitchen door, frustrated. He will close his eyes, and because he won't open them again immediately, she will wonder is he a bit pissed; had he and Jean gone for a drink while she was out.

Elin won't say that she was trying to find her mother's life in the gable-end walls of empty houses and the attic skylights of railway cottages. In the sudden gloom of unexpected tunnels and the uneasy glare of the lake in the park. In the joyous clanging of the silver masts in Dún Laoghaire harbour, in the new building by the pier that made her think a giant buoy had washed ashore.

What she will say is: 'I saw the same things she did, Ray. The same people, maybe. Everything.' Her voice will crack as she explains. 'I wanted to see everything that she would have seen when she left here on Monday.'

'But why?'

Elin won't answer at first. The clock in front of the kitchen window will be a metronome, issuing seconds to both of them in turn and no one. And in the silence he will open his eyes and she will see that they are full of tears, salty water washing around the blue. Then she will begin to cry, too, and say, 'I wanted her memories.'

1.30 p.m. Time to go back to Shankill. Raymond is waiting for Elin to get off the toilet and Jean to get off the phone. His phone beeps. Liz. *Stuck at shop waiting 4 a delivery. Sorry. Will catch u up there asap.*

He is alone in his mother's front room. Cluttered with her stuff, her belongings spread around, shed like flakes of skin. He crosses to the mantelpiece. Beside a vase of dead daffodils is a photo Elin found in the spare bedroom. A family holiday in Norway. Elin is a baby in Mum's arms, curled up against her neck. She was born in December '82, which must make this summer '83. Dad has the box for his new camera around his neck; Anita has a hand on the box. Raymond remembers that camera. It was heavy and complicated, and Dad was very proud of it. (His instructions to their neighbour at the campsite, who was taking the photo, were so long and over-complicated that Mags had butted in: 'Per! Just tell him to point the camera at us and click the bloody button!') He wonders why he remembers that holiday so clearly, when so much of his childhood is a blur. Not a miserable they-burned-me-with-cigarettes-till-I'd-faint blur, more of a shrugging so-what. Perhaps that holiday is a learned memory, one he has convinced himself he has simply because they looked at Dad's photographs so often. He stares at the lake behind his nine-year-old self and forces memories to the surface: the black shock of the cold water when you jumped in; the way the light inside their tent was the colour of Fanta.

Mags spent the entire trip exhausted by baby Elin and bitten alive by midges. She must only have been in her early forties then. Not much older than he is now.

'Mum,' he says, and again, feeling the pleasing, palindromic softness of the letters warm his mouth. It's gentler than *Mags*, than *Ma*. Losing *Mum*, that was his mistake. Not *Mummy*: that word must be left behind. That is the job of growing up, to put it aside with the careworn teddies. No, that's not quite right, he decides: it's not solely the child's job, it's the parent's too. His mother should have reclaimed the 'my' but left the 'mum' behind, for him. Dropping *Mum*, *Ma*, for 'Mags' was *his* wrong turning. He understands that now.

Liz told him how annoyed her dad used to get sometimes, when he had flashes of what he had lost and what he was yet to lose. He used to repeat jokes, she said, and though she'd try to laugh fresh every time, it just wasn't possible: he could see the desperation, the attempt to lie in her face. 'You've changed,' he'd said to her once, angry and tearful when she didn't have it in herself to muster up a smile at the same terrible pun being repeated over and over. 'There's not a one of you in this house with a sense of humour any more. You're no fun.' It wasn't only he who was disappearing slowly from his family: it was working the other way around too. She would catch him looking at her, puzzled. Strangers to each other. Is this what will happen to them? Where has she gone, his vanished mother?

It is clear to him that he lost her years before. He desperately needs to find her, to explain and apologise and promise. He allowed her to spend her days alone in this house, this room.

In his heart, he knew she was lonely, yet he did nothing about it. He claimed he loved her yet he never gave her the chance to ask for help; neither did he offer it. He didn't care: this lack of love is a spotlight on him. A glare to disorient him before the torture begins.

He will face it. He will. Whatever is in Mags's future, he will meet it head on. All he wants is for her to stop being scared of whatever is to come and to return home. If he can just have that, he will make it right. He will swear an oath of allegiance to her. Whatever it takes.

He won't be a son to his mother, he will be a daughter.

He puts the photo back. There is another picture on the mantelpiece behind it. It was taken in front of the house in Kilmarth Road. He is sixteen in this one, frowning at the photographer. Elin is next to him, her head leaning against his arm. Mum is next to Elin with Anita on her left. They are oddly posed, formal. Raymond had made a fuss about having to be in it at all. This is the photo Dad took on the day he left for Oslo. It was the last thing he did before Mum drove him to the airport. (He sent them a copy of it – Raymond remembers the letter arriving and Elin's tears when she saw she was smiling in the picture, worried that Dad would think she was pleased he had gone away. 'I wasn't happy, Ray,' she sniffed and wiped her nose on her sleeve, 'but everyone always says smile for a photo.')

The previous October, he and Jean had gone to Barcelona. When they were checking out of the hotel he discovered he had left his book behind so he went back up to the room. The door was open, a cleaner already in 'their' bathroom. From further along the corridor he could hear the hum of a vacuum. It was no longer their territory; the illusion was broken. It wasn't someone else's either: it was just an ordinary room, with a messy bed and empty bottles lined up beside the wastepaper bin. It was nothing special. Whenever he thought about that trip – and it was great, they'd had a real laugh – that was all he could think of: the empty bedroom from which all traces of his holiday were being scoured. Back at Reception Jean was flicking through the photographs on her phone. Delete, keep, delete, delete . . . curating her memories of the holiday. Archiving their visit before it was even over. Before long they would forget the details of the weekend entirely, and her edit of images would become their joint memory of the trip.

His mother was a woman who joked that a dead president holed up in a cupboard used to chat to her. How had he ever found that funny? It was tragic. *You treat her like she's some old dear you barely know but visit out of the goodness of your heart.* Anita was right about him.

Jean sticks her head around the door. 'Sorry. I'm ready to go now.' She frowns. 'You okay?'

He shrugs. Nods. 'Who was on the phone? Is everything okay at work?'

'A meeting I had to cancel. It's fine. When did you last speak to Pauline? She'll have seen the news and be wondering what's going on.'

'It's okay. I called her.'

Jean walks over and stands in front of him. He often has the sense he's looking at her from afar, viewing her as though she was at the end of a long platform, or on a stage, at an angle to him. It is only when she is standing completely still, facing him, that he sees afresh how slight she is, barely level with his shoulder. He looks down at her. There are times when she seems as unfamiliar to him as a punter in the library, and he finds himself wondering who she is, and who he is, and why do these two strangers lie next to each other every night in the dark. But this is not one of those times. At this moment Jean is wonderfully, thankfully, completely familiar. She reaches out and gently puts her fingertips to his face. The pressure is a caress against his jaw. The doorbell rings but neither of them moves. He hears Elin on the stairs, then the sound of her feet on the tiles in the hallway.

'Elin had headlice once,' he says, wondering where this is going. 'She was seven, I guess. I remember getting home from school one day and Mum had finished delousing her with that horrible shampoo when she noticed that she had caught them herself. I heard her ask Anita to help her but she refused, said she wouldn't go near either of them in case she got nits too.'

'Lice used go round my class like a Mexican wave. The fine-combing drove me nuts.'

'I was going to my room and I saw her reflection in the bathroom mirror. She was trying to stretch around to the back of her hair to comb it out. It was a few weeks after Dad first went away, and she looked so horribly lonely standing there with a towel around her shoulders, not able to see what she was doing and without anyone to help.' He frowns. He had glimpsed her in the mirror but she hadn't seen him and he'd gone to his room, closed the door and put a CD on as loud as he dared.

'You hardly ever talk about when your dad left.'

'What is there to say? He met someone else, he never came back.'

'If breaking people's hearts was that straightforward there'd be no music industry. There are a million things to say, if you want to say them.'

'We always stuck out a bit, you know? Being half Norwegian. There was a kid in my class who'd moved from Belfast, and he got treated like he was an alien, so imagine the shit I got for having a family that was half Scandinavian. *Your dad's a big hairy Viking robber*. I hated it. And then our house was that big . . . dump is what I used to think. Coming home from school in the dark by myself down the laneway used to creep me out.'

'Did you all feel like that? The otherness bit, I mean, not the creepy bit?'

'Yeah, I think so, in our own ways. Not that we ever talked about it. I told Dad once about the Viking shit and he said he'd call round to their parents! Jesus, that would have made it so much worse I never mentioned it again. His accent and the way he was so black and white about things – more "no way" than "Norway", I said to him once. But weirdly, being different made us all a unit, you know what I mean? It gave us an identity. And then he . . .' he swallows a sudden sore lump in his throat '. . . he . . . The very thing that made us different, made us stand out, was gone. So we stood out even more.'

He stops. Falls silent. He had been annoyed with his dad for going away, but why had he taken it out on Mags? Wasn't she trying to make sense of it all from the start, doing what she thought was best for them? And all he did was push her away when she needed him.

He won't write a screenplay, he can see that now. Never would have. He would never have been brave enough to sully those white pages with whatever crap he'd have come up with. And then the dawning shock that that was all it was: crap. No, he'd never have had the courage to take that risk.

He just liked being the sort of person who was going to write a screenplay, who was all potential, if only they had the time. Right now, he can't imagine ever walking through the door of the library again. The sight of all those spines, lined up like soldiers. Row after row of lives spent typing, reworking the same emotions over and over. Shelf after shelf of sweat and desperation. He has nothing to add to those constructed lives. He would be reshuffling the deck of himself and hoping the cards would fall in a more interesting way. Jean knows who she is. She doesn't pretend. With her, the cover tells the same story as the pages inside. And it doesn't make her uninteresting, or shallow, or a soft touch. Far from it. It makes her true. He has seen it in her frown when he's said something mean but funny and she's figuring on which side of the line connecting the two has he fallen. He has seen it in the flicker of her eyes on those occasions in the past when they are both a couple of pints in and he brings up the subject of – maybe – having a baby. *You?* her eyes say. *You want to be a tiny person's parent when you're not even sure who you are yourself?* Jean would be a wonderful mother. Any child would be lucky to have her. Is the truth of what she means when she says she doesn't want a baby that she doesn't want one with *him*? He's been going around for years feeling misunderstood by the world, and maybe this one person has understood him perfectly all the time. Just as his mother had always done.

'I meant what I said, you know,' he says. 'About looking after her.'

'Yes,' Jean replies.

'I don't know what that means for us.' Is he asking her or telling her? It is impossible to decide which, even as he knows that he must. That not deciding is an answer in itself. He backs away from it, leaves it to her. Even as the words hang in the air he is sure that something has already changed, and he's not sure what. But in this uncertainty is the conviction that it will become clear when it has to. She moves away to pick up her jacket from the sofa and the absence of her fingers on his skin is almost painful.

Ray and Jean are waiting for her downstairs. Elin is dreading the prospect of going back to Shankill again today – she's only back from the place, what, an hour? The scrabble from despair to hope and back again that comes every time she has to knock on a stranger's door or stop someone in the street to show them the poster. The quick *no* had become easier to deal with during Thursday's grim, rain-sodden house-to-house. They were a swift transaction, an easy dismissal. But the head-scratching *yes-I-might-have-now-does-she-have-a . . .* were exhausting. All these, the slow *no*s, were by far the hardest to take. And then that woman in the car park! A drawbridge had been lowered for the briefest second only to be pulled up again.

From the top of the stairs she hears Jean answer her phone and walk towards the kitchen. 'No problem, Professor Morrissey,' Jean is saying. 'Just let me check my diary.' That's bound to buy her a few minutes. Ray has told her before that when Jean isn't actually *at* work she spends most of her time on the phone *about* work. Elin goes into her mother's bedroom and sits down on the bed by the pillow. She leans over and pulls the string on the bedside lamp. The *ping* is soft, so she does it again. Off and on, a few times. She knows that both Anita and Ray have been through this room already looking for anything that might be a clue. Sergeant Corish, too. Elin opens the drawer in the little table next to the bed. Tissues, nail varnish, pens and notebooks, bookmarks. The usual jumble of stuff, it's no different from her own at home. She flicks through the notebooks. Out of habit she opens a blank page and draws a big, careful M, then stops herself. Some are empty, some full, with every page a blur of crossed-out lines. She wonders why her mother kept them. Why retain a tiny archive of daily chores once she was finished with it? Why the need to keep such humdrum proof of the day's activities? She picks up the topmost one. Each page has a picture of a panda and as she flicks quickly through the pages the bear's arm waves at her. The most recent date is last Sunday, 6 April. *Toast in toaster at lunchtime. Earrings in cutlery drawer. J card. Raymond?* How cryptic. Maybe Mum writes in code in case someone should read it. Someone like me, she thinks, and blushes. She hears Jean in the hallway downstairs, her phone call finished. Elin closes the cover and returns the little bear back to his bed in the drawer.

Elin is on the stairs when the doorbell rings. The door to the sitting room is ajar and Ray and Jean a faint murmur from behind it. It's probably Liz. Just before lunch Elin had opened the front door to the Chinese girl from Centra. Her first reaction was stupid guilt – though she'd only taken a photograph of the card; she had left the card itself untouched on the shelf. 'Killian sent me,' the girl said, handing her a plastic bag. Wafts of rashers and sausages and the sharp vinegar of warming coleslaw rose from her arms. The girl turned to go. 'Wait,' Elin said. She wants to say, *I heard how rude that man was to you earlier and I'm sorry, we're not all like that.* But she doesn't. Because whatever she says, she knows it will come out patronising and wrong.

'Yes?' the girl said, at the gate already.

'Nothing,' Elin replied. 'Sorry. Thank you.'

But it's not the girl at the door this time. Time speeds up and contracts in a flash. Her body registers his presence before her mind does. He is pale and unshaven and his eyes are red. She wants to grab him and pull his arms around her. To duck under his jumper and stay there, her feet planted on his shoes, her cheek pressed to his heart. To push her fingers up his sleeve as far as the *Hearts* tattoo on his forearm. He doesn't say hello. He doesn't reach out for her. It is so incongruous to see him there. Behind him, the house across the street is painted purple with leafy green panels in the door. If only she could point at it and go, *Look, we painted the street in heather to welcome you.* But she can't. She returned the right to say it the day before, when she phoned him. *It isn't working out*, she said. Having to come home had made her see it. She was sorry and at the weekend would he please take any of his stuff in her flat and return anything of hers and leave her keys? She had hung up then, thinking what a fool she had been, for years. Trying to hold them both in a state of suspended animation, deliberately living light, like a student, and always keeping just enough space between their lives. Agreeing when Marty's mum referred to her as a free spirit, letting that become the accepted definition and explanation of her, when in fact it was so far from the truth. If he got close to her family, he would have been told the truth about her. She had hated herself and her cold, mean voice. She was a stranger to them both.

Ray and Jean appear from the sitting room. Shit, they're meant to be going to Shankill now. She must get Marty to leave, quick. She'll have to think of something to tell Ray. Oh, Christ, but it's all so confusing because now Ray is stepping past her and . . .

'Good man.' Why is Ray acting as though he was expecting to see Marty, a man he has met only the one time at a rugby match? Shaking Marty's hand and introducing him to Jean? 'You made good time in the end. Come on inside. Elin, call me when you're ready to follow us out.' But he's looking at Marty not her when he says, 'I've left my car keys on the mantelpiece. It's a heap of shit, but you're welcome to borrow it.'

'Your brother reckons you owe me an explanation,' Marty says. They're alone now, in the sitting room. Jean and Ray have gone to Shankill to meet Sergeant Corish. 'And he's not the only one.'

Ray had got his number from her phone and called him on Thursday night, Marty tells her.

'What did he say?'

'That your mam was missing and you need my help. That I wasn't to let you break up with me like that. That you'd panic and fuck everything up if you weren't careful.' He's been standing in front of the window but now moves to sit on the sofa next to her. 'I added that last bit myself.' He puts a hand on her arm. 'I don't believe all that bollocks you said about *it isn't working out*. What is "it" supposed to be anyway? We aren't a fucked-up country that doesn't know its arse from its elbow and needs a bailout. We are you and me. *Us*. Ray's right. If you think we aren't working out, then you owe me an explanation as to why you think we're fucked and why you have decided that now, when you're here. But you can shove your *it isn't working out.'*

What is she to do? He's sitting next to her, this man that she loves, that she has cried endless tears for. That she has lied to, yesterday and for years. And of course he's furious and upset and bewildered, but in one way, isn't that better than the alternative? To believe he has spent years loving a monster? Is that not a bigger punishment? If he would only get up and walk away and hate her! That would be better. Because he will get over it, and meet someone else, and in time decide it wasn't his judgement that was flawed, it was her. It was *it*.

'Neep and Nucho,' he begins, his accent revving up the names the way it always does, giving Nucho a long *o*. 'I've always thought they're us. A puffin and a posh fish.'

'What do you mean?'

'They're so different, yet they're always on the same side. No matter what. I want to help you, with your mam. You just had to ask.'

She pictures Neep and Nucho in this room instead of them. Two creatures toddling around together, having their adventures. Solid, side by side. Ordinary and unlikely. And happy. Always desperately happy, even when things are going wrong.

'Talk to me, Elin. I will, I can, help.' He sounds desperate. His words are stuttered, fragments of sentences that sound unsure as to whether they're wanted or not. 'Please, please, tell me.'

Imagine a world where she could and he wouldn't hate her for it! One in which he would put his arm around her. Clutch her. Kiss her. His clothes would have that bookie's smell of cigarettes and desperation and the promise of success next time. Always next time. If only she could take the chance. What odds would Marty give her?

Of course she can't tell him. She would lose, he would lose. For his sake, she must protect him from the truth of her.

Beep beep. A text from Liz. *U still @ house? Leaving shop 4 S'kill in 10. Need lift?*

'I have to go,' she says.

'No!' He grabs her arm. 'You're not going until we sort this out.'

Elin has been living Jack's death since it happened. Even though she no longer relives that last moment over and over, she has been trapped within those seconds for years. They are the paper on which the pages of her days are printed. Everything, she sees now, that she has tried to do since has been tied to that moment by string. Her life is controlled by millions of pieces of string, all too short for any other purpose than to Gulliver her to the earth. This city used to be her home, family. Her life. That morning, on the DART to and from Shankill, she had kept seeing Jack. In kids in the playground, houses, school yards. She thought she was listening for the missing voice of her mother, but there was more to it: she was trying to catch Jack. And Dad, too; everything would have been different if he was there, she was sure of it. She had been trying to unravel the yarn all the way back to the start in the futile hope she could knit it again in a different way.

Anita's son died and it was my fault.

She imagines saying it. Taking each word from the dark of a locked vault. The shock of hearing aloud that which is a constant thought. It would be like a dream in which you are on a busy street and look down and discover the pavement is gone and you are falling down a dark hole. She and Ray rarely speak about Jack in their infrequent conversations, and with Mum the subject is dealt with through euphemism ('that awful time'; 'when we lost our boy'), a comforter that blunts the knives and prevents them stabbing her. What would she say? *So that's why I was in Tobermory. That's who I was when you met me. Who I still am, no matter how I try to hide it.*

She shakes her head.

'Elin! I know . . . I know about your nephew.'

And all she can hear is the dark pounding of her own blood in her ears.

'Fuck's sake, Elin, did you never Google someone? I decided a long time ago not to mention it, that you'd tell me about it when you were ready. If you ever were. When Ray rang me last night, I asked him. Did you not think it odd I never pushed you about meeting the rest of your family?'

'So why have you wasted your time with me if you knew who I was? What I did.' She is rotten to the core. Unworthy, unlovable. This is her truth and now he knows it too.

'What you *did*? Elin, it was an accident. Awful, shitty, crappy. There aren't words for it. But it was an accident. You're allowed to forgive yourself.'

'I'm not. Because my sister doesn't.' Anita is right to have nothing to do with her. She knows that Raymond and Mum think Anita's treatment of Elin has been so harsh as to be cruel. But Anita's right. Elin doesn't deserve her forgiveness. That's why, since the day of the funeral, she's never asked for it again, not once.

'Elin, I love you more than life itself, so please believe me when I tell you: yeah, okay, your sister gets to decide whether *she* forgives you. But she doesn't get to decide whether *you* forgive you.' He sounds angry finally, as he stands up. 'And until you believe that, you know what? You are fucked.'

He knows. He *knew*! All this time.

And she's lost him anyway.

Still three o'clock. She's sick of looking at her watch. It was three the last time she looked at it, hours or minutes before. Derek is going on about work again. Work seems to be getting more airtime than usual since Mum went missing. Or maybe it's the same amount, and she's not noticed it before because it's been so long since she has felt the need to interrupt, to talk about something herself.

'So,' he is saying, 'then Gary turns around – you remember Gary, don't you? You sat next to him in Tabacs that time? – and he goes, *We'll have to run the figures from scratch.*'

Anita nods. She remembers Gary well. She was sitting beside him at the annual senior management team night out in February. Pleasant guy, early thirties maybe, well-dressed and polite. Derek is very taken by him, seems to rank him as a future . . . She pauses in her thoughts. A future *what*? A future Derek, she supposes. To be honest, spin the clock back twenty years and she'd have been taken by Gary. She had made a big effort for that dinner. Got her hair done that morning, expensive dress, manicure. The lot. She'd worked really hard at the SimpleSlim all week so that she would be able to eat and drink without having to police every mouthful or, worse, be feeling too bad about herself to eat much at all, and be aware of Derek frowning over at her plate, presumably embarrassed that his fat wife wasn't eating.

A couple of years before there was an ad on TV in which a woman at a fancy dinner party introduced herself by warning her companions what a bore she always was on the subject of her kids. The first time they saw it Rebecca had nudged her and said, 'I bet that's you, Mum, isn't it? Going on about us all the time,' and Anita had laughed and said, 'As if!' and looked over at Derek to catch him laughing too, but he wasn't. So now she tries not to talk about the kids. Hardly at all. Instead, sitting next to Gary in her new dress (it was quite comfortable until she put the Spanx on, but even though they gave her a much better shape, the flesh that she hated around her waist got squashed up higher, slowly crawling up her body to her throat to strangle her), she talked about movies, and TV programmes, and what Christmas-present box sets they each had watched. 'My mum loved that one too,' he said, when she offered him the bread and she told him she'd just finished the second series of *The Killing*. 'No way!' he exclaimed when, over the starter, she commented that the jazz spilling from the speaker above their heads was something she'd heard Gay Byrne play on *Lyric* the week before (she'd heard it in the car when she was dropping Cuan to a football game in which he'd scored a goal, but she didn't mention that). 'Isn't that funny?' Gary said. 'My mum really loves that show too.' *My mum, my mum, my mum.* She didn't even have to talk about her own children to be reduced to the status of *Mum*. Shaking his head good-humouredly at the coincidence, he noticed her wine glass was empty again and refilled it. She felt herself blush. It was hot in the restaurant and fresh wafts of her own perfume assailed her. God, why had she put on so much?

She glanced along the table to where Derek was joking about something with Siobhan, the new business manager who probably wasn't any older than Gary. You can be sure she wasn't telling him, 'Oh, my dad loves *Match of the Day* too, when he can stay awake for it!' She pictured herself from Gary's point of view: the frumpy missus of the boss, put next to him because he's the office charmer and can be counted upon to get her housewife's heart beating a bit faster for an evening. Anita excused herself and went to the toilet. In the cubicle she tugged off the Spanx and shoved them into the bin.

So, yes, Anita thinks, as Derek extols his virtues. *I do remember Gary.*

People often say that women marry their fathers, but there are times when Anita wonders did she in fact marry her mother? Derek has an easiness to him that Mum has. A light touch to life. Rebecca has it too – maybe that's why she gets on so well with her granny. Derek is able to move around his own life in a way that Anita doesn't in hers. He knows how to divide his world out; everything isn't carried around in a pot on his head. 'I hope the kids are okay,' she says. 'And the girls keep an eye on Cuan properly. Are you sure your dad will get there before half three? I'll phone him again in a while to check he's arrived.'

In addition to the garda teams, there are seven volunteer search parties. Anita and Derek are walking down a narrow and muddy path through Shanganagh Park, heading in the direction of the old house on Kilmarth Road. She knows it well anyway, and has been over this route already this week

– twice, in fact, as has Raymond – but Rena has asked them to walk it again. 'Think smaller,' was what Rena said. 'Anything might be important.' Raymond texted to say he and Jean are here too: they are starting from the opposite end of Kilmarth Road and will meet them along the way. She's glad to be away from Jean for a while. Patronising cow. Raymond talks about how great she is at her job, how efficient, how highly her team rate her. Anita reckons her team must detest her. Jean thinks Anita is a waste of space, Anita is sure of it. Jean's two sisters and her sister-in-law – with seven children between them – work full time: two GPs, one engineer. 'God, no,' Jean said to her once. 'In my family we've no stay-at-home mums!' Anita hates that expression and its sly suggestion of laziness. Of pointlessness.

Anita has her eyes on the ground as they walk along, not really sure what she's doing, but this is what she's seen on TV in such situations. She's not so much looking as staring, but it's all she can do so she keeps going, putting one foot in front of the other. It's chillier today and the ground is still wet and sticky from yesterday's downpours. 'Winter's after coming back,' she'd heard one of the guards say earlier. 'Last thing we need.'

'The kids will be fine,' Derek replies. '*Are* fine. Why shouldn't they be?'

'I worry, that's all.'

'I know you do, but there's no need to, honestly, Anita. You need to cut them some slack, Cuan especially.' As with the path under her feet, this too is old, potholed ground. As any couple can attest, ancient territory can be the scene of the longest battles. Nothing brings old wounds to life like a sniff of fresh blood. Why does Derek continue to refuse to understand how important Cuan's welfare is? She knows how incessantly cruel, how vicious and disregarding, the world is, and she doesn't understand how her husband can be so blind to it. How can he not see it the same way? As if he can read her mind, he continues, 'Nothing is going to happen to Cuan, and you can't keep acting like it is.'

'You don't know that.'

'No, of course I don't. No more than I know nothing is going to happen to you, or to me. The point is that I have made the decision to go about my days *believing* it to be the truth. And you haven't done that, Anita. I watch you not believing it. And so do your children.'

Your children. The loss of Jack hadn't brought them closer together, the way the grief counsellor they had seen a few times had told her it could. They coped in parallel, the lines of their lives zigzagging, sometimes touching, overlapping, but generally just roughing along as two tracks next to each other. She pictures her marriage as an escalator in a vast shopping centre. Two lines stretching out, rising side by side to the top of the building. Interdependent yet completely separate. One track can break down even as the other glides swiftly along without missing a step. But the escalators do an important job, don't they? Carrying their children to adulthood and what passes for safety within it.

'They're your children too,' she snaps. 'Why is everyone so keen to drop everything on my shoulders all the time? First Raymond with Mum, now you.'

'No one is doing that. You're not listening to me. Or to Raymond for that matter. And whatever is going to happen with Mags, well . . .' His hands rise and fall from his sides. 'When we find her, she's going to need all our help. And, yes, it's going to have a massive impact on you, of course it is. That's the reality of the situation. But you are the one who is taking everything on yourself, only to get upset because you feel put upon. I'm sorry, Anita, but you're doing this to yourself, and you've got to stop it, for your own sake as much as the kids".'

It's *The Generation Game* all over again, she thinks. It was her and Raymond's favourite TV programme when they were little. The contestants were in pairs, each couple made up of a parent and their adult child. They were shown how to do something by an expert and then had to copy it. The expert would judge who was best. That is Anita's adult life. Trying to make a perfect copy of something she's glimpsed only once. Waiting to be judged by a stranger in front of her parents and sure to be found wanting.

'That is just so typical of you,' she says. She knows, of course she knows, that any sentence beginning, *That is just so typical of you* never ends well. But she can't help herself. She's exhausted. Tired of trying, of being good. Bad just happens anyway, so why bother tiptoeing around trying to avoid it? It will land on you if it chooses to. There is nothing she can do to stop it.

'Don't start that, Anita. We're all in this terrible situation together, so please let me and the kids help. Raymond too. He's a lazy sod, sure. Fair enough, we all know that, but so what? If he's willing to help, then let him. You've got to stop expecting everyone's participation to be on your terms.'

'You don't understand.'

'Jesus, Anita, that's always your fall-back, isn't it? It's

always that the rest of us don't understand *you*. Never the other way around.'

'I knew you'd be like this.'

'Right, of course you did.' He is sarcastic. 'And let me guess, because of Jack, isn't it? Because of how I feel about Jack, how I acted when he died. Because I didn't want to punish everyone in sight, to make Elin suffer. That doesn't mean I didn't care. I was as broken-hearted as you were. I still am. If it had been me in the car with Jack that day, what would you have done? Or your mother? Would you have blamed either of us the way you blame Elin?'

She hates Elin. She hates herself too. Something of her son is kept alive within her relentless anger. Her guilt at the broken door – that child lock! That bloody child lock! She *had* told Elin about it. So why, in her secret, darkest-hour-of-the-night heart, is she not sure? And in her lack of certainty lives her own guilt. And that is too big, too painful, too overwhelming. To allow that in would drown her. No, no, she thinks, in every waking night. *No, I did tell her.* Locating her fury entirely in Elin was the only way she could keep it from spilling out and corroding everything. Her refusal to allow herself ever fully to accept his death is the air at the heart of the flame. She knows rage could have flooded her existence, submerged her love for her husband, her twins. Even – from before his birth – Cuan. So she gathered it all into a single casket and dropped it on her sister's doorstep. The sister who had come along and pushed their family of four into a new shape. Who had absorbed their mother's time and their father's attention. Who had been so like him, special to him in a way that Anita had never felt she was. She cannot forgive Elin because she wouldn't know where to start or where to end.

She has walked on a step before she notices that Derek hasn't. She turns on the path to face him. They are almost at Kilmarth Road now. It is flanked by tall trees on either side, which makes it darker than the path they are just about to leave. She can see figures moving about in the distance, luminous jackets flitting about like moths. Through the trees to her right, steps lead down to the sea. The cliff path is narrow and crumbling, with tough, scrubby grasses clutching the rocks. She's seen children play on that path before, though she can't hear anyone on it now. They used to mess about there themselves as kids. Madness. No way would she ever let Cuan near it. The sound of the sea hitting the stones of the beach far below rises and calls to her.

'You never did understand that my feelings could be as real as yours,' he says. He doesn't sound angry any more. His face is flat somehow, suddenly older-looking. 'Because you were his mother, you thought your right to grief was more valid than mine.'

Is this true? She stares at him, at the two decades spent together that are written across both their faces. The years have been lived together by the bodies standing facing each other. She did believe she had grieved more: that was true. More than anyone. And did she have a bigger claim to mourning? *Yes.*

'I don't believe that we were equal in his life, Anita, because you were with him all the time and I wasn't, and I hate myself for every day of his life that I missed. But we are equal in his death. And I won't continue to let you take my son's death away from me. Not when that's all I have left of him.' Standing there, two feet away from her, tears fall down his cheeks. His nose runs and he lets it. His arms are flat by his sides. It's a long time since she saw him cry and it's oddly shocking. Derek isn't being himself. She needs people to be themselves, because if they are then she knows who *she* is. It is *The Generation Game* all over again: she needs an expert to show her what to do. How else is she to find her way?

Ham-fisted because of her gloves, she fumbles in her coat pocket for a tissue and steps forward to give it to him. His hands are bare, his fingers cold and waxy. She tugs her gloves off, shoves them into her pockets. His cheeks are wet and drops of snot hang from the end of his nose. She presses her hands together, capturing his. The tissue is squashed between his palms.

'Anita, if it had been you in the car with Jack, would you blame yourself as much as you blame Elin?'

She has seen broken escalators in shops, the steps pulled up smooth, like a bike chain, revealing the grey, oily, cavernous space beneath. She nods. It is the barest movement at first. She can feel her head moving down to her chest and back up again, her face turning to Kilmarth Road and the branches, and the straggle of sunlight desperate to flicker through them. Her eyes are closed. She is making herself dizzy. Up and down, her head goes. Up and down. She can't stop. Tears flow from her closed eyes, washing down her cheeks, her lips and into her mouth, salty and warm.

'Ssssh,' he says. 'It's okay, it's okay.' He pushes her hands apart and puts his arms around her. There are more tears in her than there is water in the oceans of the world, she is sure of it. She is aware of someone else approaching from behind on the path and overtaking them, a voice speaking to Derek and his louder, normal, *yes-yes-all-fine-thanks* in return. 'Anita?' he says, quiet once more. 'I wouldn't have blamed you.'

And so the motor whirrs into life again. Silver teeth gleam as the escalator steps flatten then fall just before they turn in on themselves. Up and up, down and down. Gliding on, in tandem for ever.

As soon as Liz starts the engine a man's voice fills the car. Elin recognises the fragile, breathy sound.

'Crap.' Liz presses something and the voice cuts off mid-word. 'Sorry. The CD player is jammed. It comes on automatically now. Same song every time. Danny keeps at me to get it fixed but it's one of those things I know I'll never get around to. *Way to Blue* used to be my favourite album and all.'

Danny had waved them off from the door of the shop. Elin wonders did she look surprised when she saw him there because Liz said, 'He has a half-day,' in an unconvincing way before adding with a shrug, 'It's only double Irish. I'll do him a note.'

The car smells as strongly as Best Buds and is as untidy as the little office at the back of the shop. It is littered with scraps of paper and twine, and green foam squeaks under her feet. 'Oasis,' Liz says. 'It gets everywhere. Just kick it to one side. We're going the long way, if that's okay? I have to drop off posters in Dún Laoghaire on the way.'

Liz's car reminds Elin of her untidy studio in Meadowbank and its smells of ink and paint. The building was partitioned cheaply and all day she is an unintentional eavesdropper, hearing voices from other rooms and on the corridor outside. All the light in the world bounces in its windows. It is probably chilly in there today, she thinks, picturing a half-finished Neep and Nucho lying on the long white table and waiting for her to appear and colour life into them. She wishes she were back there. This transplanted existence is too frightening. She shouldn't be here: not in this car, not on this road. She has tried, she really has, but it's just not possible to live a straightforward life when the past is complicated. Complexity follows us around, it becomes part of us. It changes how decisions are made, and why. This is why she loves Neep and Nucho so much, she thinks. The ease with which they see the world and believe it is theirs, that it will revolve around them for ever. They are her children. If only she could quietly escape, like the *Fox Plays Dead and Is Thrown Out of Pit* story in Dad's old book. But she can't. What a terrible daughter she is, even to be thinking of escaping when her mother is out there somewhere, lost. Worse. *Go on*, she thinks viciously. *Run away again, you coward. That worked out so well last time, didn't it?* Her life is contracting, returning her to its beginnings. If only, she thinks. If only I could start again. *If only if only if only.*

She cries for most of the journey. 'Sorry.' She sniffs, as Blackrock Park zips past. Her voice is thick with tears, her own words muffled inside her head.

'No need to apologise,' Liz replies. 'I'd be crying too, if it was my mum.'

Elin shakes her head but doesn't speak, until 'You must think I'm nuts,' she says, as they pass Seapoint DART station.

'Nuts? Nah, you're upset. Bawl your head off, if you need to. Better out than in, that's what I tell Danny, not that he listens. Here, take these.' As she tugs a packet of tissues from her pocket the car veers over the middle of the road. Liz swears under her breath and returns her hand to the steering-wheel. Her hand is stained, marked with thin scratches. There are two Quink-coloured stars on the back of her wrist. Elin has to resist the urge to touch one when she takes the tissues. She is still crying as they drive past the marina in Dún Laoghaire and Liz swerves left to pull into a parking space.

'Fuck off!' she calls. 'No, not you, him!' She glares at the driver, who shoots past, horn blaring. 'Look, Elin, we'll be there soon and I think it won't help the others to see you arrive in such a state.'

Elin stares out her window at the harbour while Liz nips into the shopping centre. The silver masts are those she saw a few hours earlier from the DART. Distant figures make their way down the pier, striding its length with no other purpose than to turn around and walk back. She envies these strangers, that retracing their own steps is all they have to do on a Friday afternoon. The water ripples gently in the breeze, slapping against the sides of the boats. She watches a man help a young boy into a dinghy. The boy is laughing, his arms held awkwardly out from his sides, lagged by his lifejacket.

'This is to do with that bloke, isn't it?' Liz is back.

She stands her mobile in the cup holder. It beeps repeatedly and she glances at it, over and over. A man had called into Best Buds to ask for directions earlier, she explains. 'I guessed it was him. Raymond said your boyfriend was Scottish.'

'Marty, yes. We broke up,' Elin says. So he knew all the time but wanted to be with her despite it? His complicity in her crime makes him a stranger to her. *Forgiveness?* The word makes no sense any more. But she is lopsided without Marty. She will keel over without him, sink without trace.

'Shit timing.' Liz winces. 'But hang on – if you broke up, then what's he doing in Dublin?'

'No, I mean, we *just* broke up. Yesterday. Today.'

'So where is he?'

'I don't know, back at the house. I said I had to go.' He was crying as she left. They both were.

The car is warm and stuffy and she opens her window. Elin forces herself to stare at each boat in turn until she can feel her breathing return to normal. The music of the harbour slips in on the cold air. With clinks and crackles the glittering spires sing, their chorus a celebration of the sea. A dog barks; a flame-haired child in a passing buggy wails, disconsolate. 'Go on, then,' the woman pushing the buggy says. 'Have them, make yourself sick.' She fires a packet of sweets down to the child without breaking her stride. Elin closes her eyes and leans her head back against the seat rest. It, too, reeks of old flowers. If Miss Havisham had a car it would smell like this, she thinks. She is aware now of the slow rise and fall of her chest under her coat. Her head feels heavy, and when she inhales, the air whistles through her tears.

Her grandparents are buried in a family plot in a tiny graveyard in Wicklow on a hillside overlooking the sea. She has a memory of being brought there as a child. Of standing by a wall in winter and looking out at the water and tasting salt, cold and fresh, in the air. It must have been an anniversary, though she has no idea whose. Ray was there, too, but sulking because Mum wouldn't let him stay at home by himself even though he was thirteen. ('You have to be fourteen to stay home alone,' Mum said. 'That doesn't make any sense!' Ray retorted, angry. 'I mind Elin when you go to the shops even though Anita is never here.' 'Babysitting is different,' Mum snapped.)

Mum had walked to the far side of the cemetery to the water tap and left the two of them standing at the grave. Elin remembers that she was trying to make out the words on the headstone letter by letter, the way they did in school: *Dappy Duck, Iggy Igloo, Emma Elephant,* then *Dappy Duck* again. Ray hung around next to her, picking up handfuls of gravel and throwing them down. She wished he wouldn't do it: the splat-splat of the stones against the words felt a bit mean.

'That's Granny and Granddad under there,' he said, pointing at the ground. Elin looked down, imagining a comfy bed hidden under the grey stone with Granny and Granddad asleep inside it, next to each other. Holding hands even, the way she's seen her parents do when she's gone into their room in the night and they're lying side by side in the dark. 'Nope. Not possible,' Raymond dismissed her idea. 'Granny and Granddad aren't facing the same direction. Anita told me.' She remembers how she had looked up at Ray, bewildered. He never lied to her, she knew that. So it had to be true. They weren't together, not properly. Granny and Granddad were separated under the grey ground.

Elin opens her eyes. She leans forward and wipes condensation from the windscreen with her sleeve until the road that will lead them out of Dún Laoghaire appears in front of her. 'Ready?' Liz asks, and Elin nods. The car and Nick Drake start in harmony. Liz reaches out to switch off the CD.

'No, please, leave it,' Elin says.

There is a TV crew at Shankill DART station, filming volunteers busily giving out leaflets. Liz has worked hard to manage as much of that as she can by herself, to keep it away from the family. Elin overheard Liz telling Jean that everyone seems to have a missing-person story to tell. Urban myths, the lot of them, she reckons. A missing brother walking in the door after a decade; an elderly man wombling away from his care home and spending the night in the baby-change room in a shopping centre . . . 'They mean well,' Liz said, 'they really do, but people, really! Think before you speak.'

It's impossible to get used to seeing her mother's face wrapped around streetlights and being given from hand to hand so easily. She looks too old in the photo. It misrepresents who she really is. The picture illustrates a missing-old-lady story. No, more than that: it is part of the creation of the story. But that's not who her mother is. Elin watches as a young guy, not much more than the twins' age – his face is familiar but she's not sure from where; he must be from Booterstown, she supposes – stops a young woman leaving the DART station and thrusts a leaflet at her. She takes it from him and almost immediately throws Mags on the ground. She didn't even glance at her! Elin dashes over and picks it up, flattening it out again between her hands. The rush of anger she denied herself earlier that morning just a few feet away from this spot rises within her.

'You didn't look!' she shouts.

'What?' The woman jumps and turns around, frightened. Elin grabs her arm with one hand while she waves the sheet high in the air with the other. Mags flutters to and fro above their heads. 'You didn't even bloody look! Would it have been so bloody hard to take a bloody look?'

Liz runs over. 'Elin, please! Sorry, sorry,' she says. 'That's her mother on the poster. She's very upset.' She drags Elin away. 'For fuck's sake, do you want to end up on the news too?' She tugs at Elin's arm and Mags drops slowly down, surrendered.

They are leaving the DART station when a journalist stops them. Elin recognises him as the man who interviewed Sergeant Corish on the TV the day before. He wants to talk to Elin for the evening news. 'Liz,' Elin says, 'I can't. You do it.'

'I don't know, Elin, hadn't we better check with Anita first?'

'All publicity helps in these situations,' John FitzGerald says. 'But we've to leave in five minutes or else we'll be too late to make today's editorial meeting. So . . .'

'All right, then,' Liz says. 'But I'm not family.'

Elin stands to one side and listens as the woman she met for the first time this week talks about her mother. About how active she is and, yes, she is aware that concerns had been raised recently about her memory, but her physical health is excellent. About how popular she is in their community. How special. 'She knows us all,' Liz says. 'And she has time for us all. Which is quite something these days, isn't it?'

'And Margaret has been missing now since Monday?'

'Yes, she was last seen on Monday here in Shankill.' Liz sounds oddly formal, like a guard. 'Other sightings have been reported, and I know every one is being looked into, though none of them has led to anything definite yet.'

'This is a very difficult question, I know, but the last confirmed sighting was four days ago. As time goes on, you must all be getting concerned about the outcome.'

'We're very worried for Mags, yes, of course we are. However, the gardaí and everyone involved remain hopeful that we will find her soon – the worse for wear, I'm sure, but soon. We have no reason to think otherwise.'

About a mile down Kilmarth Road they catch up with Ray and Jean. They parked at the DART station and have spent nearly an hour getting this far, Jean tells them.

'No,' she replies, to the question asked by Elin's raised

eyebrows. 'Nothing.' Together, the four of them turn onto the lane, a point at which suburban Shankill seems to hold up its hands and say, *Yeah, fair enough. Let me keep from here back as far as the supermarket, and you can have the field and the cliffs and the sea.* The ditches on either side are heavy with rain, and brown muddy water has spilled out onto the path. Elin can see Sergeant Corish fifty yards or so ahead, walking alongside another guard. They are both wearing high-vis vests, and what little sun can poke its head through the trees that line both sides of the track catches them as they bend and stand. On the left-hand side of the path a metal fence runs most of the way to the end of the road. It breaks here and there for access to the path. The cliff top is that direction, but invisible behind the trees that run along the far side of the fence. On her right, and set back from the path down long driveways to protect them from the winter winds and salty air, there is a scatter of houses, each one a different style, as though every twenty years a new one was beamed down. Through the trees Elin glimpses a bungalow that she remembers being built. ('Who'd put their house back this far?' Mum had sniffed. 'That sea view is wasted on them!') The bungalow is inhabited still, but dishevelled, with red paint peeling from the front door. The venetian blinds in the front window – she remembers the day they appeared: Mum had been more impressed with them – hang in a crooked line. A single slat swings down, like a broken limb. She glances up. A formation of dark clouds scurries out to sea, revealing fresh, whiter ones behind them. The sharp movement makes her think of the lid on a yoghurt pot being peeled back.

Further ahead is their old home. It was warm when they walked around it on Wednesday, much warmer than today. It was so horrible to see the house like that, to climb around it so tattered and sad and forlorn. She won't go in again today, even if Ray wants to – she couldn't bear it. She'll stay on this side of the wall. She rubs the side of her hand, where she had cut it on the fence. The red tracks are a faint line, stitching scratched into her skin. She pulls the edges of each thin scab until it tears off and exposes a fresh red mark.

'I've never been to your old house before,' Jean says. 'But Mags has shown me photos.'

'How recent?' Ray asks.

'From when you were kids.'

'You won't recognise it in that case.'

Ray hangs back for a second so that he can drop into step beside Elin. She can tell he's trying to suss out from her face what's going on. He lifts his hands to pull on a pair of gloves, reminding her of what he did at the graveyard years before, when he told her that their grandparents were buried head to toe. Remembers how he had held his arms out level with her eyes until his hands were flat, the tips of his fingers facing each other. Held his forefingers side by side but looking in opposite directions and slowly moved them forward until each nail was tucked into the webbing on the opposite hand. Granny and Granddad. *Till death do them part.*

'Well?' Ray is at her side now, his voice quiet.

'Marty knew, Ray. About Anita, about Jack. He's known for ages.' Everything, contained in a single name. The whole, horrible mess of the last seven years.

'And he's right about it too. Fuck Anita. Why are you insisting that she decides how you live? What happened to Jack was awful. Horrific. Awful things happen.' His face falls.

'They just do, and I'm sick of acting as though they don't, bouncing around pretending that I'm different from the rest of the world, as though I know more, or care less, or deserve something else. Because I don't.'

'You phoned him.'

'Yes.'

'Why?'

'If what happened with Jack forced you to take a wrong turning, you can't go back and change direction. That's not the point of figuring out what the wrong turning is. Believe me, I've tried. If you think everything in your life is shit, there's nothing Marty or me or anyone else can do about it. But it's all you've got to work with. He's right. Why continue to deny it to yourself?' They stop walking and he turns to her. 'Please, Elin, please. If you never do one other thing to mind yourself, please do this: listen to Marty. He's right and he loves you. There's nothing to be afraid of.' His hands are raised, as if he's conducting a choir that no one else can see. He drops them again. 'That's why, Spuddy. That's why I called him.'

Spuddy. He hasn't called her that for years.

The sounds around her shift and change when Ray leaves her side to catch up with Jean and Liz. There is a muddy suck from her trainers as she moves on again, slowly. The sound of Ray's voice calling to the others to wait up gives way to faint birdsong. She can hear the low growl of the wind picking up in the trees and the sea breaking over the rocks at the bottom of the cliff, drenching the stones below. As a child, she walked this road alone to and from school for years. Mum never knew about the times when she used to walk on the cliff path rather than the road so that she could watch the sea change the colours of the stones on the beach. It was like a magic trick, watching them go from dull grey to petrol blue as the water grabbed them. And then the waves would recede and the stones would revert back to their own colour, their true nature. Unchanged, after all.

Raymond hurries on. Marty won't have given up yet, he's sure of it. He'll *make* sure of it, if he needs to. He is aware of Elin standing behind him on the path, that he is walking away from her. It makes him uncomfortable, reminds him of what happened on the afternoon of Jack's funeral. Only this time he isn't letting her down, even though he is the one walking away. But this isn't about Jack. It's not about any of them separately, as adults in their own lives. This is about them as a family, if they can ever be such a thing again. About them as grown-up children. He glances over his shoulder. She has her phone out, turning it over in her hand. *Go on, Spuddy*, he thinks.

Further ahead Rena's high-vis vest flares as she moves in and out from the sides of the path. She and the young guard disappear off into the ditches and copses on the left, only to reappear a minute later a few yards further up before vanishing up a driveway on the right. He hurries, wanting to catch up with Jean. Another young man appears out of a driveway. *Civil Defence* is written across the back of his jacket. Everyone stares at the dog with him, but no one speaks. The man falls into step with them.

'I knew I knew you!' he says to Raymond, after a minute. He rests one hand on the dog's head while he chats. 'Didn't you used to be in *Baysiders*? Years ago, mind. My ma loves that programme, we used always have it on when we were having our tea. Better than *Emmerdale*, she says. She was mad about Tommy.'

'No,' Raymond says, 'sorry, not me.'

'Oh.' He looks crestfallen. 'Cos you're the head off him, only older. You must get that a lot, do you? That you look like him?'

'No.'

Jean asks the man something as she bends down to pet the dog. 'Not at all.' Raymond hears the reply but not her question. 'We use the dogs for all manner of situations.'

'Liz?' Raymond asks, suddenly remembering something from Wednesday evening. Jean and the man are distracted by the dog. He turns to face her, feeling awkward. 'What's a *five-pint decision*?'

'In my experience, Raymond,' she gives him a small smile, 'the wrong one.'

Then the dog strains at his leash and leads the man up another driveway. A minute later Raymond is aware of Elin getting closer behind them again, just as Liz is saying, 'It's not much of a birthday for you, though, is it?'

'It's okay,' Jean replies. 'We don't really go in much for birthdays, do we, Raymond?' His initial reaction is to read this as a criticism. *He*, she must mean, he doesn't. *Heads or hearts*, he thinks, and tosses the sentence up into the air again. This second time, it lands the other way up. Yes, it's true, they don't make a fuss of each other's birthdays. Why not? he wonders. They should. The child Raymond would have been shocked to hear his future self wouldn't 'go in much' for birthdays. Why isn't he better at their relationship? Why does he always expect it to stand or fall on its own terms, despite him? No wonder she doesn't want a baby. He wouldn't have a baby with this version of him either.

'Sorry, Jean,' he says. 'I could have managed a card at least. I should have. I'll make it up to you. Promise.'

'It doesn't matter.' Jean looks surprised. 'But thanks.'

'The card was for you!'

'What's that?' he says, as they all turn and look at Elin.

'The one Mum bought in Centra. I saw a list in her bedside locker,' she blushes, and he wants to tell her, *Don't worry, we've all had a root around in there, why wouldn't we?*, 'and it had *J card* on it. I didn't know today was your birthday or I'd have made the connection earlier.'

'What list?' Raymond asks. 'I didn't notice any list.'

'In that cute notebook, the little one with the panda illustrations. It was at the back of the drawer. Oh, shit!' Elin says, and then again, but louder, more strident: 'Oh, shit – the panda!' Mud splashes from a puddle as she pushes past him. 'The page! The page that stuck to my shoe! Ray, come on,' she shouts over her shoulder as she rushes ahead. 'Mum's been at the house. She has!'

Raymond runs after her, panting to keep up with his little sister. Jean and Liz follow behind. Anita and Derek come into view from the opposite direction. They are walking closely together in a swift one-two, one-two, a blurred shape getting clearer in the darkening afternoon.

He hears a shout from twenty yards ahead on the right where a dense thicket of trees separates Kilmarth Road from the cliff. Then another, louder. Even the still-bony fingers of the topmost branches seem to shudder in the air, to register the commotion far below them. 'Sergeant Corish!' a voice calls, then again, more urgently the second time. A yellow jacket flares, then disappears behind a hedge. A whistle blows, sharp and shrill. Elin glances back at him, her eyes wide and frightened. 'Hurry,' she says, gasping for breath. Anita has begun to run towards them, towards the disturbance. Her coat flaps, each lift and fall that of broken wings.

The whistle blows three times.

He hears it as a cry to each of them, a single voice calling him, calling his sisters. Calling them home.

MONDAY, 7 APRIL 2014

Mags is nearly at Blackrock when she wonders what she's doing on the DART at all. Didn't she intend to walk there? It's Monday. She's feeling a bit tired today: that must have been why she got on the DART without even thinking about it. She could do with a pick-me-up. She usually drops into The Red Hen for elevenses on a Monday, when the cakes are sure to be fresh.

Mags has a theory about this since she spotted the same scone three days in a row at the back of the Red Hen's serve-over cabinet a few months before. Anita hadn't believed her. 'How could you possibly have recognised a pastry?' she'd said, when Mags mentioned it on the phone.

No need to be so *sconeful*, Mags had thought, thought here was little point in sharing the joke with her daughter. 'Meet me there tomorrow and I'll show you,' Mags replied. 'The currants look like eyes and a mouth. It's definitely the same one.' Anita had sighed and *Mum-that's-nonsense*d her. Mags wondered what had Anita said to Derek about it, because when he called by to pick up Rebecca to bring her to her grinds the following Saturday, he'd laughed and said, 'Did you see on the internet, Mags, that slice of toast with Jesus's face on it?'

'*Daaad, shut uuup!*' Rebecca hit him on the arm as she got into the car.

Yet it's a nice day to be on the DART, so she decides not to get off at Blackrock after all, but to keep going while it's lovely and quiet and she has a perfect view out on both sides. Passing the park she notices the empty buggies lined up by the gate to the playground, their erstwhile occupants busily hurling themselves around the swings and slides. Women toddle after their toddlers, bent double over the littler ones. They'll be the mums, she thinks, recalling Anita's theory that you can always tell the au pairs in a playground because they're the ones leaning against the railings staring down at their phones. There is a lake in the park, with a tiny island in the middle. The wooden house on the island is covered with graffiti. Enterprising, she thinks. It must take a bit of effort to get yourself and your spray cans out there. The water is bound to be filthy, though it's probably not that deep. It would have been nice to live around here when the children were young – they'd have loved this park. Apart from the beach – and it was a stony one, which wasn't much fun to play on – there wasn't much for them to do in Shankill, now that she thinks about it, though she'd never have agreed to leave back then. She loved that house too much. Still, she's glad she had the sense to see that it wasn't a house to grow old in. Not alone. Too isolated. Almost everyone in Kilmarth Road had been burgled at one time or another. More than once, many of them. The compulsory purchase of the back garden for the new road wasn't the worst of it, because at least she got a good price for it, and it's not as though she'd have been able to keep maintaining that garden herself for long. No, it was catching that lad breaking in through the kitchen window had proved the last straw for her.

'Get out of my kitchen!' she had shouted at him. 'Now, or I'm calling the guards.' She was glad her voice stayed strong, though her heart was pounding, fit to explode. She got such a fright that a squirt of wee landed in her knickers and she had to clench her muscles hard to stop it at just the squirt. She put her hand in her pocket for her mobile, though, of course, it wasn't there – she never knew where she'd left it last. He stared across the room without really seeing her at all. His head bobbed from side to side and his eyelids drooped, sweeping up and down. Drugged up to the gills! He was standing on the rockery, with one knee up on the sill (Raymond had been right after all when he'd said she might as well leave a ladder outside the house as build her herb garden in a rockery underneath the kitchen window). The largest pane was shattered and his curled fist pointed at her through the shards of glass.

The sensation in her pants was horrible as she walked closer.

'A'right?' he said, his breath smelling of cherries, of cheap lollipops. 'I'm, eh, looking for me, eh, granny. She said she'd be, eh, here . . .' He trailed off, blinking. Swaying slightly. She stretched out and shoved. Heard him fall backwards, soundlessly, into the plants, one leg doubled up awkwardly beneath him. A gust of rosemary and lavender chased her as she closed the window and ran out of the room. Her hands were shaking so much that when she picked up the phone to call the police it fell on the floor twice before she could dial.

She made sure to go upstairs and change before the guards arrived. Her pants and tights were cold and already stinking. Betrayed by her own body like that! The mortification. And for days afterwards she'd had that jittery feeling you'd get when something bad happened. Not bad-bad (not *Jack-bad*), but just awful enough to shock you out of yourself and you'd hear yourself talking about it to everybody for days, even when you didn't intend to, as though you should sluice the upset out of you, dilute it away in the retelling.

Yes, you should always leave on your own terms.

And then Salthill & Monkstown station has slipped past too, and she's still on the DART. Seeing all the empty apartments reminds her of the time she got the DART home from visiting Maria in Glenageary. She'd stayed longer than she'd intended and just caught the last train. All those sitting rooms glowing into the dark night with a television on and a single person sitting in front of it! Everyone alone and watching other strangers.

She opens her bag and checks her list. All fine. She's plenty of time for a jaunt and she'll still be home to meet Anita. She can always get a taxi from Blackrock if she's running late. She should get a little thank-you for Liz for the daffodils, she thinks, and takes out her pen to add it to the list. Maybe one of those fancy herbal teas she likes. Liz always has a new one on the go. Mags has wondered sometimes what it would be like if Liz was her daughter. She feels desperately disloyal even having the thought, but once it was planted in her it kept growing, no matter how little she watered it. They'd suit each other well, she thinks. Wouldn't it be great if you could choose your parents? Mags's own parents are so long dead that although she remembers she loved them there is no freshness to the emotion; she can no longer call up the active feeling of love that once existed. Perhaps that's what happens: you love someone and they you, but when they die the love can go no further. Her feelings for her parents are a pressed flower kept neatly between the leaves of a once-favourite book.

She imagines a giant computer somewhere, a sort of dating agency, and once children grow up and are running their own lives, they'd be matched up with a new parent, one who suited them better, adult-to-adult. Once she'd asked Raymond what he thought of that idea. Not meaning to upset him, Lord, no, but she thought he'd be interested in the concept of choice that lay behind it. Only his face had fallen and no matter how she tried to explain it, he had taken it personally. With your own children, she supposes, how can it ever be anything else?

She smiles at the memory of Liz waving to her from behind the shop window earlier, her two hands a funny cabaret, wriggling from side to side. Mags has a particular affection for people who wave with two hands because it looks so daft to everyone except the recipient (the wavee, should it be?). Apart from Liz and her flowers, Best Buds had been empty. It nearly always was. 'I feel as though I'm the one going to seed, Mags,' Liz said one day last week, sounding uncharacteristically gloomy. 'We're all on the shelf in this place.' She was biting her nails again too. Mags had privately tut-tutted.

Liz had set up the business with a few bob she'd inherited after her dad died. Frankie had arranged it with her mother years before, when he was still in control of his finances. They had put money aside that was to be given to Liz, her brother and sister when he was gone. 'It was as if,' Liz told her, 'he understood how long a journey it was going to be, and he wanted to thank us when it was over. He didn't know who we were by the time he died. Not a clue. He guessed that a day would come when we were strangers to him, so he sorted it all out in advance, as soon as he had a diagnosis.'

Is this what will happen? Mags recalls the consultant and his questions. *Pity you weren't as good at remembering the answers a few weeks ago, wasn't it?* she scolds herself. It's impossible to imagine following Frankie into the same dark tunnel, disappearing the way he had. She just doesn't feel *different* enough. She has her moments, sure. But doesn't everyone? He must have been in her shoes once. He must have looked in the mirror and thought, *No, not me. It's not true. It can't be me.* He must have been aware of his thoughts shying off, bucking like nervous animals under his attempts to control them, and he must have felt the same terrible fear – the panic of a child caught out in a terrible lie – that had begun to wash over her when she least expected it.

Mags hasn't wanted to talk to Raymond and Elin about it yet. She'd had to with Anita, because her GP had said it would help to bring someone with her to the consultant's. Even so, when Mags had suggested they do nothing until after all the tests, Anita had jumped on the idea: she'd have shaken its hand and kissed it on both cheeks if she could.

She'd had a good chat with Liz instead. More than one. 'Fear can be the worst bit,' Liz told her. 'Once I decided not to be afraid of the illness or what it was going to do to him, it did help. It's very hard to train yourself to be different with someone you love, who you're used to being a certain way with. He'd repeat the same question over and over and I used to get so annoyed sometimes, though I knew he wasn't doing it to irritate me. It was weird. He wasn't himself but I kept on reacting to him as though he was. When he was going on about something I used to hear myself turning into the stroppy teenager who used to shout and slam doors just to piss him off. Dementia doesn't just change the person themselves, that's what's so vicious about it. It changes the entire family, the world of that family.'

They grieved for the loss of the small things of their lives as well as the big. It wasn't about the holidays-of-a-lifetime they never took, Liz told her. Who cares about them? Losing the daily currency of existence, that was the hardest. His illness sucked the joy out of life for them, made them all feel as though there was a shifting, fictional version of each of them, a stranger they, too, had to be when they were with him.

'After a while, I began to imagine him as a toddler,' she said. 'Like Danny, when he was little. So if I needed to lie to him about where Mam was, or what day it was, I did. I didn't talk to him as though he was a child, that's not what I mean. But I kept my expectations at that level, and didn't ask too much of him. So if he wanted to play some old song over and over, fine, that was what we'd do. I never got angry with Danny when he wanted to play the same game for hours, so why should I with my dad?'

'After the funeral,' Liz has told her, 'not on the day itself, like, but in the weeks after, a few people said to me wasn't he better off in the end, to have died, that there's people with Alzheimer's living for twenty years, not knowing their own name or are they awake or asleep. Everyone can come up with a statistic, a fact. We're all becoming bloody experts. Too much information about nothing is a disease of itself. And I know they were trying to be kind but I'd think, *No, fuck off. Go bury your own father and then come talk to me.* Because we didn't bury an illness, we buried our dad.'

Death returned Frankie to them, Liz believes. Death set them free to remember him as he had once been, not as the body in the coffin. To so many people, he had become only a man-with-dementia, a stranger dressed in familiar clothes. People don't say it, but she was sure plenty of them thought it: what a relief for the family, that his death spared them such an expensive problem. Liz detected a casualness, a distraction, in many of the mourners at his funeral: as though he had been buried in their minds for years and the service was no more than a final formality.

Liz was right, of course: Mags is afraid. And right now, that is the worst part. Frightened about what she does know, frightened about what she doesn't. Because how can this work? She loves her children dearly but they have such little feeling for each other. How can she contemplate forcing them together for her future? She might as well try to jam them back in the womb and start afresh. That must have been her fault. That she failed them as children in some way that gave them permission to fail each other as adults. *Ah, sure you'll forget*, she thinks blackly. *Sure you won't know a thing.*

What is the expression Derek sometimes uses? . . . *Circle the wagons*, that's it. She doesn't believe it's her children's job to circle their wagons around her indefinitely. And yet, she thinks, if not them, who? How are we to be responsible for the world if we don't have the ability or the bravery to put an arm around each other? She was wrong to accept Anita's determination to cut Elin out of her life: it's not a mother's job to shield her adult children from each other. She blames herself for that, has done so for the longest time. When Jack died, Anita had needed her more. That was the truth of it. Anita was lost within herself; no one could reach her. It was shocking to see her like that, a house-trained pet suddenly turned feral and vicious.

Mags had been furious with Elin for going off to Scotland. 'You're running away, Elin,' she'd said. Not in their first phone call, of course not. But in the third, the fourth, when Elin still hadn't come back and it was a month, then six, seven, weeks later.

'I just can't be there. I can't look at them. I can't bear the way they look at me.'

'You're just like your father!' Mags was angry when Elin returned for the inquest only to say she'd be leaving again the same day. 'You always were the most like him of the three of you.' It felt as though a steel door had burst open inside herself to reveal a raging fire behind it.

'Well, good,' Elin retorted, equally stung. 'I loved Dad and I'm glad I'm like him, whatever you think.'

And then they hadn't spoken for three months. And later, when Anita seemed to be improving, getting tugged slowly back from the cliff edge by Cuan's little hands, Mags was confident Anita's rage at the world couldn't last, because it would have to encompass Cuan too. She should have known her eldest better. Her anger became contained, stuffed up like a jack-in-the-box into a single word: *Elin*. And there was no swaying her. Mags had tried, God knows. So she'd stopped trying for a while, thinking *softly-softly* and it will come right of its own, time will heal it.

Time had cemented it. Raymond had surprised her by taking himself off to Cork and she was left with the one of her three children – Mags permits herself a disloyal thought – whom she got on with the least. She has kept trying over the years, suggesting to Anita that Elin could write to her. Or maybe meet up at Christmas, or on Mags's birthday. She got Elin's books to show to the twins in the hope that Anita might be curious. Nothing. Raymond had been no ally: he dodged the subject, hiding under cover of some feeble nonsense about respecting their decisions. That was the difference between sibling relationships and parent–child ones, she thinks. Parents will care, will try, for ever. It's the birth contract, signed in blood. So what was she to do? If she insisted on Anita seeing Elin, it would be a disaster for everyone. How could she *insist*, anyway? They were all adults. No, the way to do it, she had decided, would be to work on Anita over time. Wear her down. And, in her guilt and shame, Elin never forced the issue either. From the day of the funeral she seemed to have accepted Anita's viewpoint as the truth.

The mistakes I've made, Mags thinks. Three spools of thread hurtling out of sight in different directions over the horizon and she can't chase after one without abandoning the others. She tried to support them all in the way they each asked her to, only for it to feel as though she has failed each in turn.

Can her own future be a force to reunite Anita and Elin, a falling wall that the two opposing sides can climb over? Can her dying brain bring Raymond back from his blackness, his world where, because everything is a joke, there is no need to take anything seriously? It feels so unlikely that her children can come together to fuel the rest of her life. That enough love exists there somewhere to ensure they will be in front of and around and behind her all at once, all the time. No. There is no light to be bled from her failing star.

The DART stops at Dún Laoghaire and still she doesn't move from her seat. A woman stopped her on the street in Dún Laoghaire once, oh, years before, and asked the way to the Victoria Hotel. She liked that people often asked her for directions – she must have had a local sort of look to her, no matter where she went. Mags pointed the woman in the right way, using the disused sea baths as a signpost. 'Do you know,' she added helpfully, 'those baths date from the 1790s. Imagine that!'

The woman, impatient to grab only what she needed and move on, frowned. 'Is that interesting?' she asked.

When was the last time someone had stopped her for directions? Last year sometime? That's ageing's invisibility cloak right there, she thinks. She remembers sitting under the table while her grandparents and their friends played bridge. Granddad would smuggle bits of scone and fruitcake down to her and she would lean against his legs and listen to the dull, tea-drinking, circular conversations above her head. Who'd be an old person? she would wonder. The boredom of it! The dullness of them, pushed out from the golden blessing of youth. What possible use could they be? And now it's her turn. Yet she still doesn't know what she's meant to be doing, or what use anyone might think she is any more. To be of no use to anyone is the fear the world pushes on us, every day.

She stares out at the sea. Per is dead fourteen years. What would their lives be like if he was still here? She might be living in Shankill yet, if he'd never gone. Never left her. Never not-come-back. Never had a heart attack. Oh, there are too many *nevers* when it comes to him: which one should she stop at? It was her decision not to go with him to Oslo, it's true, and she blamed herself for it for such a long time. Even though his contract had had the option of a second year, she had been sure he'd only last the one; his decision to see it through had surprised her, not that she could admit it. She should have been worried then. Should have known. And the morning that letter from him arrived – imagine! The first warning that her husband was detaching himself from their life came in a letter! – she could have destroyed the kitchen in her rage. Her fear. He was unsure, he wrote: *I believe we have grown apart, become people separated by more than distance. I don't know how I feel about you any more.* She had never heard him express doubt before. Only when she spoke to him – that frantic scrabbling, sweating phone call; her fingers pushing the dial around, furious that it couldn't turn quicker – had she understood the steel foundation to these words: *But I do know how I feel about someone else.* Her heart in her mouth the entire time. That's an odd expression, she thinks. As though your heart is escaping, shoving its way out while some darker, meaner emotion shoves impatiently against the revolving door.

Did it happen because Per felt pushed away from his family? *You fool, Mags,* she thinks. *You coward.* She could never excuse what he'd done, yet she felt she deserved his doubt. It was no more than she had done to him. He would never have met Nina if she'd gone with him. Mags's secret truth is that she had been scared of moving to a new place, where the few people she knew were in-laws, and not many spoke English. How stupid. Home *was* him: it was all of them together, the family. She'd convinced herself that he'd be back after a year anyway, so it wasn't worth the effort of moving everyone. Anita was about to go to college. Elin was only in primary and could have moved easily enough, but Raymond was starting the Leaving Cert cycle and so easily distracted that he was in danger – she had taken no satisfaction in being proved right – of making a complete bags of it.

And then, that terrible winter, when the truth of it sank in. He wasn't coming back to them at all . . . Elin, her father's little pet, sad and bewildered, the weight of the world on her thin shoulders; Raymond, furious and taking his anger out on Mags; Anita, freshly in love with Derek and not seeming to care. Mags had tried so hard, she really had, to keep everything normal. To act like it was okay; to swallow the pain and humiliation and tell them how much he loved his children nevertheless. And how they could visit him, and he would them. And the lies and the phone calls and the having to stand over Raymond to make him write to his father. And her own hidden rage and fear all the while.

What settled in her – and stayed for many years – was a despair that didn't leave her until after she'd sold the house. A sense of being exposed, raw, with nothing to mediate between her and the fierce stupidity of the world. This is life, she thinks: we are the ruination of one another even as we are completely dependent on each other's drawn breath.

The DART pulls into Shankill station. That was quick. *You were miles away, Mags*, she says to herself. *And now here you are, miles away.*

She pauses at the ticket booth to adjust her beret. 'Nice hat, love. My missus has the very same,' the man behind the counter says. 'You might need an umbrella as well, mind, it's looking dark to me.' She checks her bag. Yes, there it is. Two brown eyes in a brown face peer up at her from an envelope.

Don't worry, she thinks. *I'll not forget about you.* Her canvas shopper is rolled up in the bottom of her handbag, with just the words '*I am*' visible. She spies a birthday card in there too. Who could that— Oh, yes. For Jean. Of course. She's very fond of Jean. When Mags sees an article in the paper about Jean's bit of the college she sometimes cuts it out and posts it to her. 'But if it's relevant she'll have seen it online,' Raymond said once. 'There's no need to bother.' But Jean always thanks her for them. Jean understands why she does it, Mags is sure of it.

The ticket man must wonder why she's still standing there because he says, 'The main exit is out to the left there, through the car park.'

She walks to Kilmarth Road and towards her old life, tucked away at its end. It's a long time since she was last here. The road is quiet, apart from the bark of an unseen dog, the sound cut through with a chain's clink and rattle. At the far end, car tail-lights flash red before disappearing up a driveway, she can't make out which one. She hears the engine fall silent, and when it does, the sound of the sea slips through the trees on her left, the beautiful repetition of the waves calling to her from down below. The tide must be in. She'll go up as far as the old house, then onto the sea path, she decides. If the clouds clear and the tide isn't too high she might even have a stroll on the beach while she's at it, if there's time.

The sun rises in spite of everything. The world is constant, except for us. And yet here we all are, made from stars yet buzzing about as though our human pursuits are what really matter. As though our relentless distractions will save us. Who am I to be? Mags thinks. Who can I become, when I can no longer be myself?

'You've no list for *that*, Margaret Jensen,' she says aloud, and a tea-brown sparrow on a nearby hedge twitches and flies off.

The wind in the branches and the crashing of the sea are suddenly so alike that she can't be sure what is air and what is water. She decides to walk into the thicket of trees on her left to get closer to the sound of the waves. The ground is muddy and uneven and she stumbles at the edge of a ditch. After a moment she rights herself and continues on through the trees, her head bowed under a high, green canopy.

Will I miss myself? she wonders. Will I miss me when I'm gone?

ACKNOWLEDGEMENTS

A very big thank you to: my editor Ciara Considine for her insight and support with this book (and its big sister), and to Breda Purdue, Joanna Smyth and Siobhan Tierney at Hachette, who along with Susie Cronin have been a pleasure to work with; Margaret Halton at United Agents for her ever-sound advice; those who improved this book at various stages of its early life: Andrea Carter, Denise Judge, Paula McGrath and Catherine O'Mahony and Mary Reynolds; James Ryan, Carlo Gébler and especially Éilís Ní Dhuibhne for the many, many wise words; and finally love and thanks to Feargal and to Clare, Tony, Ronan & Johnny.